Survival
Chain of Deceit, Book 10

By

David McIntosh

The complete "Chain of Deceit" Series

Survival, Chain of Deceit

Book 10

ISBN: 978-0-9987139-2-2

Dedication

As with all my novels I dedicate my stories to the men and women who wear the uniform of the military and first responders and the families they leave behind when called to duty. They are the true Americans and deserve our respect and loyalty for their dedication to our country, flag and freedom.

Table of Contents

It had been three months since Amber Pierce was released from the hospital after being shot and losing her brother to a gang of killers. She was looking for revenge for her loss. Being only 22 years old and having to cope with almost losing her father and mother and then the death of her twin brother, Josh, was almost too much to bear. The story she told her mother, Connie Pierce, was that it wasn't revenge but vengeance, which was a kinder way of saying she was going to kill those that caused her harm and a lot of pain. Fully recovered from her physical wounds, but not her mental trauma, she was about to set out on a quest with Andi and Ivy, her two new partners.

Andi and Ivy were unique in many ways; both were androids that looked and acted more human than most humans did. They were completely built and programed by the CIA to be highly trained field agents and so far, had proven to be the best of the best. They did not show emotion like a human would, but feelings had been programed into their systems so they could and often showed emotions that looked real.

Amber was standing in the kitchen looking at her mother as she told her the plan and that Andi and Ivy would be arriving later that day.

"Amber, have you consulted with your father?" Connie asked as she was slicing a tomato for the sandwich she was making.

"Yes, he said he would do whatever he could within the company to assist," Amber replied quickly.

"Don't be in too much of hurry, young lady. I know the FBI and CIA are working around the clock to locate the killers and they will. I talked to your godfather Josh yesterday in anticipation of you wanting to get involved. He told me about Andi and Ivy coming and that they had information for us. And you know that your father will not let you go alone. That is why Josh sent Andi and Ivy over. And you are not going to like what I am about to say, but it is going to happen. Davin and I are going to be following a couple of leads, while you, Andi and Ivy follow others. It is time we found Monica Teach and put that bad chick down."

"I don't have a problem with that mom, just that I want to kill her. Josh was my brother and we were connected a lot closer than, well a lot closer than you or dad," Amber responded angrily.

Monica Teach, is a terrorist, killer, ex-CIA Research and Development technician and direct descendant to Blackbeard the Pirate also known as Edward Teach or as some knew him as Edward Thatch. Edward was an English pirate born around 1680 and died on November 22, 1718 when killed in a conflict that went very bad for him and his crew. His ship, the *Queen Anne's Revenge*, was recently found off the coast in shallow water near Beaufort Inlet, North Carolina. Monica decided at a young age to follow in Blackbeard's footsteps in as many ways as possible. So far, she had killed, blown up a major hotel, stolen various high-tech equipment including the holographic emitter and that was just the short list of her crimes.

Because she was financed by a large drug ring, she was able to purchase or steal the things she required to complete whatever she planned. Blackbeard was not into drugs unless you wanted to call rum a drug. At least, as far as we know, he didn't use, sell, or condone drugs. But that

8

was a long time ago and without documented proof that he used drugs there really wasn't any way of knowing. Monica, on the other hand, saw a way to make money to finance her group and jumped on the drug market with both feet. And in doing so, she was able to buy politicians, police, FBI and at least one or two CIA employees.

At an earlier time, Monica thought she had the perfect assistant; almost too perfect Ivy Wadsworth had worked in the Research and Development Lab at the CIA with Monica and was convinced to join with Rocky Soto and Monica when he was fired from the CIA. At that time, Ivy had no idea that Rocky had stolen the holographic emitters; she would only discover that later after Monica killed Rocky and took the emitters for herself. Eventually Monica did learn of Ivy's deception; Ivy was as an under-cover agent for the CIA. Monica didn't let on that she knew; and while flying to Los Angeles on their stolen C-123 cargo plane, she shot and killed Ivy. And to add injury to insult, Monica had opened the cargo loading ramp and dumped her out from about 12,000 feet.

Who was really Monica Teach? Was she the great, great granddaughter to Blackbeard the pirate, a terrorist, half-sister to Amber Pierce, or an innocent victim of circumstances being in the wrong place at the wrong time? It really seemed like she had a split personality and was two completely different people, one loving and caring, and the other a murderous terrorist. Who was she, really?

Saturday morning broke with a bang. The thunderstorm was raging with vengeance. There were frequent storms on Kauai, but this one was one of the worst recorded. The wind was blowing at a consistent 35 miles per hour with gusts of 60 mph. There was so much rain that Amber could not see past the patio deck just outside her window. Yesterday had been so beautiful with its bright blue sky, a few clouds, and a light wind, but today was almost like hurricane weather. Reports stated that the storm would blow through in a few hours. Hopefully the report was correct; she and her partners needed to go. They had a lead, a weak one, but one they would follow.

Andi and Ivy had arrived via the CIA's private business jet late last night, about four hours before the storm hit. They brought files and information about Monica Teach and her team. It was decided that Amber's father and mother would take the company jet back to Washington to assist her uncle Josh, Director of CIA, and then check out a possible trail in England. But no one could leave until this storm ended or blew out to sea.

Amber slept nude and had just slid out of bed when the crash of thunder woke her up for the tenth time during the night. While standing at the window, Amber watched the storm and said a silent prayer to her brother. Not being a very religious woman, she wished things had been different. She was driving the car when attacked; she should have been able to prevent the accident and death of her brother. At least that is what she believed in her heart. If only things had turned out differently, maybe her brother, Josh would still be alive. But was killing the people that started that chain of events going to help? Probably not, but she was determined to find out. Josh was dead and there was nothing that she could do to bring him back; all she could do was go out and kill the ones that did it.

"Amber, are you up and dressed?" Connie called as she knocked on Amber's bedroom door.

"Yes, I'm up mom, not dressed, come on in," Amber called back without turning from the window.

The door opened and in walked her mom. "The report is the storm will let up by lunch; come on out for breakfast. Your dad wants to talk to you and your team. Oh, Ivy and Andi are in the living room."

"I'll be right out, let me get some clothes on," Amber replied and then turned to see her mother standing by the door, not smiling, but looking very concerned.

"Is everything all right mom?"

"No, but your dad will explain; now get dressed," Connie said, then turned and left, closing the door behind her.

Ten minutes later Amber, Andi, Ivy, Connie and her dad, Davin, were sitting at the breakfast table waiting for someone to say something.

"Dad, what is going on? Mom said you would explain," Amber said finally breaking the silence.

"This is not easy for me to say, but you have to know. Your uncle Josh is in the hospital. They say he had a stroke; and well, the outlook is not good. You know we were going to Washington when this storm breaks, but not to follow up on any leads. I have been named acting director of the CIA until Josh gets out of the hospital. Connie being FBI will continue as liaison between us and them."

"Is he going to be all right?" Amber questioned.

"Not sure, but the doctors are hopeful; in any case, he is out of commission for a while. How long we don't know. Our stay in Washington is now open ended. You three will have the total support of the company and full use of one of the company jets until you catch or kill Monica Teach and her team. I would prefer alive to stand trial, but we know that may not be possible. Just be careful."

"Andi, Ivy, where do we start?"

"That is a good question, Miss Amber. The last reported sighting of Monica was in Vietnam. I suggest we start there," Ivy answered confidently.

"Sounds good to me; can we get support from the local police or our people in country?" Amber asked quickly.

"Already on it, the local company office has several very good agents that have been assigned to assist us with whatever we need," Andi replied.

"Good, as soon as this storm is over, we leave. You did bring your weapons, didn't you?"

"Of course, and a few extra on the plane in case we need something a bit heavier," Ivy answered smiling.

"Ivy, I can't believe you are really an android."

"Well to be honest, I am not completely an android; my brain is half human and half computer. My, or rather, our bodies are grown in a lab with real skin, blood vessels, human organs and much more, but our skeleton is titanium and we both have a titanium under body. Kind of like a dog having two layers of hair, one thick under coat to protect them from the elements and the outer coat that grows and provides further protection. Our undercoat is titanium and acts a kind of armor protecting our vital organs. Remember the movie '*Terminator*'? Well, we are more like the 'Terminator' Arnold Schwarzenegger played."

"And they said Hollywood was all make believe."

"Well, the writers thought of it; and we made it work. Just like the tricorder, flip phones and many things that came out of *Star Trek*, *Star Wars* and other sci-fi and horror movies," Ivy replied and then paused while she thought for a moment, "Watch this," she said and then transformed into Connie Pierce.

"You can do that without touching any buttons?" Davin asked.

"Yes, built into our matrix," Ivy said and then returned to her real self.

"That will be very handy. Can you do that too, Andi?" Connie asked.

"Yes, we are programed with clothes on; but they are only a holographic projection, over our bodies. I would show you, but we are almost nude under this clothing," Ivy responded.

Several thousand miles away from Kauai and the Pierce home, a lone figure known only as The Colonel sat quietly in her suite at one of the finest hotels in Bangkok sipping a Long Island Iced Tea. No one knew exactly who she was or what she looked like because anytime she went out, she would use her personal holographic device to hide her appearance. She was contemplating her situation and what she needed to do next. Her drug business at several university campuses around the world were doing very well and the guys there were really enjoying all the sex they were getting. The drug Sexiticy was a hit with both male and females on campus, the ladies were making tons of money and getting satisfied nightly and the guys were having more fun than ever.

Sexiticy was more powerful than Viagra or any other sexual stimulant on the market with or without a prescription. Of course, there were some serious side effects. The deadliest was if you took too much of it there was only one out come, death. There had been 32 recorded deaths directly related to the misuse of the drug, and not all were men; at least 6 were ladies that were experimenting and over dosed. Sexiticy had been developed by several noted chemists in Thailand and deemed safe by their standards if taken in moderation. The United States Food and Drug Administration thought otherwise and would not give it the customary stamp of approval. So, it fell into the hands of less than notable parties and hit the drug market anyway. The Colonel learned of the drug, experimented with it, and loved the effect. With the help of her team, she was able to corner the market and take over as a major distributer of the drug. Concentrating on colleges and universities, she helped set up sororities as on campus brothels and had her pushers sell the drug to as many male buyers as she could get. Word spread and soon her business was growing across the nation. She did have one set back thanks to the Pierce twins, so she had ordered the hit of the twins and was almost successful. But Amber was still alive and would be coming after her soon. However, she had plans for young Miss Amber; and Amber would not like the outcome.

A knock on the door broke The Colonel's thought process. Instead of turning on her holographic emitter, she just stood and walked to the door, then stopped and looked down at herself. *'Oops, guess I need to put something on before opening the door.'* She was only dressed in black bikini panties which she usually did when home alone, not thinking that anyone would bother her. She peeked at the door camera to see who it was and decided that this visitor was safe, and she would not need to get dressed or use the holo emitter. Opening the door, she let Hannah Brickman enter.

"Wow aren't we casual today," Hannah said and then kissed her on the cheek.

"Didn't feel like getting dressed, what brings you to my humble home?"

"There is nothing humble about this place, boss. We need to talk; I have information which will be of interest to you. But first I need a drink and get comfortable," Hannah said as she walked over to the wet bar, poured herself a tall Scotch and added a couple of ice cubes, kicking off her shoes as she walked over. Hannah was casually dressed in a tight leather mini skirt with a white sheer blouse cut very low in the front exposing her ample breasts. She was a tease and loved men and women looking at her; but she was also a very good spy, which is why Amber loved this woman and wanted to keep her around a long time.

"What have you got, Hannah?" The Colonel asked as she sat down on the sofa. When Hannah sat down beside her with their knees touching, she placed her arm on the back of the sofa, looked at her straight on and smiled. "Come on out with it."

"You were right, Amber Pierce with a couple of new partners is coming to Vietnam on the company jet. They are experiencing a storm on Kauai right now but should be leaving sometime later today, going straight to Ho Chi Minh City. Should arrive later tonight," Hannah said smiling. After sipping her drink, she said, "I needed that, may I have another?"

"Sure, help yourself," The Colonel answered, "Is that all you have?"

"No, babe, there is more; give me a sec and I will tell all," Hannah replied as she poured another tall Scotch. "By the way, this is great Scotch."

"Okay, drink up. What else is there?" The Colonel asked getting a little impatient with her friend.

"I don't have names or descriptions yet, but Josh Randel has sent two new agents to Kauai to join up with Amber. Also, I got word that Josh Randel had a stroke and is in the hospital; my contact said they don't expect him to survive."

1963, Berkley University, California

Years earlier at various university research and development laboratories there was in-depth research into the use of drugs to control and enhance individuals to be used as super soldiers and other classified uses. The use of LSD and other hallucinogenic drugs on subjects proved to enhance brain functions, strength and agility but had some serious side effects which would not come out until years later.

"Doctor we have a new crop of volunteers. They will be here at one this afternoon. What do you want to start them on?" Laboratory assistant Robert Henshaw asked his boss, Doctor William March.

"Briefing first, they need to know the risks, and well, many other little details of this experiment. Have you been testing the drugs yourself; or are you just that stupid?" March questioned his assistant as he looked closely into Henshaw's dilated eyes.

"No, sir. I would never do that."

"You had better not, but why are your eyes dilated?"

"I just came back from the eye doctor and she dilated them for a test." After pausing for a second, she continued. "I have the list of names of the volunteers, do you want to see it?" Henshaw asked handing a clipboard to March.

"All these are graduate students, right? Have they signed the non-disclosures and waivers? We don't want to be sued for malpractice. What we are doing here is sanctioned and paid for by the government, but things happen. Let's get the lab prepped; and wait, it is almost noon now, we have work to do to prepare for their arrival."

"Right, sir. I will have them assembled in the classroom next door for the briefing and bring them in for their individual doses, half placebos and the other LSD, right?"

"Make sure you keep track of who gets what. We don't want any screw ups like last time."

"Fer sure, fer sure," Henshaw commented as he walked over to the cabinet that contained the drugs and started to set up the test.

Two o'clock that afternoon, six volunteers were receiving doses of LSD and placebos. The tests were supposed to show increased cognitive and brain function; dexterity and response times were also being measured. Each test lasted about three hours and each volunteer, locked in a secure room with multiple stimulus items in the room, such as building blocks, mathematical problems, stationary bikes, treadmills, and weight sets, was being watched individually. Each volunteer was given certain tasks to complete and were measured and compared to the volunteers on placebos.

"This is a first; one of the volunteers is the son of a Navy Admiral and another that of a congressman," March commented as he looked over the results of today's tests.

"Didn't notice, who are we talking about?"

"The Admiral's son is Albert Hunnicutt and the congressman's is Ted Graves. Interesting. Which one got what?"

"Hunnicutt got placebo and Graves got a low dose of LSD, both first timers."

"Well I guess if it got out that either one was using drugs or was in this program, they would not get elected into politics, now would they, so let's change each name and save their future. Let's be fair about this; change every volunteer's name and resign them," March said and then scratched through each name on the list, changing Hunnicutt to Albert Glass and Graves to Theodore Carson. He then pulled their paperwork and ran it through the shredder, twice; pulled out some blank forms and filled in the new names. "Get each to sign these, explaining we need to cover up who they are for security reasons."

"Right on, sir."

"Amber, before you go, you need to know a few things about your father and me," Connie said looking at her daughter and getting a confused look back.

"Mom, I have been living with you for over twenty years and know what you do. You are a retired senior FBI agent; and dad, well he is second in command at the CIA. What else is there to know?" Amber questioned as she poured herself a glass of soda.

"Yeah, that's what you know, but you don't know our history; and knowing the entire story may just keep you alive."

"Now you are trying to scare me. Our plane doesn't leave until six tomorrow night, so I have time if you want to tell me my family history," Amber said almost like she really didn't care but wanted to please her mother.

"Some of the details I don't know but let me go back to the beginning before I met your father. He can, well he may if he wants to, fill you in about his two tours in Vietnam. That is where he met your Uncle Josh. Both were assigned to the 138th Radio Research company. I think I have the right name; but anyway, what they did over there was to help the infantry locate the enemy. How they did that I am not sure of, but they both survived and returned home early in 1972 when everyone was returning. The unit was reclassified as a reserve unit and based in Orlando, Florida where it took on a new mission. The boys did go to the reserves for a short time to help get it started and then punched out. Josh joined the CIA. Your dad got involved with the FBI working undercover in Palm Beach as an Insurance Investigator, mostly researching missing ships, such as the *MaryJean*. We found her and became independently wealthy over night, but that is another story for later."

"I knew they met there but didn't know they were in the same unit; that's cool," Amber said between sips of her soda. "Go on."

"First, where are Andi and Ivy?

"Oh, they went down to the hotel to rest. Wait, do androids need sleep, or do they recharge?" Amber asked.

"Good question, I don't know. Maybe you can ask your dad when he gets home."

"When is he coming home?"

"In a couple of hours; let's move into the living room and I will continue with the story."

"Okay, it is a bit more comfortable in there anyway," Amber agreed and the two of them left the kitchen and got comfortable in the living room.

"Where was I? Oh yeah, both guys left active duty. Davin joined the reserves while Josh headed off in pursuit of wealth and fame. He ended up being recruited by the company and worked various field assignments until one day he needed help while in Palm Beach. That is when he contacted his old friend Davin. Your dad was working as an insurance investigator and was an undercover detective for the local FBI office, which Josh did not know. And your Aunt Stephanie was Davin's secretary and partner. They worked various black market and insurance fraud cases together for several years, racking up an impressive record."

"That I didn't know, when did you enter the picture?"

"Not long after Josh contacted your dad, they were working on a case of military cargo showing up in a warehouse in New Orleans which was discovered by the FBI.

I was assigned the case and that is when I met both Josh and your father."

"Is that when you located the *MaryJean* and recovered all that gold?" Amber was getting more interested in her family history by the minute.

"Yes, that was the beginning of a beautiful relationship that has taken us to many exotic places and almost got us killed more than once," Connie stated.

"So, what in your history is so important that I must know to help keep me alive?" Amber questioned.

"I will get to that shortly, just be patient young lady. We have all night. I need something stronger than a soda; I'll be right back; do you want a beer or something?"

"No, I'm good."

Five minutes later Connie returned with a tall glass filled with some unknown liquid. "Okay now that I have something to drink, I can continue with this and I will tell you what you need to remember. We recovered the gold and some classified documents from the German high command. We have been putting together a case from those documents, adding more over the years and now have a solid case against some people in high places. Those documents are in our safe and will stay there for now. If anyone finds out we have them, it could get us killed. But I am getting off the story, let me start from the beginning and you will understand why you need to know."

"Okay, what's in those documents that is so dangerous to have?"

"I will come back to those. Not long after finding the ship and gold, your father and I married. Stephanie and Josh married not long after that, and we became the fantastic four, well at least in our minds. But we did work on many cases together over the years and progressed up the chain of command in both the CIA and FBI. Stephanie became an FBI agent and the four of us were a team to be reckoned with."

"Cool, then Josh and I were born, and everything changed, right?" Amber questioned.

"No, not quite. Let me take you on a little trip through some of the missions we did, and you will understand better," Connie stated and then leaned back on the sofa and thought for a moment.

"I need to take a trip to the bathroom; I'll be right back," Amber said as she stood and headed toward her room, returning a few minutes later wearing a bath robe. "Thought I would get a bit more comfortable."

"Good idea, I will change shortly. My story really starts right after you two were born, prior to that we were field agents working whatever cases they would throw at us. We both remained field agents for a while, but eventually became agents driving a desk. However, that was not until you were six years old. The missions we did until then were very tame, as it were, investigating the disappearance of agents, stolen documents, and such. Your father got involved with Research and Development to bring out some new gadgets to help in the field. He loved working with the head of the department, Rocky Soto, and his team. You already know about Rocky and his team and I will fill in some blanks for you. Let's start shortly after your sixth birthday."

May 1965, Berkley University Medical Research

"Mr. Graves, we wish to thank you for your participation in our program. Remember we have no record of you ever being here so your time in the military should not be affected. We wish you luck and safety during your tour. Did you say they were sending you to Vietnam?" Doctor March said as he shook Graves' hand, the day he was leaving the university and heading to Vietnam as a reserve commissioned second lieutenant in the Army.

"Yeah, finished ROTC and got a commission as a 2nd Lieutenant and now assigned to the 82nd Airborne Division. I will be getting further assigned when I arrive at Fort Bragg. I leave in two days. I guess jump school is in order then most likely on to Vietnam. I did my basic training last summer; and well, I guess I am ready to go fight," Graves stated before he started to leave.

"Wait, Lieutenant, I have something for you," March said and reached into his pocket and withdrew a pocket watch. "I carried this during World War II, and it brought me luck, saved my life, literally. I want you to carry it while over there and if you return alive, I would like it back. Is that okay with you?"

"Sure, be honored to carry your good luck charm," Graves said, really feeling silly about the gesture, but not wanting to alienate the doctor; he might be able to supply him with more drugs when he returned and possibly other things too.

"Good, be safe and see you when you return," March said and watched his best subject walk out the door, knowing full well that that young man was now completely addicted to LSD and would do almost anything to make sure he got his fix. Graves knew from talking to soldiers that had returned from Vietnam that drugs were easy to get, and the supply was almost endless. If only he could make his small supply last until he arrived in Vietnam. He already had names of suppliers and locations of where to make contact. He just needed to get in country to be refreshed and hopefully survive the war.

Graves arrived at Fort Bragg on a Friday and immediately was sent to Fort Benning for airborne training which would last three weeks. He then returned to Fort Bragg where he boarded a MAC flight (Military Airlift Command) plane to Fort Lewis, Washington and then on to Vietnam where he was assigned to be the executive officer to a Major Donald Ingram of Bravo Company 101st Infantry Division. This assignment didn't last long. He was a combat trained officer and that is where he wanted to be. Bravo company was not on the front lines; it was only acting as advisors to the local government and military. Graves got his wish on November 10th, 1965.

October 30th, 1965, Vietnam, Fire Base Alpha

"Lieutenant, this is Lt. Colonel Hal Moore and he is commander of the newly formed First Battalion of the 7th Air Calvary unit located north of us. He has something for you; and well, sir, please this is your show."

"Pleasure to meet you, sir," Graves said and saluted. "El Tee, you have been here in country for what now, 5 months and from what I have heard you have been doing a great job with your team, maybe it is time to pin these on," Lt. Colonel Moore said as he pinned on 1st Lieutenant's silver bar on Graves collar.

"Thank you, sir. I have been here over two hundred fifty days and looking forward to going home soon," Graves stated smiling. "I don't know what to say but thank you."

"Nothing to say; you have been doing a great job and deserve the promotion. Sorry we don't do a complete promotion ceremony; but being in a war zone, it is just not safe to line up all the troops and do that sort of thing, could get troops killed. I know you understand. Now get out there and, wait, here is your next mission. There is one more thing, you and Major Ingram are being transferred to my new unit, First Battalion of the newly formed 7th Air Calvary. Major Ingram will be taking over Alpha Company as commander and you will be one of his platoon leaders. The commander there had to take emergency leave due to a family incident; he was always short a platoon leader which you will become once you move your things over there. Keep in mind we are not a battalion that is destined to stay in the rear; we are a combat unit and expect to move out in the next few days. I expect you two to report by eighteen hundred today, ready to run. You are both dismissed, I will see you at 1800," Moore said. He saluted and left the bunker.

Minutes after receiving his promotion and placing his new rank on his bunk, Graves called his team together to give them the good news. Not about his promotion which they already knew about, but about their mission. While waiting for his men to assemble in his tent, he slipped a small white tablet on his tongue, just a small dose of LSD to get him through the day and hopefully return alive from this mission.

"Okay men, time to rock and roll again. Sergeant pack up some extra rations and ammo, we may need it this time. And have the helos ready to leave in thirty," Graves ordered Staff Sergeant Henry Link. He then looked at his men and added. "May god have mercy on our souls. Now go get ready, we leave in thirty."

November 10th, 1965 Ten days after reassignment

"El Tee, you look like shit, what the hell happened out there?" Major Ingram questioned his newly promoted Lieutenant standing at attention in front of him, after a two-day mission into hell.

"Short story is the gooks had a whole battalion waiting for us and our choppers were being hit with small arms fire before we got to the ground. Chopper two got hit with an RPG; it exploded, no survivors. My chopper took multiple hits; the pilot was able to put it down and we off loaded. We had started to return fire, but before the chopper could get off the ground, it was hit. The co-pilot was killed, and the pilot joined in the fight with the rest of us. We were able to hold our own for a while, called for help, got a couple Sandy's in which pushed back the gooks. We spent two nights in heavy fighting, I lost over half my men, including Sergeant Link, my radio op and medic in the first few hours. Finally, relief came and evac got us out, but not without heavy loses. Sir, I can't do this anymore. Can we finish this debrief later; I need to check on my men? We haven't eaten or slept in 2 days."

"Yes, El Tee, get cleaned up, eat, get some sleep, we can talk about this later," Major Ingram ordered as Graves saluted, turned, and walked out of the command bunker. Graves returned to his bunker where he immediately poured water on his dirt incrusted face. He then reached into his pocket and withdrew a plastic packet containing small white pills; slipped two out, quickly put them in his mouth, and swallowed. The LSD would take affect shortly. In the meantime, he would check on his men, get a bite to eat and sleep for a couple of hours, maybe. The LSD might have other plans.

While he lay in his bunk, Lt. Graves relived the two days of fighting and the loss of eight of his platoon. He hated this war and everything about it; he hated the drugs he was taking just to get through the day. His commander suspected he was on drugs but had not confronted him about it. Most of the men in his platoon were taking something to get through the day and hopefully make it to the day they would rotate out. Graves had been in country for two hundred and seventy-four days; he was getting short and that meant he had to be extra careful, otherwise he would be taking that freedom bird home in a body bag and he did not want that.

"El Tee, the commander has asked me to get you, he wants you in the command bunker in ten minutes. Something has come up and he wouldn't tell me," Sergeant First Class Alfred Boxelder said to the lieutenant when he walked into Graves' bunker.

"Tell him I will be right there; let me wash the cobwebs out of my head and get my boots on," Graves replied as he slowly responded to the request.

Ten minutes later, Graves and Boxelder were standing in front of the Major waiting for orders.

"At ease, gentlemen, please sit. What I am going to tell you is not going to be easy for you or me," the major stated, paused and then took a long swig out of his canteen. "We just got orders to move out, take everything we can. The entire battalion is heading to the La Drang valley to set up and secure a landing zone for more troops to be brought in. Now, get your men packed up; we move out in three hours. Dismissed!"

November 14th, 1965 7th Air Calvary moves to la Drang Valley

First battalion of the 7th Air Calvary boarded their Huey helicopters, twelve in all and started to move into the valley. The flight would take about 30 minutes and they did not expect much resistance once on the ground. What they found was not what was expected. Upon arrival they were greeted by over 2,500 plus well-trained North Vietnamese regulars and spent the next three days in a fight for their life. After three days of fighting, Lt. Colonel Moore had a total of 75 of his men killed and numerous wounded and an estimated 3,000 North Vietnamese regulars were dead. When reinforcements finally arrived, they lost 234 additional men in the continuous fighting bringing the total of dead to 305, branding it as the Valley of Death. As Lt. Colonel Moore's position was being overrun by the Vietnamese, he ordered a Broken Arrow command which ordered any and all combat aircraft to converge on his site and do what they do best and kill the enemy to save his men. In the process there was an accident which caused the loss of several of his men when a fighter jet dropped napalm on friendlies. The battle was considered a victory by the military, but not by Moore; once they left the area, the Vietnamese returned to collect their dead and reclaimed the Valley. (See Appendix for more detail on this battle)

Young Lt. Graves sustained injuries which put him in the hospital for several months before being able to return to active duty. He finished his tour of duty in Vietnam on July 4th, 1966 and returned to the United States and was discharged with medical disabilities. Lt. Graves was promoted to Captain and participated in multiple campaigns while in country, most notable was the La Drang battle before discharge. He received the Purple Heart and Silver Star for his leadership and heroism in Vietnam, but these meant nothing to him. He just wanted to be out of the military and get on with his life. Captain Graves married his girlfriend from college, and they had a baby girl, naming her Allison after his mother. His wife was killed in an auto accident when Allison was ten years old. Ted had no idea how to raise a female child, so he placed her in a girl's boarding school with the provision that he would bring her home when she turned eighteen years old.

He continued to use LSD and now had to get a fix for Morphine because excessive use of it while in the hospital got him addicted to it. He completed his law degree, passed the bar, and became a highly respected lawyer. He eventually ran for Congress and won; then set his goal on the Presidency which he won several years later with a little help from some very corrupt friends. As a corrupt president, he was able to make sweet deals that benefited him more than the country and eventually was exposed. He took his new wife and ran. While cruising off the coast near a deserted island in the Bahama chain, his yacht was struck by a torpedo meant for another ship and he was pronounced dead, but no body was recovered. Everyone thought the President of the United States was dead and the cover up as to his corrupt political career was swept under the carpet.

Roll back fifteen years from present day to an early mission

"Davin, what do you want to do with the kids when we are in London?" Connie asked as they packed for their next trip to London. Young Amber and Josh were just turning six when Davin and Connie took this assignment, so we rolled the clock back in time to bring Amber up to speed.

"Your mother said she would come over and watch the kids."

"When did you have a chance to ask her?"

"Called before I left the office. She will be here before we leave," Davin said just as they heard the front door open and a familiar voice yell.

"Are you two still here?" Connie's mom, Betty called up the stairs.

"Yes, be right down," Connie yelled back.

"I'll be in the kitchen. Where are the kids?" Betty yelled.

"Daycare, we need to pick them up in, damn, in fifteen minutes. I'll be right back," Connie responded and ran down the stairs. "Be right back with the twins," she yelled as she exited the house and jumped into her car.

Three hours later Davin and Connie were relaxing in first class on a Boeing 747 on their way to London and another case. Two agents had gone missing out of the London office without a clue. It was their job to find out what happened and hopefully discover where the two were. What had started as a simple case of finding the two agents immediately turned into murder and a plot to blow up the London CIA office.

"Seth Conner Station Chief, welcome to London," Seth said as Davin and Connie entered the office building. After Davin and Connie showed him their credentials, he led them to the inner workings of the facility.

"Seth, what can you tell us about the two that are missing?" Connie asked as they sat in Seth's office.

"They are not missing," Seth started to say. Davin and Connie looked at each other and then back to Seth.

"Not missing! So, where are they?" Davin questioned.

"In the morgue, they were killed and dumped down near Buckingham Palace. Both were shot and then beaten to death; the coroner thinks a tire iron or something similar was used. Their weapons and credentials were missing, London Yard believes it was a robbery gone bad. That is about all we know now. We didn't find out until a few hours ago; you were already in the air."

"Okay, a robbery gone bad, we are not scheduled to fly out for a week and can extend that if need be. Do you mind if we poke around a bit ourselves?" Davin said and then looked at Connie and winked.

"I have a few friends over in the Yard; maybe we can link up and get this solved quickly," Connie added.

"Okay, we have a room secured for you at the hotel just down the street, nice place, five stars. They give us a good rate, so we put all our visitors there, I think you will like it," Seth commented. "I will have one of my agents take you down. I have a bunch of work to catch up on since this happened. The boss wants answers and updates every four hours."

"Let him know we arrived and will be assisting as much as possible. Now I need some good food and a few hours of sleep. Seth we will touch base after some sleep, a shower and food. Any good restaurants close by?"

"Yes, here is a map of the area, I marked several fine eateries in blue on there and the one marked red is the hotel. See you in a couple of hours," Seth said handing Davin the map, and showed them out to the lobby where a young female agent was waiting for them.

"Hello Mr. and Mrs. Pierce, I am Julie Thomson, your liaison while here. Please follow me to the hotel; here is my contact information and the number to the facility," Julie said and started for the door. Julie stood about five foot four and had flaming red hair. She was wearing tight black slacks with white blouse and had her hair pulled back into a long ponytail. The only thing that took away from her professional business attire were the red Converse high top tennis shoes she had on her feet.

"Hello Miss Thomson, pleasure to meet you. We have a car outside with our luggage," Connie said quietly as they headed for the door.

"Please call me Julie, and you can leave the car here; I will have your luggage brought over, leave me the keys. It is just next door, we own the hotel, so discussions of the classified nature can be discussed there if need be," Julie commented and turned right after exiting the facility.

"Nice hotel," Davin commented as they walked into the lobby and approached the front desk.

"Mr. Pierce, please call if you need me for anything, have a good evening, the restaurant here is very good. Good night," Julie said and then turned to the desk clerk, "Mr. and Mrs. Pierce will be with us for at least a week, make sure they are taken care of, William."

"No problem, their room is ready and dinner reservations are set for five, if that is too early please let me know and I will adjust it to a more convenient time, sir," William responded as he directed his comment to Davin and Connie.

"Thank you, Julie; we will call if we need anything. Oh, there is one thing; we need to see the files on the missing agents tonight. Can you get them to us?"

"Sure, I will bring their files over in an hour; is that okay?"

"Yes, fine, see you in an hour."

"Your keys, sir. You have suite 453 on the fifth floor. The elevators are on your right; your luggage will be right up. Here it comes now," William said and pointed to the elevators.

Ten minutes later, Davin and Connie entered their suite. She immediately headed for the restroom to freshen up while Davin dropped his coat on the first chair and plopped down in an overstuffed recliner and put his feet up. Glancing at his watch, he saw they had not had any sleep for the past 18 hours and he then understood why he was so tired. After kicking off his shoes and leaning back, he closed his eyes and fell asleep. Connie came out of the restroom in a white robe to find her husband sound asleep in the chair. She looked around the suite and saw a small but well stocked mini bar, walked over, and poured herself a drink. Hearing a sound behind her she turned and saw Davin's left eye open and he said, "Yes I would love a scotch, please."

A light knock on the door interrupted her pouring of the scotch, but she continued, walked over to Davin, and handed him the glass before she walked to the door. She checked to see who was there with the door camera and then opened it to be greeted by Julie Thompson.

"Here are the files you requested. Is there anything else I can get you?"

"No, this will keep us busy tonight; can we meet in your office at nine in the morning?" Connie asked, taking the files.

"Sure, nine is fine, my office is on the second lower level, next to Chief Conner's. Have a good night," Julie said and started to leave.

"No wait; come in. We have a few questions that you may be able to answer," Connie said before Julie got away.

"Okay, not sure if I can help but will try," Julie said and entered the suite.

"Would you care for a drink?"

"Sure, beer if there is any."

"One beer coming up. Please have a seat."

"Julie, you seem very young; how long have you been with the agency?" Connie asked.

"My looks can be deceiving, I'm twenty-eight, finished the academy three years ago. When asked what I wanted to do, I chose London station. I didn't want to be stuck at a desk at Langley and my language skills are not the best, so the Orient was out of the question. But here I can blend in pretty well. There are a lot of red heads in England, mostly Irish which is my heritage. My grandparents were Irish immigrants who settled in New York, where I was born." Julie answered and then took a long pull on her beer. "I love English Ale."

"Great, so you have been here long enough to get to know the two that were killed?" Davin asked.

"Yes, I knew both and am going to miss them. But from what the police said it looks like a robbery gone bad."

"We will determine that with your help and Scotland Yard. Were you close to either of them?" Davin asked.

"No, not really, we would chat, you know hallway talk; they never discussed their mission with me, and of course I couldn't talk about why I was here," Julie acknowledged.

"Why are you here?" Connie asked.

"I can't tell you, but I do have a mission and am working very close to its completion. When done I will be going back to HQ for debrief and reassignment."

"Of course, you can't tell us; we are here for another reason, to find out what is behind the death of two agents," Connie reasoned. "You know I am not CIA, but FBI, and have been authorized a clearance level equal to my husband's. Look, we just need to know more about the two that were killed. Tell us what you know of their habits, where they hung out, lived, whatever you know."

"Okay, Marvin Grossman lived in an apartment four blocks from here and Cecil Hunt had an apartment around the corner from Marvin's. They were partners of course and hung out when not working or maybe they were working, but they would usually go to the Boar's Drool Ale House located in Stratford."

"We are presently in Blackheath; why go way up there to drink when there are many great pubs around here. They must be up there working a mission," Davin surmised. "How do you know about that place?"

"Marvin said he needed a date for cover one night and asked me to join him. I accompanied them a couple times, we chatted and drank a bit, but I guess they were there on assignment because they didn't drink much and were watching the crowd. They never told me why they needed me to tag along, but the ale was great, and I was curious as to what they were up to."

"That's interesting. Okay, where were their bodies found?" Connie jumped in.

"Blackwell, which is about halfway between us and the Boar's Drool, both were face down on the banks of the river," Julie answered and then looked at her empty bottle, held it up and pointed at it while looking at Connie. Getting a nod from Connie, Julie stood and went to the wet bar and retrieved another ale. "Thank you, after today I really need to relax."

"Yeah, I guess finding out two of your friends were murdered can put a damper on things," Davin added and walked over to the bar and poured another scotch. "Now you said they found them this morning; did they say how long they had been dead?"

"No but promised to have a complete report to use by noon tomorrow."

"Is there anything else you can tell us?" Connie asked.

"Yeah, Marvin was acting kind of strange for the past week, nervous, I guess. About what I don't know, maybe they were getting too close to whatever they were investigating and that got them killed."

"Nervous, what about Cecil, how did he act?" Davin questioned.

"Like he didn't have a care in the world, nothing phased him. Cool, calm, and always smiling, that was Cecil. Kind of like James Bond, he didn't let his emotions get in the way of his mission."

36

"Tomorrow we check out the Boar's Drool, would you care to join us?" Connie stated looking intently at Julie.

"Sure, would love to."

"That's not going to interfere with your other assignments?" Davin asked.

"No, I've been assigned to assist you two in whatever you need," Julie agreed and finished her second English Ale. "Is there anything else you need tonight?"

"No, just the files and a good night's sleep; thank you, see you at nine in your office," Connie said and walked with Julie to the door.

"Thanks for the ale; I really needed to wind down. Good night."

Flying long distances is still much better than taking a ship or driving if you are limited on time, but it takes its toll on the body going through different time zones in a short period of time. Sleep is the only cure for this problem and sleep is what they did for the next twelve hours. Even with the curtains drawn tight a little daylight seeped into the bedroom. Davin was up early, well early for him, it was seven in the morning here in London.

"Good morning, sunshine, time to get up; we have a meeting at nine," Davin said to his still sleeping wife.

"What time is it?" Connie groaned.

"Seven fifteen, get up so we have time for some breakfast before we meet Julie at nine," Davin said and then headed for the shower.

"Five more minutes, wake me when you get out of the shower and leave the water running."

Five minutes to nine, Davin and Connie walked into the CIA facility and were greeted by the lobby guard. "Good morning, Mr. and Mrs. Pierce, Julie is expecting you, please your credentials and then proceed to the elevator on your left, press two down. I will let her know you are on your way down."

"Thank you," Davin said. After showing the guard their credentials, they proceeded down to level 2 and Julie was standing at the elevator waiting for them.

"Good morning, hope you slept well; please follow me," Julie said smiling.

"Didn't we just pass your office," Connie said as she saw the name on the door when they passed it.

"We are going to the war room; there has been a development you need to be aware of," Julie said as she stopped in front of a door guarded by a young Marine holding an M-4. He saluted and then opened the door behind, not saying a word or cracking a smile.

"Relax Raymond, this is Mr. and Mrs. Pierce from HQ, not the boss," Julie said to the guard.

"Just doing my job, Julie," the young Marine replied and then smiled at her.

"You two friends?" Connie asked when the door was closed behind them.

"Kind of. He is my boyfriend. Please don't tell Seth," Julie confided quietly.

"Your secret is safe, now what happened?" Connie replied with a smile.

"Good morning. Seth, what has happened since last night?" Davin asked the Station Chief.

"Well, a lot. and none of it good. Please have a seat. Julie, lock the door and tell your boyfriend to let nobody enter," Seth ordered and then stood and walked over to the large screen monitor on the back wall and clicked a remote. The picture that appeared was the complete floor plan of the facility they occupied. "This is our facility as it is shown on the construction plans submitted to the city." He clicked the button again and an overlay appeared. "And this is what was actually built. You can easily see the difference and the secret, at least, supposedly secret addition we had put in during construction. These plans are ten years old and we haven't added or deleted any of the special areas since construction."

"Okay, that is a good thing I believe, isn't it?" Davin questioned.

"Yes, it is a good thing; we haven't created anything to alert the city of London or Scotland Yard to question this place. Until now," Seth stopped and picked up his coffee, "Where are my manners, would you like some coffee or tea?"

"No thanks, we're good. Continue," Davin said, waving off the offer.

"We discovered there has been a breech in our security. Not sure how but we have our suspicions. Which I will cover in a minute."

"Why are you showing us this, we were briefed back in HQ about this facility, your bomb shelters, exits and everything here," Connie offered.

"That may be true but," Seth stopped.

"But what, get on with it," Davin said getting impatient.

"We have a mole."

"No way, everyone here has been vetted and cleared years ago. Who is it? Do you know." Connie questioned, her FBI training kicking in real fast.

"Yes, we know, and we were about to make an arrest when Marvin and Cecil were killed. Now we are not sure."

"Did you think one of them was the mole?" Davin asked.

"Yes, we believe Marvin was the mole and Cecil found out but was killed before exposing him. Ballistics show that Cecil was killed with Marvin's weapon and then he killed himself or someone else killed him because both bullets came from Marvin's weapon."

"But didn't the report say their weapons were missing along with their credentials," Connie asked.

"Yes, but they were in a garbage can a block away. Tests prove both were killed with the same weapon, Marvin's," Seth concluded. "And we have reason to believe these facility plans were compromised and this facility is now exposed."

"Okay, that's not good, but what else may have been leaked out?" Connie asked.

"We are doing a complete search of our database and have discovered at least, so far, ten classified documents that have been compromised. All ten are classified Top Secret," Seth replied.

"Okay, I guess we add a bit more snooping to our agenda and see who may have those docs and plans. Julie are you ready, we need to start this investigation now," Davin stated and then looked at Seth. "You keep looking here and make sure nobody leaves the facility alone, two or more."

"Already put that order out. And stay in contact, Julie will provide you with secure cell phones set with speed dial to my office and my second in command. You can meet her later; right now, you need to go to work. Oh, do you have your weapons?" Seth asked as everyone stood to leave.

"Yes, Julie, the phones?" Connie asked.

"My office, let's go," Julie said as she unlocked the door and exited with Davin and Connie in tow.

Boar's Drool Ale House

It took almost an hour to get to the Boar's Drool from CIA London, mostly because of traffic. The mid-day traffic in London could be easily compared to rush hour traffic in Los Angeles but with narrower streets and more stop lights. Then there was parking, because London had been a city for well over two hundred years and back when it was built, they didn't have cars, just buggies, horses and foot power, there was little thought to building parking lots. After another twenty minutes looking for a place to park, Julie who was driving finally found one four blocks away from the Boar's Drool. It was a muggy day but not raining yet, so the walk was pleasant.

"Wow, the sign says it has been here since 1789, guess they are well established and hopefully have some good food," Davin commented when they approached the Ale House.

"Oh, you are going to be greatly pleased; when Marvin and Cecil brought me here, we had dinner and several times we came for lunch and it was beyond great. I think that is why they came; the food and drink were definitely a real winner," Julie commented as they entered the old establishment.

"Now this is truly an old English Pub, I love it," Connie acknowledged as they worked their way to a booth about halfway down the side wall.

"You here for drinks or lunch?" the young waitress asked seconds after they sat down.

"Both," Davin answered looking up at the tall waitress dressed as an English Barmaid.

"What can I get you?"

"Three pints, dark ale, please," Julie said quickly. "My treat."

"Right away, Mum." And the waitress walked toward the bar, returning minutes later with three tall pints and menus. "I'll be back shortly; our special is Shepherd's Pie and for desert Yorkshire Pudding."

"What do you recommend, Julie?" Connie asked.

"The Shepherd's Pie is very good; I don't think you will go wrong with anything on the menu."

"Don't look, but I think we have attracted some attention. Does anyone know you here, Julie?"

"Not that I know of, only been here three times over the past year, and with Marvin and Cecil each time," Julie replied. She looked over her shoulder at the other patrons, just as the waitress returned.

Within minutes they had placed their order and were enjoying the dark English Ale.

"I remember the man at the end of the bar, but never talked with him. Is he the one that has interest in us?"

"Yes. Seems very interested in us. He talked with the waitress after she left our table and keeps looking this way. Maybe I should just go talk with him," Davin stated and then sipped his ale. "Guess not, he is coming over."

"Good afternoon, Mr. and Mrs. Pierce, and how are you doing Julie Thompson? Before you ask, may I sit down. I'm Reginald Knight, chief inspector from MI-6. Here are my credentials," Reginald said before Davin had a chance to ask.

"Please sit, Reggie," Davin said being a little sarcastic for the interruption. "MI-6, always wanted to meet one of your people but never had the chance. Pleasure to meet you Reggie."

"It's Reginald. Mr. Pierce or should I call you Davin?"

"Please sit, and Davin is fine, what can we do for you?" Davin asked. "Sorry for the Reggie bit."

"Thank you, sir, eh, Davin. Most of my few friends call me Reg, only my mother calls me Reggie. Seth called me and asked to meet with you. I am heading up the

43

investigation into the deaths of your two comrades. I was hoping we could work together to find the people who killed them and why," Reginald stated, signaled the waitress to return and then placed an order for Shepherd's Pie and another ale.

During the lunch, Reginald spelled out everything Scotland Yard and MI-6 knew about the murders and hoped Davin would do the same, but they didn't know anything more than what was already talked about. It seemed that they were at a dead end, literally.

"Davin, Connie and Julie, here is my contact information; I can be reached at that number anytime, day or night. My contact at the yard is Howard Smythe; his number is on the back of my card. Very good investigator for being so young. We need to get to the bottom of this soon. From what Seth told me, there may have been a security leak which could cause major problems with both our governments."

"That is a very true statement, Reg. We will get to the bottom of this as quickly as possible," Connie assured him.

"I will be in contact soon; you have a good day," Reginald said and then stood, dropped several large English bills on the table. "My treat."

"Now that was very interesting," Julie commented.

"Yes, it was; have you met him before, Julie?" Davin asked.

"Yeah, he has been in the office several times, good friends with Seth."

"Now who is this guy?" Connie questioned as she watched another man walk over to the table.

"Sorry to interrupt your meal. My name is Inspector Horace Blackstone, Scotland Yard. I couldn't help but seeing you having a meal with Reginald. Do you mind if I ask who you are and why you were meeting with MI-6?" Horace Blackstone said and then showed his credentials and sat beside Davin.

"Sir, we are here on vacation; Julie knows Reginald and invited him to join us. Nothing strange about that is there?" Davin fired back, not feeling comfortable talking to this Inspector.

"Just curious, old boy. He has been on our radar for several months; I can't say why but be careful with him. He may be MI-6 but, well, I can't say more here. Come by my office at the yard around four today and I will explain. Good day, ladies and sir." With that Horace got up and walked out of the tavern.

"Now what do you suppose that was about?" Connie asked nobody in particular.

"Well, I guess we will find out at four. Let's go," Davin said. He stood and waited for the ladies to stand and they all walked out; Davin stopped at the waitress and handed her the money for lunch left by Reginald. "Thank you, we will be back."

"Seems like everyone knows more about this case than we do, Julie. Let's stop by the hotel and office, I need to pick up a few things before we go to Scotland Yard," Davin suggested.

"Good idea, I could use a few minutes rest anyway and make a call back to the office," Connie agreed as they slid into the car.

At four that afternoon, Davin, Connie, and Julie walked up to the entrance of Scotland Yard and stopped at the front desk where they found a female and male guard monitoring everything within the lobby and perimeter of the building. There were no less than twenty monitors built into the desk in front of them. The male stood and contrary to the local police, or Bobbies as they were known, they wore sidearms.

"Good Afternoon, welcome to Scotland Yard. May we help you?" the male guard said with a very thick British accent.

"We are here to see Horace Blackstone," Davin replied.

"Your names and credentials, please."

"I'm Davin Pierce; this is my wife, Connie, and Julie Thompson, our liaison," Davin said as he handed the guard his credentials followed by Connie's and Julie's.

"CIA, welcome, we don't get many visitors from the CIA; please have a seat and I will let Inspector Blackstone know you are here."

"We would also like to meet with Howard Smythe, if he is available?" Connie asked.

"Sorry, but Inspector Smythe is unavailable. However, I believe Inspector Blackstone can help you with whatever you need. Please have a seat," the guard insisted, pointing to the chairs beside the west wall.

Five minutes later, Inspector Blackstone entered the lobby through a door behind the guard desk. He spoke with the guards for a moment and then came around to greet Davin, Connie, and Julie.

"Please pick up your visitor badge from the desk, sign in and then follow me. We have much to talk about," Blackstone said and then walked back toward the desk with everyone following. After retrieving visitor badges, they followed him through a door and down a long hallway to a small but comfortable conference room. Blackstone locked the door after everyone had entered. "Please take a seat, coffee and tea are on the table over there if you want any."

"Inspector, what is going on. We seem to be meeting with a variety of people and still have zero information as to what happened to our people," Davin said as he sat at the end of the conference table.

"First, Mr. Pierce, you need to know this has gotten much bigger than just the murder of two of your people. Inspector Smythe was found dead a few hours ago. Killed while having a meal. Shot in the back of his head. Suspects, well, we have none; just like we have no suspects for the murders of your people. Can you tell me what your people were working on?"

"I can answer that," Julie piped in.

"I thought you didn't know," Connie stated.

"I didn't until we stopped back at the office and Seth took me aside while you two were reviewing documents at Marvin's and Cecil's desk," Julie stated. "Seth authorized me to tell you and the Inspector when we got in a secure room. I presume this room is as secure as we can get here at the yard, sir."

"Yes, Ms. Thompson. This room is secure, no cameras or microphones. But you need to turn off your cell phones to ensure privacy." Everyone removed their cell phones and turned them off. Blackstone collected them and took them out of the room and placed them in a basket designed to hold cell phones outside in the hall. "Now we are completely secure. Please proceed Ms. Thompson."

"Okay, Marvin and Cecil were tracking a member of a known terrorist group with hopes of turning her to collect information as to what the group was planning. Seth thinks that she is the one that killed them, but he has no solid proof. The information they had died with them. Her identity is unknown at this point."

"What group was she supposedly attached to?" Davin asked.

"Bin Laden's," Julie replied.

"Here in London, this is not good, not good at all," Blackstone stated.

"I was told that London has cameras everywhere and maybe we can find out who she is if we can view the time our people were killed," Julie said hoping she was right.

"Yes, it is true we have cameras everywhere and we are looking at the footage surrounding the area where your people's bodies were found; we are also looking at it where Smythe was shot. Maybe, and I am pretty sure, all three are connected."

"How can you be sure?" Connie questioned.

"That was the easy part, your two were killed with one of their own weapons, a nine-millimeter issued by your organization. And Smythe was killed with the same weapon."

"But you recovered both weapons, wait, do you have a time of death for Smythe?" Connie continued her questioning.

"Yes, Smythe was killed a few hours after your people and well before we found the weapons and his body.

Ballistics prove the same weapon in all three murders. We have the weapons downstairs."

"Okay, not good, but okay. You said to watch out for Reginald Knight from MI-6. Can you elaborate on that as to why?" Davin cut in before Connie got a chance to ask another question.

"Yes, Mr. Knight does work for MI-6 and has for a number of years. He has in the past been very cooperative with our investigations and has proven to be an asset. Up until lately. We are not sure why, but he has gone dark way too often," Blackstone started to say.

"But isn't that what spies do; here now and then gone on secret missions." Davin questioned.

"Yes, but in tracking his movements, which we have been doing when asked by his section head to do so, he has not been doing the things he was supposed to do. For one, he has visited the Soviet Embassy on multiple occasions along with trips to the Middle East, most notably Iran."

"He's a spy; wasn't he tasked to go there?" Connie stepped in.

"His mission according to his supervisor had nothing to do with Iran or the Middle East in general. His mission was not disclosed to us, but we were told his mission should not have taken him out of England during the time he was gone."

"So, you think he may be a double agent?" Davin asked.

"It would seem he is up to something that is not sanctioned by MI-6. And I must add, MI-6 asked us because he may have ears within MI-6 to alert him of an investigation and they didn't want to alert him to being watched," Blackstone concluded.

"Do you have any proof or just speculation? And would you consider him a suspect in the murders?" Connie asked and then leaned forward in her chair.

"Speculation on our part, but yes, I would consider him a possible suspect in the murders. We have cameras scattered around the city and he has been seen in the general area where the bodies were found," Blackstone replied.

"Is it possible the killer was a female friend or contact of our guys?" Davin asked.

"Very well could be, but again we don't have camera footage of the area where they were killed. For some reason, which we are looking into, the cameras in that area malfunctioned for a two-hour period during the exact time the coroner estimated they were killed."

"So, we have someone that can hack into your video monitoring system and shut down the cameras when and wherever they wish. This is just getting better every minute," Connie stated.

"What next?" Julie asked after being quiet during the whole conversation.

"That is a very good question. For sure we need to dig and hopefully not our own graves," Davin replied.

"Be careful who you trust?" Blackstone commented.

"So, can we trust you?" Julie asked.

"That is up to you. I am a trusted Inspector with Scotland Yard, but we are all human and can be bought. Depending on the price and motivation. You decide but be careful outside of this facility and yours as to who you put your trust into. I believe you can trust me. I must ask if you would keep me informed as to your progress, and I will do the same."

"We will as best we can; somethings may fall into a classified area which we will not be able to disclose, but anything related to the murders we will be happy to tell you," Davin stated and got Julie's agreement with a nod.

"Fair enough," Blackstone agreed.

After leaving Scotland Yard, the three started to walk toward Julie's parked car, enjoying the sights and smells of London.

"Why don't we just can the case and take a vacation. It's been years since we have had a vacation and even longer since we have been in London. What do you say, Davin?" Connie teased as they approached the car.

"Would really love to but with three murders and two of them our people, we can't just drop it. And it is looking like it goes much deeper than just a robbery gone bad. Let's get back to your office, Julie. I want to talk to Seth, and I need you two to dig up all the past cases our guys were working on and see if there is anything strange or out of place," Davin ordered.

"Roger that boss," Connie acknowledged, getting a smile from Davin.

"Everything is on the server; I'll just need to check Connie's clearance level before accessing it with her."

"Trust me, her clearance is probably as high or higher than yours, Julie. But please verify, I don't want any other breaches in security. Also, now that I'm thinking about it, make sure only you two access the files. If Seth thinks there may be a mole in the house, we don't want to expose ourselves too much, at least not yet."

"Good point," Julie agreed and then climbed in behind the wheel and started the car while Connie and Davin strapped in. Forty-five minutes later, she stopped the car in front of London CIA facility and turned off the engine. Seth was just walking down the steps toward them when he looked up and saw them pull in. He waited for all to exit the car before he walked over to them.

"Good evening, I hope you have had a productive day. I know we did. Please come inside, I have information for you," Seth said. He turned and started up the steps, just as it started to rain. "Just in time, I would say," he said once they were in the lobby. "Down to my office. Do you need to use the restroom? I have drinks in my office." After pausing, he then said, "No, okay." "Level two down," he spoke to the elevator automated system and the doors closed behind them and started down.

"Seth, what is going on now?" Davin asked when they reached his office and sat across the desk for him.

"Got a call from Reginald Knight; he told me that you met, and he offered help in the investigation. And before you say anything, he is with MI-6; and he is not to be trusted. We have had dealings with him before, and every time the operation went sideways. Remember the old movies with Inspector Clouseau; well, he makes him look good. This guy has screwed up no less than three of our covert operations, and he will screw up your investigation too. Keep him at arm's length if possible," Seth stated quickly.

"He didn't come off as a screw up, but we only talked for about ten minutes; then he left, and an Inspector Blackstone visited us. He seemed pretty straight," Davin commented before he looked over at the Scotch bottle on the table near Seth's desk and pointed at it. After getting a nod from Seth, Davin stood and poured himself a drink after offering to pour for anyone else and got a no from all. "Okay, your loss." He paused to take a sip. "Ahh, good scotch; Knight said you called him to join us. Is that true?"

"No, I did not call him; haven't spoken to him in weeks. He actually said that I called?"

"Yes, and said you asked him to assist us if possible," Connie interjected.

"Okay, don't feed him any information without clearing it with me," Seth ordered and then stood and poured himself a scotch. "Changed my mind. Julie, if you want one, it's okay."

"Sure, thanks sir," Julie replied. "I kind of like Agent Knight, but I would compare him more to Agent Smart of the TV series Get Smart. Not as much as a bumbling fool but trying too hard."

"I partly agree, but, in any case, you clear everything through me before giving him anything."

"Roger that, Seth," Julie agreed.

Present Day

"Amber, you see this mission was not just a quick missing person, it turned into multiple murders, espionage and much more," Connie told her daughter.

"So far I can't see what could get me killed. Is there more?" Amber asked and then stood. "I need a refill, you?"

"Yes, I'm getting to that," Connie replied and then headed to the restroom. "Be right back."

"Good time for a break," Amber agreed.

Five minutes later, with fresh drinks and refreshed bodies they sat and stared at each other for a moment.

"Amber, since the loss of your brother, you have to understand that your father and I cannot lose you too. We want you to be careful out there; the person you are hunting is deadly and will show no mercy. She tried to kill Ivy and then pushed her out the back of a plane from 12,000 feet, which almost killed her. But you already know that. Let me continue with the story and you will understand and be able to make your own decision about what's in the safe."

Back in London, CIA Facility

"Connie, come with me and let's leave the boys alone," Julie said, standing and heading for the door.

"Right behind you, Julie," Connie replied and closed the door behind her as she and Julie left the office.

"We can use the big screen in the conference room to compare the files. My access code should allow us access there. This way," Julie said and headed down the hallway.

Meanwhile Davin and Seth discussed the latest information provided by Blackstone and got his thoughts on Blackstone. From everything Davin was hearing, he concluded that there was a little tension between the three organizations and very little trust.

It took until ten o'clock that night to go through all the mission reports and files from the two agents. What they found raised some questions. Several reports by Marvin were not the same as Cecil's; there were some minor discrepancies in several of the after-action reports. Each member of the team had to submit their own version without consulting or comparing what they wrote with any of the other team members.

"Davin glad you decided to grace us with your presence. We have found some minor differences in the after-action reports for both our guys. Look at this." Julie brought up a file dated April 10th of this year, just three months ago.

"Wait, did I read that correctly. Marvin said he met with his informant at eight in the evening and Cecil was not present during the meet. Cecil's report says he met with the informant and does not mention Marvin being there or not. Why would Marvin or Cecil lie on an after-action report; don't they know these will eventually be read by Seth or someone. Or were they hedging their bets that, like the military, these reports rarely ever got read?" Davin questioned what they saw.

"There are other differences, look at this." Connie brought up another document. "This time Marvin says the mission went off without any problems and they got all the information they needed, but Cecil says they had a problem with the informant not producing the information they needed."

"Julie, when did Marvin and Cecil arrive in country?" Davin asked.

"Marvin was assigned here Feb 4, 2019 and Cecil on Sept 7, same year. Marvin is ex-Navy Intel linguist and Cecil ex-Army Intel communications. Neither one was assigned as field agents. So why were they working as field agents?" Julie asked as she scanned their personnel files.

"Was it a match made in heaven or hell? And more importantly who assigned them field duty?" Connie questioned.

"That is a question I need to ask Seth," Davin replied quickly.

"I wasn't here at the time, but I did hear through the grapevine that it was a match made in hell and dictated by Seth. But when I got here, they seemed to be working good together; but maybe that was just an act," Julie answered as she continued to look at Cecil's file. "This is interesting?"

"What did you find?" Davin asked but continued to read more after-action reports.

"Says here that Cecil was married but came here unaccompanied. I didn't know he had a wife. Wait, there's more; he was unaccompanied because his wife died in an auto accident shortly after they were married. I will get the details of that and let you know what I have found."

"What about Marvin, was he married?" Connie asked.

"No, not according to his file. Never married," Julie replied as she skipped over to Marvin's file.

"Okay, we need to know the details of the accident," Connie said and then added, "I will contact my office and see what they can find out about both guys. Something just doesn't feel right. Why were two ops guys assigned field duty when they were not trained as field agents, or were they?"

"I need to know of any lapse in time from leaving the military and joining the CIA. No matter how short, where they were and what they were doing. Connie can you follow up with that too?" Davin asked.

"Sure, that should be easy; they both would have had an update on their clearance paperwork. I will contact DIA and see what they have," Connie promised.

"Good, it's late; let's call it a night and get a fresh start in the morning. I'm hungry and I bet you two are also. Dinner is on me if the restaurant is still open," Davin said and then stood and stretched.

"It stays open late for us all night workers," Julie commented as she started to shut down the computers.

Present day, Pierce Living room

"Mom, I'm getting pretty tired, can we continue tomorrow?" Amber asked between yawns.

"Let me wrap up this part of the nightmare first; I will condense it," Connie agreed and then looked at the clock on the wall. "Yeah, it's almost midnight. But anyway, I'll wrap up this now and shorten the rest of the nightmare in the morning."

"Deal! Now don't get me wrong; I want to know, but I want to be awake to listen and ask questions."

"Okay, well we continued to do research on Marvin and Cecil and came up with a plethora amount of stuff that just didn't make sense. First, when Marvin got out of the Navy, he disappeared for about two months; his clearance docs says he went for a hike in Alaska and was completely off the grid. I had my friends at my office check flights, hotels, rental agencies, everything they could think of to get a true picture of Marvin. It turns out that there were no flights, hotels, camp stores or anything that showed he did in fact go to Alaska. What they did find was a round trip airfare to Singapore and then he fell off the grid. No trail to follow, just dead air."

"So, where did he go?" Amber questioned.

"Sources have confirmed he met with several Chinese businessmen, whom we have recently learned are legitimate businessmen, but who also work for the Chinese Intelligence Agency. It looks like Marvin may have jumped ship and gone over to the dark side."

"Okay, so where does Cecil fit in and I am still wondering about the Station Chief Seth?" Amber's eyes lit up when she heard about Marvin.

"Cecil was just in the wrong place with the wrong person at the wrong time. He was as clean as a snowflake and got caught up in a bit of bad espionage. And got killed for it," Connie concluded.

"What about Seth?"

"That is another nightmare, Seth turned out to be Marvin's handler and he did assign Cecil to him to help cover up the fact that Seth and Marvin were working both sides as double agents."

"One last question before I go to bed. Why do I need to know this and how is knowing all this going to keep me from becoming dead; and why aren't you and dad dead because of this, whatever it is?"

"This was just the beginning of the nightmare and I told you all this, so you will understand what happened six years later when you and your brother were on vacation with us in the Bahamas. But as Paul Harvey used to say, *'That is another story.'.*"

"In the morning, mom. Oh, what happened to Julie?"

"Julie, well, she was shot when Seth met with two Chinese agents to deliver a disk with classified information on it. From what Julie said, it was suspected that Seth was selling classified information to the Chinese and for some unknown reason one of the Chinese agents pulled a gun and shot Seth. Julie had followed Seth to the meeting site, not knowing what was going down until she saw the Chinese agents, which she had recognized from a report that had been sent to her office just the day before. Being a good agent, she charged in to try to save Seth but was shot for her effort. She told us what happened. Seth and one of the Chinese agents were also killed and that is part of the nightmare which I want to forget."

59

"What happened to the documents or disk? And again, did Julie survive?"

"The other Chinese agent left his partner and ran. Julie recovered the disk and it is in the safe. She is now the Deputy Director of the London Office but not without complications. Her left arm is completely paralyzed, the damage from the bullet was too extensive to repair. That is only part of the problem; what is on the disk would bring down governments, ours, and several others. So, you see why we haven't let it out. But there are still people looking for it. They don't know we have it," Connie explained.

"Do you know what is on the disk?" Amber asked, not expecting an answer and left Connie deep in her thoughts.

"Yes, I do and sleep well," Connie said and watched Amber walk to her bedroom.

"See you in the morning, mom," Amber said quietly as she headed for her bedroom.

Six Years later, CIA HQ

"Good morning and welcome back Mr. Pierce. How was your trip?" the guard at the front desk lobby of CIA Headquarters said as he greeted Davin Pierce.

"Trip was good; do you know if Josh Randal is in his office?" Davin queried.

"I know he isn't; he is in the cafeteria with Mary Henderson, his new secretary and Ms. Stephanie," the guard replied and then handed Davin his badge.

"Good, I need a cup of coffee anyway," Davin said and then headed to the cafeteria to meet with Josh Randal, the Assistant Deputy Chief of Covert Operations for the CIA.

Minutes later, Davin was standing behind Josh holding a cup of coffee when Josh slowly turned around.

"You know Davin that if we were not in CIA HQ and you had snuck up on me like that, I probably would have killed you," Josh said laughing, "Good trip. Anything I need to know before I finish my breakfast."

"Not here. But it is more like lunch," Davin commented. "Hi, I don't think we have met; I'm Davin Pierce Chief of Nothing and I like it that way," he said in order to drop a heavy hint to Josh to leave him out of the politics of management.

"I've heard a lot about you and your lovely wife, Connie, isn't it? I'm Mary Henderson, I believe you know my father and brother," Mary commented.

"You are Bear's daughter; finally get to meet you. And yes, both have pulled my backside out of the fire several times. So, you are the younger sister; pleasure to finally meet you. But please tell me that you are not working for this bozo."

"As a matter of fact, I just started this week working with Mr. Randal," Mary said with a smile.

"I'm so sorry for you; you know he is a workaholic and does not appreciate anybody. He will..." Davin started to talk smack about Josh when Stephanie stood up and looked Davin in the eye.

"That's enough, you will scare her away," Stephanie scolded, with a very angry look.

"Okay I will stop; he really is not a bad guy once you get to know him. May I join you?" Davin conceded.

"Yes, but no more bashing or I will start on your bad habits," Josh replied smiling.

"Let's not go there. Josh, we do need to talk, privately in your office. Yes, I know both of these fine ladies have very high clearances but not for what I need to tell you and you alone."

"Okay, give me time to finish my breakfast and then we'll go up. Until then tell me about your trip," Josh requested.

"That is what we need to talk about, but not here."

"How's Connie?" Stephanie asked.

"She's fine, recovering from jet lag but doing fine," Davin answered.

Small talk continued for another twenty minutes before Josh finished his breakfast. "Let's go; you have my undivided attention for the next forty minutes when I have to brief the boss. Maybe you should go with me and tell him your story too. Is it good enough for the boss?" Josh asked, referring to the President of the United States as the boss, not the Director of the CIA, who would also be at the meeting.

"What happened while I was away that gets you a meeting with the boss?" Davin asked as they entered the elevator.

"I'll tell you upstairs."

Josh Randal's Office, third floor

"Have a seat, coffee?" Josh offered as he walked around behind his antique desk.

"Nice desk, how did you get it in here?" Davin asked as he admired the century old wooden desk.

"That was the tricky part, but it's here and I love it. But we are getting away from the purpose of this meeting. You want to know what happened while you were playing in

Panama. Well, a lot; first, the President has ordered troops to the southern border; seems that we have another group of terrorists wanting to cross the border illegally, and he wants it stopped."

"That doesn't involve the company. What has happened that I need to be aware of?" Davin interrupted.

"The most important thing is I'm being promoted, again. I tried to talk the Director out of it, but failed."

"You are already Deputy Director of Covert Operations, what next? Director?" Davin joked.

"Yes, the Director of Covert Ops is retiring; says she has had enough of the cloak and dagger stuff and just wants to relax at her cabin and watch the sunset," Josh stated.

"So, congrats to you for becoming the new Director of Covert Ops. Now I get the funny feeling that it doesn't end there. My answer is no."

"You don't know the question, but yes you will and that is an order. And I will throw in this desk. I know you want it; and it is time you stepped out of the field and learned a bit of the political BS that I have put up with for the past two years."

"And a case of fifty-year scotch may help seal the deal," Davin teased.

"Done. I knew you were going to say that, and the case is in that cabinet right there," Josh said pointing toward the cabinet.

"Do I get to keep Mary, too."

"Yes, but we have to share her. Due to budget cutbacks, we are down to one secretary for the both of us," Josh said. He then stood and walked around the desk to shake Davin's hand and congratulate him on his promotion.

"When?"

"Effective immediately. I have already moved into the corner office with the big window, this one is yours," Josh replied and then started for the door.

"Wow. Don't you want to hear what happened in Panama?"

"I'll read your after-action report; have it on my desk before close of business. Oh, the computer there is clean with all the proper accesses and programs. Enjoy old friend," Josh said. He left the office leaving Davin to think about what just happened.

'What the hell have I gotten into now, another nightmare,' Davin thought to himself. When he walked around behind his new desk, he noticed that the stuff on it was from his bull pen desk.

Four Hours Later

"Davin, can you come into my office?" Josh said when he stuck his head into Davin's office. "I just read your report. What do you mean when you say that Miquel Sanchez was released by the police? Did I read that right?"

"Yes, we set up a sting and allowed the local police to make the arrest to keep our involvement a secret; and within hours of arrest, they let him go. Our local agent asked why and was told to mind his own business, that Sanchez was a trusted businessman within the community and was released without bail. He has fled the country already, in the wind, as it were."

"You spent a year tracking this guy only to lose him to the Panamanian police. What's your next move?"

"Well, before he was released, he had a large meal provided by the police, but prepared by one of our gourmet chefs complete with a small amount of radio-active tracking ingredient, so we know where he is and until that wears off, we can track him. Right now, he is in Miami, Florida."

"This man is a gun runner, drug king pin, and sex trade dealer just to name a few things on his list of crimes; when do you propose to pick him up?"

"Actually, I just talked to the US Marshalls in Miami and they are moving in as we speak. He should be in custody within the hour," Davin replied smiling.

"Good work. You are going to make a great Deputy Director," Josh said. "Oh, before you go, can you bring me up to date on the London job that you and Connie were involved in with Julie Thompson and the death of three agents. It's been six years, anything new on it?"

"I have nothing but nightmares about that one and no I don't have anything new on who that Chinese agent was or how Seth and Marvin were involved with him. But as far as the deaths of Marvin and Cecil, it looks like they were meeting with someone that somehow got Marvin's weapon, shot Cecil, and then shot Marvin with his own gun. What the meet was for or anything beyond that is still under investigation. Seth, on the other hand, was working as a double agent with the Chinese. How this was related to the death of our two agents is yet to be determined. But we feel they were related and are looking into that; keep in mind this case is now six years old and very little information is coming up. Julie Thompson has been keeping us posted on any information that comes up. We are hopeful we will get to the bottom soon," Davin concluded, not telling everything he knew just yet or the fact that he had the disk that disappeared that day.

"Is that everything, Davin?"

"Yep. That's it."

"Keep me posted," Josh said. He then looked Davin in the eye and added. "Get back to work."

Present day

"Amber I only have a little more to tell you and then I will show you the disk. You need to know this; it may save your life or get us all killed," Connie commented and then waited for her daughter to sit and sip her coffee.

"Okay, mom, I'm ready. Remember Andi and Ivy are picking me up at three."

"I know, this will not take long. Let's go back to when you and Josh were twelve and your dad just got promoted to Deputy Director of Covert Operations. He really wasn't happy about it, but your dad, like always, dove in headfirst. He did make some changes and recruit some new talent and told Josh that he was still going to work in the field when he felt the need."

Day after Promotion Day, years ago

"Davin there is a Julie Thompson on the secure line for you," Mary said to Davin when she poked her head into Davin's office.

"Good, been waiting for her call. Please close the door, Mary," Davin said. After he picked up the secure phone, he said, "Good evening, Julie, how are things in London?"

"Hello boss. I just heard you were promoted to Deputy Director; congrats are in order, right?"

"Not yet, I don't feel like the new DD. But you didn't call me to wish me well for becoming the new Deputy, did you?" Davin shot back.

"No, I didn't, but what's the possibility of you flying over here soon. We have some new information that you need to see," Julie asked.

"Can't you just send it; I'm kind of busy here."

"No can do, boss. Too big, you will understand when you get here. Oh, and bring some old clothes that you wouldn't mind getting dirty. I will send a couple of pictures to spark your interest."

"Okay, I will call and get the company jet and be there by morning. Should I bring Connie?"

"Yes, for sure, she will be interested in this too."

"See you tomorrow. I will let you know when we will land, and you can pick us up."

"Roger that, boss," Julie said and then broke the connection.

Davin stood and walked over to Josh's office, knocked on the door and then entered. "Josh, boss, I need to go to London tonight. Can I borrow the plane?"

"What? That is for company business and no you can't borrow the company jet. But wait, does this have anything to with the murders six years ago?" Josh asked quickly.

"Yes, but I can't tell you why until I get back from London."

"You can't, why not?" Josh asked.

"Because I don't know, yet. Julie Thompson called and asked if Connie and I would fly over tonight because they have found new information about the case and she needs to show us and explain in person," Davin answered and sat down across from Josh.

"Show you, why? Is it so big she can't send it over in an email?"

"Yep," Davin replied just as there was a knock on the door.

"Enter," Josh yelled, and Mary stepped in with a small stack of papers.

"This just came into the office over the secure fax, I do believe you need to see them. They came for the London office," Mary said and handed them to Davin.

"Wow, okay now I see why we need to go. Look at this, Josh," Davin said handing Josh a couple of the pages.

"I would say so. Mary call the pilots and put them on standby to depart for London in two hours," Josh ordered as he studied the pictures of a submarine and what appeared to be a Navy destroyer parked next to it. It did not say when or where the pictures were taken.

"Go find out what they know and report back as soon as you can. I know you three have been working this case for the past six years; it is time you got to the bottom of it," Josh ordered, and then added, "This looks and smells like the same boat that you and I had the pleasure of being on years ago. Could it possibly be the same one? No way, I thought we sunk that one."

"After we brought it back to Norfolk, the Navy took charge and I really don't know what happened to it, but I will find out. I will call when I'm in London," Davin said, then stood and left the office. He stopped by his office to retrieve his weapon and some notes, taking the photos, and headed for the elevator. Once in his car, he called Connie to alert her of the trip and told her to pack bags for the kids too; they can go on this trip. Nothing dangerous can happen on a look and see trip.

Present day, Pierce house on Kauai

"Okay, now you know how your dad started moving up the ladder at the company. As you know now, he is acting Director and hopefully will step down as soon as Josh gets better. He was planning on retiring this year. But you need to know a little more; then you will understand that no matter what you do in life, you will have a target on your back. People have been trying to kill your dad and me for years and luckily they have failed."

"It was on to new business at the company, so he thought," Connie added. "What we found when we got there directly linked new evidence to the murders of three agents and more."

"I remember that trip. Josh and I were only twelve, but you treated us like adults. When we got there, you had us stay with friends while you worked. Almost not fair, but we understood. You never told us what you found out; is that what you are telling me now?" Amber questioned.

"Yes, when we were in the air, your father called an old family friend and they agreed to let you stay with them and to watch you two while we went with Julie to see what she found. Let me pick up from when we landed."

London Heathrow International Airport General Aviation hangar

"Welcome to London, are these your kids? It is a pleasure to finally meet the both of you. Davin and Connie. We have a helicopter waiting to take us to the site. Your kids can go, but it would be best that they didn't," Julie said to Davin.

"Not a problem. Admiral Henderson will be picking them up. There he is now," Davin said as he saw Admiral 'Bear' Henderson with his wife walking out the lobby door.

"Bear, how the hell are you?" Davin said giving his old friend a big hug.

"Doing fine, Davin. Connie, you still hanging out with this loser?" Bear said and hugged Connie. "Amber and Josh, you two have grown since the last time I saw you, how long has it been?"

"Five years, three months and seven days, Admiral," Amber jokingly said and hugged her second godfather. Josh Randal was their first godfather, and they loved both.

"Couldn't be that long," Bear said thinking.

"Yeah," Josh agreed and shook Bears' hand.

"I have a car waiting and I know Davin and Connie have a helo waiting, so grab your things and let's go," Bear said and then turned back to Davin and Connie, "You do remember where the house is, don't you?"

"Yes, don't know how long we will be. I will call and keep you posted. We must go. Thanks for taking care of the kids," Connie commented and then hugged both kids and started toward the helo after Julie.

"Bear, again thanks. I will call soon," Davin said before he turned and ran toward the waiting helo.

Once onboard the helicopter, the pilot lifted off. Julie turned and looked at Davin and Connie with concern and then said, "We are going to the coast where there is an abandoned submarine base. Some hikers stumbled on this; and well, what they found was scary. I remembered a report I read about you and Josh Randal and a Soviet Missile submarine; and well, this may be the same boat."

"That is interesting," Connie said.

"Is the pilot one of ours?" Davin asked.

"Yes, and so is the chopper. I will fill you in with more when we get there," Julie said as she leaned back to relax.

"Are the hikers still there, or available? And what coast are we heading for?" Davin asked as they crossed over the Cliffs of Dover and were over water.

"The hikers are available but sit back and enjoy the ride; we have a long way to go."

"Where are we going anyway?" Connie questioned.

"An abandoned Nazi Submarine pen located at Ijmuiden, Netherlands," Julie commented calmly. *(see appendix for information on U-Boat submarine pens built by Nazis)*

"Netherlands, how the hell did a Soviet missile boat end up there after all these years?" Davin questioned.

"That is the six-million-dollar question, and there is more. But I want to show you when we get there; don't want to spoil the surprise," Julie said as she smiled.

"Okay, if you insist. We will wait," Connie said and then leaned back in the comfortable seat and looked out the window at the English Channel below them.

Two hours and twenty minutes later, the helicopter set down on a dock a hundred yards from the abandoned submarine pen. The doors opened, and they were greeted by several uniformed police and two men dressed in coveralls.

"Welcome back, Ms. Thompson," the taller of the two said, "Please follow us. We will brief you in the trailer over there." He pointed to a camper trailer parked near a wall.

"Please have a seat; first let me introduce myself. We briefly met six years ago at the Boar's Drool Ale House, Reginald Knight, MI-6, Chief of Operations now. And this is my partner James Wittman. We have been working on the case of your three murdered agents; and with this discovery, we may have a solid lead behind what actually happened when the two hikers stumbled into this place. They had no idea that what they were seeing. Deep inside this facility is now a fully operational, and very old Soviet missile boat. It's one you may recognize. I understand you have been on board her, along with a small crew, and were able to disarm the explosives on board and quite literally save the world. Be that as it may, here she sits. We were able to capture two dozen Chinese nationals working on her in an attempt to make her seaworthy again. We are not sure why, yet, but have a good idea. In addition to the Chinese, we were able to recover this." He held up a small 'S' disk. "On this disk is the classified report that was filed with your FBI and CIA. How they got it, we believe was part of the exchange that may have gotten Seth Connors killed. But at this point we can't prove that; it may have been one of the other two that passed it on to the Chinese. We are questioning the prisoners and will get an answer soon."

"This is deeper than I thought," Davin commented.

"It just gets better and better doesn't it, Davin?" Connie replied.

"To quote a phrase that you Americans like to use, *'You ain't seen nothing yet,'*" Reginald replied, smiling.

"What else do you have?" Connie asked.

"Not me, Ms. Julie has more information for you," Reginald replied.

"That's correct, but first I think we need to go out and look at your boat. We need to be on board. Let's go," Julie said and started for the door. She stopped when she saw Reginald hesitate. "Are you coming Reg?"

"No, go ahead. I have had enough of that boat for one day."

"Okay, but you won't know what I know."

"Really, MI-6 knows everything," Reginald teased.

"No, they don't, come on," Davin said.

As they walked slowly down the pier toward the submarine, Davin had flashbacks to when he and Josh almost died on that boat causing him to slow his pace and fall behind the rest.

"Davin, are you okay?" Connie asked seeing him falling behind.

"Yeah, just remembering what we went through on that thing." After pausing for a second, he yelled up to Julie, "Julie are the missiles still on that boat?"

"No, when we got here all the missile tubes were empty," she replied.

"Didn't that send up a red flag? Where are the missiles?" Davin asked as he stopped at the gangway with the rest of the team.

"We don't know, and yes, we are trying to find out. Hopefully, the Chinese that were working on her know the answer. And yes, we are very concerned. Come on board; I have something you need to see," Julie said and then opened the hatch to the control tower.

Present Day

"Let me wrap this up really quick, you need to get ready to go, Andi and Ivy should be here shortly. There were heavily armed Marines surrounding the boat and at each entrance. This was understandable and expected, but the amount of security was over whelming; we didn't have this much security at the London office. We entered the old boat and Julie took us down to the main deck and into the Officers Lounge where she asked us to take a seat. On the

74

table were six file folders marked Top Secret. Not sure of what was going on, Davin opened the one in front of him and then closed it quickly. He asked Julie "Is that what I think it is?"

"Yes," Julie responded and then took a seat at the head of the table.

"Why are the pictures of my kids in this folder?" Connie asked being very concerned.

"When the local police arrived and assisted in the capture of the Chinese nationals that were working on this boat, they allowed our men to enter the boat first. In doing so they located and captured three more in this room. They had no idea of what had taken place outside and were just sitting here drinking tea and reading and most likely discussing these files. When two of my men entered the room with weapons drawn, they just leaned back in their chairs and one spoke asking, "Who the hell are you, and how did you get on board my boat?" "Julie said and paused to let that sink in.

"After a few minutes, Julie came on board and entered the lounge and asked the speaker to explain what they were doing on a Soviet missile boat and why they had our photos and stats on the table. He refused to answer, and they were removed from the boat and put in holding cells which are conveniently located within the base. That is when Julie called us, and we flew over. After hours of interrogation, the leader finally admitted that they had been hired to get the boat seaworthy and to assassinate us, including you and Josh," Connie said quietly.

"Okay, so they were captured and are probably sitting in jail somewhere which tells me that we are safe, right?" Amber asked.

"No, not exactly. They are in Guantanamo and will be until someone in a much higher paygrade decides otherwise. But the people that hired them are still out there; they would not disclose who they are or how we could capture them. Those files are locked away along with other information."

"So besides you and dad having a bunch of crazies wanting to kill you, what is the point of this story?" Amber asked.

"Well there is more to the story, but you don't have time for it now. The bottom line is that we did piss off a lot of bad people over the years and they have tried and failed many times. The current threat is Monica Teach, ex-CIA Research and Development technician along with her ex-boss, Rocky Soto. But he is dead. She has inherited the mantel and sword to go after all of us. She is very good. And before you ask, yes, she was paying the Chinese to recondition that submarine. We didn't find out that little tidbit until just a few days ago. Her plan is still unknown; the boats missiles are gone, no torpedoes or other weapons; the reactor was still functional, so she might have wanted to make the boat a floating bomb. We just don't know, yet."

"Wow, I guess I need to take her down before she succeeds in killing the rest of my family," Amber agreed.

"Yes. Now go do what you were trained to do and do it fast," Connie ordered.

"You didn't say what was in the safe?" Amber asked as she stood to leave, pausing to ask.

"Popcorn."

"Popcorn? I don't understand," Amber questioned.

"You will soon. Now go."

Twenty hours after departing Kauai, Amber, Ivy and Andi landed in Ho Chi Minh City, Vietnam. Stepping out the door of the company Gulfstream business jet into the one-hundred-degree heat of Ho Chi Minh International Airport was a shock to the system, Amber's system. Kauai was hot but this hot seemed hotter. Ivy and Andi didn't notice any difference. They wouldn't since they were both androids. Waiting at the bottom of the air stairs was a man and woman, both dressed in shorts and light-colored silk shirts.

"Welcome to Vietnam, Miss Pierce. I'm agent Todd Black and this is my partner Ginger Burns." Todd introduced himself and his partner to them and showed their credentials. "We have a car waiting, would you follow us?"

Forty-five minutes later, after fighting through heavy traffic, the car pulled up to an estate located on the north-east corner of the city in a very Hollywood style area. A guard walked over to the car and when seeing the occupants, he signaled for the gate to be opened by another heavily armed guard.

"A fortress of sorts," Ivy commented at seeing the guards, gate and the M1 Abrams tank parked on the lawn about fifty feet from the gate.

"Yes, the war isn't really over out here, there are some diehards that keep trying to restart it. So, we just stay prepared," Todd Black said as they drove up the driveway to the front of the house.

"Do you get many attacks?" Andi questioned.

"No, lately it has been quiet; last month there were three attempts, all failed with the capture of two of the attackers and the death of six others. They don't come in force, more guerilla tactics and for the most part they haven't been able to penetrate much beyond the gate. We officially can't repel the attack until they have fired at us or entered the grounds. We lost a good man to the last attack; he was shot when he stopped a car trying to enter the gate. The attackers were killed."

"But the war is over?" Amber was puzzled.

"True, I will explain once we get inside," Black said when he stopped the car in front of the mansion. "We have rooms set up for you and lunch will be served on the half hour. Come, meet the team."

After entering the mansion and shown their rooms, they all met in the foyer to be escorted to the dining room, where lunch was being placed on the table.

"Todd, you were briefed as to why we are here, correct?" Amber asked between bites of her lunch.

"Yes, and after lunch we will go down to the command center and discuss your plans and tell you what we know. If that is okay, with you," Todd answered.

"Sure, isn't this room secure?" Ivy asked.

"Yes and no, we scan it daily and have discovered it has a weakness. Mostly the windows, anyone with a hi-tech listening device sitting outside our walls can still hear us. We are in the process of turning the entire building into a secure facility but because of budget cuts by our politicians, it has been slow rolled. I hate politicians, they are only there for their own agenda," Todd stated.

"I know what you mean, I am very happy that term limits were approved a few years ago and some of those old lifers have been replaced. Hopefully our government will get its act together in our lifetime," Amber agreed.

After lunch, the five of them walked over to a door in the back of the dining room and entered, climbed down a spiral staircase, and exited in front of a vault door guarded by two armed Marines. After showing their credentials, the one at the desk pressed a button causing a small buzzing sound and the door unlocked. The other Marine pulled the vault door open and allowed the five to enter, closing and locking the door behind them. Once inside they were greeted by three more Marines and another door; this time the guards were behind a glass, assumed to be bullet proof, and again, they had to show credentials and subject themselves to iris scans before the door was opened.

"Wow, some security you have here Todd," Amber said eyeing the amount of security check points they had to go through.

"Can't be too safe here; this door takes us to the SCIF and that one to the bomb shelter and escape route," Todd said pointing toward a door to his left. "No security check except the first one outside to access that one, until you get inside. Once in, you must identify yourself to stay. If not on the list, you are asked to leave."

"You're kidding, aren't you," Amber questioned.

"Yeah, inside joke. We will save as many as possible in there. It can hold about 100 people safely for at least 30 days, plenty of food and water," Todd said smiling as they entered the SCIF.

In the SCIF (Secure Compartmented Information Facility)

"Wow, impressive," Amber commented as they entered the facility. "How long has this been here?"

"The mansion with this underground cavern was built around 1900; we updated it when we got sucked into the conflict. CIA has had the building since 1958 and modified it in the early 60s. This place has saved a lot of lives. And hopefully will continue to do so. Come on in here; we have some things for you to help catch Ms. Monica," Todd said leading Amber and her team into a room near the end of the corridor.

Once inside they saw a rack of weapons, handguns, and various survival gear along with four manila folders marked Top Secret.

"Please have a seat, you are welcome to take anything in this room for your mission except the folders. Read them, memorize what's in there, but they cannot leave the facility. Top Secret you know," Ginger said as they sat down, speaking for the first time since they arrived.

"Thank you, Ginger," Ivy said politely.

"I will be doing the briefing here. Todd has some work to do upstairs, so shall we get on with it. Todd, keep me informed as to your progress, please?" Ginger asked and watched as Todd started for the door, with a nod and wink at Ginger.

After Todd left, Ginger flipped a switch on the table which dimmed the lights and lit a sign outside the door stating the room was in use and to not disturb.

"Okay, now we get down to business. My name is Ginger Burns, I have been with the agency for twenty-two years. My function here is Chief of Station, Todd is my second. I know you thought the other way, but we do it that way for many reasons which I will not go into right now. I worked with your father before being assigned over here. You are here to learn all we know about Monica Teach, her location, her team and whatever else we know. So, this meeting will be kind of short because we don't know much. Her team consists of approximately sixty mercenaries; she has a large amount of cash handy to purchase people, weapons and whatever she wants. We have tried to put a freeze on any accounts she may have, but she doesn't use banks or anything within the system that we can freeze. You were told she was in Vietnam; well, that is incorrect. She is in Bangkok, Thailand. Our office there has been trying to track her but are failing. She has that holographic device and uses it when she travels. There have been sightings around Bangkok, but when approached she virtually disappears right in front of our agents. The bottom line is that we are not sure she is even in country," Ginger stated. "We can get you into and out of Thailand without much difficulty but locating Monica and taking her down will be your problem."

"But if she isn't there, why bother going?" Andi asked while he was reading the file.

"Yeah, why not set a trap and have her come to us?" Ivy asked.

"Okay, what do you think will get her to come to us?" Ginger asked.

"Well, my mom told me a story which she didn't have time to finish, about a Soviet missile boat that they found in the Netherlands that was linked to Monica. It was a few years ago, do you know what happened to that boat?" Amber offered.

"Yes, as a matter of fact, I do. It was taken to Norfolk Naval Yard, which is where I saw it last. As far as I know, it is still there. That is a long way from here; and it has been six years since it was moved there. It may be scrap now anyway."

"Yeah, you are probably right about that. But there was something about that boat that she wanted and had those Chinese workers there to either find something or get it ready for sea. Only they know for sure and they are not talking," Amber said and then looked at the unopened folder again.

"We need to attract her here or go there to get her."

"How about this? She wants to kill my parents. Let's set it up so she can, here, or maybe, in Thailand," Amber offered as a possible solution.

"That is a good idea, Amber," Ivy agreed. "Andi and I can be the decoys and with the help of this facility and Ginger's personnel we should be able to trick her."

"But how?" Ginger asked and watched as Ivy and Andi transformed into Davin and Connie Pierce right in front of her eyes.

"How?" Ginger asked, not knowing that Ivy and Andi were androids with holographic devices implanted within their systems.

"I guess you were never told, and this is very Top Secret, Ginger. Both Ivy and Andi are androids and have very specialized systems," replied Amber letting out their secret.

"It is true, Ms. Ginger, we are androids designed to blend in and do things human agents cannot do. Our systems have the holographic device built in. We are human in all respects. We bleed, can simulate death, eat, drink, and even digest food; although not like you do, but with the use of chemicals in our system, we can digest food. We are programed in many things that we cannot discuss here."

"I heard the company was working on building robots to help in our work, but I had no idea; androids, wow, you look so human," Ginger stated.

"We are human in every aspect and anatomically correct in every way. Remember years ago, there was a few companies building human-like dolls to be used as sex partners; well, we took their work a lot farther," Ivy said smiling.

"Wow, we could succeed with this plan. You two can be Davin and Connie Pierce. We will set you up in one of the best hotels in the city. Since you are here to help track down Monica, you need to be seen around the country. Maybe you two should travel to where Davin was stationed during the war here in Vietnam. We will leak that they are here and hopefully draw Monica out. Amber you need to contact your parents and tell them the plan. Have them go undercover back at home." Ginger stated this out loud even though everyone already knew the plan and she was only stating the obvious. "You also have to be seen with Amber on occasion, but you know all that; I guess I am just setting it straight in my mind. Okay, let's get to work."

"There may be a minor problem with the plan. Dad is now the acting director of the company. Josh is in the hospital; he had a stroke."

"I got a message about that but didn't know that your father was the acting director. That could complicate things a little; tell him to keep a low profile and for he and Connie not to leave or have contact with anyone outside the company. Have him send the company jet here with two holographic replacements. We need to make it look like they are really here."

"Yeah, that will work. Is there a secure phone down here?" Amber asked.

"Yes, I will take you to it in a few minutes. But Andi, how long can you stay as Davin?" Ginger asked.

"Indefinitely!" he replied.

"Great! Amber, come with me to make the call."

After a lengthy conversation with her father, Davin agreed to the plan and started to make arrangements to fly two decoys to Vietnam. He and Connie would use holographic devices to change into two analysts with the company for the duration of the plan. Josh Randal was in the hospital, and Stephanie spent most of her time with him.

Washington DC, CIA Headquarters

"Connie, we have to go undercover for a while. Amber has a plan in place to draw out Monica Teach and we are part of the plan," Davin said handing Connie a small personal holographic generator.

"What has she got planned?"

"It's complicated, but I agreed it may work. We will become two agents that are posing as us and we stay here as them; they go to Vietnam as us. Once there, Ivy and Andi will become us and start a tour of the country helping Amber draw out Monica, while the two agents back up Amber as themselves. We will become the two undercover agents here and continue to work assisting Josh and keep this place running," Davin said quickly in the privacy of his office.

"Wow, when do we start?" Connie questioned.

"Our replacements are on their way up now. They will leave this office as us, and we will be them," Davin said just as Mary announced that the two agents had just arrived. "Send them in, Mary," he replied to the intercom.

"Come on in and have a seat; thanks for coming on such short notice. I have a very special mission for you two.

Oh, before I forget; this is my wife Connie, please meet Barbara and Clyde Hines," Davin said to introduce them before continuing. "This mission is classified Top Secret and you are to discuss it with nobody outside this office with the exception of Mary and Connie when I am not here and only them."

"Not a problem, sir," Clyde stated and looked at his wife and got a nod of approval from her.

"For the next hour, you will study the folders in front of you; learn everything there is to know about me and my wife. You are going to be us for a short period. I hope you have some sunscreen packed because you have won an all-expense paid vacation to beautiful Vietnam. As us, you will stay at the local CIA owned safe house and hotel. Once in country, you will meet with our daughter and her two assistants. Go to the local CIA compound and switch places with our two agents already in country. They will assume the duties of being Connie and me. They will be attempting to draw Monica Teach out of hiding and try to kill her. Do you have any problem with being targets for a short period?" Davin started attempting to lighten the assignment a bit with humor. "Our daughter, Amber, is running the operation and you will back her up completely."

"Targets?" Barbara questioned.

"Yeah, I know, but as targets we may be able to catch a criminal that has been causing a lot of damage and death. It is a dangerous assignment, but you will only be targets for a short period, just long enough to get in country and change places with the two agents already there."

"Why don't they just assume being you now and not send us?" Barbara asked.

"Won't work; she has spies everywhere, and we need to be seen boarding the company jet flying to Vietnam. If they suspect anything, this op goes south real fast, it may not work as planned, but we need to put on a good act. Are you prepared to be targets for a short period, if not we will have to kill you now, because you know the plan?" Davin said as a joke.

"Oh, then it doesn't sound so bad. I know about Ms. Teach. Been following the reports of her activities and we are both in on the capture of her," Barbara said answering for the both of them.

"Good, I was hoping you would agree. As back up, you will take orders from Amber. Yes, she is new to the company, but I have complete confidence in her ability and with you two as backups everything should go as planned."

"Only one question, Davin. Why us?" Clyde asked.

"Good question and I have a good answer. You two are about the same build as we are, and I have known you for years. You are the best choice to play us. And you will only be us for the trip over and transport to the hotel. After that you will become yourselves again. Connie and I will become two different agents once you have changed with Ivy and Andi. We will worry about who while you are in transit."

"Fair answer. Okay, I guess we need to read these files and then," Barbara said, "I assume we are going to get a couple of those highly classified Holographic devices to use for this, unless you just want our gifted make up department to change us."

"Once in country, you will give the holo devices to Amber. Yes, they are highly classified; and we don't have time for the graphic department to do a complete makeover of you," Davin commented. "One other thing, you need to watch a short movie to see how Connie and I walk, talk and act, only about a half hour long," Davin said and then sat back in his chair and smiled.

"Okay, let's get started," Clyde said picking up the folder.

27 hours later

"Welcome to Vietnam, mom, dad. We have a car waiting to take you to the hotel. I would like to meet with you after you get settled, say two o'clock in the library. We have a room ready for you at the compound," Amber said as she hugged her parents, climbed into one of the waiting SUVs and headed for the CIA compound on the edge of the city.

"We know where the library is; two o'clock is fine," Clyde as holographic Davin said glancing at his watch which he had already set to local time. "Let's go, I would love to get a shower before we meet."

"You have plenty of time, dad," Amber said as she led them to the waiting car.

After a quick shower and change of clothes, the two holographic copies of Davin and Connie came down to the foyer of the compound and walked up to the guard's desk, who stopped them, informed them of a change of meeting location and redirected them to the elevator where they were to press B2 for the sub-basement second level.

"Welcome to the inner-sanctum of CIA Vietnam. But I believe you have been here before, but mom you haven't, right. Follow me, the conference room is down the hall," Amber said. She turned and started down the long hallway.

Once inside the conference room, they were greeted by Andi and Ivy.

"Why the change to the pit?" Clyde asked as he sat down across from Amber.

"It is of no concern of yours, but there has been some leakage of information; we believe they may have a mole or a new undetected listening device upstairs. So, to prevent any possible leakage, we moved down here where it is much safer for all. Now can we move on. This is Andi and Ivy, your replacements. It was decided, by my dad, that you two will become Andi and Ivy for the duration of the op. Your holo device has already been programed to be them. Mom and dad will remain as you back in the States."

After spending an hour going over the details of the plan again and discussing any possible scenarios where it could screw up and how to recover, they were ready to put it into motion.

"Okay, you know the plan, time to switch," Amber ordered and then watched as Andi and Ivy became Davin and Connie, and Barbara and Clyde became Andi and Ivy. "Wow, that is so cool. Now Barbara and Clyde, you will stay here with me and be my back-up as planned. Mom and Dad, good luck, I really hope this works."

"It will," Andi as Davin said and then he and Ivy as Connie stood up and walked out of the conference room and headed out to the visit Ho Chi Minh City. Ivy and Andi could easily mimic the personalities of Davin and Connie since they were both androids and could adjust their personalities quickly and could completely fool most anyone to believe they were the real Pierces. They could not completely fool a medical exam or even x-rays because of their inner structure. But being in Vietnam and not needing a medical exam, everyone felt confident they could fool Monica Teach into exposing herself. So off they went to explore the city, a city that early in Davin's life when he was single, wild, and very much into completing a mission, he had been assigned as a soldier in the United States Army.

Secure Conference Room, CIA Headquarters

"I really hope this works, I knew Amber was smart and this plan of hers is downright brilliant," Connie stated.

"Did you tell her about our missions and what to expect?" Davin asked while in the privacy of the secure conference room.

"Yes, but didn't get a chance to finish. She has a better understanding of how we got here and that there is a price on our heads from multiple bad guys. But she doesn't know what was on that sub."

"We have to tell her," Davin insisted.

"I know and I was about to when she had to leave. Ivy and Andi had just shown up and well, she had to catch her flight," Connie apologized.

"When she gets back, we both will sit down with her and tell her. Deal?"

"Yep, deal."

"Let's get on with this charade. Amber is counting on this to work," Davin said just before he pressed the button on his holo device and changed into Clyde Hines while Connie became Barbara Hines.

Many miles away far away from CIA HQ

"Good. So, Davin and Connie are in Vietnam, keep an eye on them. I will be in country tomorrow," Monica Teach told her contact in Ho Chi Minh City. She broke the

89

connection and looked out upon her team in the warehouse they occupied in Bangkok, Thailand. *"This has just gotten much easier,"* she said to herself. She stood and walked around her desk to the door and stepped out on the balcony overlooking the work bay where her team was working on their weapons and vehicles.

"Wan, come up and bring two of your team," she yelled down to Wan Chang, one of her lieutenants. Minutes later Wan and two of his team stood in front of The Colonel smiling; they knew she was about to send them on an assignment and had been waiting weeks for this.

"Wan, I need you and your two teammates to get on a plane and go to Ho Chi Minh City.
Our arche enemy is taking a little vacation, and we need to mess with their itinerary when I arrive tomorrow. That is when we will kill both of them. I also have information that their daughter, Amber, is also in country; we will take her out too. My contact there is Arnold Wilson, ex-CIA and now working for the highest bidder, us. Get with him and he will put you on the Pierce family. Right now, I want you three to follow, log what and where they go. Do not interrupt! I want to be sure we know what they are up to before I get there. Questions?" The Colonel ordered.

"Yes, why not come now and just kill them or let us have that pleasure?" Wan questioned.

"No, they are tricky, and I want to see their face when I kill them. So, no killing, but you will be with me when I do," The Colonel stated firmly.

"Yes, boss. We will not kill until you are there," Wan agreed.

"That's all, now go, you have a plane to catch."

Shanghai, China

Deep inside a large, highly classified facility located on the outskirts of Shanghai, three bio chemists were chatting about the new bioweapon they had just completed testing.

"Chang, the test was a success! We now have a weapon of mass destruction that the world will never see coming," the junior lab tech boosted.

"Yes, we do, but we still need to come up with an antidote before releasing it to the world. Otherwise, we could wipe out our own population too," Chang, chief bio chemist and weapons developer stated to his two technicians, as he studied the results of the test. "And we need to determine the best way to deliver the virus. And we also need approval from, well, everyone before we go any further."

"But if we wait, we will never be able to bring down America. That was the whole reason we were tasked to develop this virus. Bring America to her knees and institute a new world order, ours. Don't you agree, Chang?" the technician proclaimed.

"We wait!" Chang ordered, then closed his notes and stood, bowing to his technicians and left the lab. He knew that his technicians would go behind his back and do something stupid, but he was in no position to stop them. They were young and had little patience for anything like waiting for permission; they figured that asking for forgiveness was easier than asking for permission.

"We really should wait. If this gets out that we exposed this virus to America, they will execute us without a second thought," Melissa said, looking very concerned that she might get exposed if Han removed even a tiny sample from the containment chamber.

"No, I am taking a sample out and going to the airport. I will expose it to one traveler that is heading to America and we will call it a beta test. What harm can it do, just one traveler?" Han stated then walked to the containment chamber and started to put on his protective bio suit.

"I'm out of here, you are on your own," Melissa said as she hurried out the door. She slammed it as she left and headed to Chang's office, hoping to catch him before he left the building.

Han entered the containment room and took a small sample of the virus and placed it in a vial. He closed the lid tight and then left and resealed the room. After removing his bio suit, he placed the vial in his pocket, turned off the lights and left the lab, heading directly to the exit. Minutes later he was on a bus heading for the International Airport.

After arriving at the airport, Han immediately entered and stopped at the first coffee vendor he could find, thinking that he would put the virus in the coffee and then accidentally spill it near or on an unsuspecting passenger that was heading to America. His plan seemed fool proof, but only a fool would attempt such a plan; it had failure written all over it. But being the fool that he was, he got his coffee and opened the vial while sitting in the waiting area. He poured it into his cup spilling a little on his hand. He was now infected and almost cried out with the thought that he would be dead before his plan had infected the millions of people in America. The virus was fast acting, and he started to immediately feel ill. He was thinking about how he would still be able to complete his plan, when he saw four police officers walking toward him. The lead one held a picture, which Han assumed was of him, and he was correct in his assumption. He stood up, picked up his cup and started toward the boarding gate for a flight that was heading to Los Angeles, California. He tripped and fell, spilling his coffee on the shoes of a businessman heading for the same gate. He was successful in making contact but was also immediately surrounded by the four police officers.

"Han So Wang you need to come with us," the lead officer said not knowing the virus had already been delivered and that he and his men might also become infected. "Where is the vial?"

"What vial are you talking about, sir?" Han answered as he attempted to stand up but could not because he felt extremely weak. Two officers reached down, helped him up and escorted him to the exit.

"Get him out of here," the lead officer ordered.

Six hours later while sitting in the interrogation room being questioned by the police and Dr. Chang, Han placed his head down on the table and died.

"Quarantine the building, I believe we found our missing virus. Anyone who had contact with this man needs to be quarantined immediately," Doctor Chang ordered when he examined his dead technician.

Hours Later in Los Angeles

A tall Chinese businessman exited his trans-Pacific flight from Hong Kong to Los Angeles. He was unaware that he carried a virus that was fast moving and very deadly. He would be dead in two weeks and didn't know it.

Somewhere over the Pacific Ocean, the businessman who had the coffee spilled on him felt a little ill but didn't think much of it because he hated to fly and it usually made him sick every time he flew. He developed a hacking cough on the plane where he unknowingly spread germs to over three hundred passengers who had connecting flights to various cities around the United States.

Over in China, the government and medical facilities were in a heated battle to control an outbreak of a virus that they had developed in their research and development sector for use as a biologic warfare virus. But it was only to have left the laboratory after development of a cure for it. The virus escaped the lab on the hands on a technician and was now in full rampage in China. Over 12,599 people were infected within the first couple of days and now 310 were dead from the virus. Within weeks, the virus had spread to Italy, France, Britain, Russia, Spain, and Africa and now in the United States.

Morning came in the usual way in Ho Chi Minh City, fast, hot, and muggy. The city was much like Las Vegas, Nevada. it never slept. There was always something happening in the city, night clubs which sprang up during the war were still in business taking care of the locals and the millions of visitors that came to the city to learn more about what their brothers, fathers and sisters did in an attempt to stop the spread of communism. They would visit the bars, brothels and war zones that were now tourist traps instead of killing traps.

Davin and Connie, aka Andi and Ivy, exited their hotel and climbed into a taxi for a day trip into the jungle. Davin wanted to show Connie where he was stationed during the war and have lunch and possibly dinner in Da Nang. The trip was planned to get to the airport and take a helicopter to Da Nang, spend the day and fly home after dinner. After arriving at the airport, they met with retired Major Brent Miller, their pilot for the day. Major Miller had flown sixty-seven combat missions in Hueys, both as medivac and later in gunships. He had been shot down four times. Since he had no family back in the States, he decided to return in 1982, and continue to fly, working part time for the CIA and with a local charter service.

"Good morning Mr. and Mrs. Pierce, welcome to Vietnam," Miller said when they walked up.

"Good morning Major, long time," Davin said casually.

"Huh, long time, did we serve together; my memory is a little fuzzy these days," Miller replied.

"We met once shortly after I got in country, I was with the 138th R&R Company and I flew with you once on a short hop down to Ho Chi Minh out of Da Nang. I was a NUG, New Unexperienced Guy, back then and they wanted me to pick up a diplomatic bag and bring it back. You were available and provided the transport," Davin related to Miller.

"Yeah, I think I remember that. We got to Ho Chi late in the afternoon; couldn't make it back to Da Nang safely, so we stayed, and if I remember correctly, we hit almost every bar in town before morning. Yeah, Sergeant I remember you now, pretty wild night," Miller recalled leaving a lot of details out of the reply because of Connie standing right there.

"I know you were single and young, but you will tell me about that night," Connie insisted.

"No, I won't. What happens in Vietnam, stays in Vietnam, end of story. Let's get airborne, Major," Davin stated and then turned to follow Miller to an older military converted Huey.

"Is that old bird safe?" Connie questioned as they walked to a Huey that still had bullet holes in the door and two M-60 machine guns mounted inside.

"Just for show, a lot of the younger tourists want to fly in a real Huey with the guns. It makes them imagine what the ride was really like. They do function, I occasionally run with DEA and the local police to help slow down the drug trade," Miller said as he climbed into the pilot's seat. Davin, you can ride up front if you like. Connie, please strap in; my ground crew will close the doors before takeoff. Oh, this is Rhonda, my co-pilot and ground crew, she will ride in the back with you Connie. She is not working today, just needed a ride to Da Nang; hope you don't mind the extra passenger?"

"No problem, Major," Davin replied as he looked over at the very shapely lady wearing short tight shorts and a loose blouse unbuttoned to the knot that tied at the bottom, exposing her waist and almost all of her breasts, leaving little to the imagination.

"Rhonda, what takes you to Da Nang?" Connie asked.

"The beach up there is awesome, and I can work on my tan without being bothered. The beaches down here are always crowded and well, I sunbathe nude and there I can, not here," Rhonda commented as she slid the right door closed and then walked around the front of the Huey, gave a thumbs up to Miller, climbed in with Connie, slid the door closed, tapped Miller on the shoulder and then sat, strapping in across from Connie, smiling.

Connie sat across from Rhonda and wondered. She was a highly trained FBI agent for many years and had worked with her husband while he was on assignment with the CIA; something was not right with what she was seeing. She could not put her finger on what was wrong, but she didn't feel right about it. Was it the fact that Connie was really Ivy and her android brain was seeing something that was not there, or was the programing of Connie's vast training and experience causing conflict? She let it slide and decided she would just keep an eye on Rhonda and Miller. She sent a text to Davin/Andi to let him know her feelings; he replied that he felt it too. They could use the new Disrupter, a device that would disrupt any holographic generators within range, which is about 50 feet from the device. Since their android installed technology would override the effects of the Disrupter, it would not affect their plan if they needed to use it, so Connie and Davin both agreed to let it play out and see what happened.

"Connie, why are you and Mr. Pierce here, in Vietnam?" Rhonda asked.

"We had been working so hard that when we decided to retire, Davin suggested that we come here to see where he started his career. He knows all about mine, but his has been a secret for so long I really wanted to know," Connie answered.

"That is pretty cool, did he tell you what he did or is that still a secret?"

"He hasn't told me everything, yet, but I'm working on it. Some things he says he will never tell, secrets, you know," Connie replied just as the Huey lifted off the pad and started to climb to altitude. She glanced up front to see Davin at the controls, she didn't know he knew how to fly a Huey. Surprises, well, it really wasn't Davin flying, but Andi; and he was programed to fly anything that flew.

The trip to Da Nang was just short of 400 miles and would take about three and a half hours. They could have taken a plane but what fun was that, flying at twenty-five thousand feet, you couldn't see the scenery as well and the old Huey would be more like being there during the war.

About halfway up Rhonda slid open one of the doors to allow the air to rush in; the rush of the wind ripped open her blouse exposing her small but perfectly tanned breasts. This small act worried Connie for a few minutes, not knowing if Rhonda had ideas of pushing her out. However, she calmed when Rhonda sat back down and buckled in, not closing her blouse but letting the wind caress them.

"Does this bother you, Connie?" Rhonda asked indicating the door and her exposed breasts.

"Not a bit; wish I could join you, but Davin wouldn't approve," Connie replied.

"It does make me feel freer. You should try it; the boys up front can't see us," Rhonda challenged.

Connie reached down and unbuttoned her blouse and reached around behind her and undid her bra, removing it slowly and let the wind caress her too.

"Does feel great, how much time do we have?"

"About an hour or so, just relax. Davin is having fun flying; and Brent is asleep, I think, looks like it anyway. By the way, the M-60 beside you is loaded with blanks. If you want to fire a few, go for it. We load it that way to give the tourist a thrill," Rhonda offered.

"No, I would rather just look at the jungle below and be thankful I never was here during the war. And this does feel great."

Three and half hours later they landed at Da Nang airport and Miller shut down the engine as Rhonda opened the door and helped Connie out. Conversation during the flight was minimal but Connie enjoyed the view out the open door.

"Davin, what time do you want to return? We can fly at night if you want, but I would prefer a daylight return if you don't mind," Miller asked as he tied down his Huey and signaled the lineman to come over.

"Maybe we will stay the night; go back in the morning. If that works for you," Davin suggested.

"Sure, there is a nice hotel down on Main Street, not too expensive, clean and the restaurant is pretty good too. We can walk from here, only a couple of blocks." Miller paused a bit before he looked at Rhonda and asked, "Are you okay with spending the night?"

"Sure, why don't I meet you for dinner at seven at the hotel restaurant." Rhonda agreed.

"Good, let's go; just need to tell the lineman our plans and then we can head on to the hotel," Miller stated.

Twenty minutes later, they were checked in at the hotel and parted ways, Rhonda to the beach, Davin, and Connie to the military side of town or at least where it was years ago, and Miller headed for the bar.

Walking away from the hotel Davin and Connie were playing the tourist very well when they stopped and entered a curio shop on the corner.

"Did you notice we are being followed, not sure but ever since we left the hotel there has been an oriental lady following us," Davin said to Connie as they walked around the shop.

"Yes, not Rhonda, she was not oriental, not sure who this is, but let's see what happens when we leave here," Connie said and then headed for the door. "Must have been a mistake, she passed right by the shop and well, gone."

"Maybe we are expecting too much, too soon. Let's just have fun and enjoy the city. The compound I was in is just a couple miles outside the city, if it is still there," Davin said as they left the shop and turned north up the sidewalk, stopping for a moment to flag down a cab. "The city has grown a lot and they probably tore down our base."

"Do you speak English?" Davin asked the driver of the cab.

"Yes, very well thank you, where to?" the driver replied.

"The old Army compound north of town, is it still there?"

"Yes, it is our number one tourist destination, were you stationed there?" the driver asked.

"Yeah, good, take us there. Can we get a cab back from there in a couple of hours?" Davin questioned the driver as he pulled into the traffic flow.

"Yes sir, cabs are in and out of there all the time."

Fifteen minutes later, Davin and Connie were standing in front of the gate that allowed visitors to reconnect with their past. Of course, it was only programed memories for Andi and Ivy, but none the less they could enjoy what Davin had experienced all those years ago. Davin watched as the cab drove away in a cloud of dust and wondered again if they were walking into a trap, a trap they were hoping would happen soon. From the memories that Davin had downloaded to him, he was able to escort Connie to the barracks, operations center, and various other parts of the compound. Of course, most of what really happened here was classified and those areas had been demolished before the war ended. After two hours of exploring and chatting, they decided to catch the next cab back only to find there were no cabs available and no one around to assist them.

"Where is everyone? When we arrived, there were at least twenty tourists and several locals milling around," Connie commented.

"Yeah, something is up," Davin/Andi agreed. "It's going to be dark soon, and we don't want to be walking through the jungle to get back in the dark. There has to be a phone here."

"I saw a phone outside the operations building," Connie said and started to walk toward operations. When she reached for the phone, she saw the cord had been cut and it looked like it was recent.

"That will do us no good," Davin said and looked over toward the barracks where he saw a woman standing on the first step, dressed in a pair of very short tight shorts and a blue loose-fitting flowered blouse. "Maybe she can explain and help."

"It's about to happen, Davin. Be careful," Connie said seeing who the woman was.

"Hello, Monica, what brings you to Da Nang?" Davin said as they approached Monica Teach.

"Oh, you know, I love the weather and the fact that you two are here without any protection. I could kill both of you right now, but really want to enjoy the moment," Monica said and lifted her arm, pointing a Desert Eagle fifty caliber pistol at them.

"Mighty big gun you have there, Monica. Can you handle that much power?" Connie teased, knowing that Monica had used that same pistol to kill her and drop her out of an airplane from 12,000 feet over the desert.

"You know very well I can handle it. And didn't I kill you once already; can't you just stay dead," The Colonel/Monica replied.

"You tried but failed then and will fail again," Connie shot back.

"No, I won't," The Colonel/Monica stated. "You have no idea why, do you?"

"What do you mean, Monica?" Connie replied questioning that comment.

"Oh, I guess they never told you, did they?" The Colonel/Monica answered smiling.

"Who never told me; what are you talking about?" Connie looked confused.

"How can you be so sure?" Davin asked, looking more confused and wanted to distract Monica and her henchmen. As he scanned the entire scene, he saw several of her minions slowly walk out of their hiding places. They were surrounded and unarmed, not very good odds but at least Monica didn't know who they really were, or did she? She did mention killing Connie once or did she mean Ivy? Monica did try to kill Connie several times and Ivy once.

"I guess you missed the clue I left on the sub. Go back and look; oh, wait, that will not be possible because you didn't go to the sub. They didn't tell you what they found on the sub, a bit of the past that has been kept secret all these years, a secret that you should know about but I have to go now," The Colonel said as she looked at her watch.

"What secret? We were on the sub," Connie/Ivy said.

"You know Davin, you were here standing most likely exactly where you are standing now and didn't die then, hopefully you will not die in this beautiful country. I suggest you don't move from where you are standing until I am gone, there are some very bad people wanting you dead. You need to be very careful, Andi," The Colonel/Monica stated changing the subject and then started to turn back toward the door of the barracks.

"Why did you call me Andi?" Davin/Andi asked and then looked to his left where the gate stood open. It was over 100 feet away, even with his speed he would never make it. Then he looked at Connie/Ivy and winked.

"Because I know you are not Davin and Connie Pierce, and you need to know I am not the one out to kill you. But you probably already know that Andi. Got to go now, be safe and tell Amber to watch her back, they are after her too," The Colonel/Monica said then turned and entered the barracks, quickly running to the rear exit to a waiting Jeep and left the compound. Her four assistants quickly turned and exited the compound and climbed into the several Jeeps that pulled up to the gate, never dropping their aim on Davin and Connie.

"Ivy, what did she mean about the secrets of the past?" Andi/Davin asked.

"I have no idea. Connie did not program anything prior to working with Davin on that *Mary Jean* case many years ago. We need to get back to HQ."

"Yeah, but you know we are miles from town, and it is getting dark," Andi/Davin stated. He paused for a moment and then added, "We don't require sleep, let's just cut through the jungle and get out of here. If Davin's memories were programed correctly, there is a short cut through the jungle that he and his buddies took to get to town quickly and back before roll call in the morning. According to his memory bank, he only missed bed check and roll call, ah let's see six times in the first tour of duty."

"Let's go, I don't want to get shot by Monica again," Connie/Ivy said and started for the gate with Davin/Andi close behind. It was only five miles to town and the walk should not take long.

Amber walked out of the Vietnam CIA HQ with Barbara and Clyde Hines posing as Andi and Ivy and headed toward the cafe' across the street to grab a bit of dinner. They had not heard from their decoys since they left for Da Nang earlier that morning. But worrying about two androids on a mission was a moot point, they were both stronger and faster than any human alive and were programed in more ways of survival than any person on the earth. But none the less, Amber was worried.

"Amber, when were they supposed to check in?" Barbara asked.

"Three o'clock. Just a couple of hours overdue, nothing to worry about yet; they went to Da Nang and one of the old compounds that my dad served in. They may not have any phone service out there; it is several miles from the city."

"Okay, if you are not worried then we aren't," Clyde replied.

"Didn't say I wasn't worried," Amber replied and then added, "Let's sit outside, it is a beautiful day and I want to be able to see all around us."

They took a table outside under a colorful umbrella. They had just started to sit when two shots rang out. The first hit Clyde in the chest, and the second took down Barbara, both were dead before hitting the ground. Amber, fearing a third bullet for herself, dove for the ground and drew her pistol, looking for the shooter. People were diving for cover all around her and running away from the café. She never saw the shooter; and after a few minutes, the local police showed up and took control of the area.

Clyde and Barbara's holo device immediately stopped working when it detected no heartbeat and both holographs dissolved exposing Clyde and Barbara as themselves. Lucky for Amber, they fell behind the table and nobody saw the transformation except Amber. She pulled the tablecloth down and covered their bodies as best she could without exposing herself to the shooter.

'So that's what happens when you get shot and die,' she thought to herself.

"Are you okay, Miss?" a tall local police officer asked. As he reached down to help Amber up, she slid her weapon back into its holster and took his hand.

"Yes, fine," she replied and then looked at her two agents, lying dead on the ground.

"You are armed; you know that it is not legal in the city to carry a weapon," he stated as she handed him her credentials and authorization to carry.

"Ms. Pierce, welcome to Ho Chi Minh City; and I am very sorry about your friends," he said quietly as three CIA agents ran up to the café' and saw what had happened.

"Amber, what the hell happened?" Agent Todd Black asked as he and Ginger Burns approached the bloody scene.

"Sniper," Amber said as she looked again at her dead friends and then walked away. The local police officer tried to stop her but was unsuccessful.

"We will get you a full report, officer," Ginger stated and then turned and tried to catch up to Amber. Todd stayed at the scene and identified himself and agreed he would get a statement and have it at the station by morning. The officer gave Todd his business card and then proceeded to yell at his men to secure the area and wait for the coroner to show up. Todd stayed because the victims were American CIA Agents and he wanted to be sure their bodies would be handled properly and to recover their credentials and weapons before being carried away by the local coroner.

"Amber, wait," Ginger yelled at Amber as she entered the gate to the CIA compound but stopped immediately before going up the steps into the building. Ginger caught up and hugged Amber. "We will find out who did this."

"I know who shot them, Monica Teach, and she would have shot me, but Barbara was in the way," Amber replied quickly.

"How can you be sure?" Ginger asked.

"She promised she would kill me and my parents; that is why I am here. She killed my brother and almost killed mom twice. She is relentless and I will not stop until she is dead, or we are. We have no safe harbor, it's either us or her. Mom was about to tell me why she is so set on killing us, but didn't get a chance."

"Oh, I didn't know. Let's get downstairs and see if we can contact Davin and Connie," Ginger said pressing the elevator button.

"If they are still alive," Amber said quietly.

Ten minutes later, Amber and Ginger were sitting in the secure conference room. Amber was dialing the secure phone to connect to CIA Headquarters in Virginia. The building always was busy, the staff duty office would pick up the phone and locate her parents, but they were in disguise as Clyde and Barbara Hines, she had to ask for them.

"You have reached Central Intelligence Agency; how may I direct your call," the operator said in a very pleasant voice.

"This is Amber Pierce, I need to speak with Clyde or Barbara Hines, can you locate them for me? I will hold," Amber said trying her best to control the anger she had building up within her.

"One moment please, I will connect you, they have been expecting your call," the operator said. There were a few clicks and Clyde/Davin answered.

"Hello Amber, how is Vietnam?" Clyde/Davin said casually.

"Not well, are you in a secure room and is Barbara with you?"

"Yes, on both, what's happened?" Clyde/Davin said.

"Dad, Clyde and Barbara are dead; a sniper shot them less than twenty minutes ago," Amber blurted out and then started to cry.

"Amber, wait, what happened, how?" Clyde/Davin asked quickly and then signaled for Connie to sit.

"We walked across to the café' on the corner near the compound and before we had a chance to sit, two shots, and they were dead. I wasn't shot; don't know why, but I am all right. All I can figure is that Barbara was blocking the shooter. Can mom hear this?"

"Yes, she is sitting here, and I have it on speaker. Calm down, we will be there as quickly as we can. Are Ivy and Andi doing okay?" Davin asked.

"We don't know. They went to Da Nang this morning, and we haven't heard from them. They missed their check in time," Amber said and then looked over at Ginger sitting at the end of the conference table. "Ginger

Burns is trying to contact them now but not having any luck."

"Okay, look, we will fly out tonight just have a car pick us up," Davin said.

"No, don't come here, I don't want you two killed. We may have lost four good agents today, and there's a good chance of losing more. I just don't want you to be in that number. Stay there. I will call if I need more help. Right now, I have Todd and Ginger as back up. and there are three other agents here that can help if need be. You two stay there, and don't leave the building."

"Okay, but you be careful. Monica is not going to give up."

"Yeah, dad, I know. I will call tomorrow, be safe. I need to go. Talk to you tomorrow," Amber said then hung up the phone without waiting for a reply.

Two miles away a group of men and women were sipping cold beers in a local bar when the television news came on and described a pair of murders not far from them. The Colonel smiled and lifted her beer in a toast with her men. The Colonel was a perfect holographic simulation of Monica Teach and all the men and women around the table thought she was truly Monica, as they had never seen The Colonel as anyone else.

"Four down, three to go, maybe more," The Colonel said to the men and women around the table. *'Looks like Harvey completed his mission or at least most of it. Which two did he get?'* she thought to herself as she smiled and then added out loud, "Drink up; we have work to do. Get back to the warehouse and load up, we have a plane to catch."

"Where to, boss?" one of the women asked.

"Hawaii, actually we are going to Kauai, then on to Los Angeles. But first the family cottage on the beach. They have something in their safe I need to retrieve."

"Roger that. I just got a new bikini and want to see if the boys like it over there."

"I have a new one too; we can lie on the beach while we wait for our targets to catch up with us. Now let's go boys and girls," she ordered. She stood and started for the door after leaving a hundred-dollar bill on the table to cover their drinks. With that said, the group left the bar and headed back to their hotel to pack and then to the airport where The Colonel had her jet parked. "We can spend a few days on the beach; it will take some time for them to figure out we are no longer in country. After killing four of their people, two of whom are very high ranking, they will be looking deep and hard to find us."

"Where is Harvey going to meet us?" Alice Crenshaw, a perky young blonde woman with a murderous attitude asked as they walked to their parked Jeeps. She had a crush on him, loved everything about him except he didn't like woman in general, preferring men and wasn't ashamed of letting everyone know it.

"He will catch up to us at the airport, don't worry your pretty little head Alice. You do know he is gay?" Monica said as they exited the bar.

"Yeah, but I will convert him back to liking women."

"That I gotta see," The Colonel as Monica said as she climbed into her car with Alice and two of her team; the rest climbed into the second Jeep.

"When he sees me in my new tiny bikini, he will not ever want another boy again."

"We shall see, Alice."

"Amber, we just got a report that indicated Monica Teach and her team landed in Kauai on a private jet," a team chief said when he came into the conference room where Amber, Ginger and Todd were discussing their next move.

"How the hell did that happen? Well, I guess it is already decided; we go to Kauai. Chief, call the airport and have the pilots get the company jet ready for departure in two hours," Amber ordered and then asked Ginger and Todd, "Would you two like to tag along? Since we haven't located Ivy and Andi, I need back up; and you two are my first choice."

"Before I go and call the pilots, I wanted you to know we have a lead on your two decoys," the chief added.

"Well, what have you found out?"

"A man and women were found badly injured outside of Da Nang wandering around in the jungle. I have sent two agents up there to see if they are our missing agents. It will take a while before we know anything. Da Nang is several hours by air from here, and we don't have any agents local up there," the Chief continued, "Didn't want to say anything to get your hopes up until we were sure."

"That's okay, Chief. As soon as you know, please let me know," Amber said and then looked back at Ginger and Todd, "How long do you need to get ready?"

"We can be back here in an hour," Ginger said before she stood and started for the door.

Hundreds of miles away in the emergency room at the Da Nang General Hospital, two unknown people were being treated for severe burns, trauma, and broken bones. Neither one of the patients understood what had happened to them and could not tell the doctors who they were.

"Did you look at the x-rays on the male patient?" asked the lead emergency room doctor.

"Yes, looked like an artificial arm," pausing the nurse handed the doctor more x-rays, this one belonging to the female.

"They are American, we probably need to call someone," the doctor said looking at the x-ray.

"Whoa, they are human, but their skeleton is metal and there are numerous other abnormalities that I can't explain," the doctor said, "Get me the number for the U.S. Embassy; maybe they can help."

Four hours later Agents Henry White and Diane Bear walked into the Da Nang General Hospital Emergency Room lobby.

"Good afternoon, I'm Agent Henry White and this is my partner Diane Bear. We understand you have a pair of patients that showed up without identification and are badly injured. We are missing two of our people and are here to help identify your patients. May we see them?" Henry said when they walked up to the nurse's station, showing their credentials. "Are these the two you have here?" he continued and showed the nurse a photo of Andi and Ivy.

"Just a moment Agent White," the nurse said; she then picked up the phone and paged the duty doctor.

"Would you come with me," a tall doctor said as he walked up to the agents.

"Right behind you," Henry said as he and Diane turned to follow.

"I'm Doctor William Hun, head of emergency care here at the hospital. They are still in recovery, both have multiple bruising, cuts, and abrasions. Nothing broken internally, but neither one knows what happened or who they are," the doctor said as they walked down the long hallway toward the recovery room. He stopped just outside the door. "May I see the pictures of your people?"

"Yes, Doctor Hun, are these two here?" Henry asked.

"Yes, these are the two we have in here. Come on in," Doctor Hun said, "I'm curious, what are they, we did x-rays, and their internals are not anything like we have seen. Almost like robots but look like humans. Are they robots?"

"Doctor Hun, may we go to a place where we can talk and please bring anyone that has seen those x-rays with you. Before we go there, may we see them?" Henry said.

"Sure, I will get the nurse on duty that worked with me on them and meet you back here in a few minutes," the doctor replied. After a pause he added, "My office is two doors down on the right."

After checking on Andi and Ivy to be sure they were their missing agents, Henry and Diane walked down the hall to Doctor Hun's office where they met with him and two nurses.

"Doctor, we appreciate you meeting with us. The two you have in recovery are our missing agents, and we need you to understand that what you saw in the x-rays is highly classified. They are both human, but were severely injured years ago and had to have extensive surgery to include the replacement of limbs with experimental artificial arms and legs. Their survival is paramount to our work and

114

any discussion about what you saw is strictly forbidden. Agent Diane will remain here to monitor their condition and await our team to arrive to transport, when you deem them in safe condition to move, that is. I cannot stress enough that you are not to discuss that they were even here to anyone, ever," Henry stated and then looked at Diane and back to the doctor and his nurses. "Do you understand, doctor? If anyone discovers that they are still alive, the people that tried to kill them will return to finish the job; and they don't care if anyone else gets hurt in the process. So, please protect yourselves, and do not discuss the fact that they were ever here; or if you should happen to slip up, make sure you follow up that they came in dead on arrival. We will move them as soon as we can. Again, Agent Diane will remain here until they are moved," Henry concluded. He then paused and added "We will need you to sign a non-disclosure statement if you don't mind. It is for your own protection and ours, stating that if you do disclose anything you have seen or heard can be punishable by severe prison. I know it sounds harsh, but it is a matter of national security and required by our government."

"We understand Agent White. Are we in any danger?" the lead nurse asked.

"You are not in any danger as long as the people that hurt them doesn't know they survived. So, again, do not talk about them to anyone and you should remain out of danger," Diane commented.

"Agent White, we understand, and will make sure they are comfortable and taken care of," Doctor Hun said. He then turned to Diane and gently said, "I will have a room prepared for you and your injured people where you will be safe and out of sight."

"That will be fine, sir," Diane said and then looked at Henry.

"I have to call HQ," Henry said as he pulled out his cellphone and stepped out of the office.

"Can I go see our patients, doctor?" Diane asked.

"Yes," Doctor Hun said. He then pointed at one of the nurses indicating she should take Diane to their patients.

Ten minutes later, Diane and Henry met again in Doctor Hun's office.

"Change of plans, doc. We have a team coming in to pick up our people. Can you make sure they are ready to travel in about three hours?" Henry asked.

"Sure, not really sure if they are stable enough, but I assume you will have a doctor with your team to take care of them?" Hun asked.

"Yes, of course," Henry commented. He then turned to Diane and said, "We need you to stay here until our transport arrives; should be within three hours. They are flying in from Ho Chi Minh City and then driving over to pick up our people."

"They don't look too good, Henry, almost looks like they were blown up or were close to an explosion. I know who they are, do you?" Diane said quietly to Henry.

"Yes, I was briefed, now we need to isolate them and wait for our people to get here."

"Are you okay, Henry; you seem very distracted. Is it because they are, you know, I don't want to say it here, but are you okay?" Diane pressed.

"Not really, there seems to be something going on that we haven't been briefed on. We are senior agents; we should have been told," Henry answered looking more confused.

"Get over it, Henry, you know as well as I do that there is that little saying that goes with every mission, you know, 'NEED TO KNOW'. And obviously, they felt we didn't need to know until now. I'm okay with it and you should be too," Diane said and then walked back to the recovery room to be with Andi and Ivy, hoping they would wake up so she could find out what happened.

"Amber, we will be landing in Kauai in twenty minutes. The weather is warm with a slight breeze, usual weather for this time of year. Please make sure your seat belts are fastened and well you know the drill. Flight crew prepare for landing," the pilot announced over the intercom.

"Good, maybe we can catch up with Monica here and end this," Ginger said to no one in particular.

"I'll drink to that. And we need to call back to find out about Andi and Ivy. They should have been picked up by now and are heading back to the States," Amber said to Ginger.

"Ms. Pierce, we got a call a moment ago about your two agents. They have been picked up and are airborne, heading to Washington. Their condition is critical, but stable. Ivy woke up and told Diane Bear that they accidently stepped on a land mine and that Monica Teach was there. That's all she said before passing out again," the stewardess said prior to her returning to her seat in preparation to land.

"Thank you! Now, let's get Monica," Amber said getting angrier by the minute.

The landing was smooth as always with this crew and after climbing into the three waiting SUVs Amber ordered them to drive to the family home located an hour from the airport.

Pulling into the driveway, Amber quickly noticed the front door was open. Pulling her weapon and signaling for her team to do the same, they approached the house slowly. Ginger started to the right and Todd to the left. Two other agents followed Amber to the door. One agent pushed open the door wider and glanced inside. Seeing nothing unexpected, he stepped in with Amber close behind followed by the third agent. Nothing appeared out of place as they cleared the house, until Amber reached the master bedroom and found the safe open and the contents, or what she knew was supposed to be in the safe laying scattered on the floor. It was obviously not a robbery for money because there was a stack of money amounting to about five thousand dollars along with a pair of diamond earrings and other jewelry.

"What the hell? What was so important that they left the money and jewelry." Ginger said as she looked at the stash on the floor.

"It was Monica and she just wanted the item that my mom told me could get me killed," Amber said quietly.

"What was it?" Todd asked.

"I don't know, mom didn't get a chance to tell me. Guess I need to call her," Amber said. She then pulled out her cell phone and paused before she said, "I need a secure line."

"There is one at HQ Honolulu," Todd said quickly.

"Hello," Amber said answering her cell phone.

"Hello Amber, this is Monica, we need to talk and soon. Can you meet me in an hour?" Monica asked not really expecting a positive response.

"Oh, sure, so you can kill me, right? I will be right over," Amber replied.

"No, we need to talk; I promise I will not kill you, at least not yet. But you need to know why I am after you and your family. Your father is too much of a coward to tell you; and mom tried to tell you but chickened out too. So, it is up to me. Be at Pier 14 at the café' in one hour. You can come armed if you like; I will be there alone, almost anyway. Let's

119

do this, you can bring Ginger with you and I will have my backup, no others; and we can have a nice quiet drink and I will educate you. Be there, or I will kill your father, Oh, I know the decoys you sent to Da Nang are Andi and Ivy. Sorry for killing them, but, well, I will explain. See you in an hour, don't be late," The Colonel said and then broke the connection.

"Where is Pier 14 Café?" Amber asked to anyone.

"Not far, why?" Ginger replied looking around at the cottage. "Nice place you have here."

"My parents' house, they bought it years ago after finding a large stash of gold on a sunken ship."

"I heard about that, so your parents are the famous gold divers; didn't Josh Randal assist in that?" Ginger asked.

"Yes, and they really don't have to work, but love what they do. Speaking of Josh, has anyone heard how he is doing?" Amber questioned and then picked up stuff on the floor and put it back in the safe.

"Aren't you going to call the police about the break in?" Todd asked.

"No need, I will call Valerie Lake shortly, but nothing is missing of value except whatever Monica took and Val is a lieutenant in the local police and close family friend," Amber said and then relocked the safe. "Let's go! Ginger, you, and I are going to Pier 14 Café', and the rest of you back to the plane and wait."

"Wait, is Pier 14 because of that call?" Todd asked, looking very confused.

"Yes, and Ginger and I can handle it. Todd, take everyone back to the plane and wait for instructions from me or Ginger. We have it covered," Amber ordered and then walked toward the front door; after turning around she added, "Make sure the back door is locked; we will secure the front." With that she exited the house.

An hour later Amber and Ginger walked out on the deck of Pier 14 Café' and saw Monica sitting alone at a corner table sipping what looked like a Fu Fu drink of some kind, complete with a slice of lemon and a tiny umbrella.

"Good afternoon, Amber, please have a seat. I assume this is Ginger Burns, your back up. Pleasure to meet you two, finally," Monica said pleasantly and then signaled for the waitress. "Please order anything, I'm buying."

"Ginger Ale for me," Amber said, and Ginger indicated to make that two. "Don't want to drink and miss this great opportunity to hear what you have to say. Now what is so important that you risk being shot or captured, Monica?"

"I will get to that in a minute, first enjoy this beautiful day and know that you are perfectly safe sitting there. But rest assured, if you try to shoot me or act foolish, it will be the last thing you do. I have a sniper within range to take you out if I signal him to do so. I just want to talk and pass on some very important information to you. Information that you should have been told a long time ago. Information that your father would have told you if he knew sooner; he knows now and only learned when he and mom visited my Soviet Nuclear Submarine and found some papers that I left there," Monica explained between sips of her drink. She glanced down at the table at an envelope and then back at Amber.

"Okay, you have my attention, what is it?"

"Well, sis, it's like this. Back before you were born, and even before dear old dad and mom got together, there was another man in mom's life. A man that served his country in Vietnam and died when his helicopter was shot down. But before leaving this world, he fathered a baby girl. His name was Edward Teach the eighth. That baby girl is me; the bottom-line girl is that I am your half big sister; and well, since we are related, I really wanted you to know before you got yourself killed."

"No way, you are not my sister. Mom would have told me," Amber protested.

"Oh, she was about to several times; here is the proof, sis," Monica said as she slid the envelope over to Amber. Inside she found two birth certificates, one for Monica Teach, daughter of Connie Young, the future Mrs. Davin Pierce, Amber's mother, and it appeared to be Monica's mother too. The other, dated the same day and with some differences, her name was Monica Henshaw, daughter of Daniel and Darcy Henshaw dated the same day as the first. The death certificate for Monica Teach was also dated the same day as the birth certificates. "It got complicated during my birth. You see the doctor and his wife wanted a daughter, but she was not able to have kids. So, he faked my death at birth and produced another birth certificate with his name; and, well, he stole me from our mother. She didn't find out until years later when I left those copies for her to find on a Soviet Missile boat that I was having worked on as a rouse to draw mom and your dad to investigate. The plan worked; they searched the boat and found the documents you hold in your hand. She didn't know until then that I was her daughter and your half-sister."

"Where are this doctor and his wife now?" Amber questioned.

"Well, they are dead. Car crash a few years ago, seems he liked to drink and insisted on driving home after a party. Speeding and excessive drink don't go together very well, I miss them. Lucky for me they had huge insurance policies and a lot of money in the bank and investments, so I was set pretty good afterward. But I still miss them. He did our mother wrong, but they treated me well, raised me, and never told me the truth until I found those documents after they died. He kept them in the safe at home and I was never allowed to open it until they were both gone. So, you see I was kept in the dark all my life too. I know how you must feel right now."

"How, no, you are a terrorist, murderer and who knows what else you have done. How can this be?" Amber responded almost in tears as she looked at the birth certificate and date of birth. "You can't be my sister, half or otherwise. Josh is my only brother and you killed him."

"To set the record straight, I had nothing to do with killing our brother; that was a group of men that used to work for me but decided to go rogue. As for our mother, she was young, in college and fell in love with a man that had a past. After she got pregnant, they split up and I was born. He went to Vietnam and got himself killed, but I found out he died a hero saving several wounded soldiers before they got him. Our mom graduated from college. She thought she had birthed a still born baby, but the doctor had lied. My father, Captain Edward Teach the eighth, was a descendant to that notorious pirate Black Beard, Edward Teach. I changed my name from Henshaw to Teach after who I thought were my parents died. Mom became a Miami cop before she joined the FBI. The doctor that stole me from our mom died from injuries in a car accident when I was sixteen. Been on my own ever since."

"You are going to be killed or arrested someday; you may as well give yourself up now," Amber said trying to understand what she had been told. "Sister or not, you are a criminal and need to spend the rest of your life in jail."

"Let me make somethings clear to you, little sister. I am not the one that needs to go to jail, I haven't done anything wrong in the United States short of breaking into our mother's house and retrieving those documents. Everything to date was done by Rocky Soto and his band of terrorists. Yes, he is dead, but his team is still out there," Monica confessed.

"I don't believe you; do you believe her, Ginger?" Amber said and asked Ginger.

"No, she is lying. I am not sure she is your sister; that can be forged," Ginger stated.

"True, but you can do your homework and find out it is all true. Here are the names and places you can check. As for Soto's team, well, they will be dead before much longer, not by me but by you and your CIA and FBI. I have informed them as to where to find them; and well, they will be no longer real soon," Monica stated. Then she stood and added, "I have to go now; enjoy the rest of your day sister. Keep an eye out for me, but I promise you this, you are not on my hit list. I never planned on killing you; just scare you into meeting with me. It doesn't pay to kill you," Monica said, and placed a hundred-dollar bill on the table.

"Wait, what did you do to my parents?" Amber asked as Monica stood up and turned back to face Amber.

"I did nothing to your parents; they are still safe back in Washington. As for Andi and Ivy, I talked to them yesterday and left them standing in the middle of Davin's old Army compound. The last I saw of them they were standing watching me and my team leave. Why, what happened to them? "Monica stated looking confused. She looked Amber directly in the eye, winked and started to smile a little.

"It looks like they were blown up, severe injuries, cuts, broken bones. Are you sure you didn't do anything to them?" Amber insisted.

"Look, I saw they were not your parents and decided to just leave before Andi decided to do something stupid like try to catch me. Their holographs were perfect, but I worked with your parents for years. They almost fooled me, but my contact tipped me off about your plan. I was no closer than fifty feet to them but saw through your deception. I hope they will be fine, really, sis, I had nothing to do with causing them harm. No reason to, besides, I helped design and build Andi, he is my second-best creation. There are still a lot of old land mines and unexploded ordnance buried around that country, they may have stumbled on one and it exploded, but it wasn't me. Look, I must go. Tell the waitress to keep the change. Bye Sis. Oh, that birth certificate is a copy, so keep it and do your homework," Monica said, walked across the deck, entered the café and disappeared.

"Nothing to do with almost killing Andi and Ivy; I am not sure I believe that. There is still unexploded ordinance out there, so it could have happened that way. If she didn't do it, then what happened? Guess we must wait until they are repaired and ask what happened. Anyway, look at this birth certificate. Wow, I lose a brother but gain a villainous half-sister. What the hell is going to happen next?" Amber

125

said as she picked up the birth certificate again and looked closely at it.

"Looks real," Ginger said picking up the other evidence Monica left them. "College degrees in Microbiology, Robotics and Computer Science, two master's degrees and a PHD. Wow, border line genius. But something just doesn't add up. Why confront you now, and why the wink and smile. She is up to something and I can't put my finger on it, but I don't trust her.

"Yeah, pretty impressive, and she worked with Rocky Soto in the R & D lab for the company. Right under my parents' noses, and they didn't know who she really was."

"I need something stronger than this, waitress," Amber stated and called for the waitress.

Meanwhile Monica entered the café and was greeted by two rough looking characters, standing near the door who stopped her. "Very good performance Monica; now let's go, The Colonel is waiting. As promised, we will let her live for now, but if you cause any trouble, she will die," the larger of the two men stated and then escorted Monica out to a waiting SUV.

Out on the deck, Ginger and Amber were sipping their stronger drinks and looking at the documents left by Monica.

"What is this?" Ginger said as she scanned a birth certificate and felt something taped to the back. Removing a handwritten note, she read. "Help me, I'm being held captive by The Colonel and did not do anything wrong. Please help me." It was signed Monica Teach.

"What do you make of that?" Amber asked and then drank the rest of her margarita.

"I have no idea, but it does throw another link in the chain of events," Ginger stated as she looked at the note and turned it over to see that it was on a piece of stationary from the Grand Hilton Hotel in Bangkok Thailand. "Interesting, look at this," she said handing the note to Amber.

"They must have held her there before coming to Kauai," Amber said, "Let's call it in, and see if we can get some agents over there to check it out. Maybe they will go back or left some kind of information to lead us to their next location."

Los Angeles International Airport

"Shanghai Airlines Flight 458 arriving from Shanghai, China at gate 15." The announcement was heard in the international arrival wing of one of the busiest airports in the country. It was 8:15 in the morning and a lot of flights were arriving from their long cross ocean or country flights. The term used in the aviation community was 'Red Eye' because most passengers arrived with blood shot eyes from not getting much sleep in their 12 to 16-hour flights. This was no exception, over 300 passengers disembarked from flight 458 and over half of them did not feel well, whether from the long flight, poor food, or possibly from the young businessman that boarded the flight feeling a bit under the weather himself and who may have spread his possible head cold to a lot of the passengers that were crammed into the Boeing 767 jumbo jet. The young businessman exited and went to the men's room to freshen up before his next flight which would take him to Washington DC. He had an appointment with his boss, NSA Director Phillip Wilson tomorrow and the information he carried was sensitive and extremely volatile. His three-hour layover would give him just enough time to stop in one of the many restaurants and get a good airport breakfast before boarding his next flight.

"Okay, let's get back to the plane, I need to call my mom," Amber said standing and starting for the car.

"Wait, Amber. We need to go after her. Stop her before she gets away," Ginger said following Amber into the parking lot.

"No, she is not the problem right now, no wait, what am I saying. She is testing me; she doesn't think I will kill her. But I need to talk to my mom and dad. This is all wrong; if she is my sister, why would she want my family dead? It doesn't make sense," Amber questioned as she climbed into the car's passenger seat.

"True, something is not right with this. If she is your sister, why would she want you dead?" Ginger agreed and then started the car's engine.

"I need to talk to mom; get me to the plane so I can use the secure phone," Amber ordered.

"Right," Ginger said and then sped out of the parking lot, a little too fast.

Twenty minutes later, they were sitting in the company Gulfstream. Amber immediately picked up the secure phone and dialed CIA HQ and waited.

"Hello, you have reached the office of Josh Randal how can I help you?" Mary asked when she picked up the ringing secure phone in Josh's office.

"Mary, this is Amber, is my mom there?" she asked.

"No, I can locate her and have her here within the hour," Mary replied.

"Would you please get her and my dad in the office so I can speak to them on this line," Amber asked referring to the secure phone she was on.

"Sure, are you on the plane?" Mary asked.

"Yes."

"I will have her call you as soon as she gets here," Mary replied, "Is everything all right?"

"No, everything is not all right; please, get my mom," Amber pleaded, tears flowing down her cheek.

"Okay, as fast as I can. Just wait by the phone," Mary said and then broke the connection.

Forty-six minutes later, the secure phone buzzed indicating they had an incoming call.

"Mom?" Amber said quickly.

"Yes, baby, what's wrong?" Connie asked, paused, and before Amber could say anything, she continued, "Monica told you, didn't she?"

"Yes, why didn't you tell me; I'm out here looking to kill my sister. You should have told me!" Amber yelled in between bursting out in tears.

"Honey, I tried, many times but just couldn't; I am sorry you had to learn this way," Connie replied as she tried to calm her down.

"What now?" Amber questioned.

"Come home."

"I am home; well almost, we are on Kauai. I plan on going to the house and stay there for a while until I figure out what to do. But why, why didn't you warn me."

"I did, sort of," Connie admitted.

"You did, when?"

"I told you that what was in the safe could get you killed."

"You didn't tell me what was in the safe and by the way it is gone now. Monica broke in and took whatever it was," Amber told her mother.

"It was a copy of her birth certificate and death certificate. The doctor that delivered her told me she had died and issued the death certificate. He took her and raised her for his own. I didn't know about her until we discovered Monica's briefcase on the Soviet sub a few years ago. It contained the certificates, school records, college transcripts, and degrees from several universities. She is highly trained and unknown to anyone at the agency she was hired and worked with Rocky Soto in his lab. She helped design Andi and many of his other projects. Her IQ is over the top, higher than Soto's and many others in the lab. Then when Soto got fired and brought up on charges, she disappeared with him and Ivy," Connie broke down and told Amber.

"Damn, I need to think about this, but what do I do? I can't kill my sister."

"Go to the house; we will be there as soon as we can," Connie volunteered.

"No, don't come out here; I need to be alone. My team is here. I will keep them close, but I want to be alone for a few days. Don't come," Amber insisted.

"Okay, but just call if you need to talk; there is a secure line in the house."

"Where?" Amber asked being a bit confused.

"In the den behind the picture of Diamond Head," Connie told her.

"Never knew that. I will call if I need to talk. There was a strange note in with the documents she left, saying she was being held prisoner by a person known as The Colonel and to help her. It came from the Grand Hilton Hotel in Bangkok, Thailand. Got to go now, Goodbye mom," Amber said then hung up the phone.

"Goodbye baby," Connie said to the dial tone.

Hilton Hotel, Kauai

"How is our guest?" The Colonel asked her second in command, when she entered her hotel suite and dialed him on her cell phone.

"She is doing fine. No problem," he responded and then added. "What's our next step?"

"Not sure, I need a drink and time to relax," she said, kicking off her shoes and walking over to the wet bar in her hotel room. "Take the boys down to a pub and relax, I will call when I need you."

"Sure boss, we were just heading out for dinner. Jackie is staying with our guest," he said quietly.

"Good, enjoy the night," The Colonel said and then hung up her cell phone and tossed it on the sofa. She wanted to sit down to enjoy her scotch. As she walked over to the sofa, she took off her clothes preferring to relax nude. After clicking off the holographic device, she sat and put her shapely legs up on the coffee table and leaned back to enjoy her drink.

CIA HQ

"Davin, she knows," Connie told him when he walked into the office.

"Did Monica tell her?" Davin asked as he sat down behind his desk.

"Yes, she didn't give me details, but they must have met; and she told her. What do you want to do?"

"Nothing, that was a long time ago and Monica has become a criminal. If Amber continues with the mission and

132

kills or arrests her, then this is over. We do nothing. Have we heard anything from the hospital?"

"Yes, Mary told me they are going to release Josh tomorrow. He is getting stronger and is out of danger. But he needs to retire and relax, this job is going to kill him and saying that you need to retire too. I don't want you dead again. Because this time it may be permanent," Connie said.

"Okay, as soon as this Monica thing is done, I will retire. We can go to the island and sit on the beach, drink and relax," Davin agreed.

"Promise?"

"Yes, promise; I am getting too old for this shit," Davin replied as he quoted a saying that Danny Glover used in the movie, *Lethal Weapon*, and again in the movie, *Maverick*.

"Amber, have you given any thought that the Monica we met is not the real Monica?" Ginger questioned as they drove to the airport.

"Yes, as a matter of fact. She did have proof as to who she is claiming to be. But since that damn holographic projection system has come into play, it is really hard to tell the difference. What do you think?" Amber agreed.

"I just don't know, she seemed quite real and with those documents, which could have been forged; well, they looked very authentic," Ginger said and turned into the parking lot of the general aviation side of the airfield.

"I need to talk to my parents again and then we fly to L.A," Amber stated, looked at Ginger and back to the Gulfstream VI that would take them back to the States. Beyond the company jet stood another Gulfstream, a little older than hers but not by much. The paint job is what caught her eye, white with blue and gold strips, painted like a class A motorhome, jazzy but not over the top. "Check out the paint on that Gulfstream next to ours."

"Yeah, pretty jazzy, maybe we should take that one."

"No, ours has the secure phone and our weapons; and besides if we traded down, no matter what it looked like, Josh would probably take it out of our pay. Let's go. I need to make a call," Amber said and then climbed out of the SUV. "Go ahead and turn in the keys, we will not need it anymore."

"Wait, I thought you were going to rest at your mom's house for a bit, did that change?" Ginger questioned looking sternly at Amber.

"Yeah, it did. I have a feeling we need to be back in LA, and soon."

"Okay, it's your call, I will meet you on the plane," Ginger said and climbed out and walked to the operations desk inside the terminal and turned in the keys, telling the clerk that someone would be by later today to pick up the SUVs.

Sitting at a side window on the jazzy Gulfstream was Monica Teach looking out at Amber walking to the company jet, as a tear ran down her face. She was a prisoner of the android and holographic impersonator of herself. She had helped Rocky Soto design and build several androids, Andi was the first, they only recently discovered that Ivy was also an android a few months earlier when The Colonel shot and pushed Ivy out of an airplane. She did not know about the third android, the one sitting in front of her. She did not know the true identity of this Monica aka The Colonel, never exposing her true self. The only time she saw The Colonel, she was using the holographic projection to display another Monica or other person. All she knew was that this android was programed to kill and deceive, a prototype of sorts, designed by Monica herself but built and programed by Rocky Soto. This android had been given a program to kill and the ability to learn and adapt. Artificial Intelligence and the ability to be whomever she wanted to be just by thinking. Her holographic device was built in and had a vast library of people hardwired into her system. The perfect killing machine designed and built as a test to replace humans on the battlefield.

Monica Teach knew that she would be dead soon or worse, blamed for the killing of Davin, Connie, and Amber Pierce. Josh and Stephanie Randal were also on the hit list and unless she could stop it, they would all die soon.

135

"Yeah, that is your half-sister walking over there. If she only knew how close she was to us, I am sure she would get her troops and storm this jet, killing or capturing all of us. And quite possibly killing you too," The Colonel/Monica stated as she looked across the tarmac at Amber.

"Are you really going to kill them?" Monica asked.

"Oh, yeah, but not yet. I need to play a bit more and drag your name down through the gutter. You know, if this were a movie, the background music would be something mysterious and foreboding."

"I would prefer something happy and upbeat, but this is your show not mine."

"Monica baby, this is your show. I am doing all this just for you and your sicko family. They have been causing trouble for all of us criminal types for too many years and it has to stop," The Colonel/Monica said.

"Look, it's over, mom and dad are going to retire, and I will make sure Amber quits the company. I don't know how but will find a way," Monica pleaded.

"It doesn't matter; if it isn't them, it would be someone else. I need to make a statement and using you as the statement is the best way. Killing them and blaming you sends a strong message to back off," The Colonel/Monica stated.

"That's where you are wrong, they will just step up the search for you."

"No, they will have you in jail or dead and I will be someone else. Remember, this is just a holographic projection of you and when I'm done, I will become, well, not sure who I will be, maybe Josh Randal or Stephanie and just cause more problems."

"You are a sick person, whoever you are," Monica stated and then looked out the window again. Tears ran down her face as she watched Amber's jet start to taxi out to the runway.

"No baby, you haven't seen sick yet. We will be leaving in a few minutes; and when we get to L.A., you are going to be seen blowing up an historic icon, well, maybe several. The Queen Elizabeth is in the harbor and has many tourists visiting daily; you will make sure she sinks," The Colonel/Monica stated smiling.

"You can't do that; you will kill thousands of innocent people," Monica yelled. "Wasn't blowing up the Honolulu Hilton enough destruction for you."

"I won't be doing it, you will; and you will then be labeled a terrorist again," The Colonel stated, smiling.

CIA Gulfstream at 38,000 feet heading to L.A.

"Hello, mom. What do you and dad want me to do, Monica said she is going to kill us but not yet. Not sure what she meant about that," Amber said when Connie picked up the secure phone.

"Come back to Washington and we will figure it out together."

"We just took off a couple of minutes ago and are headed to L.A.; after that, I don't know. She seems to be one step ahead of us. Is it possible someone is telling her our moves?" Amber questioned.

"Very possible. Who do you have with you?"

"Ginger Burns, Todd Black, George Esteban, and Charlie Wan. Why do you ask?" Amber wondered.

"They are all good agents and I trust them, so it has to be someone here at the company. Monica had a lot of

137

connections while working in the R and D section, could be almost anyone. I will ask Davin to do a deep dive into everyone that may have associated with her," Connie said thinking out loud.

"That may help, we need to find out who she is working with."

"Just a sec, mom, the pilot just said we are going to have to go around a storm which may delay us, nothing serious. I will call back when we get past the storm," Amber said and then hung up.

On the Gulfstream that had been sitting next to them before departure, Monica stared at herself sitting across from her, she couldn't believe what was happening.

"Why are you doing this? I never did or I, hell I don't even know who I am talking to. You look and act like me, but I know you are a holographic projection over a sick person. Who the hell are you?" Monica yelled.

"You may as well know, and I will tell you a little story, but wait," The Colonel said as she closed her eyes briefly, smiled and instantly transformed into someone that Monica had never met or even knew. "I normally don't pose as you because I am too tall. I do have a lovely lady friend built very much like you and she will do anything I ask of her. Now you know the real me. I will introduce you to Sally soon; she is busy setting up the next phase of my plan," The Colonel said but not being completely truthful.

"Is this the real you? If so, who are you? I don't recognize you," Monica questioned as she stared at the woman that sat across from her.

"No, you probably don't recognize me, you may remember my father. He was killed before you were born, or rather almost killed. You may know his name; he was Ted Graves and I'm his daughter Allison. He used to be the President of the United States, well up until they tried to kill him."

"I have heard of you. We talked about you in one of my high school civics classes. He was reported killed over twenty years ago. They said he was corrupt and deceived the American people; they have proof you embezzled millions of taxpayer's monies. Basically, he got rich off the American people. Where has he been and why are you doing this now?" Monica asked becoming very curious.

"All true but let me tell you my story. As President, he was not exactly looking out for the interests of the America people but more so making sure I could live a long and profitable life after he left the White House. At the time, he figured the population would not miss several million dollars that were hidden away in secret funds to be used for covert operations and other not so popular government run programs. Well, some young overzealous investigators discovered what he was doing; so, he fled the country, taking my mother, who happened to be working undercover for these investigators and left. To make a long story short, he was sailing in the Bahamas and ran into a bit of trouble with a torpedo that was fired at another ship but hit his. He was blown off the boat and was able to swim to shore. He had multiple burns, broken bones and was barely alive, but survived. He must have lain on that beach for several days before some fishermen found him and took him to a hospital in Nassau. It was months before he was able to leave and even then, was still a mess. Because he had planned well, he was able to tap into one of his off-shore accounts and get enough money to pay for his medical bills; and with the help of some very talented plastic surgeons in Europe and South America, you see him almost back to his former self. I was in a private boarding school while all this happened, but once he recovered to a point that he could move around the world with ease he brought me home and set me up in the business."

"That's amazing Ms. Graves," Monica commented when he stopped to take a sip of wine.

"Please call me Allison, Miss Monica," Graves insisted, "Would you like some wine?"

"I would love some."

"Well, after many years of medical procedures and recovery, he decided it was time to reinvest in his past and go after the two gentlemen that destroyed his life. That's when he brought me into the family business, as it were, to help."

"Those two wouldn't happen to be Davin Pierce and Josh Randal, would they?"

"As a matter of fact, you have it correct; you win a prize, more wine," Allison said with a chuckle and poured her some more wine.

"So, what now. I guess I know why you have kidnapped me being the daughter of Connie Pierce, but why? Amber and I have done nothing to you; we were not even born when your father was almost killed."

"Oh, because we can do anything. But let me go on, so you can better understand the sequence of things." Allison sipped some wine and then stated, "Damn good wine, don't you think?"

"Yes, very nice." Monica said quietly, thinking *'The timeline isn't right. She should be much older if born while he was in the White House, or before; but she is so young. Must be the holo device not showing the real Allison.'*

"Once he was able to move about safely, he started to recruit help in his quest. First, he recruited Rocky Soto, who was a junior scientist with a small company where he was not appreciated. He made him famous, got him hired at The Company and he worked himself up to lead research and development scientist. He was very smart which allowed him a lot of latitude in his inventions, his best being Andi and the holographic generator. He was an ingenious inventor, but he got greedy and had to be removed. I sent in one of my trusted female assistants to be you and kill Rocky, which she did rather well. You were never the wiser as to what was going on, but now, I need you to just be you, while I go into the next phase of the destruction of Pierce and Randal."

"You won't tell me what you are planning, will you?" Monica asked, hoping that if she knew that, somehow, she could stop it.

"Now if I told you, how much fun would that be. I would prefer you just being surprised. Just sit back and enjoy the ride; we are off to Los Angeles and then, well not sure exactly, but I will keep you informed," Allison said and then picked up the phone next to him and ordered the pilot to take off as soon as cleared by the tower.

"Where is dear old daddy now?" Monica asked between sips of wine.

"Not far, actually he is sitting in the back of the cabin smiling at you," Allison commented smiling. "The one in the wheelchair is dear old daddy. You will get to spend more time with him later, but now we have work to do in Los Angeles. So, sit back and enjoy the ride."

Ted Graves, multi-millionaire, past President of the United States, he could almost do anything he wanted to, but his life changed over the years. Having control of a holographic device developed by Rocky Soto and his team gave Graves a major advantage over his targets. He could be anywhere, posing as anyone, at any time, and be completely hidden from his adversaries. He knew this and had been taking advantage of this for several years, ultimately getting in position to rescue Monica Teach. His plan was working at least up until he was confined to a wheelchair. He now relied on his loving daughter Allison to follow through with his plans. Who was The Colonel that Monica talked about and why had he or she sent Monica to confront Amber and tell the family secret? That only threw gasoline on a fire already blazing.

The man sitting in the back of the business jet in the wheelchair was not Ted Graves, but a holographic simulation of him. Ted Graves was sitting in his office outside of Los Angeles with his daughter Allison discussing the events that were happening around the world with their names attached to it. Ted was dying. He knew it and so did Allison. They needed to end the killing and clear their names and soon before anyone else got killed. But how to do it without getting killed themselves was the question.

When The Colonel's plane landed in Phoenix, he/she did not know the person he was turning Monica over to was not one of his people, but an imposture with an updated holographic device. This slip up allowed Ted to rescue Monica without firing a shot, which he had planned on doing if need be. Now Monica was safely with his sister in a maximum-security prison for women in Arizona and would stay there until he felt it was safe for her to come out.

"Captain, how long before we land in Los Angeles?" The Colonel as Allison asked his pilot as they left Kuai and started over the eastern Pacific Ocean.

"Just a bit over 5 hours, sir," the pilot replied.

"Good, have the steward serve lunch when ready. Do we have enough fuel to get to Phoenix without stopping?" Allison asked and then turned to Monica, "How would you like your steak, Monica?"

"Yes, we can get to Phoenix, no problem," the pilot replied.

"Good, don't go to L.A., go to Phoenix and land, we need to pick up a friend and drop off our passenger. Then on to Los Angeles."

"Yes, sir."

"Medium with a baked potato with butter would be nice," she replied after Allison finished with the pilot.

"Good," she replied and then into the phone, "two medium steaks, salad and baked potato. Serve when ready," Allison ordered and then added, "Let the steward know what you want up there, captain."

"Yes, sir," the pilot responded.

Fifteen minutes later a shapely stewardess in a short mini and low-cut white blouse carried a tray to Allison and Monica and served their lunch. "Wine, sir?" Allison had re-activated her holo generator becoming The Colonel again.

"Yes, please," The Colonel and Monica said in unison. "Thank you."

"I thought Ivan was working today," The Colonel said to the lovely stewardess.

"He's here, flying right seat today so they asked if I would fill in. I am Melodie," she replied.

"Didn't know he was a pilot."

"Yes, he fills in when we are short pilots and then they call me."

"Okay, didn't know. But it's okay. Check back in a few minutes if you would and keep the wine flowing."

"Yes, sir. No problem," Melodie replied smiling then turned and returned to the galley.

Twenty minutes ahead of Graves Jet

"When do we get into L.A.?" Amber questioned the pilot when she stepped into the cockpit.

"If all goes as planned, we should be on the ground in about four and half hours. Sit back and relax, the weather is clear just passed this storm, no storms or anything that would slow us down after this little build up. Louise loaded some nice Rib-eyes why not get her to fix you one. And the bar has some good wine and beer if you like."

"Sounds good, is there enough steaks for everyone?"

"Yep, she planned ahead for the entire team," the pilot commented then picked up his intercom and called for Louise. Seconds later she stepped into the cockpit with Amber, discussed lunch and then headed back to the galley.

After enjoying a great steak at 38,000 feet and some red wine, Amber stood up and walked to the back of the jet and laid down on the large sofa. Moments later the stewardess covered her with a blanket and dimmed the lights. Amber was exhausted and the wine and steak just helped her sleep. Four hours later she woke as the pilot informed the team, they were on approach to Los Angeles International Airport and to please buckle up for landing.

Thirty minutes behind Amber's jet was Ted and Allison aka Ted and The Colonel with their captive Monica Teach, on their way to cause more trouble for the Pierce and Randal family.

After touchdown, Amber and her team were met by a local FBI team to be escorted to the area headquarters. The ride would take about forty minutes with the prevailing traffic around the airport and LA in general.

"Miss Pierce, I'm FBI Senior Agent Malcom Drumming and this is Agent Pamela Grayson, you need to come with us. There has been a development that you need to be aware of. Your dad asked for me personally to take you and your team to Headquarters. They are waiting there for us," Agent Drumming stated after showing his credentials and then indicated they should leave immediately by pointing to the three Chevy SUVs waiting on the tarmac for them.

"What are my mom and dad doing here?" Amber questioned.

"They will explain when we get there; I am not at liberty to tell you anything except that it is urgent that you get there as soon as you can. Please, this way." Drumming pointed to the SUVs again.

"Why not just tell me over the secure phone on the plane?" she asked again.

"I don't know, Miss Pierce," Drumming said and continued to walk toward the SUVs.

"Okay, let's go."

Forty-five minutes later Amber and her team along with Drumming and his team entered the conference room where Amber was greeted by her parents and Josh Randal.

145

"What is going on, dad?" Amber asked as she hugged her mom and dad.

"Please have a seat, we have a lot to talk about," Davin Pierce said and then sat at the head of the conference table. "Agent Drumming please stay, you need to know this also, since it is your city."

"Secure the door and don't let anyone in without Mr. Pierce's permission," Drumming ordered a junior agent.

"Amber, your team has stirred up a hornet's nest and it is about to come to a head," Davin started to say. "Wait, before you say anything, we have intercepted information that our ex-President Ted Graves is alive and behind a lot of the crime spree going on. He teamed up with Monica Teach and you know what she has been doing."

"Ted Graves, wasn't he killed or supposedly killed over twenty years ago in the Bahamas?" Drumming asked.

"Yes, but his body was never recovered; it seems he did survive and has been running the show. We are not sure but believe he was working with Rocky Soto and several high-level politicians to cause us trouble. He is dangerous and extremely well connected. He also has access to many of Rocky Soto's inventions."

"What makes you think that Ted Graves is still alive?" Drumming asked.

"We are not completely sure, but we do believe he is alive and is the one behind all the damage that we thought Monica Teach was doing on her own. But it looks like he is really running the show. The information we have translated from multiple sources leads us to him and Monica Teach is working for him."

"Wow that does change things a little. But the bottom line is Monica needs to be captured or killed; and if

Graves is behind her, then he will fall too," Amber said confidently.

"Wait, you need to see this," Connie said and then picked up the TV remote. "We received this yesterday and well, just watch."

"Hello, you already know me but for those that don't, I'm Monica Teach the great granddaughter to Black Beard the pirate. I sent you this video to let you know what we going to do if we do not receive a hundred million dollars in unmarked bills by noon tomorrow. I will let you know where and when to deliver our money. Yes, our money, we figure that since your government has been supporting illegal aliens, terrorist countries and countries that hate the American way of life, then you can afford to pay a small non terrorist group to be able to keep your country safe. What do I mean? Well, it is easy. You pay us, and we eliminate the competition, the illegal aliens, the countries that hate America, we will destroy them all! Starting with Iran, at five o'clock Tuesday, the capital and their entire government will no longer exist. Your first thought is that this will start World War III. Yes, it will, but there will be nobody over there to fight; they will all be dead. Wait for my email Mr. Pierce, I will send it at eleven o'clock Tuesday. Bye for now, daddy."

"Wow, it is almost eleven, dad, have you got the money?" Amber asked.

"No, we don't. The President would not authorize the payment, saying we do not negotiate with terrorists. That has been the country's creed all along and I knew he wouldn't pay."

"But she will start a world war, and nobody wins if that happens."

"That is a very true statement, so we need to find her fast. We also intercepted a communication from a person we had not heard from in over twenty years. He was talking to Monica over an unsecure satellite phone, giving orders and checking on the status of what she was doing. It took a while, but we finally were able to identify the voice as our supposedly deceased past President Ted Graves. All indications are that he is running the show, not Monica. And to top that off we don't believe that is really Monica, there is just something wrong with how she is acting."

"Not Monica, you think it is someone posing as Monica using a Holo device?" Amber questioned her dad.

"Yes, there is something wrong, I can't put my finger on it just yet."

"Okay, say it isn't Monica; where is she.? You know she met with me in Hawaii and told me about mom and her. She could have killed me right there but didn't. What is she up to and why?" Amber asked to nobody in particular.

"That we need to find out and soon," Connie said quietly.

'Yeah, this is getting really weirder by the minute. Ted Graves, didn't he get killed or supposedly get killed over 20 years ago in the Bahamas?" Amber asked to nobody, really just stating a fact that everyone in the room already knew.

"Josh and I were working a case against him and he fled the country on a private yacht which just happened to get in the way of a torpedo fired at one of our ships and missed, but hit the yacht. It was assumed, incorrectly as it seems, that Graves went to his grave, a watery one on that day but we were completely wrong. No body was found, several of the other passengers, mostly his bodyguards, were found but no Graves." Davin completed the story about his involvement. "Oh, his wife wasn't on the boat; she and a bodyguard and one other female were on the beach when the boat exploded. She survived and went on to complete several more years of service with the Secret Service, under cover and was killed during a mission a couple of years later. Great loss, she was a very good agent and did a lot for the country."

"Wow, so if Graves is still alive and running the show, who is posing as Monica and by the way, where is the real Monica Teach?" Amber asked her father, knowing he didn't have a good answer.

"That is the six-million-dollar question of the day, young lady," Davin replied.

At eleven o'clock Davin Pierce received the expected email from Monica Teach, stating that the money was to be delivered by armor truck to a location ten miles outside of Los Angeles. The place was remote, and they were to provide no armed guards with only one escort vehicle to take the driver away from the location. The truck was to be left unlocked. Davin responded that this was not going to happen, they were not going to pay the requested ransom.

Ten minutes after receiving the response from Davin, four F-35 fighter bombers took off from an airbase in Saudi Arabia armed with nuclear weapons. They were escorted by eight FA-18 Super Hornets from the aircraft carrier USS Enterprise. They had orders to destroy Tehran; the orders had come from the President of the United States, just not the current one. The crew of the aircraft and airbase did not know this and were following orders as directed.

"Ranger 1 this is home base, you are cleared to drop," the commander of the Joint Strike Force based in Dharan, Saudi Arabia ordered.

"Roger, base, ten minutes out, Ranger 3 and 4 are three minutes from target," Ranger 1 acknowledged the two targets. The first being the city of Tehran, Iran and the second Iran's nuclear testing and weapons of mass destruction facility located ninety miles from Tehran.

"Ranger 1 be advised you have six bandits approaching from the south."

"Our escorts will make short work of them. Let them come on up."

Two minutes later four FA-18 Super Hornets dove down to intercept the bandits. One minute later Ranger 3 and 4 acquired their target and released the first of two nuclear weapons on the facility, then accelerated to maximum and climbed to 48,000 feet and sped out of the area with their escorts in tow.

"Bombs away, Ranger 1," Ranger 3 reported as they headed back toward their base in Saudi Arabia.

"Roger, two minutes to drop, our escorts have a few bandits to handle but will be far enough away when we drop," Ranger 1 replied with a smile and then switched to his escorts' channel and reported 1 minute until drop and to get out of the area pronto.

"Roger, Ranger, consider us gone, two bandits down and the others are heading toward you. Drop and go," the lead escort stated.

"Bombs away and we are out of here," Ranger 1 replied; then he and his wing man accelerated to max speed, climbed to 48,000 feet, and headed out of the area. The four remaining bandits had no idea what would happen when they got to where they thought Rangers 1 and 2 were.

One and half hours after takeoff, the four F-35s dropped their weapons of mass destruction on Tehran and videotaped the destruction. They had very little opposition from the Iranian military and what there was were shot down almost immediately by the FA-18s. The nuclear explosions could be seen and heard hundreds of miles away, the destruction was complete. Tehran was completely destroyed along with their government and multiple civilians. More than two hundred thousand people died instantly and with the fall out another half million would die within weeks. The four Iranian fighters arrived over Tehran just as the WMD hit the city destroying the city and all four fighters were blown out of the sky.

"She did it. Tehran and the testing facility are gone, somehow, she got our navy to launch a mission with nuclear weapons to level the city and destroy Iran's nuclear facility. I think World War III just started," Davin said as they watched the reports come in along with live coverage via satellite coverage.

"Holy hell, what is she going to do next and how the hell did she get our own Navy to do this?" Amber questioned.

"That must have been Ted Graves doing the string pulling. He knows the codes; and with his knowledge of the system and the right amount of cash and technology, he could have pulled it off," Davin added. "We need to find him and put him down."

"Incoming call Mr. Pierce, video call," a young agent said as he answered the secure phone.

"Put it up on the big screen," Davin ordered.

"Long time, old friend," Ted Graves said when his image came up on the screen.

"You are not my friend. What the hell are you thinking, Graves. You just started World War III," Davin said as he viewed Graves on the screen.

"Ok, I admit we are not friends, but Monica asked nicely for some money and you refused. Did you think that I was bluffing? Look, before you say anything else, I have the power, the resources, and the hatred for what you and your buddy Josh did to me. I had a good thing going and you destroyed it and almost killed me. So, Monica and I are going to destroy another city every day until you pay up. Oh, one other thing, it is no longer one hundred million, the fee is doubled. You have two days to deliver or another city goes away."

"Don't know how you did it, but you won't be able to use our military again," Josh Randal finally spoke up.

"I won't need them; they will be too busy defending the homeland. When the world finds out that I can destroy a city any time I want, they will be coming after you with guns blazing; of course, blaming the great United States for starting the war. Sit back and watch the show; it will be a best seller. Goodbye ladies and gentlemen," Graves said, and the video ended.

"Damn, did we get a trace on the source of that call?" Drumming asked his technician.

"No, sir. Sorry," the technician replied.

"What now, Mr. Randal?" Drumming asked looking at Josh Randal sitting across the table from him.

"Actually, I don't know, Agent Drumming." After pausing for a moment, he then turned to Davin, "What do you think? We almost killed him once; do you think we should try again?" Josh asked casually of Davin.

"Yeah, I think so, but this time we will not miss," Davin answered smiling.

"Dad, how are you going to do that? We don't even know where he is," Amber questioned both of them.

"Not yet, be we will. He is smart and has had a long time to plan, but we are smarter and have more resources than he. We will find him and end this. In the meantime, we need to make sure our military is on full alert and to not attack anyone unless fired on first or at least threatened," Davin stated and then stood and started for the door.

"Where are you going, dad?" Amber asked watching him head for the door.

"I need a drink, be right back," Davin replied and then Josh stood and followed.

"I need a drink too, be right back," Josh said and followed Davin out the door, closing it as he left.

"Don't worry, Amber. They know what they are doing, even if we don't," Connie said looking a bit confused too.

Washington DC, Walter Reed Military Hospital

"It's been a long time, how are you doing?" Director Phillip Wilson, NSA said as he entered the hospital room where Agent Winho was quarantined and being treated.

"Sir, I am not feeling very well, so I would like to make this briefing short if you don't mind," Agent Winho replied from the inside of the plastic enclosure he was inside.

"Sure, tell me what you can in the next fifteen minutes, and then put the rest in your after-action report. I can read it when you get it filed. But don't worry about the report until you are out of here."

"Well, sir, as suspected the Chinese are working on a bioweapon that could be considered extremely dangerous and could cause a pandemic if released. I got wind of it through my contact in the lab. She was worried and even mentioned that her lab partner was considering releasing it without permission. And honestly, sir, I believe he already did."

"How can you be sure?"

"On the news, which leaked out on one of the Chinese radio broadcasts that was being retransmitted on board the plane. It seems that the technician was caught at the airport with a vial of the bioweapon. They didn't say that he released it; but when they showed his picture, I remembered seeing him at the airport and saw the police arrest him near the gate that I was boarding. If he released the virus on that plane, it is highly possible that I may have been infected."

"That is why we are talking here in your hospital room instead of in my office. Do the doctors know what kind of virus it may be, and if it has been transmitted to others on your flight?"

"I told the doctors about the flight and they notified the airport to hold all the passengers from my flight in quarantine until tested. But I know some people caught connecting flights and others may have got out of the airport before being stopped. We may have a pandemic in the works, sir."

"We got the passenger list and are rounding everyone up as we speak. Don't you worry about it; just get well. We need you in the field, not in a hospital bed," Wilson commented and then asked. "Is there anything else you need to tell me?"

"Just that I think my cover in China has been compromised and would prefer to not go back there for a while."

"Sure, that I believe we can make happen. Now get some rest and we will talk in a few days," Wilson replied. He then left the hospital room and headed back to his office.

"Davin, do you really know what you are doing?" Josh asked.

"Josh, I have no forking idea what we're doing, but we are going to do it anyway" Davin responded.

"Well, you know, it was the same stuff 25 years ago trying to get him out of office; and we did that. But this time, we're not sure where he is, or how many people he has working for him; and with Monica, he could do almost anything he wants. He could be anywhere posing as anyone."

"Josh we will make this happen; we will get it done. Don't worry," Davin stated.

"Davin, do you know something I don't know?" Josh asked as they walked down the hallway.

"As a matter of fact, I do," Davin stated matter-of-factly.

"So, when are you going to fill me in on all this extra information that you have?" Josh demanded as he stopped in front of the elevator.

"As soon as I get a tall cold scotch," Davin said, and he pushed the button for floor number one.

"Don't you think we should tell the rest where we are going?" Josh said as they stepped into the elevator.

"Sure, you can call them once we get there."

"Where is there?"

"I don't know, the closest bar," Davin stated.

Fifteen minutes later Davin and Josh were sitting at a table in a bar two blocks from the FBI headquarters building. Josh called Connie and told her where they were and invited them to join if they liked, or wait, and they would be back in about an hour.

"Dad, we thought you were going to be gone a few minutes, but here you are having a drink with your old buddy. What are you not telling us?" Amber questioned when she walked into the bar and saw them sitting at the table.

"Honey, there were just a few things I couldn't say in that room with all those extra people. Most of which is highly classified, and Josh knows it, but will not admit that he does. We'll have this one drink; would you like one. And then we'll go back up to the conference room and I will lay out the plan," Davin said and then took a sip of his scotch.

"Sure, I will have a scotch on the rocks."

Thirty minutes later, they were walking back into the building and up to the conference room. Upon entering Drumming stood and questioned where they had been.

"Sit down Drumming, I will tell you everything in just a minute," Josh said as he took his seat at the head of the table.

"Ted Graves the past President of the United States 22 ½ years ago. He committed multiple crimes against the country to include murder, extortion and many other crimes that are too lengthy to mention here. He fled the country on the yacht with his wife and several Secret Service agents that were under his personal payroll. His wife, may she rest in peace, was one of our operatives. Her death came unexpectedly, and we believe is linked directly to Ted Graves. Davin and I pursued Ted Graves to the Bahamas and the Soviet submarine that we recovered recently was on station and fired a torpedo at our ship but missed and inadvertently hit the yacht that Ted Graves and his people were on. Several bodies were recovered; Ted Graves was not one of them. We believed his body was destroyed during the explosion. It has been unknown to the CIA, FBI, or any law enforcement agency that Ted Graves was still alive until now. Our plan is to draw him out into the open and remove the problem before he can destroy another city. We do know that Monica has been working with him making sure his technology is up-to-date. She is a computer genius and was a faithful follower of Rocky Soto. We will use her as bait, but we need to use Amber to get to Monica since they are half-sisters. Amber are you up to this?" Josh stated and asked.

"Mr. Randall I am a dedicated CIA agent; Monica's team killed my brother I want revenge," Amber said as she looked at her mom and dad across the table.

"Amber, be assured that you may have to kill Monica. I truly hope it doesn't come down to that," Davin added.

"Amber honey, you don't have to do this, if you don't want to; she is your half-sister," Connie stated as a tear dropped down her cheek.

"Mom, I know she is my half-sister. We have talked, and I don't believe she is doing this willingly. I will not kill her," Amber stated and then added, "we don't even know where Monica is much less how we are going to catch her."

"But we do know where Monica is and how to get to her," Davin said.

"So, where is she?" Drumming asked.

"Agent Drumming, we need you to secure this building and the surrounding area," Josh ordered, "Please go take care of that now. This operation begins now."

Meanwhile 6 miles from the FBI headquarters, the holographic image of Ted Graves and Allison Graves posing as Monica, and Sally Howard, were sitting at their own conference table discussing what to do next.

"Sally I need you to go to Las Vegas," Ted Graves said.

"Ted what am I going to do there?" Sally asked.

"You're going to go as Monica and gamble, have some fun, make yourself be seen and videoed."

"Sounds like fun when do I leave and what are you going to be doing?" Sally queried.

"While you'll be having fun, and take hundred thousand dollars with you, I'm just going to do a little bit of destructive criticism of our government system."

"You're not going to destroy a city in the United States, are you?" Sally questioned.

"No, my dear, just putting the ball in motion to destroy Moscow or maybe Berlin. I really haven't decided yet. But I don't want you involved in this one, I want them to see you in Las Vegas having fun."

"Okay, if you insist, I will go have fun. I'll pack my bag and head that way within the hour. May I take the car?" Sally asked.

"Sure, take the white convertible Corvette," Ted insisted and then watched as Sally stood and walked out of the room.

"Sally, before you leave, send Carlos in; I need to speak to him," Ted asked. Then he smiled at his daughter posing as Allison now.

"You called Sir," Carlos said as he entered the conference room.

"Carlos, we have a mission to set up and you are going to be the lead to make this one happen," Ted Graves said as Carlos sat down across from him. "How would you like to go to Europe?"

"Haven't been to Europe in a long time, Sir, sounds like a good vacation."

"Won't be exactly a vacation; you are going to go to make sure we destroy Moscow."

"That will not be a problem, Sir. The bomb is already in place. I can detonate from anywhere in Europe if I have a computer. Actually, I could detonate from here if you so desire," Carlos stated.

"I know Carlos; you could detonate from here; but I need someone on the ground there to ensure the public is duly panicked. And I know you are so good at creating panic," Ted stated smiling.

"When would you like me to leave, sir?" Carlos asked.

"Tomorrow morning would be fine, no rush," Ted stated.

"Am I to go alone or take my team?"

"Oh, take your team and cause panic. I know you enjoy that. I will let you know if and when to detonate. Make sure you and your team are far enough away before you press the button," Ted Graves ordered.

"Oh, rest assured we will not be within the blast zone," Carlos agreed smiling.

"Now go and get ready, this phase is about to get very interesting."

"It sure is nice to have a bunch of trained monkeys to do what I want," Graves said at Allison after Carlos left the room and was way out of hearing.

Graves did not know that Carlos was not a trusting person and had planted a listening device in Graves' office and bedroom to listen in on things said, and Carlos was not pleased at being called a trained monkey. He would let Sally know how Graves really felt about them and see what she wanted to do about it. Sally didn't trust Graves either. Although she and Carlos were not lovers, they were very close friends and trusted each other with their lives, which in this case if Graves found out about the deceit, he would kill both without hesitation. Sally and Carlos were walking on very thin ice, as it were, because Graves knew of the deception and had plans for them and Carlos's team too.

"Colonel, where are the real Allison and Ted Graves right now?" the fake Ted asked.

"Our last communication with our person at the estate confirmed they are in his office with the doors closed," The Colonel replied and then switched from his Allison holograph to a male in a business suit with a smile and small trimmed bread.

"Stop that, stay as The Colonel or Allison, quit playing around, I never know who I'm talking to when you do that," the fake Ted ordered.

"Sure, thing boss. What next?" The Colonel asked.

"Inform the FBI as to their location and set up a raid for day after tomorrow. And then let slip that there is a raid planned and see that Allison and her father leave the estate before the raid. I will project my image there for the capture, or rather the almost capture."

"Sounds like fun, I will make it happen," The Colonel replied and then left the suite as Allison.

"Captain, the weather is turning pretty rough, what do you suggest?" the first mate on the freighter *Stratahorn* asked as he watched the brewing storm on the horizon.

"Ned, that is a good question, let me check the forecast and let you know in a minute. We are due in New Orleans by morning to start unloading this cargo and if we want to get paid, we need to be there. But as you know as well as I do, Mother Nature doesn't abide by schedules, except her own. Be right back," Captain August said as he turned and walked back to the radio room.

"Captain, I think you need to see this," the radio operator said as he handed him a printed weather report.

"Damn, Ned, what you see ahead of us is the edge of a rapidly forming tropical depression. NOAA is predicting this could quickly turn into a hurricane. Contact the engine room and order full speed; let's see if we can get to New Orleans before that thing hits us. The report says it is moving at 15 knots on a northerly course directly for New Orleans. If we can get 20 out of those old engines, maybe if we are lucky, we can beat it."

"Don't know sir. We have been nursing those engines for months now, they really need an overhaul," Ned responded and then ordered more speed from the engine room and got the same response he had just made to the captain.

"Sparky keep an eye on the weather reports and let me know of any changes. It's going to be a rough ride, fellows. Alert the crew to batten down the hatches and secure any loose cargo."

Two and a half hours later, the Gulf of Mexico was turning up the heat on all shipping. The *Stratahorn* was caught right in the middle of it. Even though the Gulf was small compared to the Atlantic and Pacific Oceans, it still could cause major damage to shipping and coastal communities. And today was no exception. Seas were starting to peak at eighteen feet and tossed the five hundred and fifty-foot *Stratahorn* around like a cork.

Four hours after getting the initial report, the winds were at a constant velocity of seventy-five knots gusting to over ninety. The latest report showed that the tropical depression which started just over four hours ago was now classified as a category 2 hurricane. If it continued to intensify, she would become a category 3 and maybe 4 before night. She was officially named Hurricane Billie.

"Captain we are losing steering; the rudder is not responding!" Ned yelled over the storm.

"Do your best, son, keep her heading for the coast, maybe we will survive yet. How far to the coast?"

"Twenty miles, plus or minus," Ned yelled back just as a large wave broke over the side causing the freighter to list to port and almost capsize. Ned was fighting the best he could with the captain assisting with the wheel.

"The winds and seas are pushing us toward the coast, and we have no control of where we will end up," the captain yelled over the winds. "May god have mercy on our souls."

The crew had been through a lot of storms, but this one came up quickly and seemed like it was out for revenge. Survival in the Gulf of Mexico in a storm like this was going to be extremely risky. They could not turn back; the seas and winds were too strong to turn the ship around. If they attempted to turn, they would most likely capsize when a large wave hit them broadside. The crew was doing everything they could possibly do to save the ship and themselves, but hope was all they had left.

Minutes seemed like hours as they fought the raging weather. Visibility was down to about fifty feet with the rain coming down in sheets so thick you would think you could cut through it with a knife. The wind was clocked at over one hundred and eighty-five miles per hour. The captain knew his ship was doomed, but still he fought with all his might to try and save her. Land was approaching rapidly, and they had no idea where they would finally hit, but it was going to happen and very soon.

The sound of the ship striking land was barely heard over the raging storm but what happened next flashed in an instant through the crew's eyes as the ship literally exploded into the dike surrounding New Orleans. Within minutes, the ship was nothing but a pile of metal and cargo being washed into the city. There was nothing left of the ship or the dike as the Gulf of Mexico poured into the city just as it had done years before when the dike failed to hold back another hurricane.

There is a saying about Las Vegas, and it goes like this, *'What happens in Vegas, Stays in Vegas.'* This is almost always true for the millions of visitors that come and play in the other city that never sleeps, New York being the other one.

Sally also sometimes known as Monica Teach arrived late in the afternoon at the MGM Grand Hotel located on the famous Las Vegas strip. After giving her car keys to the parking attendant, she walked into the main lobby to check in. She had reserved a suite on the top floor and planned on having a lot of fun both in the casino and her suite. Her assignment was very simple this time, pose as Monica Teach, spend a lot of time in the casino and be seen. If threatened, she could easily change her identity to almost anyone else and virtually disappear right before your eyes.

Her suite was large and complete with a fully stocked mini bar, awesome view of the city and a king size bed which she planned on using a lot with whomever she wanted to play with.

"Thank you," she said to the bell hop that brought her luggage up to the suite and tipped him twenty dollars, receiving a big smile from the young man and an offer to assist in anything she wanted. "I will keep that in mind, what is your name?"

"Matthew and I get off work at midnight," he replied smiling at the beautiful lady standing in front of him.

"Give me a contact number and I may just call you later," Sally as Monica replied and smiled. She closed the door, kicked off her shoes, and started to undress. She needed a shower and then would head to the casino to play a little and see what she could find for entertainment. After clicking the holographic device's button, the holo display disappeared and she was once again Sally Howard from Chicago and only wearing very short tight black shorts and matching top, which she immediately removed and walked over to the window to gaze out, naked. She turned and walked over to the mini bar, pulled out a beer, and then returned to the window, sitting down just to enjoy the view before her shower. Sipping her beer, she contemplated the evening and what she may or may not wear to enjoy a night on the town. Finishing her beer, she stood and walked into the bathroom to shower and then to unpack.

After her shower, Sally picked up her holo device and pressed a couple of buttons to transform into Monica Teach and a couple more to cover her naked body with a very short red dress that accented her figure with a front that barely covered her breasts and left a lot of cleavage showing. Gazing in the mirror she smiled and thought to herself, *'This should get some attention.'* She slipped on a pair of spiked heels, picked up her purse with her gambling money, and headed for the door. She would be completely naked, if the holo device failed at any time, but she really didn't care. She wanted to be sexy and available if she found a play friend for the evening. The device was carefully slid into the tiny pocket of her dress.

Sally took the elevator down to the casino and located an empty seat at a Blackjack table, laid two hundred dollars down and took her chips, placing ten dollars out as her first bet, to test the waters, as it were. Three hours later and up a thousand dollars and four margaritas, she cashed out and stood, handing the dealing a fifty-dollar chip.

"Leaving so soon?" the man that was sitting next to her asked.

"Yeah, a little tired, need to hit the bed. Does that excite you?" she replied.

"Yes, it does."

"Sorry to disappoint, but my batteries are low, and I need to recharge, maybe later," Sally said and then turned and walked toward the elevators. She was not kidding about the batteries. But it was not her body needing to recharge; it was the holographic device that needed to recharge. It had just given her the mini vibration indicating batteries were low and would shut down in about fifteen minutes. She really didn't want to walk through the MGM casino naked, not just yet anyway.

As she entered the elevator, the holo device quit completely. Her dress dissolved, just as the doors closed, leaving her naked in the elevator. At least she was alone for the moment. Her holo device dropped to the floor from the holographic pocket in her now dissolved dress. Sally leaned down to pick up it up, smiled and hoped she could get back to her suite without being seen; but then the elevator stopped at the eleventh floor, and the doors slid open. A young couple who stood in the hallway, stepped in, and pressed 19 to go up.

The young man looked at Sally standing in the back of elevator and smiled. He was punched by his girlfriend for looking. He turned and faced the front of the elevator smiling.

"Maybe a threesome?" he said to his date, loud enough for Sally to hear. Sally just leaned against the back wall, smiled, and shook her head no to the comment.

"No, baby, you paid for me and I will treat you right," the young girl said as she looked up into his eyes smiling. She was wearing a very short mini skirt and low-cut blouse that left very little to the imagination. "You are mine tonight."

Sally smiled at the young man and stood in the back of the elevator and waited. When the elevator stopped on the 19th floor, the young couple got out and a middle-aged man stepped in. He smiled at the sight of a naked woman in the back of the elevator.

"I've seen a lot in Vegas, but you are the first nude in an elevator I have encountered. Are you okay?" the gentleman said and then added. "If you are looking for company tonight, I may be able to help."

"Lost at the Blackjack table. Thanks for the offer, but I am heading to bed, alone," she replied smiling. Finally, the door opened on her floor and she quickly walked to her suite wearing only a smile, and her black spiked heels. She carried her small purse and holographic device that looked like a smart phone. The gentleman just smiled and watched the door close between them. Upon reaching her suite, Sally immediately walked over to the mini bar, pulled out two scotch bottles, and downed them both quickly. "Damn that was embarrassing. I should have known not to go naked under the holo projection. When will I learn?"

Sitting down in front of her window she drank and leaned back to rest and think. While looking closely at the device she wondered; it seemed to be working fine now and the battery indicator showed a sixty percent charge. She pressed the device to change herself into Monica and it worked perfectly.

'*What the hell?*' she said to herself.

Los Angeles Late the same night

"Allison, did you get the message off to Mr. Randal?" Ted Graves asked his daughter as she entered his office.

"Yes, sir. Mr. Randal was not available, so I spoke with his secretary, Mary. She said she would relay the message as soon as Randal checked in," Allison Graves said and then took a seat across from her father. She was wearing white skintight spandex slacks with a matching white halter top accenting her perfect body. Smiling at her father, she was happy to finally become part of his life. For the first eighteen years of her life, she didn't even know where he was, only that the money to support her showed up at the boarding school each month and she lived very well, learning four languages, martial arts and a multitude of other life skills. Now on her nineteenth birthday, she was brought to Los Angeles to meet with her father and join his organization.

"Dad, why are you telling the CIA about Monica? Is she in trouble?"

"Yes honey, she is a bad person and the CIA has been looking for her for a long time and I am just trying to help them locate her. I got a call from a friend of mine at the MGM Grand in Vegas telling me she was seen gambling earlier tonight. I felt it is my duty to help when I can."

"Okay, I guess that's good. If she is bad, then she should be arrested," Allison agreed. "I'm tired and it is late. Is there anything else you need me for? I want to go to bed."

"No, go on, I have a few things to finish up and then I will be heading to bed myself," Ted Graves said and smiled at his beautiful daughter. He waited until she left and closed the door behind her before he picked up his cell phone and dialed a number. "Nat, how is our guest doing?"

"She is doing fine, sir. Sleeping soundly. Do you want me to wake her?" Nat replied. She was a tall older lady with long black hair and deep blue eyes. Natalie Henson was the warden at a private woman's prison located near Phoenix, Arizona. Twenty miles deep in the desert making it very difficult for escapees to actually escape. The real Monica Teach was being held there, unwillingly, as a favor to Ted Graves, her brother. There were no records kept on Monica at the prison, she was one of the ones that just disappeared and would be impossible to locate. At least until the right time to let her go.

"Good, keep her in good health, I will need her soon," Ted stated and then thought for a moment adding, "Is she in solitary?"

"Yes, as you requested. Nobody knows she is here except a couple of the guards and they don't know her except by the name of Nancy Smith. She gets three meals a day and use of the exercise room only. Gets all her meals in her cell and nothing more," Nat stated sounding a bit disgusted with the situation. But he was her younger brother and she would do anything for him. Well, almost anything, and right now he was getting very close to stepping over the line, again. She supported him when he ran and won the Presidency and cried when she thought he had been killed, only to discover he was alive a year after he was supposed to have died. He had been living in Columbia under an alias where he received multiple medical treatments for his injuries sustained from when the boat he was on blew up. He contacted her only after being in the hospital for a year. She was happy and relieved that he survived, and also understood his injuries were not just physical, but mental too. He was different and his anger and aggression were apparently gone; he was a changed man, maybe because he was dying, or maybe he just wanted to stop running. This made her very happy and scared at the same time.

"Good, just a few more weeks and I will come get her," Ted said and then hung up his phone. He was happy and satisfied that all was going as planned. He would win his war or die trying, again.

Ted had gotten lucky with the tip from his informant that The Colonel was stopping in Phoenix to pick up another one of his team and to drop off Monica to be placed in a safe house that he controlled. Ted's team intercepted The Colonel's team had been replaced with his team and so he had been able to rescue Monica. He then moved her to be with his sister, a warden at a max security prison in the desert outside of Phoenix where she would stay until it was safe for her to be freed. Monica agreed to this and went with Natalie to the prison.

The temperature outside had approached 110 degrees with a humidity factor of about 90 percent. Threatening dark clouds had moved in rapidly. It definitely looked like a very bad storm on the horizon. Nothing out of the ordinary for south Texas, but this wasn't south Texas; it was New Orleans, and there had recently been enough rain in the area to fill an ocean, which it had done several times over. The last storm like this had cost the residents millions of dollars and the insurance companies even more with flooded homes and businesses.

Amber and her team had just arrived when they got the report that the sighting of Monica Teach in New Orleans was a mistake and the woman that looked like Monica was a female impersonator from one of the drag queen clubs located downtown. So now they were stuck until the storm passed since winds had increased so much that all airplanes and airports had shut down for safety reasons.

Amber stood in the private lounge at the executive terminal where she had watched the storm arrive and wondered how long before they could leave. She had been waiting for the company jet to arrive, which was overdue now. The lounge had a small mini bar for them, but she did not want to partake until she knew their next move. She pulled her cell phone out of her pocket and pressed the speed dial for her dad.

"Ms. Pierce we just heard the airport has closed and diverted all incoming traffic to Dallas, until the storm passes. It has been upgraded to a category three hurricane and getting worse. You are not going to be able to leave today, sorry," the attendant told her while she waited for her father to answer her call.

"Dad, we arrived yesterday when the hurricane was on the east coast of Florida; now we want to fly out and the airport has just closed because that storm turned west and is headed straight at us. We are grounded at the airport until it passes. The person identified as Monica was just a female impersonator on her or his way to work. We talked and enjoyed his show. He didn't think it was a problem impersonating a known criminal for his comedy act, actually though it was truly funny. Little did he know that he came very close to getting shot," Amber said when Davin Pierce answered.

"Nothing new, we got your report on the confirmation that the Monica sighting down there was a female impersonator walking to work. Good work! So, are you going to get out of there?"

"Well, we might have shot him if he hadn't cooperated, but he did," Amber said with a small chuckle. "We're stuck here until this storm passes."

"Yeah, anyway, your mom says to be careful; the Big Easy can be a dangerous place during a storm. And if you see Agent Pride, say I said hello and glad he survived his kidnapping," Davin joked, referring to the TV series NCIS New Orleans where Agent Pride was kidnapped and almost killed.

"Sorry dad, I missed that episode. Thanks for spoiling the ending," Amber laughed.

"Oops, it was a good one, I have it recorded; you can watch it when you get home."

"I will." Amber paused as the storm reached the airport with a vengeance. "Wow, the storm just hit, and two small Cessnas just flipped over, broke their tie downs and... Got to go. I'll call later," Amber yelled into the phone as the intensity of the storm increased. A large window exploded when it was hit by flying debris not more than twenty feet from her. She picked up her bag and along with everyone else in the room moved quickly away from the plate glass windows.

"What happened to your storm shutters?" Amber yelled at the attendant.

"They took them down to clean and paint the building and were scheduled to be reinstalled next week. Bad timing," the attendant yelled back as they ran to the back of the lounge.

"Everyone to the back of the room, NOW!" screamed the lounge attendant and then ducked down behind the bar just as another window exploded inward. Several of the crew and guests were struck by the wind hurled shattered glass pieces. "The safest places are the restrooms, go in there."

"... please seek shelter, this storm which started off the coast of Florida as a topical depression has just been upgraded to a category 4 hurricane. Sustained winds of 135 miles per hour and gusts over 150. I repeat this is now a category 4 hurricane and you must seek shelter immediately..." the TV announcer just reported before a large piece of glass shattered the TV. It was knocked off the wall and crashed to the floor.

Everyone ran toward the restroom doors and only half of them made it before another window exploded inward sending glass into the group. Three died instantly when the glass struck them in the back; the lucky ones dove into the restrooms.

"Where is Henry?" Amber yelled to anyone that would listen.

"I don't know," was an answer that came back.

Amber turned, opened the door, and looked out at the carnage. She saw Henry laying in a pool of blood beside two other people. Grabbing the man next to her, they ran out and picked up the injured and carried them into the bathroom. Rain and debris were streaming into the lounge and within seconds everything that was once a comfortable lounge was a total wreck. Ten, soaking wet, would be flyers were crowded into the small ladies' restroom, huddled against the inner wall.

"How is he?" Amber asked almost yelling over the sound of the storm screaming outside. Two of the biggest men leaned their backs on the door to hold it closed as the wind attempted to blow it off its hinges.

"Not good, he has a lot of glass in his back and I am trying to stop the bleeding but... get me some more towels." The attendant was working hard on Henry to stop the bleeding, but it was a losing battle. Without medical attention soon, he would not survive.

"Does anyone have a working phone?" the attendant asked the group.

"Mine is wet, but still functioning," a young lady in a short mini skirt said as she looked closely at the face of the phone.

"May I borrow it? I need to call for help?" the attendant asked and took the phone when she handed it to him. After punching in 9-1-1, it rang a couple of times and abruptly stopped. Looking at it, he was confused; but it only took a moment to realize the circuits were probably down.

"Look, there is water coming in under the door," Donald Vickers, US Marshall said pointing to the base of the door. "Get some towels to stem the flow." He grabbed some towels and pressed them under the door in an attempt to stop or slow the water flow.

"Did you get in touch with your dad?" Jake Miller, US Marshall, asked as they milled around in the ladies' restroom.

"Yes, he knows we are here and safe at the moment, but with this storm, only time will tell," Amber replied then turned to the attendant and asked. "How strong is this building?"

"Pretty strong, she was built to sustain category 5 hurricanes and has proven to do so over and again. The last one only did what this one already has done, blow out windows and destroy the furniture. We should be safe in here until this storm blows over. If only we were upstairs, that is where the food and drinks are, and there are only a couple small windows which have automatic storm shutters on them. The people up there are safe and have food and drink," the attendant replied.

"Why don't we go up there?" Jake said casually.

"Easier said than done. The stairs going up are across the lobby and I really wouldn't recommend trying to cross over to them right now. The winds alone would most likely prevent you from getting there; but if you didn't get killed by flying debris, you might make it. Then there is a passcode you must enter to get in at the top of the stairs. With no electricity, the keypad will not work; and right now, we are on generator, but for how much longer I can't say. So, having said all that, I don't recommend trying for the stairs just yet. Let's wait until the storm dies down a bit."

"Okay, I agree with what you are saying, but the water is still coming in under the door. Jake see if you can open the door a little to check what is going on out there," Amber requested as she eyed the water level rising.

"It won't budge, Don, come help me push," Jake stated as he pushed hard on the door. "It's like there is something blocking it."

With Don's help they were able to move the door a few inches and water started to flow in for about three feet over the floor. Letting the door slam shut, stopped the water flow from the edge of the door, but not from under the door.

"Sally, this is Carlos, I need to tell you something that you will not believe, but trust me when I tell you this is the truth," Carlos said into his phone while flying to Frankfurt, Germany.

"What is it now, Carlos. Ted sent me to Vegas to have some fun and be seen. What is so important that you had to call in the middle of the night," Sally asked as she rolled out of bed.

"Look, I know you and I haven't seen eye to eye much and you don't really trust me, but believe me this time, your life depends on it."

"What are you getting at, spill it; I'm tired and want to get back to bed."

"Look, I planted some bugs around the house and overheard Ted plotting to have you and me killed. He sent me to Europe to cause trouble and to detonate a few well-placed bombs and he sent you to Vegas to expose yourself. His plan is to have you captured or killed by the FBI, and me to detonate a few bombs with one or two of them killing me. He is crazy and I just wanted you to be aware. I am going to disappear in Europe, and you should consider disappearing too," Carlos stated and then paused for a moment to let it sink in.

"Kill us, why?" Sally questioned.

"I guess we have outlived our usefulness and he is tying up loose ends, namely us."

"But who will replace us? We have been loyal and, hell, why?" Sally wanted to know.

"I don't know but take care of yourself; be safe and run," Carlos said and then broke the connection.

Sally looked around the suite and wondered if she should believe Carlos or not. He wasn't very trustworthy, and this only proved that. Planting bugs to spy on their boss was pretty low, even for Carlos. But hell, if it were true, then how much more time did she have?

She thought about just slipping on a pair of jeans, blouse, and her running shoes, but then thought again. Maybe she should use the holo-device to hide in plain sight, at least while it worked. But could she trust it? The thing quit on her while in the casino and what if it quit again and she was seen by the people after her. No, she slipped on the jeans, blouse and running shoes, pulled a blonde wig from her bag, and pulled out her make-up bag. She would disguise herself and walk right out the back door. Sally threw her clothes into her suitcase, retrieved her 9mm Berretta pistol, checked the mag for a full load, slipped it in the small of her back and headed for the door.

She grabbed a cab at the front of the hotel and told the driver to take her to the local mall, which never closed. She would switch cabs there, head to the airport, and catch the next flight out of Vegas to anywhere. She didn't notice the woman following her out of the hotel and get in the cab behind her.

"Ted, she just left the hotel, I am following," Heather Newton said in her cell phone when he answered.

"Just follow for now, let's see where she is going; maybe she just got tired of Vegas. Is she in a cab or in the Vette?"

"Cab."

"She must have found out our plans for her. Take her out when you get a chance; she is a liability now,"

Graves ordered. "Try not to kill anyone else in the process, please."

"Consider it done, sir," Heather said and then hung up her phone, pulled out her 357 autoloader and checked to ensure the safety was off. Killing Sally in front of a lot of witnesses was not her first choice, but they would never see her anyway; the holographic device would ensure that.

Minutes later, Sally's cab stopped in front of the mall with Heather pulling up behind her. Heather paid the cabby, climbed out, and walked quickly toward the crowded mall when she pulled her weapon and yelled, "Sally, US Marshal, stop."

Sally stopped and turned around to face Heather. Seeing Heather holding her autoloader pointed at her, she immediately dove to the right. The bullet fired missing her by inches and slammed into the wall behind her. Sally pulled her Berretta and took careful aim at Heather, who was confident that Sally was unarmed, a near fatal mistake by Heather. Two shots fired by Sally buried into Heather's chest and threw her back onto the pavement. Sally immediately stood and ran into the mall. She ducked into the first lady's clothing store she came too, before the police had a chance to identify her as the shooter. Sally quickly picked out a new outfit, paid the cashier with cash. and stepped into the changing room. A couple of minutes later, Sally stepped out of the changing room into the store again as a brunette in a short mini dress and red blouse. Her weapon rested comfortably in the small of her back as she eyed the police in action around Heather. Walking out of the mall she signaled a cab and asked the driver to take her to the General aviation terminal at the airport where she would hire a pilot and plane to fly her out of Vegas.

Heather laid on the floor for several minutes before rolling over and accessing her injury; lucky for her she had on a bullet proof vest under her blouse which stopped the bullets from penetrating her chest. But the bruising would be extensive. Two police officers were standing over her and another was leaning down to assist her up with a pair of handcuffs ready to put on her. He had already picked up her weapon when she protested to the handcuffs.

"No, handcuffs, I'm a Federal Marshall," Heather said almost too quiet to be heard, but stopping the officer from handcuffing her. "Here are my creds," she said as she pulled out her US Marshall badge and identification.

"What the hell were you thinking, shooting in a crowded shopping mall?" The lead officer demanded.

"The woman I was about to arrest is a wanted fugitive and was obviously armed and dangerous. I shot in defense, when she pulled her weapon," Heather lied as to the sequence of events, hoping that witnesses would not remember the exact sequence and that she had fired first.

"Call this in, Sam," the lead officer ordered his partner. "Are you okay?" he asked Heather redirecting his questioning back to her.

"Yes, did anyone see which way she went?" Heather questioned.

"She ran into the mall and faded into the crowd; we lost her inside," Sam said when he stepped back from making his call to headquarters. "She is legit. US Marshall Heather Newton from the Los Angeles office."

"Who is this fugitive? What did she do to warrant shooting in my town?" the lead officer asked.

"She killed two Marshalls in Los Angeles. I have been tracking her for the past week and almost had her. I let my guard down and expected her not to be armed. I screwed up."

"Almost got you killed, Marshall Newton. I will have Sam take you to the hospital to check your wounds."

"No, I'm fine," Heather insisted.

"No, you are not, a shot from that close could have broken ribs and you could be bleeding internally. You will go to the hospital; we will clean up around here and question any witnesses that saw what happened."

"I guess you are right, let's go," Heather agreed and then walked with the officer to a waiting ambulance.

Carlos walked toward the private jet that he had reserved for himself to fly to Europe from New York, but as he crossed the tarmac from the terminal, two men approached him smiling. His team was to catch up to him in Frankfurt, Germany. The commercial flight from L.A. had landed him in New York with a twelve-hour delay, which was unacceptable, so he had chartered a private jet to continue his journey.

"Carlos, we need you to come with us," the taller of the two said as they approached.

"What do you want? I just got here can it wait a couple minutes," Carlos asked as they approached, he looked around and saw that he was completely exposed and had nowhere to run.

"Carlos, you can come quietly," the taller of the two pulled out his US Marshall credentials and badge, showing them to Carlos.

"Oh, what can I do for you, marshal?" Carlos asked as his fear slowly dripped away, these were US Marshalls and he was safe with them.

182

"We need you to come with us. There has been a report that you may know where a Mr. Ted Graves is."

"Sure, are you going to arrest him?"

"That is the plan, but we need you to get us to him as soon as possible. Will you come with us now? We have a private plane waiting over there to fly us to wherever he is."

"Okay, let's go, my luggage?" Carlos said and then followed the two US Marshalls to a waiting Gulfstream IV business jet. There was a third Marshall waiting at the boarding steps. Minutes later they were heading out of New York.

"Tell us what city he is in so I can tell the pilot where to go," the marshal asked.

"Where are we going? Are we heading east or west, looks like east?" Carlos commented.

"Oh, yeah, when I saw him last, he was in L.A."

"Would you care for a drink?"

"I will have a beer if you have any," Carlos answered reluctantly. "What's going on; why is your weapon pointed at me? I haven't done anything wrong." Carlos asked the Marshall sitting next to him when he noticed the Marshall had his weapon out and pointed at him.

"Just sit back and be quiet; we will be landing shortly," the Marshall said but kept his weapon pointed at Carlos.

An hour and half later, they passed over Bermuda and then turned a little southwest and climbed to forty-five thousand feet.

"Change in plans, just relax, the weapon is for your protection. We have been asked to bring you to the Azores," the Marshall said just before they landed on the small island.

Forty minutes later, they were standing on a dock looking at a large yacht. "Welcome aboard," the Marshall said as the lines were cast off and the engines started.

"If Mr. Graves needed me back, he would have called, I don't understand what is going on, but have a very bad feeling about this," Carlos replied and looked around at the yacht and the US Marshalls that were on the boat with him.

"You should have a bad feeling; we will be taking a little trip to one of the outer islands to drop off a package. Then on to London. Does that make you feel better?" The marshal commented.

"Wait, am I the package?" Carlos questioned.

"Yes, as a matter of fact you are the package. We have been asked by our employer to remove you from the equation; sorry to say, Carlos, but you have become a liability to Mr. Graves and well, what can I say, he found your listening devices and you have to go. Understand it is just good business. We will be docking in a couple of minutes; please don't do anything stupid, we wouldn't want you to get hurt before we docked."

Two hours after Sally left the mall, she was on a private jet flying to Denver where she hoped she would be able to disappear completely. Once airborne, she felt a little safer and started to put together what she knew and why she was now a target. The US Marshall was a fake or worked for Graves; she knew that immediately when that woman called out her name and had her weapon pointed at her. That was not how US Marshall's acted, and she was alone, which was another factor in proving she was a fake or maybe a real Marshall being paid by someone other than the government. When the plane leveled off, the pilot announced that his passengers were able to move about the cabin, use the air phones, or any electronic devices they wished.

Sally picked up the handset and inserted her credit card to use the phone then stopped before completely inserting the card, thinking, *'If I use this card, they could possibly trace it and find me. Better wait until I get on the ground and buy a new cell phone and call from that.'*

After landing in Denver, she bought a cell phone at the first available store on the concourse; that was easy, especially if you paid cash, which she did. She still had over a hundred thousand of Graves' money in her luggage.

"You have reached the reception desk at CIA Headquarters; how may I direct your call," the receptionist said when she picked up the call.

"I need to speak to someone in charge. Urgent please," Sally said. She had immediately activated the new cell phone and planned on throwing it away at the end of the call; she would use the other new one for future calls.

"One moment please, who shall I say is calling?" the receptionist asked.

"I will only give my name to the person in charge today; it is extremely important and urgent that I speak to someone in charge immediately," Sally insisted as she looked around the airport terminal.

"Okay, one moment," the receptionist replied, put the call on hold, and buzzed the senior agent on duty.

"Hello, this is Simon Rafferty how may I help you?"

"Agent Rafferty, my name is Sally Howard and I need to surrender myself to you tonight," Sally stated almost too soft to hear.

"This is the CIA, not FBI, we do not have jurisdiction or authority to take you in; why do you need to turn yourself in?" Rafferty asked.

"I cannot go to the FBI; they have a mole in their ranks, and I would be dead before morning. I need to turn myself into the CIA tonight," Sally stated.

"Where are you now?"

"Denver," Sally responded sounding desperate.

"Denver, you know you called the Washington office. But let me see if we have an agent available to meet with you. Hold one, please," Rafferty said then pressed the hold button and looked over at his assistant and asked. "Who is on duty in Denver?"

"That would be, no, she is on leave, here, Cynthia Flower. She is the station chief," his assistant replied.

"Good, I know her, she is fantastic," Rafferty replied and pressed the hold button to return to the call. "Miss Howard, I can have you meet with our station chief out there. Her name is Cynthia Flower, and she will help you get back to Washington. But why, may I ask, why do you feel you need to turn yourself over to the Company?"

"Survival," Sally stated quickly and with confidence.

Two hours after being in the ladies' restroom, located within the executive terminal lounge, Amber and her six other trapped passengers waited as the storm picked up intensity outside. Water started to seep under the door. Within minutes, they were standing in four inches of water. Pushing on the door proved to be impossible as the water level outside the rest room was over three feet deep and growing.

"We need to stop the flow of water," one of Amber's team members stated as he looked for towels to shove under the base of the door. The towels located temporarily stopped the flow, but water still seeped in all be it slower. "That should hold it for a while."

"I thought the Corp of Engineers rebuilt the dikes after Katrina with a promise that they would be able to withstand any hurricane," Jake stated to nobody in particular. Jake feared very little; he was a Marine before becoming a US Marshall, but this had him worried.

"They did, something must have happened; or this storm is stronger than Katrina," Amber replied, standing in three inches of muddy water.

"We are trapped; if it gets too deep in here, is there another way out?" a shapely young lady in a short mini dress and nearly transparent wet white blouse asked. "I don't want to drown. And standing in this water is making me cold."

"Get up on the counter by the sinks and stay out of the water," Amber suggested. There was a long counter with four sinks they could use to stand in if they wanted to be out of the water. Amber stood in ankle deep water in her white leather mini skirt, light blue silk blouse, high heels and a light blue blazer that hid her weapon placed in the small of her back and she thought that Michelle was dressed more for a date than a plane ride to New York; she then realized that Michelle might be thinking the same thing about her.

"Sounds good to me," the young lady said and then jumped up on the counter and sat in the corner attempting to not show all the males in the room her ample breasts.

"Take this," Donald said to her, handing her his jacket.

"Thank you. My name is Michelle Brooks, who are you?" Michelle said quietly.

"Donald Vickers and this young lady is my boss, Amber Pierce," Donald said pointing to Amber. Donald and Jake were partners with the US Marshall Service and had been assigned to work with Amber, who was with the CIA, and did not have jurisdiction to arrest in the United States. Donald retired from the US Navy as a Captain where he served as commander of Seal Team Six until he retired two years ago.

"Stay calm and we will get out of here soon," Amber said to assure her.

"I hope so," Michelle said as she took the jacket and wrapped it around her shoulders.

"Okay, we need to look up to see if there is a way to get higher if that water continues to get deeper. This is a two-story building; maybe we can find a way to the second floor. Like Michelle, I really would prefer not to drown in the ladies' restroom," Amber commented and then asked, "Jake can you lift me up to the ceiling? I want to see if there is any way we can all get up and maybe find a way to the second floor."

"Sure, get up on the counter; I will boost you up there," Jake said pointing to the sinks. The water level had increased to about eight inches before they reached the sinks. "At least the building is built strong enough to stay together, at least for now."

"Donald, try your cell phone and see if you can get any kind of weather report or make contact with anyone," Amber ordered.

"What's going on, the water is still rising?" Michelle yelled.

"Amber, the weather report says the storm is just coming on to shore and the winds and rain will continue for at least the next 12 to 20 hours," Donald reported.

"That doesn't sound good. Michelle, just hang in there. I am going up to look for a way to the second floor," Amber responded. She paused and looked at Jake before telling him, "Lift me up, big guy."

After reaching the ceiling tiles, Amber pushed through the one directly over her head and looked up, first toward the men's room next door where she saw a solid concrete block wall extending to the true ceiling four feet above the drop ceiling. Shining her cell phone flashlight around the area, she saw ventilation and air conditioner ducting but could not see very much because of the weak light. She yelled down to Donald, "Do you, or anyone else, have a mag light; my cell phone light is not bright enough."

Seconds later a hand raised up beside her, tapped her on the hip, and handed up a mag light.

"Thanks," she replied.

"We may have a way, but it will be tricky. Push me up. I think I can walk on the girders up here and check the

AC vents," Amber said to Jake and then started to hum the tune to the Titanic.

"Stop humming that Amber; we are not sinking, at least not yet," Jake responded to her humming when he recognized the tune.

After ten minutes of pulling and cutting open AC ducting down and not finding a good way, she almost gave up until she saw another large air conditioner duct coming down in the far corner of the room. Making her way over to it she started to pull the ducting down. As she hummed the tune from the Titanic, she continued to cut and pull at the insulation and exposed a grate at the top and light coming down. Reaching up, she pushed on the grate and it moved. Amber pulled down the air conditioner ducting opening a hole big enough to crawl through and stood pushing the grate away from the hole. Seconds later as she poked her head up through the floor she was greeted with a smiling face.

"Well, hello, welcome to the second floor. Are you alone?" the elderly black man said as he reached his hand down to help Amber up.

"Hi, no, there are others down here," Amber said quickly.

"Amber, hurry up the water is rushing in now and is almost waist deep. Michelle is now sitting on the other end of the sinks all wet again. The rest are either standing waist deep in water or standing on the toilets," Jake yelled.

"I found a way up; start sending people up. I will help them to the exit," Amber called back, then turned back to the man and said. "I'll be right back; I have others that need to come up."

Jake turned to Michelle and said, "You're up first; come over here and I will boost you up and Amber will help you up there. Come on, no time to be slow."

Michelle stood on the sink counter and walked over to Jake as he leaned down. "Climb on my back."

"Okay," she said, kicked off her 4-inch spiked heels, put her legs around his neck, and sat on his back. Jake stood and then put his hands on the bottom of her feet and started to lift. "Loved those shoes, but ruined now; whoa, go slow please." Within a few seconds, Michelle had her bare feet on Jake's shoulders and was reaching up through the drop ceiling to Amber's waiting arms.

"Next!" Jake yelled and another woman started to climb on the sink just as the water started to cover the top of the counter. Jake proceeded to help her up through the ceiling and then looked down at the two remaining men. "Okay guys, come on; this water is not going to slow down, and we need to get out of here now."

The first man dressed in a business suit climbed up on the sink and Jake attempted to help him up, but he was too heavy. The last man was even heavier.

"We may have to wait until the water is higher and just swim into the ceiling," Jake said with a small chuckle.

"At the rate it is rising, that will not be much longer," the man in the suit commented as the three stood on the sink counter. The water was up to their waist by then and only a few feet below the drop ceiling.

"Let me try," the younger of the three said, "Just a little help from the two of you and when I get up there, I can help pull you two up."

"Sounds like a plan; up you go," Jake said as he and business suit pushed the younger man up. Once up, he spun around and laid on his stomach to help Jake and the final man up.

"Be careful where you step, only step on the girders," Amber yelled to the men. It was a warning that came a second too late when the business suit slipped off the girder and dropped back into the rest room full of water, hitting his head as he fell.

Jake quickly looked down through the broken ceiling tile for the business suit and did not see him. "Hell, stay here I may need help." Jake slipped through the hole and back into the water. He located the injured man within a few seconds and pulled him back to the surface. When he pushed his head through the broken ceiling tile, he shouted, "Pull him up; he's unconscious."

"Got him. What about you?"

"Pull me up now," Jake yelled as the water started to overlap the ceiling tiles. "Let's get out of here."

Five minutes later, Jake and his two male survivors were sitting in waist deep water at the AC Vent that Amber had found and had the other women crawl up to the second floor and hopefully dryer conditions.

They exited through a floor vent into the upstairs lobby near an exterior wall. It took the ladies several hard pushes to get the vent cover to move, allowing them to exit into the lobby where they met several more stranded passengers. Luckily some had dry clothes to share. Ten minutes later, all were sitting on the floor on in one of the few chairs available listening to the storm raging outside. Their luck held with this being a nearly windowless lobby set up with computers and comfortable chairs. The passengers that were already there had blocked the glass window as best they could with furniture and carpet.

"Damn that was fun!" Amber commented being very sarcastic.

"Yeah, brings back memories of survival school," Jake agreed.

"Amber, I was able to make a quick call before the water trashed my phone. The person I spoke with said she would get information as to our situation and location to Red Cross and hopefully rescue will be sent as soon as the storm lets up," Donald told her.

"That's good news, thanks Don," Amber said and then added, "Did anyone find any food stored around her, I could use a drink."

"I second that," Jake and Donald agreed.

"Put me in for something tall, cold and very alcoholic," Michelle added.

A few seconds later, a tall black man stepped in front of Amber and handed her and the rest bottles of water and three small bottles of scotch. "Glad you made it up here; we have food and drinks when you are ready. There are more water bottles just around the corner; should last the thirteen of us for a few days."

"Thanks," Amber said taking the bottle of water and scotch.

"Name is Jerry, was hoping to be home tonight with the family but my ride home like everyone else's got cancelled with the storm. Stay dry, and if you need anything, don't hesitate to ask," Jerry said.

"Thanks again, Jerry. Where is home?" Jake asked.

"New Orleans, of course. I live just outside of the city; been here all my life. Could never leave this beautiful city; well, hopefully, she will still be beautiful after this one. Hurricane Katrina was bad enough and this one is trying to destroy us again, but she will fail just like Katrine failed. Now you relax, I'm here if you need me. Can't provide much, but whatever is in the pantry, we will share. I will call you for dinner rations when ready." With that Jerry turned and walked away.

"Michelle, where were you heading when this storm interrupted everyone's day?" Amber asked as she and Michelle sat leaning against the wall on a dry floor. The storm was still screaming outside, but at least they were safe. And they were able to locate a floor grate that allowed access to the men's restroom to save the few men stranded there. Overall, they lost two of the group, one from being impaled by flying glass and another drowned when the water level in the men's room reached the ceiling.

"New York, my agent has me auditioning for a part in a Broadway play. Guess I'm going to miss that one too," Michelle said quietly.

"You are an actress?"

"More of a wanna be, I have had a few parts in plays, nothing great but I keep trying. What do you do? You are so up and active."

"I work for the government," Amber said, not disclosing that she, Donald, and Jake were CIA field agents.

"Must be exciting. Do you carry a gun? I think I saw it when you were boosted up into the ceiling."

"Yes, but please keep that our secret."

"No problem. I bought this outfit to go to the audition and guess it is ruined now. How long do you think we will be stuck here?"

"A couple of days I suppose. But we are alive, and Jerry said they have some food and water in the kitchen around the corner, so we will not starve. We will survive, Michelle," Amber assured her.

It was Saturday morning and the clouds were grey and dark, threatening rain, unusual for this time of the year but anything can happen in the west. That's why they called it the wild west. Cynthia Flower woke from a deep sleep to the sound of her cell phone ringing repeatedly. Rolling over she looked seriously at it and almost didn't answer the call. Looking at the caller identification on the screen convinced her she had better respond, it was her office and it was Saturday, her normal supposedly day off. Which was rare because she tended to work seven days a week and ten to twelve hours each day. Dedicated as she was, she needed a short break and today wasn't going to be it.

"Yes," is all she said into the cell phone.

"Cynthia, we have a situation which needs your immediate attention," the voice on the other end said.

"Can you give me a hint?" knowing full well this was not a secure line and the caller could not say much more than to come to the office.

"You will be briefed when you get here, meeting in one hour, your conference room," the female caller said and then broke the connection.

"Damn, what now?" Cynthia said as she crawled out of bed and headed for the shower, shucking her extra-long tee shirt as she went. She showered and dressed in her conservative jeans and grey blouse, she slid on her business jacket, put her Colt model 1911 Officers model into the holster on her hip after checking for a full magazine, and headed for the door. Two other full magazines were in her back jeans pocket along with her cell phone. The office was just a few blocks away from her apartment and did not require her driving; besides, her car was parked in the secure garage under her office building.

Minutes later, Cynthia was walking into her conference room to be greeted by four of her partners and someone she had not seen in months.

"Davin Pierce, what brings you to my city?" Cynthia said as she hugged her boss.

"Please sit, and I will explain; and then let you get on to fixing the problem," Davin suggested as he indicated she should sit next to him at the table.

"Okay, can I get some coffee first? I haven't had any this morning."

"Sure, please, it is fresh," Davin said, and then sat and waited for her to pour herself a cup.

"Cynthia, before you ask, Connie is in Washington with Josh; he is just barely out of the hospital but doing well. But you have a more serious task and are going to need the help of everyone on your staff. I invited your department heads to this meeting so they can be up to speed as quickly as possible."

"Wow, what a way to start a weekend," Cynthia interjected.

"It only gets better. We have reason to believe and the evidence to back it up that an old friend has come back from the dead. And he is the one behind everything that Rocky Soto committed. Do you remember President Ted Graves? I'm sure you do; he was in office when you were in high school; We thought he died in a boating accident over twenty years ago. We have, or should I say, we will have a person working with you that has firsthand knowledge of his existence and where he is."

"I read about him, crooked to the bone, stole millions from the America public, faked his death only to be discovered on a yacht in the Caribbean. Wasn't his yacht torpedoed by a Soviet submarine?" Cynthia added, "Yeah, I know the scumbag and you say he is still alive?"

"Very much alive, at least that is what our source tells us," Davin said.

"Where is our source now?" Cynthia asked.

"That is where you and your team come into play. She called the Washington office and requested us to help her."

"Why us, and not the FBI?" She asked wondering why the CIA.

"She said she doesn't trust the FBI; Graves has a mole in there, and her life would end as soon as she turned herself over to them. She wants you to meet with her today at noon. She will call this office with the location; you are to go to her and take her to a safe house. Make sure she is safe; she will answer any of your questions. She has already told us that a US Marshall attempted to kill her when she was entering a shopping mall."

"Why me?"

"She is here in Denver to start, and you are the most logical choice," Davin stated.

"Not trying to get out of an assignment, but we are on United States soil and really don't have jurisdiction in this."

"You are not arresting her; she hasn't committed any crimes that we know of. You are just taking her in for protection. If she has done anything illegal, we will handle that later. Now it is nine-fifteen and she is going to call your private number at ten. Go get her and make her safe and comfortable," Davin ordered. "I need a full report on everything she tells you as soon as possible. We need to track down and stop Ted Graves as quickly as possible. We cannot let the public know that he is still alive and is now considered a terrorist."

Davin and Cynthia sat in her office sipping coffee and waited for her private phone to ring, it was five minutes to ten and the waiting was the hardest part. At exactly ten o'clock, the phone rang, and Cynthia picked up the handset.

"This is Cynthia Flower, is this Sally?" she asked.

"Yes, Miss Flower, this is Sally Howard. I need to meet with you as soon as possible, my life is in danger."

"Miss Howard, where are you now?" Cynthia asked hoping to get an answer.

"I'm at the Denver International Airport on a pay phone near the food court," Sally said quickly, "Please hurry."

"I can be there in thirty minutes," Cynthia told her.

"I will be at the bar next to the Pizza Hut. I'm wearing a short black skirt with a white blouse and pink sneakers."

"Okay, I will be in blue jeans, grey blouse and a light grey blazer. And there will be two other agents with me for your protection. But you will not see them directly. See you in thirtyish minutes; don't drink too much, we need you sober," Cynthia said laughing.

"Thank you," Sally said and then hung up the pay phone.

Thirty minutes later, Cynthia and her two agents were walking into the Denver terminal; another agent sat in the Chevy Tahoe SUV at the curb and waited. Walking into the terminal the two agents split up and were walking down the sides of the baggage claim area while Cynthia walked down the middle. After taking the escalator up to the food court, they converged at the top and split up again. Cynthia saw Sally at a table in the bar talking to a woman dressed in jeans, blue blazer and knew something was not right. Quickly Cynthia told her agents to close in because there was an imposter with Sally. Cynthia walked up behind the imposter and from a few feet behind her she pulled out her weapon and kept it low on her leg.

"Sally, I'm Cynthia Flower," she said.

"Lower your weapon, Miss Flower; I'm US Marshall Heather Newton here to arrest Miss Howard. You have no jurisdiction here."

"She has requested us to protect her from you and the FBI; and that is what we are going to do; now, YOU, lower your weapon. We don't want any blood spilled in here," Cynthia said bluntly just as two airport police walked up along with Cynthia's two agents.

"What the hell is going on here?" the officer asked when he saw the weapons pointed at each other as he and his partner pulled their weapons in a three-way standoff."

Cynthia flipped out her credentials and had her two agents do the same. "We are Federal agents here to escort this woman out of the airport; she is a material witness to several crimes," Cynthia said quickly to the officers.

"And who are you?" the officer directed the question to Heather Newton.

"I'm US Marshall, Heather Newton, here to arrest this woman for murder."

"Marshall against Federal agents, who the hell do we believe, B.J.?" the lead officer said.

"Maybe we just take all of them down to the station and have the captain sort it out," B.J. said.

"That may be the best idea. Okay all of you lower your weapons and either holster them or give them to my partner. I'm not going to ask twice."

While the officers, agents and marshal stared down at each other, not moving, or lowering their weapons, Sally saw an opportunity and took advantage of it. She slowly slid off her stool, turned and ran out of the bar and into the crowded terminal. Cynthia watched and didn't do anything until Sally was well into the crowd, then she lowered her weapon and smiled.

"Guess we all lose, she ran," Cynthia said as she watched Sally run.

"You bitch, you saw what she was doing and let her go, I should arrest you for obstruction of justice, but I need to go after her." Newton holstered her weapon and started to follow Sally into the crowd but was stopped by the officer.

"Good luck and don't call me bitch. Officer, thank you for your help; we will fill out any report you need on this," Cynthia offered.

"Agent Flower and Marshall Newton, both of you need to come down to the station and tell the captain what the hell is going on," the lead office stated holstering his weapon. "Let's go, NOW!"

An hour and forty minutes later, Newton and Flower were walking out of the airport police station. Cynthia was smiling, and Newton was not.

"You let her get away. I really should arrest you, but don't have the time right now. But get in my way again, and I will not hesitate to shoot you on sight, understand? And what agency did you say you were with?"

"I didn't say, you figure it out. Now get out of my sight or I might just shoot you for the hell of it," Cynthia replied, returning the threat. She pulled her cell phone from her pocket and called her third agent to bring the car around to the police station to pick them up.

Ten minutes later, the Chevy SUV stopped in front of the police station. Climbing in Cynthia noticed that there was a person laying on the back seat. Leaning over the back of the seat Cynthia said, "Miss Howard, I presume?"

"Yes, please get me out of here. That women works for Ted Graves," Sally said quickly without raising off the seat. The other two agents carefully slid in the back with Sally.

"We got lucky today, kids. Somehow Graves is monitoring all phone calls to the office. How did she know where to catch up with you Sally? We need to check the security of our supposedly secure phones. There is a leak somewhere," Cynthia stated to no one in particular, thinking of who knew of the meeting and what she was wearing.

"Miss Amber, can I get you anything?" Jerry asked as he walked around the room of survivors.

"No thanks, Jerry. Any news on the storm?"

"Last report said it is now downgraded to a Category 2 and the levy holding back the ocean is gone; that is why we are flooded. They did say to not get in the water, as it is not healthy for several reasons which you can imagine. The biggest problem is the alligators have moved inland and are hungry; so, staying here is probably the safest bet for a few more days. At least until the water level drops. The phones are still out; and cell service is marginal. I have been trying to reach search and rescue to see if they can come and get us out of here but no luck yet."

"Thanks for trying, Jerry," Amber said.

Twenty minutes later, a search and rescue helicopter flew over the building, but did not stop to check for any survivors. Amber thought they would at least stop to check, but maybe they were already full of survivors from other locations.

"Jerry, is there any way we can get on the roof?" Amber asked.

"Yes. but until the rain stops, I would not suggest going up there. A lot of antennas and electrical wires which don't mix very well with water are on the roof."

"Good point, as soon as it stops, let me know; I want to get up there and maybe get a signal to search and rescue. We need to get out of this place to safer, dryer ground," Amber commented.

"I agree. We will run out of food in another day and the available drinking water is pretty low too."

"My point exactly," Amber said. She stood, walked over to the empty sofa, and laid down.

Two hours passed without the rain letting up; then suddenly, it stopped. The eye of the storm was sitting directly over the flooded airport.

"Miss Amber, the rain stopped; come," Jerry yelled across the room. Amber, Jake and Donald jumped up and started running toward Jerry.

"Donald, stay down here; I may need you to help the injured up," Amber ordered.

"You got it, boss," Donald agreed and then slowed his pace to watch Amber, Jerry and Jake enter a door in the back of the room to expose a stairway.

"This way, hurry. Don't know how much time we have." Jerry said as he hustled up the steps, slipping as he went on the wet stairs.

"Be careful, we don't want you hurt," Amber said, catching Jerry from falling backwards.

"Thanks, Miss Amber," Jerry replied.

Amber reached out for the handle and started to push the door open but could not. "The door is stuck," she stated.

"Let me at it; there is no door in this world I can't get through," Jake said as he stepped past Amber and Jerry. "Yep, stuck, not much of a landing here to get footing on; can you two hold my back and let me kick it open?"

"Wait, Donald, come up; we need your muscle," Amber yelled down to Donald.

"What's the plan?" Donald asked in the dim light.

"Door is stuck, something may be blocking it. Jake needs us to keep him from falling backwards while he puts

204

the force of his size thirteen boot into the door," Amber explained.

"Okay, I will stay on this step and lean forward holding your backs while you hold his. Go for it, big guy," Donald said as he did his best to maintain stability while leaning forward into the backs of Amber and Jerry while they held Jake. Jake leaned back as far as he could without tipping over his helpers and cocked his left leg and slammed it into the door just to the right of the door handle. The door did not move more than a half inch.

"Something large and heavy blocking, let me try again," Jake said, kicking four more times without success. "Damn, guess there is a door I can't get through."

"Okay, what next?"

"There may be another way, I really don't like the idea, but it may be our only way out," Jerry commented.

"We are open for any ideas, good or bad," Amber said as she and the rest walked back down to the main room.

"Well, there is another set of stairs to the roof, but, well, you are not going to like where," Jerry started.

"Don't tell me, it's outside?" Jake asked.

"Yes, on the north side of the building; and the only way to get there from here is to swim."

"I'll go," Jake volunteered.

"No Jake, I am the better swimmer, you know that. I'll go," Donald said. "The last survival class you almost drowned, remember."

"Oh, yeah, forgot about that; yes. you are the better swimmer, but I am stronger and whatever is blocking the door may be too heavy for you to move. I need to go," Jake shot back.

"Wait guys, I will settle this. You both go. Donald, you help your weak swimming buddy; and when you get there, the both of you remove whatever is blocking that door and let us out," Amber directed to settle the discussion.

"Okay, which way is the north end of the building," Jake asked.

"That way." Jerry pointed to his right. "This is a big terminal, so you will have to swim about one hundred yards and then turn right. The stairs should be, if still there, about twenty feet away and attached to the wall."

"Okay, where is the door to get outside?" Donald asked as he looked around the room and did not see any exit doors.

"That is your next problem. The exit doors are downstairs, and the stairs are over there," Jerry said pointing to the stairs that went down to the lower lobby and the water that was up to the top step.

"You've got to be kidding. We have to go down there; swim underwater to the exit door or an open window, and then back to the surface without drowning," Donald stated.

"Yep, that's about it. I can point you to the exit closest to the stairwell, so you can go directly to it. Hopefully, you will be able to see enough to find it," Jerry offered.

"Wow!" was said in unison by both Donald and Jake.

"You have your weapons, right?" Amber questioned.

"Yes, Glock model 30 forty-five caliber," Jake answered.

"I carry a Glock model 19 in nine-millimeter," Donald replied.

"Both will fire underwater if need be; so, you will be protected, sort of," Amber stated.

"Who are you people?" Jerry questioned after hearing that.

"Please keep it between us, but the three of us are members of the federal government on assignment. That is all I can tell you right now. So, please do not tell anyone," Amber said and then looked at her two agents. "Are you ready for a swim?"

"Well, yeah, I guess so. Keep my jacket dry; I think I will need it soon," Jake said handing Amber his blazer.

"Let's go, big guy. I am not looking forward to this, but we need to get that door open and standing around in here just isn't going to make that happen," Donald said and handed Amber his blazer also and walked toward the stairway to the ground floor, kicked off his shoes and started to walk down the stairs with Jake close behind, shoes off and not smiling.

Michelle Brooks sat in the corner watching everything; she was almost completely dry and had given Donald back his jacket. The weapon she carried was hidden in the small of her back and she hoped it would still function if she needed it. She had a job to do and it would soon be time to complete it.

"What the hell?" Cynthia Flower said as they approached the home of Denver CIA, an unmarked, private little-known building on the edge of the city. Smoke was billowing out of the top floor and a crowd of people were standing on the street behind the fire crews spraying water on the building.

"Looks like our home is burning," said her driver, agent Phillip Gentry.

"But how? Turn down this street and stop, I want all of you to stay in the vehicle and drive to the backup office. I'm going over there to find out what happened," Cynthia said as she started to step out of the vehicle.

"Do you want me to come?" Agent Heidi Cruz asked and started to open the door.

"No, there is plenty of help over there. Just go and protect Sally," Cynthia ordered. "I'll catch up shortly." She turned and started to walk toward the rest of her team that were watching their office burn from across the street, seeing only six of the twelve that were supposed to be working today. "Monty, what the hell happened?" she asked seeing blood on his shoulder and smoke stains on his hands and face.

"We were attacked. Don't know who they were but they will not be a problem anymore. We lost a few people and the attackers had thermite grenades which they used as they died. That's why the office is on fire," Monty replied.

"Are you hurt, that blood looks bad."

"Not my blood," Monty stated and then looked at the other members standing there. "Six-armed terrorists somehow gained access to our floor, started shooting and throwing grenades. We were lucky to make it out; they did not make it. We were able to shoot them but not before they destroyed the office and killed four of our team. Don't know where Kathy and Megan are, they had gone to the break room for coffee just before the shooting started. Hope they made it out."

"Me too. Look, the police are going to want answers too. And here comes the detective now. Answer his questions and then go to the secondary office, open, and get cleaned up. Sorry but we need to get answers and quick. I have already sent my team over there. Be careful, make sure you are not followed, we have a very nasty enemy, so don't take any chances."

"Detective Dan Weston, Denver Police, who is in charge and what can you tell me about this?" Weston asked pointing toward the burning building.

"I'm in charge, detective, Cynthia Flower, but I just got here and don't know much about the fire. This is Monty Jorgenson; he is my office manager and was here when it started. He can answer your questions."

"Mr. Jorgenson, there is an awful lot of blood on your shirt, are you hurt?" Weston asked.

"No, it's not my blood."

"What happened up there?" Weston asked again.

"Detective Weston, I guess you need to know a little about who and what we do. Can we talk in private? Monty come with us; the rest of you go, you know the assignment," Cynthia said and then turned and walked away from the crowd.

"Right behind you Cynthia," Monty said and followed her and Weston.

"Okay, here is the scoop, what I am about to tell you cannot go into public reports, but you will understand in a moment. I am the director of operations for the Denver branch of a large diamond and gold exchange. We buy and sell large quantities of gold and diamonds from around the world and it is stored in our office in a large vault. Our office is, well, was a secure facility and each of my people are trained agents, and yes, they are armed. According to Monty, my second in command and office manager were attacked by six heavily armed, what I would call terrorists. There was a fight where we lost several of my people; all the attackers were killed, but not before throwing thermite grenades into the office, which started the fire. Is that about it, Monty?"

"Our offices are behind reinforced steel doors with multiple security systems. They must have had inside information or a safe cracker that could bypass our systems. We never heard them coming. Before you ask again, this blood is from one of our people; he died in my arms just before an attacker threw a thermite grenade down the hall and into Cynthia's office. I had to leave him but shot the attacker before I dove out our escape exit. Detective, when they get the fire out you will find the bodies of six attackers and four of our people."

"I understand why you wish to keep your facility a secret; wow, I knew you had an office in the area but not the location. Okay, I will get with the fire chief and we will list it as a failed robbery of a, what, financial institute or what? Is your vault locked?"

"Yes, it is on a timer and in the event of a breach to the facility it automatically locks and cannot be opened without a special code which only Miss Flower and I know. We do not have customers visiting the building; it is all done via internet and deliveries are done with armed guards and high security. And yes, we do that for real. Our vault was not breeched, otherwise we would have lost millions," Monty added with Cynthia's approval.

"Okay, not sure how I can cover this up. It looks like a simple robbery gone bad. I will make sure your new location will not be disclosed. How soon can you move the contents of your vault?" Weston asked.

"Monty will make the arrangements and as soon as you and the fire chief give us the okay to enter, we will move all the contents to our backup location. And no, I cannot disclose that location," Cynthia said.

"How can I reach either of you if we have more questions?" Weston asked.

"Our cards have our cell phone numbers; don't try the direct number that office just burned up," Cynthia said as she and Monty handed Weston their Diamond Reserve cards.

"I will call you when you can get into the building. Do you want to stick around to guard the place?" Weston joked.

"Nobody can get in there now, so no need. Call me when it is safe to enter," Cynthia said as she saw the fire crew rolling up their hoses and packing up to leave. The fire was out; the building was being checked by the fire marshal who would deem it safe to enter soon.

"I will be in touch," Weston said and then walked back toward the fire chief.

"Monty, was this a simple robbery or did someone know we were here and wanted to make a statement?" Cynthia asked.

"I don't know, but I plan on finding out. We need to identify those attackers; maybe that will give us a clue."

"Most likely not, my bet is that they were hired guns and don't even know who is paying them, no contact, no trail," Cynthia commented as they walked to the corner. "Hell, we don't have a car, mine is in the garage over there and yours is?"

"Mine is down there too. Let's get a cab to a car rental agency and rent one," Monty suggested.

"No, too risky; most of the rentals have tracking devices so the agencies can find out where their cars are at any time. There is a used car dealer a block from here, I will buy us a used car, and then we go to the backup facility. Call Megan; no, wait, she is not accounted for yet. Hope she and Kathy are okay. Don't call anyone, our phones may be tapped. Let me have yours. With all the available technology it would be easy to tap any phone and never touch it. You know that we have been tapping phones for years," Cynthia said taking hers out and he handed her his. After punching in a special code, she was able to wipe the memory from each phone and then dropped both in a mailbox on the corner. "We will get a couple of burn phones before we get to the car dealer. There is a department store on the next block. Oh, where did Davin go when he left this morning?"

"Said he had a flight to North Dakota to see an old friend," Monty said as they walked into the department store and looked for the cell phones.

"Cool, good safe place up there, I know who he is going to see," she said quietly.

"Anyone I know?"

"No, but maybe you should meet him; he's quite a character, and his home is really one to admire," Cynthia said without disclosing that Bryan lived in an old missile silo that had been converted to a CIA operations center and safe haven.

"is this the only way, Jerry?" Jake asked as he and Donald started down the steps into the cold dark saltwater. They had no idea what was down there; only that they had to turn right at the bottom and swim in a straight line to the wall. They would find the door or open window to go through, hopefully. Jerry had found some cord, so the two men were tied together with about six feet between them. That way they at least would be able to stay relatively close together. Donald, being the stronger swimmer, took the lead; each of them also had emergency oxygen bottles strapped to his waist. The swim was only about forty feet but in pitch blackness with unknown obstacles.

"Good luck," Jerry said as the two men started to dive under water.

"Are you sure there isn't another way?" Jake asked again just before his head went underwater as Donald tugged on the line to make him follow. Switching on the waterproof flashlight, Jake ducked under and followed Donald.

As Donald reached the bottom, he ran into a wall that was not supposed to be there. He pushed on it; the wall moved. It wasn't a wall but a sofa floating close to the ceiling. He turned right as instructed and swam as quickly as possible with Jake in tow, bumping into floating items in the water. His flashlight did not penetrate more than a few feet as they swam.

As they approached the middle of the room, Donald's light caught a shiny object on the right. As he turned the light toward the object, he realized he was looking at the white shirt of the man that had been waiting in the lounge for his charter flight to arrive. Not wanting to waste time and needing to breathe, Donald turned back toward the exit and swam faster, pulling Jake behind. Donald reached down and grabbed his oxygen bottle and took a quick breath, he was a good swimmer, but his breathing was a little ragged from the stress of this dive.

Suddenly the cord tying himself and Jake together became tight; and he was not able to swim any further. As he turned, he saw Jakes light fall to the floor and immediately swam back to find Jake starting to float to the ceiling. Donald grabbed his oxygen bottle, placed the mouthpiece over Jake's mouth, and turned on the air to max. Jake's eyes burst open when he realized he was still breathing. Donald grabbed Jake's arm and they started to swim toward the exit again only to run into a wall. After turning left and moving down the wall, they found a broken window, pushed through it, and started for the surface. Seconds later, both men popped up on the surface to find that it was raining again. "This way, Jake," Donald said and then added, "Are you okay?"

"Yeah, now. My head hit something, and I blacked out for a moment. Thanks for the shot of air," Jake said as the swam the length of the building. "Is that an alligator over there?"

"Yes, we need to get out of the water now," Donald said as they reached the end of the building and turned right to see the exterior stairs hanging partially on the side of the building. "There are the stairs, let's go."

"Right with you, big guy," Jake answered.

They reached the stairs and looked back at the alligator, that was slowly swimming toward them.

"Up now!" Donald said as he slid out his Glock.

"That's just going to piss him off; here, use my forty-five," Jake said as he grabbed the lower rung of the stairs and pulled himself up. He reached back, took his pistol back, and reached down to help Donald up to the first steps. Once both were on the steps, they started to climb, only to find the staircase was pulling away from the wall and was about to break completely away.

"Hurry, this thing is about to collapse," Donald yelled.

Just as they reached the top step, the staircase broke away from the wall and started to fall backward into the water. Both men jumped and grabbed the edge of the building as their staircase departed the area. As they hung by their fingers, they slowly pulled themselves up and over the edge and lay on the roof panting as the rain started to pelt them with large amounts of water. Laughing that they both had survived the trip and were now lying outside in the middle of a hurricane only seemed funny to them.

"You okay, Don?" Jake asked between laughs.

"Yeah, you?"

"Couldn't be better; now, let's go open that door. I need a cup of coffee."

"Maybe Jerry can rustle up a couple of beers or some scotch."

"I'll drink to that, my friend," Jake said and rolled over so he could stand.

They stood and looked around at the destruction on the roof and the flooded airport just beyond the building.

"Glass everywhere and our shoes are downstairs. Go figure," Jake commented as he saw all the damage.

"Let's get under that cover over there and survey the damage; maybe we can find a way to move that air conditioner blocking the door," Donald said and slowly stepped over the glass and many broken things to get to the leaning roof that used to be a workshop.

The rain came down in buckets and then the wind started to blow stronger with every passing second.

"I'm not sure this was a good idea, in the middle of a hurricane, Jake," Donald commented as they reached the leaning roof. "Brings new meaning to *'Hell and high water'*," he added with a dry chuckle.

"Yeah, let's see if we can move that thing and get back down below. This wind is going to rip this little roof off in a minute and we will not have any cover."

"Roger that, big guy," Donald agreed and started to pull himself toward the roof access door which was blocked by a large air conditioner unit. Reaching it with Jake close behind, he surveyed the unit and decided quickly that if he and Jake pushed in the direction of the wind, using its force to help move it. they might have a chance on getting it far enough away to open the door.

"Push here, put your back into it, Jake," Donald yelled over the wind and leaned his back against the unit. He and Jake started to push, slipping in their bare feet on the wet roof.

"I'm pushing, is it moving?" Jake yelled, hoping they were making progress.

"Wait, it's not moving; look for something we can use to pry it away from the door," Donald yelled as the wind rose to over 70 miles per hour, pelting them with rain and debris.

"There's a long pipe, looks like an antenna pole; maybe it will help," Jake yelled as he spied the twenty-foot aluminum pole about ten feet away. "Wait, I'll get it." After falling twice and cutting his hand on broken glass, he returned with the pole; and with Donald's help, they jammed it between the unit and the door housing. They both screamed, "Push!" and shoved with all their might.

While pushing on the pole, they managed to move the unit a few inches before the pole slipped and both men fell into the unit and then onto the roof. Laughing they both pulled themselves up, grabbed the pole again and slid it further behind the unit in between it and the door and pushed again. After slipping and screaming, they got the unit to move slowly. With the wind blowing at a constant 90 miles per hour and the pole jammed behind the unit, it finally moved far enough to be able to crack the door open a couple of inches.

"Hey, down below, anyone there?" Jake yelled into the open door. Seconds later a wind gust whipped around the corner and entered the crack with such a force that it tore the door off its hinges and spun it and the air conditioner unit to the edge of the building. Both men fell face down onto the roof and watched in horror when the roof that they had stood under moments ago flew over their heads and followed the air conditioner unit and door over the edge of the building into the water below.

Jake and Donald glanced at each other as they lay in the water on the roof and then at the now open door and stairwell. Without saying a word, both crawled toward the door and down the stairs to be greeted by Jerry and Amber at the bottom.

"I think we got the door open, boss," Jake said smiling through the blood pouring down his face.

"Jerry, get the first aid kit; guys, what the hell happened up there?" Amber asked as the wind and rain poured into the lounge from the now open doorway.

"Move everyone to the far side of the room," Jerry yelled as he ran to get the first aid kit. "Bring those two soaked men over here. Get them out of the rain."

After patching the multiple cuts on both men, they handed each of them a dry set of clothing. They sat and drank some fresh water leaning on the wall farthest away from the open door.

"You got anything stronger than water, Jerry?" Jake asked as he started to undress.

"Well, yes, this is the Executive Lounge, what would you like?" Jerry confirmed.

"Scotch if you have some," Don piped in.

"Two Scotch, coming right up, gentlemen," Jerry acknowledged and then hurried away to get the two soaked men their requested drinks.

"Jerry, can you bring three and maybe something for yourself?" Amber asked as she saw him pass.

"Sure, I'll have a coke; I don't drink, Miss Amber."

Minutes later, with drinks in hand and wondering what their next move would be, and not knowing when the water level would decrease, they sat quietly sipping their drinks.

"Miss Amber, we have food and water and of course a lot of booze to last several days. Maybe the storm will slack soon; and we can get up on the roof, and signal for help," Jerry said.

"That is good to know; is there a radio up here?" Amber asked.

"We only had speakers up here; the radio and music came from the stereo located behind the main desk downstairs. It is now underwater and of no use."

"So, we wait," Jake commented.

Cynthia and Monty drove off the used car lot in a ten-year-old Buick LaSabre. She bought the car because it was nothing fancy and would fit in with the traffic around their backup office; four door, light blue, with good tires and the price was reasonable. Monty drove while Cynthia made several phone calls on the burn phones she purchased. The first was to the backup office to check in and see if it had been compromised. There was no answer which caused her to be suspicious about its safety. Finally, she was able to reach Heidi from the office and found out that the backup office had been trashed and that she, Sally and two other agents were heading for the safe house.

"Go to the safe house, Monty; the office is gone," Cynthia said quietly as she thought of what to do next.

"Gone, how?" Monty questioned.

"Don't know, but I believe someone has been ratting on us. Don't know who or when, but something is damn hinky around town," Cynthia stated. "We will pick up the rest of the gang near the old airport, they will follow us. Sally is safe, for now. I told the team to split up, only Sally and two agents will meet us."

"Where?" Monty asked as he turned onto Interstate 285 heading north, not sure where he was going. He had never been to the new safe house.

"Breckenridge," Cynthia said and then added, "Stop at the first rest area on I-70; we will pick up Sally and her escorts there.

"Roger, boss. First rest area on I-70," he repeated back as he headed for Breckenridge, located about twenty miles west of Denver. A popular ski resort in the mountains, lots of cabins and things to do even in the summer. "Been wanted to go there to ski, haven't had the chance."

"No snow right now, Monty, so you will have to wait until winter," Cynthia joked.

"Ahh, I was so hoping to hit the slopes, been awhile since I have skied," Monty responded.

"Here is the rest stop," Cynthia said after about a twenty-minute silent ride.

"Right, what are they driving?"

"Red Chevy Tahoe," Cynthia replied. She paused as she scanned the parking lot, and then continued "Over there," as she pointed toward the red Tahoe.

Minutes later, they pulled up beside the Tahoe and climbed out. Sally was lying down on the back seat while her escorts, Heidi and Ralph stood guard.

"Heidi, Ralph, hope you haven't had to wait long," Cynthia questioned as they approached the Tahoe.

"No, but I think we were followed. Check out the dark green Mustang, they have been with us since we left the backup office. We had Sally lie down in the back with hopes they did not see her, but I am not real comfortable standing out in the open. Can we get out of here?" Ralph reported keeping his right hand close to his weapon.

"Yep, saddle up, and let's roll," Cynthia ordered, "Sally slip over to my car, I have the back door open."

"Our shadow is backing out and starting to head this way," Heidi stated and placed her hand on her weapon and unsnapped the safety strap.

"Sally, wait," Cynthia ordered before Sally was able to get out of the Tahoe. "Let's wait until they pass; maybe it is just a coincidence that they have been following you,"

Cynthia suggested and then said to Sally, "Stay in the Tahoe for a minute, and keep your head down."

The Mustang slowed briefly when it got close to the Tahoe and Cynthia's team, but then continued on out of the rest area. Both the driver and passenger glanced over at her team but did not stop or indicate they were a threat. There was a third person in the back seat which Cynthia could not see very well.

"Okay, let's get out of here," Cynthia ordered and had Sally climb into her sedan. "You know where the house is Ralph?"

"No, never been there; Heidi, do you know?" Ralph said.

"Yeah, been there several times," Heidi answered and then climbed into the driver's seat of the Tahoe.

"Good, you take the lead; we will be the caboose. Heidi, you or Ralph have cell phones?" Cynthia asked as she climbed back out of her car and asked Heidi.

"Yes," they responded.

"Company phones?"

"Yes."

"Have you used them? Are they on?" Cynthia continued to question.

"Yes, and yes."

"That is how you are being followed. Give them to me? And, wait a minute," Cynthia took both phones, pressed several special numbers which immediately whipped all information off the phones and set a mini self-destruct sequence to start, which would destroy the phones two minutes after hitting the enter key. She hit the enter key and then threw both phones in the nearest trashcan.

"Here take these; I will call you on these only. They are burn phones and virtually untraceable. Don't call anyone on them except for this number, mine," Cynthia said as she handed two burn phones to the agents and a card with her burn phone number on it. "Now, let's get out of here."

"Sally, we are going to a safe house that we hope has not been compromised. When we get there, I need you to tell me everything you know about Ted Graves and his last known location. Oh, do you have any electronic devices on you, cell phone or anything?"

"Everything?" Sally questioned. "And yes, I have a cell phone given to me by Graves."

"Everything and then some. Before we leave, will you give me all the electronic devices you have," Cynthia ordered.

"Sure, here," Sally replied handing Cynthia her cell phone.

"They may have been tracking you with this; is it also the holographic generator?"

"Yes, but I turned it off hours ago."

"Maybe, anyway I will be right back. I need to destroy this thing," Cynthia said and climbed out of the car, "This thing is getting hot," she said and then threw it as far as she could away from any person or car. The phone exploded before it hit the ground. The explosion was small, but enough to kill anyone close by. It did cause quite a disturbance in the rest area.

"Time to go," Cynthia yelled as she jumped back into the car. "That proves they were monitoring you and could hear everything we were saying. Let's go."

Ten minutes down the road, Cynthia turned to her partner Monty and said quietly so that Sally could not hear. "Green Mustang on our tail."

"I know; I saw him when we passed the last exit, sitting on the on-ramp side."

"Ralph, we have picked up the Mustang again; keep going past our exit and head south. We will take the next exit to Breckenridge," Cynthia ordered when she called the Tahoe.

"Roger, boss," Ralph said, hung up, and looked over at his partner, Heidi, and said, "We have company."

"Yeah, I know. What's the plan?"

"Continue past our exit and then head south. Cynthia will call when all is clear. I don't like leaving them unprotected; Cynthia will get off onto Route 6 then on to Highway 9 and head south to Breckenridge. We can take the second exit onto 6 south which will link us to 9 further down and come in behind the Mustang."

"Timing is going to be tight and you know your cell phone will probably not work once in the mountains. Better call her now and hope she agrees," Heidi said as she drove on.

"Yep, she will agree."

"Hope so, because she just turned off of 70 onto 6," Heidi said and then accelerated her Tahoe and watched in the mirror as the Mustang turned off also, leaving only one car behind them and that vehicle was almost a mile behind them and not attempting to catch up.

"No luck on the phone, too deep into the mountains," Ralph said as he pulled his weapon out and double checked that it had a full magazine and one in the chamber.

"Okay, only a couple of miles to our turn, hang on," Heidi said as she pushed the Tahoe up to ninety miles per hour.

New Orleans had not seen a storm like the one that just passed through there since Katrina or Laura, which caused an extreme amount of damage. The U.S. Army Corp of Engineers along with other government organizations rebuilt the dikes that would hold back the Gulf of Mexico in the event of another storm. They took extreme measures to ensure the dike would hold back even the most damaging storm, category 5 being the worst. It was a massive construction job; and all calculations proved it would withstand the worst mother nature could throw at them. They did not however figure that a five hundred foot fully loaded freighter would slam into it at over seventy miles per hour. The freighter that hit made a hole over a hundred feet wide and allowed the Gulf of Mexico to pour into New Orleans while destroying the ship and its cargo in the process. There were no survivors on the freighter. The storm had passed and now cleanup was the order of business.

"Jake, is that a helicopter I see heading this way?" Amber asked as she looked toward the east to see a Coast Guard helicopter approaching.

"Sure, looks like a helicopter," Jake replied smiling for the first time in days.

"How long have we been here?" Donald asked, knowing the answer but wanting to lighten the mood.

"Too damn long. Hot shower and clean clothes would be nice right about now," Amber stated and waved at the helo as it got closer.

"This is going to be interesting; they can't land so I know they will use the cable and lift us up," Jake commented. "Let's send up the injured first."

"Agreed," Amber said and then looked at Jerry and smiled, "Thank you, Jerry, without your help we may not have survived."

"No problem, Miss Amber. If you are ever back in town, come by; we can have a nice quiet drink together, and listen to some of the jazz that makes this city famous," Jerry replied.

"I will be back and take you up on that, thanks again," Amber said and watched as the first of the survivors were lifted to the helo. One crew member came down to assist in the process; and within a half hour, all the survivors were in the helo heading for dry land.

Four hours later, Amber was sitting in a hot bubble bath at the Pensacola Naval Air Station, Florida. Jake and Donald had taken rooms at the base hotel also. Michele Brooks had tagged along and was in the room down the hall from Amber's. The other survivors were comfortably housed in the same building. Several had to be treated at the base hospital. Of the twenty-two passengers in the terminal when the storm hit, sixteen survived; the other six died when the storm hit or from injuries sustained by the storm. These sixteen were lucky; the total death toll from the storm had exceeded sixteen hundred and still climbing.

The freighter that broke the dike was destroyed and the crew of twelve died trying to save the ship. It would take months to repair the dike and get the water level down to street level again.

"Hello, dad. Yeah, I am okay. Just sitting here in a bathtub soaking away my tired muscles," Amber said into her new phone when Davin answered her call.

"I'm glad you are okay; we were worried when we didn't hear from you," Davin said.

"Where are you? You sound like you are in a cave."

"North Dakota with Bryan. I'll be back in DC in a few days. How are your helpers?"

"They are doing fine; can you do me a favor. I need a background check on a Michelle Brooks. Something is not fitting with her and I need to know it I can trust her. I am sorry I don't have a picture, my phone got trashed and this is a new one."

"I will get the info you need and send you a picture if available. What don't you like about her?" Davin asked.

"It's not that I don't like her; it's just her story doesn't fit. And I noticed she was carrying a weapon, although she thought she had it hidden," Amber stated, "How's mom?"

"She's fine, worried sick about you and that freak hurricane. Where did that one come from?"

"You know you can't fool or second guess mother nature; she was showing us that she is in control again. It is sad that New Orleans took the worst of it again. And that freighter hitting the dike was weird; we will probably never know what or how that happened. Speculation only, I guess. Anyway, I need to get out of this tub and get dressed; the boys and I are going in town for dinner, if we can find a place that hasn't been destroyed by the storm."

"You be careful, our friend has been pretty active lately; and I will call with the information on your new friend, Michelle Brooks. Bye for now," Davin said and then broke the connection.

Thirty minutes later, Amber was dressed in skinny jeans, black sneakers, and tan blouse she was given by the manager of the facility. Jake and Don were both wearing jeans, boots and white shirts also provided by the hotel.

229

There was a surprise showing of Michelle Brooks as they all met in the lobby.

"I saw Michelle coming down the hall and asked her if she wanted to join us for dinner," Jake said as he walked up to Amber, "Hope you don't mind."

"No problem, no business talk, okay," Amber said as she saw Michelle walk over, "Hi, Michelle, nice outfit."

"Thank you, my other one was trashed and there is a nice little shop just down the street; I think they call it the Base Exchange. The outfit the hotel provided just didn't fit so I walked over to the exchange. They let me go in and buy this outfit, you like?" Michelle said as she modeled the short dark blue mini skirt, with a tight light blue blouse which accented her ample breasts and blue blazer cover up and sporting black high heel shoes.

"Okay, let's see if we can find someplace to eat, I'm starving," Amber said and started for the door.

"The hotel gave me keys to a sedan; I have it parked right out front. We should all fit," Donald said and held up the key.

After driving around the base and then finally out the main gate, they made it into town where they finally found a small pizza shop still open for business. The sign above the door was bent and crooked, three front windows were still boarded up, but the sign on the board said they were open for business; come on in.

"We have a limited menu and forget the prices listed; everything is half off. What can I make for you?" the man behind the counter said when they walked in. The place was not big and there was some damage inside. A few customers sat and were eating what looked like a very large pizza.

"An extra-large pizza, meat lovers and a couple dozen chicken wings, medium hot," Amber ordered after a short consultation with the group. "Do you have beer?"

"Yes, my tap is broken but I have bottles and cans of most beer, what is your choice?" the shop owner asked.

"Two Coors, one Bud light and a Corona?" Jake ordered getting agreement from everyone.

"This sure taste good," Michelle commented taking a sip of her Bud Light.

"You got my vote on that, Michelle," Jake commented, showing signs that he liked Michelle in more than a professional manner.

"So, where are you three off to next?" Michelle asked.

"As soon as we can get a flight out, we have to get back to Washington," Amber stated just as her phone vibrated. "I have to take this, be right back."

"Hello dad. What's up?" she said when she answered the call and walked outside.

"A lot, look at the picture I just sent. Is this the Michelle Brooks that is with you?" Davin asked.

"Yes, it is. Dad."

"Good and bad. She is a Secret Service agent out of the Los Angeles office. Been out there for two years, good reviews, consistent with her reports and all assignments," Davin stated.

"That all sounds good, what is the bad?"

"She was killed in the line of duty six months ago?" Davin stated. "Now this could be an undercover assignment and they had to fake her death to get her where she is. I am still researching that and will let you know as soon as I do. In

231

the meantime, be careful what you say and do around her. We don't know what side she is on."

"Thought we were sunk in a ladies' bathroom, and now another nightmare up here. We need to find and stop the people behind this and soon," Amber said, "Anything else, dad?"

"I heard from Cynthia Flower in Denver; she has her own nightmare going. One of Graves' assistants turned herself in to us, and now Cynthia is trying to keep her safe, but has had numerous problems doing so. But more on that later; you have enough on your plate right now. Stay safe and I will call again when I learn more."

"Bye dad," Amber said; she hung up and went back for her beer and pizza.

"What's up?" Don asked.

"Tell you later; right now, I need another beer, and some pizza," Amber said and then took a long pull on her beer.

"Okay Sally, before we get killed by those following us; give me Ted Graves last known location," Cynthia asked as they slowly drove around Breckenridge, Colorado with a Mustang following.

"He has a penthouse in a hotel in downtown Los Angeles. I last saw him there three days ago when he asked me to go to Las Vegas and make sure I was seen as Monica Teach. I drove there and played Blackjack and had some fun, but then a U.S. Marshall tried to kill me. That's when I called you."

"Have you got an address?" Cynthia asked again.

"Yes, here it is," Sally said handing Cynthia a business card of the hotel, "His penthouse number is on the back."

"Monty, I think it's time we lose our tail. How about you get back on the highway and head back toward Denver. And don't worry about speed. If they follow, we will lose them in the city. Then go to the safe house on Magnolia Street."

"Roger that boss," Monty said as he accelerated the Buick to the speed limit and turned to head out of Breckenridge on the shortest route. The Mustang accelerated and started to pull up closer to them.

"Looks like they have some power under the hood. I'm glad you opted for this x-police cruiser; she has plenty of life left in her. Hang on," Monty said and pushed the pedal down to the floor, leaving the Mustang in cloud of dust. After leaving town and heading north again, Monty pushed the car to over a hundred miles per hour. He glanced in the mirror on occasion to see if the Mustang was keeping up; sadly, it was, and starting to close the gap.

"Looks like they also got the big engine model. Watch the curves; and when you can, hand me you weapon," Cynthia said casually and then looked back at Sally, who had pulled her weapon from her waist band. "Didn't know you had that."

"Sorry, I didn't think to tell you, but I do know how to use it. Took lessons from my dad; he was a cop. And I do have a permit to carry," Sally said and looked out the back window at the fast-approaching Mustang.

"Well, we may have to use it. How many rounds do you have?"

"Twelve in the mag, one in the chamber and a second fifteen round mag."

"Good, between mine and Monty's, we have about thirty rounds also," Cynthia said. She looked at the road ahead and saw a dark Tahoe headed toward them; she watched as it passed heading toward Breckenridge, then slowed and finally turned around just as the Mustang passed them. "Why doesn't anyone follow orders now a days?" she exclaimed.

"Look at it this way, boss. We now have the Mustang outnumbered and boxed in; should we play our cards now?" Monty said as he sped through the mountain curves.

"Yes, there is an overlook coming up, pull in and stop near the end," Cynthia agreed.

"What, you want them to kill us?" Sally protested.

"No, we want to stop them; and if need be, kill them."

Slowing down quickly Monty turned into the overlook and slammed on the brakes as he closed in on the northern exit. They were lucky there wasn't anyone at the overlook; they had it all to themselves. The Mustang, seeing them pull in, immediately pulled in and stopped about halfway into the overlook. Cynthia, Monty, and Sally had climbed out of the car and took up positions on the north side keeping the car between them and the Mustang's occupants. Seconds later, the Tahoe pulled in and stopped near the entrance blocking the south exit and both Heidi and Ralph jumped out and took up positions on the side of the vehicle and aimed their weapons at the Mustang.

The doors to the Mustang opened and two men stepped out with hands raised then a third person, a female stepped out from the back seat. All three held up their credentials which were too far away to see. The female started to walk towards Cynthia's car, hands held high and no weapon visible.

"Ms. Flower, I am Secret Service Agent Lenora Henderson; you may know my sister Mary, and father, Admiral Bear Henderson. May I approach without being shot?"

"Come on over, Lenora," Cynthia said, but did not lower her weapon.

"Ms. Flower, we were asked discretely by Davin Pierce to assist you. Please verify with him or with my father, the Admiral. My sister, Mary, works for Davin now; and, well, we are here to help."

"I never got notification of your assistance, so why the deception?"

"We were supposed to stay discrete; and you were not supposed to know we were here. But when you left Denver and headed out of town toward Breckenridge, there were no other roads we could follow on. Is that Tahoe part of your team?"

"Yes," Cynthia said as she pulled out her cell phone, and prayed they had service. She had three bars, thankfully. Dialing Davin's private number, she waited hoping he would pick up, since this was a burn phone and he would not recognize the number.

"Hello, who is this?" Davin said when he picked up.

"Cynthia Flower, sir."

"Cynthia, is everything all right?"

"Yes and no; did you task a Lenora Henderson to shadow us?"

"Yes, and I tried to call you, but your phone is offline," Davin said.

"Had to dump them, we were being tailed; and well it's a long story which will be in my report. Can you send me a picture of Ms. Henderson?"

"Just did."

"Good, it's her, thanks, boss. All is well, for now. We are going to the safe house and relax for a bit. Before I forget, here is the last known address for our friend in Los Angeles," Cynthia said and then read off the address from the card.

"We will check it out," Davin said and then added. "Anything else?"

"No, I will call again later, once we get settled."

"Good," Davin said and then hung up his cell phone.

"Okay, Ms. Henderson, you checked out."

"Call me Lenora."

"Cynthia, here," she said just as a bullet slammed into the side of her car. Lenora and the rest dove for cover, not knowing where the shot came from, but hearing four more. Looking up Cynthia saw one of Lenora's assistants laying in a pool of blood and the other one crawling behind the Mustang.

"Where did those shots come from?" Lenora yelled.

"On the ridge over there," Monty said pointing toward the ridge about two hundred yards away. "Too far for a pistol shot. We are sitting ducks here; we have to move."

"How did they find us?" Cynthia questioned. "Start the car and keep low."

Two more shots rang out, the first hit the left front tire of the car and the second slammed into the door, barely missing Monty.

"This car is down," Cynthia yelled and then took two shots at the ridge, knowing it was useless at that range. "Here comes the Tahoe, stay down. Where is your driver, Lenora?"

"Both are down, and the Mustang is on fire. The shooter hit the fuel tank," Lenora yelled and then fired three shots at the ridge. She saw an SUV bouncing into the overlook, firing a machine gun at them, hitting the side of the car and not much else. Aiming a machine gun from a moving vehicle is difficult even for an experienced shooter. "We have more company."

"Headlights. Shoot the headlights and tires," Monty yelled, just as their Tahoe braked beside them.

Cynthia, Lenora, Monty, and Sally all fired at the rushing SUV, hitting the headlights and front tires. The airbag inside the SUV inflated and the blown tires caused the SUV to swerve toward the railing on the edge of the overlook, crashed through, and plunged into the valley over a thousand feet down.

"Get in!" Cynthia ordered and all four jumped in. Before the doors were closed, Heidi accelerated out of the overlook and down the highway; several bullets hit the back of the Tahoe, but nobody was hit.

"Damn, that was close," Lenora said as she looked around at her new friends.

"Yeah, too damn close," Monty agreed. "What now?"

"Not sure, but we do have a need to go back to see if your two agents are alive. They will need medical attention, for sure."

"Do you have any rifles or anything that can reach out a bit further than our pee shooters?" Lenora asked.

"No, didn't plan on a gun fight today. Probably should have," Cynthia said and to Heidi, "First place you can hide this truck, make it happen. I will call the local police and report what happened."

Ten minutes later, Cynthia had reported the incident and medical was dispatched to the site; they were asked to stop by the local police station to make an official report, Cynthia said she would as soon as she could, but it would not happen today.

Thirty-five minutes after Cynthia reported the incident, the medical team and two patrol cars arrived at the overlook to find a burned-out Mustang, a Buick LaSabre with multiple bullets holes, a broken guard rail and an SUV at the bottom of the cliff with no bodies in it and no bodies anywhere. Evidence everywhere indicating there was a fire fight, but it looked like someone hurried in and cleaned up, removed any bodies, and just didn't take the time to remove the vehicles.

"What the hell do you make of this, Mat?" the lead sheriffs officer asked his partner. "No bullet cases, no bodies, just two shot up cars and one at the bottom of the canyon. Janet, you, and your team can go; you have nobody to put back together and probably have someone needing your help in town. Thanks for driving out; sorry for the wild goose chase."

"No problem, we love to drive up here. The views are great, and really, I am very glad we didn't have to fix up anyone with bullet holes in them. Take care; and see you at the pub tonight?" Janet replied and climbed back into her EMT van.

"Yep, see ya," he said and then to his partner, "Call for a couple of tow trucks; and let's get these wrecks outta here."

"Bryan, I have to go, can you get my plane serviced and ready to fly in an hour?" Davin asked his friend and coworker while sitting in the mess hall of the North Dakota CIA safe house.

"Yeah, where you headed?"

"Denver, I need to send the plane down to pick up some of my team and a key witness."

"Cynthia?"

"Yep, seems she has been having trouble with protecting a key witness; and well, I think it is about time that I stepped in to help. Been lounging around here too long, drinking all your scotch, and staying safe. By the way Connie, Josh and Stephanie will be here tomorrow. Keep them safe."

"You know I will; now wait, while I contact the hanger to get your bird ready and notify the pilots. They are over in the rec room," Bryan said and then picked up the phone to call the hanger and then the rec room.

"Hello?" Davin said into his cell phone after it buzzed three times. "Who is this?"

"Davin, hold for the President," the voice said quickly.

"Mr. President, what can we do for you today?" Davin asked when the President came online.

"Davin, I don't have all the details of what you are working on, but something even worse has come to our nation. You most likely have heard that there is a virus spreading in many countries around the world; well, now it is here, and we don't have an antidote for it. It is working its way into a full-fledged pandemic and whatever you are working on, drop it and get you and your team to a secure facility now. I assume you are going to North Dakota."

"Yes, sir, we were just about to leave to pick up my team in Denver," Davin commented. "How serious is this?"

"Very. We are ordering everyone to keep at least six feet from anyone else, only go out if necessary and go into voluntary isolation for at least the next fourteen days. That includes you and your team."

"Okay sir, we will stay in contact; we should be in North Dakota by late this afternoon."

"Thanks, Davin; be safe and listen to the news. I will have updates as often as I can. One other little twist, since we bombed Iran there is a lot of flak coming in from other middle eastern countries and a few of our loyal allies, at least we thought they were loyal. War hasn't started, yet, but we have gone to high alert and the reserves have been called up. Don't watch the news; they are reporting only what we tell them; and they, like always, bend it to suit themselves. Bye for now."

"Goodbye, Sir."

Seconds after Davin ended his call with the President, the phone rang again.

"Hello."

"Lenora Henderson, Davin, code alpha Charlie six twelve," Lenora stated before going any further.

"Did you catch up with Cynthia?" Davin asked quickly.

"No, I'm with two of her team that barely escaped from a burning building. Do you know where she is?" Lenora said becoming very worried.

"No, got a call from her about two hours ago saying you already met with her and were outside of Denver. Haven't heard from her since. Where are you?"

"Denver, two blocks from what used to be her office. I think we have a problem, sir."

"No joke. Look, I will be down there in three hours. Take the two agents with you and your support and head for the Hilton Hotel downtown. We have a suite reserved under the name of Helen Masters. Go check in and stay there until I catch up to you. Keep your team close; we are dealing with a very nasty bad guy and his team is far reaching. And now there is a possible pandemic threating the country, and a war back in the sandpit. Iran is pissed and so are several other countries. Stay sharp and wait for my call."

"Roger that, Davin."

"Talk to you soon," Davin said before he broke the connection.

"What's up?" Bryan asked.

"We have another imposter in our ranks. Seems that Henderson did not meet up with Cynthia as planned, but another fake did; and Cynthia doesn't know she is with a fake Lenora Henderson and I have no way of warning her. They are in the mountains outside of Denver and no service available at the moment."

"Are you kidding? That damn holographic device is going to get more people killed than the invention of the bomb."

"I am not kidding. Do you still have a couple of those holo disrupters that I left here a while back?"

"Yeah, in the safe; do you want a me to go with you to help? I can bring a team with us and we'll be your backup."

"Might not be a bad idea," Davin agreed.

Three hours later, Davin, Bryan and Chili, his German Shepherd, were on their way south to Denver in the company Gulfstream VI. As usual, the flight was uneventful, and they had time to discuss their plan. With an imposter with Cynthia and their witness, they had to play it carefully; otherwise, someone could get killed.

Meanwhile outside of Denver, Cynthia, Sally, the fake Lenora Henderson, Heidi, and Monty were travelling back toward Denver hoping that whoever attacked them was not closing in.

"Sally, may I call you Sally?" Lenora asked.

"Yes, please, and who are you again?" Sally asked quietly.

"Oh, sorry, with all the shooting I only had a chance to identify myself to Agent Cynthia. I'm Agent Lenora Henderson, President's Secret Service. Those two agents with me were also secret service. I will have to contact my office soon to report their deaths."

"Pleasure to meet you; do you get to work close to the president?" Sally questioned.

"No, I am usually on assignment, such as this one to bring you in safely. I was asked for by Cynthia's boss, Davin Pierce. He and my father are good friends."

"Who is your father?"

"Admiral Henderson, commander of the Pacific fleet. My brother is David; he runs a nuke boat out of Hawaii."

"Cool, must be nice to have relatives in high places; and with your brother, I guess he is in low places," Sally said trying to make joke.

"Haven't thought of it that way, but you are right; I have relatives in high and friends in low places," Lenora said laughing. Pausing for moment she turned to Cynthia and asked. "Where are we going?"

"Airport. Our ride should be arriving in about an hour," Cynthia commented as she tapped Monty on the shoulder and said, "Take the scenic route."

"Roger that, boss," Monty replied. He then turned to Heidi who was driving, pointed to the tablet on the console, and tapped three times. This was a special code they used when things were not exactly right; and Heidi knew to take the highway to the airport and avoid the city traffic. They did not need the stop and go traffic, but to keep moving as fast as possible toward the airport.

"Boss, we have picked up a tail. Black Chrysler sedan, about a quarter mile back; been following since we came through Golden," Monty reported and then quietly checked his weapon and extra magazine.

"Got it. How did they pick us up so quick?" Cynthia said to nobody in particular.

"Good question," Lenora said as she pulled her weapon out to check the load.

"Nice piece, not government issue," Cynthia commented when she saw the black Desert Eagle 50 caliber pistol. "Kind of large isn't it?"

"Yes, but I never have anybody challenge me when I pull it out."

"They let you carry that?" Sally asked becoming worried; she had seen a weapon like that a few days ago when a U.S. Marshall tried to arrest her. Was it possible that two people have the same type of weapon; no, couldn't be, just a coincidence?

"Had to bend a few rules, but they finally gave in and said I could. Had to show them I could handle this much power," Lenora stated before she slipped the big weapon into its holster in the small of her back.

"What do you carry as a backup?" Cynthia asked, becoming suspicious of Lenora.

"Small Beretta nine, ankle holster when in slacks and thigh holster in a dress, but I don't normally wear a skirt."

"What is our tail doing?" Cynthia asked Monty.

"Still back there, we just got on the main road to the airport; should be there in about forty minutes, barring any delays," Monty reported.

"Good. Stay sharp," Cynthia commented and then thought to herself; there is something not right here. I just don't get a good feeling about Lenora Henderson.

"Davin, we will be on the ground in twenty minutes; buckle up and you know the drill, prepare for landing back there. It will be a little bumpy, but nothing we can't handle," the pilot reported as they approached Denver International Airport.

"They should be arriving at the airport about the same time as us. You did bring a weapon, right?"

"Yeah, I brought Chili," Bryan said, and Chili stood up and walked over to Davin and sat, placing his paw on Davin's knee.

"No, I meant a pistol, knife or something to defend yourself."

"Oh, yeah, got my Glock Model 30 and three extra mags. Do you think we will need them?" Bryan teased, acting silly.

"I hope not, but make sure you have the disrupter turned on after we land and are in the terminal. Keep it in your pocket. I will only turn mine on when we get more than fifty feet apart."

"Yeah, I got it. Chili will be with me to help if needed."

"I know and I pity the person that tries to run," Davin replied and smiled at the thought.

Minutes later, they heard two squeals of the tires touching down on the runway. And the big jet taxied toward the general aviation terminal. Out the side window, Davin could see the Tahoe just pulling into the parking lot.

"They are here," Davin said as he watched. "Look we know that Lenora Henderson is a fake, maybe you should keep that disrupter turned off until we get her in a secure place and then expose her."

"That may be a good idea; we don't want any civilians injured."

"We're here, Monty and Heidi. You two check our ride; we will stay in the Tahoe until you give us the all clear," Cynthia ordered as they pulled into the parking space beside the general aviation terminal and saw the Gulfstream business jet pulling up to the front on the tarmac.

"Right boss," Monty replied as he and Heidi slipped out of the SUV and started walking to the terminal. Cynthia, Sally and Lenora watched as they approached the jet and waited until it stopped, and the air stairs were lowered. They immediately headed up the steps into the plane, disappearing inside.

"How long should we wait?" Lenora questioned after a five-minute wait.

"Not much longer," Cynthia commented as she reached behind her back to remove her weapon. "Sally, are you ready?"

"Yes, boss," Sally replied and pulled her weapon from its holster and pointed it at Lenora.

"What the hell is going on?" Lenora yelled.

"We don't believe you are telling the truth, Miss, ah, whoever you are," Cynthia stated with her weapon also pointed at Lenora.

"I'm Secret Service agent Lenora Henderson, dispatched by the President to assist you and Mr. Pierce," she stated quickly. She slowly tried to raise her weapon but stopped short when she saw everyone move their trigger finger to the trigger. Anyone that knows about weapons realizes that you cannot out draw someone that has their weapon pointed at you. It is impossible, but many have tried and died trying.

"Put your hands on the back of the seat and just wait," Cynthia said as she caught out of the corner of her eye Davin walking up to the SUV. "Hello Davin, have you got it?"

"Yes, shall I turn it on?" Davin said as he held up a small black box with several switches on it. He paused, and then flipped a switch. Instantly, Lenora's and Sally's holographic devices turned off and their real identities were revealed. Sally became Heidi as planned, and Lenora became Heather Newton, US Marshall.

"What, how?" Heather said confused.

"A little device we put together to deactivate any holographic devices within the area. Neat, huh," Cynthia commented and held out her hand. "Please, very carefully hand over that hand cannon that you carry and your Berretta too."

Knowing she had lost this battle, she slowly with two fingers handed her Desert Eagle to Cynthia. Cynthia handed it to Davin and then took the Berretta and passed it to Davin also.

"Okay, Heather, let's go; we have a plane to catch. No tricks, don't try to run, my bullet does travel faster than you can run, and Heidi is an expert in more ways of killing than anyone I know, including me; and she doesn't use a weapon, just her body."

"When did you suspect me, and when did she and Sally switch? Oh, must have been at the gas station when we got fuel and they went off to the ladies' restroom. Nice. But when did you suspect I was not Lenora?"

"I have been in this business for a long time, both under cover and now department head, and I know many Secret Service and FBI agents; and never, has anyone gotten permission to carry a hand cannon like that one you have. That was my first tip; and the second was Admiral Henderson retired from the Navy four months ago and is now living the good life in London. Yes, he was commander of the Pacific Fleet, but not anymore, which you would have known if your information was up to date."

"Damn, Graves, that S.O.B. set me up."

"It's hell when you can't trust your boss; you picked the wrong side," Davin said as they approached the jet. "In more ways than you know."

"What is that supposed to mean?"

"I'll explain on the way."

Twenty-five minutes later, the Gulfstream left Denver on its way to North Dakota. Davin sat in the front of the cabin thinking of his next move. They had half of the suspects on board, a pandemic starting on the ground, and a possible war in the Middle East. Life as a member of CIA and the United States just got a little more difficult. As soon as the pilot turned off the seat belt sign, Davin stood and turned toward his team and captives. He was not wanting to tell them what had transpired but was obligated to do so. They were going to be spending a lot of time together.

"Ladies and gentlemen, I have some good news and some really bad news. I want to put this as simply as possible, but there is no real way to say it so here it is." He paused for a moment to take a sip of his beer. "We have among us Sally Howard, ex call girl and formerly in the employ of Ted Graves; we also have a young lady that was sent out to kill Sally but failed and is now in our protection. We will identify her later unless she wishes to tell us everything. Now that is the good stuff. The bad is that we will be spending a long time together at our secure compound up north. Some of you know where it is and please don't say anything to our guests. While everyone was doing their job, and I might say doing a very good job, some things happened around the world that has put our country, or rather the entire world, in jeopardy. In the recent past a flight from China brought with them a virus, a very deadly virus, and it has spread to the world in massive proportions. Thousands have died from this and thousands more are sick and there is no cure yet. We have been asked to stay in our secure location for an indefinite time. Don't worry we have enough provisions to last more than a year. We also have a medical staff there to treat any, well almost any, condition.

Oh, yeah, before I forget, Ted Graves somehow got our navy to bomb Iran with nuclear weapons. Tehran is gone and so is their nuclear development facility. We are on the brink of another war in the Middle East. That's all the news for now, stand by for further developments when I know them."

"You have to be kidding, right?" Cynthia piped in.

"Wish I was. We will be on the ground in about an hour, sit back and relax," Davin paused while waiting for everyone to sit down. "As for your families, we will have them transported here if you wish. And as I get more information, I will let all of you know. Oh, the bar is fully stocked and open, help yourselves," Davin concluded and then sat down.

"Amber, I need you and your team in North Dakota as quickly as possible," Davin Pierce ordered his daughter from the secure phone on his Gulfstream company jet as they climbed away from Denver International airport.

"But dad, we are close to catching Monica," Amber protested.

"No buts about it; you are not as close as you think, and there have been a few twists of which you are unaware. Just fly up here as quickly as you can. Your pilot knows the location. You are in the company jet, right?"

"Yes, well, we will be in about an hour; they are fueling her now," Amber stated, not being very happy about the change of plans. But her father was the boss, and he had information that she didn't.

"See you in a few hours; I'm glad you didn't get hurt in that storm. Pretty nasty and came up quicker than any I have seen in years."

"I will tell you the whole story when we get there," Amber said holding back what she really wanted to say, which was she wanted to disobey orders and go after Monica now. She knew better than to do that, so she ended their conversation with, "See you soon, dad."

Two hours later, Amber, Jake and Donald were climbing aboard Gulfstream six nine four, the newest business jet in the small fleet of planes owned and operated by the CIA. She was well equipped, and the armory alone would be the envy of any gun lover. Amber wasn't concerned that they were not safe and well protected with the arsenal they had; she was worried that Monica Teach would get away once again and attempt to kill her father and mother.

"Welcome to North Dakota, out your starboard side window, that is the right side of the plane, you will see the small town of Fargo, well known for the movie named after it. We will be landing in about, oh, let's see, say fifteen minutes, plus or minus. It all depends on how fast the runway can be cleared," the pilot announced as they crossed over the invisible line between North and South Dakota.

"How fast they can clear the runway? Is this airport that busy?" Amber asked when she stuck her head into the cockpit.

"You haven't been here, have you?" the pilot asked or rather stated. "Usually the runway is under water and they have to drain it before we can land. During the winter they must melt the snow and ice, but since it is still summer, and not quite winter, we don't have to worry about the snow, just the water."

"Why is it under water?" Amber questioned.

"Well, it is supposed to be a secret safe house or rather facility. Your dad uses it as a training base and haven for whoever needs to be safe. Your dad can explain more about it when you see him. Now go back and buckle up; we just received clearance to land and once we land, we will taxi into a hanger before shutting down; they will refill the lake, eh, runway as soon as we are clear. There is the runway, right off our nose," he said pointing to the long pavement about a mile in front of the jet. "Check list."

"Got, ya," she said and headed back to her seat.

"Flaps, 10 degrees, gear," the co-pilot read off the list.

"Flaps 10, Gear coming down," the pilot responded.

Minutes later, Amber and her team were touching down on the runway which moments earlier was a small lake. Looking out her window, she saw a lot of green grass, hills and then did a double take look at the side of one of the hills as it opened to expose a huge hanger built into the side of the hill. The business jet slowed and turned back toward the gaping hole in the side of the hill and proceeded to taxi up to the entrance before stopping. Two ground crew quickly rushed out and hooked a powered tug to the nose gear, spun the jet around, and backed it into the hanger after the pilot shut down the engines. Once inside, the ground crew placed blocks in the front and back of the main landing gear as the air stair was lowered to the ground.

"You may disembark the plane now; I hope you enjoy your stay in our little hideaway," the pilot announced.

"Wow," Amber said as she watched the hanger doors close to hide the facility from anyone who was out in this part of the wilderness. The overhead lights flickered on as she and her team stepped to the highly polished floor of the hanger and watched as a woman in jeans and tee shirt approached.

"Welcome to North Dakota, Ms. Pierce. I'm Mona Val, Assistant Director of this underground fortress. Your father and Bryan are not here at the moment but should be arriving soon. They had to go help a friend in need. I will explain after we get you settled in. Please follow me; don't worry about your luggage, my guys will bring it to your rooms," Mona said. She then turned and started to walk toward the back wall of the huge hanger. She pressed a button on the wall causing a panel to open that exposed an elevator which was completely hidden from view by the wall panel. After everyone had stepped into the elevator, Mona pressed the down button; the door closed, and the elevator dropped about a hundred feet to the lower level where the door opened to what looked like a mile-long tunnel.

"This way please; it only looks long. It is three quarters of a mile to the main facility from here. I will show you your rooms and then we can meet in the mess hall for some lunch and drinks. We have a full bar and our chef is simply awesome; she will fix you anything you want. Stole her from a five-star eatery in New York," Mona added.

Forty minutes later, they were sitting in the mess hall. They had ordered lunch and a couple of drinks and were now sitting quietly waiting for Mona to return.

"Sorry for the delay, just got word that your dad will be here in about an hour," Mona said as she walked up, "Let me order lunch and I will bring you up to date as best I can."

"Okay, now what the hell is going on. We were close to catching Monica Teach when that damn hurricane interfered with everything. And we never got an answer about Michelle Brooks. Is she real, or another decoy?" Amber questioned.

"First off, Ms. Brooks is a cop in New Orleans and an aspiring actress and is hoping to get a part in a new Broadway play," replied Mona.

"I guess that is why she carried a weapon? She should have identified herself as an officer of the law," Jake interjected.

"From what we learned, she was working undercover following another passenger headed to New York. That male passenger was killed during the flooding. But she probably didn't know he had been killed and didn't want to blow her cover," Mona added and then turned to the chef as all their lunches arrived. "Thanks, Jules."

"My pleasure, Mona," Jules said as she placed all the lunches in front of her guests.

"Dig in, don't let it get cold," Mona said as she picked up her fork.

"Damn, this steak is perfect," Donald commented as he chewed on the first bite of his ribeye steak.

Mona filled them in on the lay out of the facility and their mission here, commenting that this base was only known to a handful of agents and political figures. Due to its remoteness in North Dakota and limited access, it had been kept secret for many years.

Time flew by and soon Davin, Bryan and Chili walked into the mess hall, followed by Sally, Cynthia, Heidi, and Monty. Amber jumped up but hesitated when she saw Chili looking at her.

"Dad, I want to hug you, but not sure about your dog?" Amber said quickly.

"Chili, this is my daughter; she is safe, most of the time," Davin replied and then Chili walked over to Amber and sat in front of her, looking up smiling. "Everyone, this is Cynthia Flower from the Denver office; with her are two of her agents, Heidi and Monty. Sorry I don't know your last names, and Sally Howard, formally under the employ of Ted Graves. Please introduce yourselves while I hug my daughter."

"What a beautiful dog, did you call her, eh, ah him, Chili?" Amber said and asked.

"Yes, this is Chili; actually, he is Bryan's companion," Davin replied and then walked over to get his hug from

Amber. "I see you met Mona, Bryan's female companion and assistant director of this place."

"Cool," Amber replied as she finished being greeted by Chili with his paw in her hand. She stood and hugged her father and then introduced Jake and Donald, US Marshalls assigned to help her capture and arrest Monica Teach.

"We need to get something to eat and have a lot to tell you, which changes everything we are doing. So, get some more to drink and we will be right back," Davin said and then walked over to Jules to order lunch.

"Okay dad, why the sudden change in direction?" Amber questioned when Davin and Bryan returned.

"A lot, we have with us, well down in the holding cell, a Secret Service agent Heather Newton. She had been hired to kill Sally Howard." He paused for a moment when Cynthia Flower, Monty and Heidi came back from the restroom, and then made introductions. "And you know Cynthia, and this is Monty and Heidi, two of her agents from Denver; and this young lady is Sally Howard, ex-employee of Ted Graves." He then looked up to Cynthia and directed them to Jules for lunch.

"What?" Donald asked before anyone else had a chance to.

"Seems that the past President Ted Graves is not dead, as we suspected, but very much alive and is behind everything that supposedly Monica Teach has done. Monica on the other hand is alive and hopefully well, according to Sally and Heather. Sally was using one of the holographic projectors to impersonate Monica and draw attention away from Graves. And it was working. But it looks like Sally learned too much of the operation and Heather was hired to kill her. Am I on the right track, Sally?" Davin asked.

"Yes, my coworker Carlos and I were key figures in the organization, but we suspected somethings were not kosher with Ted. He at times seemed like two different people. We would sometimes meet at his estate and other times in a suite in downtown Hollywood, at the Hilton. Some of our other coworkers suddenly disappeared and later we learned they had died, some in auto crashes, others had heart attacks. Uncommon in young people, but nevertheless they were dead. Carlos was tasked to fly to Europe to set off a nuclear bomb and I was given a holiday trip to Vegas to pose as Monica. Not sure why he decided we should do that, but I was being paid well and he gave me an additional $100,000 in cash to play with. Then I got a call from Carlos. He said he overheard Graves putting a contract out on both of us, so I started to run. Heather almost got me at the mall in Vegas, but I got lucky and escaped. I did shoot her, but seeing her now, either I missed, or she had a vest on. I have not heard from Carlos since his call to warn me. Is there any way we can locate him? We were not close, but he did try to save my life."

"I will have our people look into it," Bryan said between bites of food.

"So, Graves put out a contract on you and Carlos. Your assassin is locked up downstairs and hopefully she will come to her senses and talk to us," Davin slipped in.

"Mr. Pierce, Jake and I can take care of her. I know her. She was a good agent; don't know why she would go rogue," Donald said.

"I heard about her, wasn't she the agent that was implicated in the scandal with one of our past congress women?" Jake added.

"Now that you mention it, yes I think she was. Something about being hired to kill the president so she could take over. Couldn't prove it, not enough evidence. Then she just walked away, and nobody has seen her until now," Donald commented.

"Guess she went to the dark side and linked up with Ted Graves, or maybe she was already linked to him," Davin stated.

"That is highly possible, what if she did and he was behind the attempt on the president's life and not the congress women that was implicated?" Amber interjected.

"Good thought, but no way to prove that, yet. I think we need to talk to Ms. Newton and see if she will give us some insider information," Davin said.

"Cynthia, is there any place I can take a shower and maybe get some clean clothes?" Sally asked.

"That is a good question, Sally. Boss, where can we clean up and maybe find some clean clothes?" Cynthia asked.

"Mona, can you show them their rooms and stop by supply to get them something appropriate to wear. We should have their sizes down there," Davin ordered.

"Ladies and gentlemen, walk this way," Mona said as she stood and started to walk like she was a sexy street hooker, swinging her backside and strutting, while twilling her long key chain, getting a laugh from everyone as Cynthia and Sally mimicked her briefly. Mona stopped and turned quickly, "Ya'll coming?"

"Right behind you," Cynthia commented when she stopped laughing. "Before you go, you need to know what has happened in the outside world." It only took three minutes to explain about the possible pandemic that had plagued the country since they had arrived.

"Holy shit, what are we going to do?" Heidi asked.

"Nothing we can do; we are safe in here but for the foreseeable future we cannot venture out into the world without risking getting sick and possibly contaminating everyone here," Davin stated. He then looked at each one of his friends and added. "We will be fine; we have enough food, and water; and the facility is airtight, designed to survive a nuclear holocaust for years."

"Do you mean we could be here for years?" Cynthia questioned.

"Let's hope not, but we can survive for about ten years without going outside or at least not past the fence up there. We have the means to do so. Now get settled in; we will be having dinner at six," Davin concluded.

"Allison, can you come in here for a minute?" Ted said into the intercom.

"Yes, dad, be right there," Allison said quickly. She stood up from the sofa, straightened her very short skirt, picked up her drink and walked into her father's study at the estate outside of L.A. "What's up, dad?"

"Not much, it seems we keep losing our people. Carlos disappeared two days ago. Sally is nowhere to be found, and four others have not reported back to work. Have you heard from anyone as to what is going on?"

"No, I haven't; would you like me to check on the missing people?" Allison said quietly.

"I would. I thought I could trust Jaime to do it, but he is gone too," Ted said to his daughter. "I don't know who to trust anymore."

"I will check on them. Do you have the list of everyone that is missing? Better give me the list of everyone that is employed by you; that way I can ensure they are all where they are supposed to be," Allison asked smiling.

"That is a good idea. I will give you access to our company roster, and where they are supposed to be. Let me know if anyone else has gone missing," Ted said as he tapped a couple of keys on his computer. "You now have access to the entire organization. Don't let anyone else see that list; it could get us in big trouble with some very unsavory characters."

"Right. I will guard it with my life, dad," Allison jokingly said.

"Don't go that far. If someone attempts to get the list, delete it from your computer. I don't want to lose my only daughter," Ted Graves said with a big smile.

"Give me a little time and I will let you know what I find out," Allison said in her sweet voice.

"Before you go, I need to fly out to Washington tomorrow. Would you like to tag along?" Ted Graves asked his daughter.

"Aren't you afraid of the virus going around? And no, I think I will pass this time, dad. I have this stuff to track down and a couple of other minor fires to put out before the weekend."

"Fires, what kind of fires? I'm not worried about that virus; I will not be getting that close to anyone while there." Ted's curiosity was piqued.

"Oh, nothing much, just that I have been seeing this guy and he is getting too clingy and I want to break it off without hurting his feelings. He is a nice guy, but I 'm just not ready to settle down and he is."

"Be kind to him; you may want to rekindle it later. I know with your mom; we broke it off two times before you were born, and it was fantastic for the many years she was around. Then I found out she was an FBI plant, and it really killed our love life," Ted admitted.

"You didn't kill mom, did you?" Allison asked pointedly.

"No, hell no! She was reassigned when I was supposedly killed in the Bahama's; she was working another under cover job, when she was shot and killed by a drugged-up junkie. I do miss her though. She was the best at her job and treated me like a king, at least a president; hell, I was the president. I had nothing to do with her death; I was already presumed dead by the government and in a hospital in France when it happened. I didn't hear about it for years after I was released and got back to the States."

"I really am glad you didn't kill mom, that would not set well with me at all, dad. But I am really glad you are alive and well."

"Good, now go and get some work done. I must pack and am pretty tired; want to hit the bed early, Good night, baby. Tomorrow I fly to Washington to meet with Josh Randel; he is expecting me, and he wants to see you too. Are you sure you don't want to go? It will do us both good to get this settled. I think they already know we have been framed," Ted said as Allison walked out of the study.

Ted finished the paperwork on his desk, slid it in the top drawer and locked it. He rolled backward and around his desk before hitting the power button on his motorized wheelchair. He had called the airport and informed his pilots that he needed his plane fueled and ready to fly to Washington DC in the next couple of hours. Ted didn't want to miss his meeting with the Director of CIA, Josh Randal; he had planned this meeting months ago and finally was able to link up with him after Josh was released from the hospital. His pilot informed him that the weather to Washington was predicted to be good all the way, so he should not have any problems getting to his meeting.

At the same time across town at the Beverly Hills Hilton, another Ted Graves was sitting comfortably in the penthouse suite. When the door burst open, another Allison Graves entered the room and stopped and looked sternly at Ted Graves.

"Tell me you have contacted that Admiral you know in Washington and have set up a meeting? Tell me you are actually doing what you are being paid to do?" Allison Graves yelled across the room, slammed the door closed behind her and immediately transformed herself into The Colonel and walked over to the man impersonating Ted Graves and asked again, "What the hell are you doing?"

"Colonel, I have already contacted Admiral Hancock and he is going to meet me tomorrow at our usual place. I will be going in as a Naval Commander David Henderson. He is the young son of Admiral Bear Henderson, retired and is presently at sea on his nuclear submarine. All my credentials are made, and I can get in and meet, then leave; and nobody will know who I am. Is that satisfactory, Colonel?"

"Yes, but I told you to report to me as soon as you made contact. You didn't which made me suspicious of your motives. Are you with me, or against, what we are doing? You are making a lot of money. I really don't care who or what your father did; you are working for me and don't forget that," The Colonel yelled and then stormed out of the suite and returned to his/her suite next door.

The following morning, the fake Ted Graves boarded his private Lear Jet and took off for Washington DC. His scheduled meeting was with the Department of Defense director Admiral John Fitzgerald Hancock, a member of The Colonel's payroll. His meeting was of course covert; and if anyone found out that past President Ted Graves was meeting with a sitting director of the U.S. government, the scandal and fallout would destroy Hancock and who knows how many others. Even a fake Ted Graves could cause major problems with both The Colonel and Hancock.

Hancock had control of all the Naval forces within the U.S. control, which is more than just the U.S. Navy. He also controlled the British, Spanish, French and Japanese Navies if ever he needed to call upon them to help in a situation.

"Good afternoon, John, how are you on this beautiful day?" Ted Graves as Commander David Henderson said as a greeting to his lifelong friend Admiral Hancock. They had been friends and coconspirators in many operations over the years since they met in Vietnam back in 1969.

"So, what brings you to Washington, Ted, or should I say Commander Henderson? Besides there are travel restrictions in place, you could get thrown in jail for that and of course if the FBI sees you, they may just throw you in jail and loose the key," Hancock said smiling.

"You know, same old thing; I need a favor and I believe you can make it happen. You're not infected, are you? Well, I will just sit over here, keep your distance," Graves/Henderson stated as they sat down in the back booth of a bar located in Arlington, Virginia. It was an out of the way place that was rarely frequented by the police, much less the FBI. The FBI had been following Hancock for many years and knew he would meet his girlfriend at this bar every day for lunch. They would eat and then go to the hotel just down the street. So, it wasn't out of character for the Admiral to be here on this Tuesday afternoon. "Where is your mistress?"

"She will be here in a few minutes; I told her I was running late to give us time to talk. What do you need now?"

"Not long ago you recovered a Soviet Nuclear submarine. I know it is sitting in Norfolk collecting dust. I would like to borrow it for a while. Oh, and I need a couple of missiles loaded too, no, make that four nuclear missiles. I want to have a little fun with the Soviets."

"You want to start World War Three?"

"Well, yeah. I don't think this Chinese virus is going to cause enough trouble and want to add to the mixture."

"Can't do it, Commander. First, that boat is not in operational condition; second, you don't have a crew to man it; and third, where do you think I can get you four nuclear missiles to arm the damn thing? It's a Soviet boat and our missiles will not fit in the tubes," Hancock stated, paused and then added, "Besides it was towed out to sea to be scuttled last year; and well, it's gone."

"Okay. True, I don't have a crew; and well it was just a thought anyway. Forget I asked for it. But I do need the use of one of your P3 Orion's armed with a bunker buster. If not that, maybe a couple of F-35s to do the job. I need some heavy hitters, and soon, before they leave there."

"And what do you want that for, to start World War Three? What country are you going to bomb?" Hancock questioned.

"No, just to go after some very persistent CIA operatives. They have a secret bunker in North Dakota; and I want to destroy it and everyone in it."

"I can't let you have a P3 to kill Americans. No way, Commander. You are just going to have to find another way. I know of the facility and it is impossible to blow up; that was a nuclear hardened missile site from the sixties. The only way you can destroy it is from within, and that is also nearly impossible." Hancock paused when he saw his mistress walking toward their table. "Look, my secretary is here; I will think about it and let you know in a couple of days. Now you better get out before she recognizes you."

Ted/Henderson stood and said goodbye to his friend and handed him a card with a number on it. "Call me at this number tomorrow and let me know." And to himself, he wondered, *'How much does she cost?'*

Moments after Ted left, a tall blonde beauty stepped up to Hancock's table and sat down after giving him a kiss on the forehead. Kimberly Jones stood five foot six inches tall and her beauty rivalled Jessica Rabbit from the cartoon *'Who Framed Roger Rabbit'*.

Ted Graves/Commander Henderson left the bar and headed back toward the small airport just outside the city, calling ahead to order his jet to be fueled and ready to leave as soon as he arrived. His meeting had the effect that he had hoped for. Hancock was a player and he knew his time in the game was getting close to an end. Hancock didn't trust Graves and he wasn't about to order a P3 Orion to bomb a CIA safe house, even if it was a closely guarded secret. He only knew about it because when he was much younger, he had been privy to a policy meeting which discussed the upgrades to the facility. He didn't realize at the time that it was a CIA compound or what it was going to be used for until years later. He was close friends with Josh Randal and Davin Pierce. They did not know of his involvement with Ted Graves and never would if he had his way.

After take-off Ted Graves reached into his pocket and retrieved a small plastic box, opened it, and looked carefully at the pills it held. Picking up two he immediately popped them into his mouth. "Ah, dreamland coming," he said as the two LSD pills slowly took effect and he drifted off into his personal dreamland. He really enjoyed playing the part of Ted Graves, especially the part where he could indulge in his favorite pastime, drugs.

Admiral Hancock and Kimberly had a nice lunch and then retired to his suite in the hotel around the corner. Three hours later Hancock walked into his office to find Josh Randal waiting for him.

"Hello, Josh. What can I do for the CIA today?" Hancock asked as he removed his jacket and hung It on the back of his chair.

"It's not what you can do for me, John, but what I can do for you," Josh commented quickly as he stood to shake the Admiral's hand and then had second thoughts. "This virus thing is screwing up a lot of friendships."

"Oh, yeah, I know. So, what is the CIA offering. It's not often that the CIA makes an offer like that to the Navy. Okay, I give, what can you do for me?"

"This is just between you and me; nobody else is aware that I am even here. So, listen carefully; I am only going to say this once. But before I do, I must inform you that I did a quick scan of your office, and found four bugs, listening devices, two were Soviet and the other two U.S made. I have deactivated all of them. Now, please sit, you are not going to like what I am about to say."

"Okay, I'm sitting, and we don't hold any classified discussions in my office so no secrets got out that I know of."

"It has come to my attention that you have recently had a visit from Ted Graves; and yes, he looked like Commander David Henderson. But David is out in the Pacific Ocean cruising around Japan in his nuclear submarine. We knew he was an imposter for that and that the real Ted Graves is sitting in my office at CIA Headquarters. And since that imposter walked in here, that alone is a dead giveaway that he is a fake. The real Ted Graves has been confined to a wheelchair for the past twenty years, ever since he almost died in the Bahamas. And he and his daughter, Allison, have been working closely with my office for at least two years. As for the guy you talked to, we don't know who he is, but will soon. We know that this imposter asked you for something and I am glad you refused his requests. That was very smart on your part. We almost caught him when he left here, but he has a new model holographic device which we couldn't jam; and he changed his appearance before we could catch up to him." Josh started to say more but was interrupted by Hancock.

"I will admit that I just met with him in a bar across town. But he..." Hancock started to defend himself when Josh held up his hand and stopped him.

"We know about the conversation. We have had that bar bugged for years; and the FBI has been tracking Miss Kimberly for months and know all about your affair. By the way, how much does a high-class call girl costs these days. You do know she is a call girl, right?" Josh paused as he got a nod from Hancock. "And let's get real; you can't expect a woman like that to fall for you. You're old, and even though you are successful, why is she interested, besides the money. We don't care about that, have your fun. But keep in mind she isn't after you for your looks; more for what you know, and she is digging to get that information, even if you didn't say anything directly. She has her way of getting information. We don't know for whom she works, but have a good idea. What I am asking you to do right now is submit your resignation effective immediately. The scandal will destroy you if you don't; and the connection to Ted Graves could put you in jail. For your own good, resign. The FBI, knowing we are friends, asked me to come over and ask you to do this," Josh concluded.

"What if I don't?" Hancock protested.

"If you don't, the FBI along with a couple of US Marshalls will be paying you a visit. You will not like the outcome. Your record is clean except for some possible misappropriations and other crimes that can be swept under the rug, but not if you continue in this position. You haven't killed anyone directly or even in-directly that we know of. Just played a little bit too much attention of ship movements to keep them away from some criminal operations that have come to light. John just resign; it all goes away, and you don't lose your retirement. Also, I must add that Mr. Graves has been losing some of his people; to put it bluntly, they have been turning up dead. We don't want you to be next. He still may come after you, so resign, and I will put you in a safe place until we capture him and put his company out of business. As a friend I am asking you to do this."

"Sounds like I have little choice in this, Josh," Hancock said sadly. "This safe place you are referring to wouldn't happen to be in North Dakota?"

"Either that or go to jail for a very long time. They have evidence to convict but are asking you to do this because of your military career and history," Josh said avoiding the answer to his question, then finally said. "Yes, why?"

"Okay, I will resign. What happens to Kim?" Hancock said as he added, "Graves plans on bombing or attacking that facility and kill everyone in it. I don't know when or how. He asked for a bunker buster and a nuclear bomb which I would not give him. He also asked for a couple of F-

35s to do the job, which I refused to turn over or direct to do the job."

"That has not been determined yet; we need to find out who she is working for and maybe use her to get them," Josh said. "I need to warn Davin and his team." After pausing to think, he then added, "Resign, go home and pack. I have a car waiting outside to take you home and then to a safe location, not North Dakota. At least not yet. The virus is dictating your new home; but believe me, you will be safe."

"Dad, I would like to interrogate Miss Newton, if that is really her name," Amber asked her father as they sat around the dinner table sipping cold drinks.

"Do you think you are up to it? I was about to send Cynthia down there to do it," Davin replied between sips of his beer.

"I am sure Cynthia would get something out of her; maybe I could watch and assist if needed. I want to find out who she is and who hired her."

"Both good information, but we need to know a bit more than that. Cynthia, take Amber down and see what you can find out," Davin ordered and then eyed his daughter with a serious eye.

"Thanks dad. Let's get this done, Cynthia," Amber agreed.

"I'll take the lead; and you follow along and jump in if you see a good opening," Cynthia said. She stood and started for the door.

"Just don't kill her, at least not yet," Davin joked.

"Right," Cynthia agreed smiling. Minutes later, she and Amber were in the elevator going down to the seventh level, where the holding cells were. If there was ever a place that was escape proof this was it, unless you had outside help and even then, you had to know this level was even there and how to access it. The elevator controls only showed five levels. To get to the lower levels you needed a special key and combination, using the five digits on the control panel to punch in the code and the access card had to be inserted in a hidden slot located below the key pad, invisible because it looked like the end of the panel, which it was, and it read the card only when swiped past number five on the pad after you entered the eight digit code.

"How do I get one of those cards and the code?" Amber asked as they passed down below level five.

"Ask your dad; he gave me this when I arrived on site and told me that if I lose it, I will be locked down here with the lights out for a long, long time," Cynthia joked.

"He wouldn't do that to you, would he?"

"You bet he would; your dad has done a lot worse, but he will never tell you that, being his daughter."

"You're joking, aren't you?" Amber questioned as the elevator doors opened to a long hallway.

"The cell is just down the hall, smile for the cameras. The cameras are monitored on level 6 in a secure area that requires the card, a special code and fingerprint scans. Only Josh Randal, Davin, Mona, Bryan, and a few others have access to that room. The operators of course have access and are ex-special forces, Seal or Marine Expo force trained. Getting in may be easy for some but getting out alive is another story. Here we are," Cynthia said stopping beside a blank wall, no window, door handle or visible access. She walked over to a hidden panel on the far wall and swiped her card passed a point; and the wall, that seemed to be solid, became transparent and showed a lone figure sitting on a bed on the far side of the cell. The wall was actually a large video monitor, like a movie screen, but just a rear projection with multiple cameras located in the cell. Cynthia pressed a button behind Amber and the wall opened and there were four chairs and a table behind it. "Please take a seat, Amber. Welcome to our high-tech interrogation room. We can see her but until I activate the inner wall, she cannot see us. I will allow her to see us in a moment."

"Wow, pretty high-tech for sure, so what is our next move, whips and chains maybe," Amber joked.

"Not quite, but close, your dad showed me how to work this stuff the last time I was here and let's see if I can remember. Oh, yeah, watch this," Cynthia paused for a moment while she entered a command into the computer on the table. Seconds later, Heather Newton's eyes popped open and her head come up as she looked around the cell for something, anything that could have startled her. Seeing nothing she let her head slump down again, but immediately picked up again and yelled.

"Whoever you are, please stop; I will answer your questions, just stop with the bee buzzing," Heather yelled with a genuine fear on her face.

"Seems she is afraid of bees," Cynthia commented and then pressed a button and spoke to Heather. "Miss Newton, do you know where you are?"

"Yes, you have me in a twelve by twelve holding cell, the likes I have never seen before. I assume you can see me, but I can't see you. Where are you and who are you?"

"First there are no bees; we just introduced that to see if you were awake. You say, you will answer our questions."

"Yes, my employer hung me out to fail. He knew Sally was armed and that the damn holographic device would fail me when I needed it the most. It is like he had control of it and could turn it on or off whenever he wished," Heather admitted.

"You say, he. Is your employer a he or she?" Amber asked.

"I don't know for sure; I would get information on my phone in a text and never spoke to him or her, just text."

273

"So, can you tell me about the operation that he or she is trying to run?"

"I don't know much; Sally could tell you more than me. She was the one that would pose as Monica Teach and travel around going wherever and doing all kinds of things. She knows a lot. I only know what was sent to me on my phone. Sorry I am not much help."

"What was your mission?" Cynthia asked.

"My mission was simple. Sally Howard knows who the boss is and knows a lot about his or her plans. I was to stop her from reaching you by any means I could. I guess I failed in my mission and now I am the target."

"Guess we really should be talking to Sally," Amber stated.

"Can I get out of here?" Heather asked, "Or at least a change of clothes and maybe a little more heat; this room is cold."

"I think we can arrange both," Cynthia said as she tapped in a few commands on the computer to raise the temperature in the cell and then looked at Amber. "There is a closet located in the back of this room, in it you will find some colorful jump suits, pick out one that may fit Heather and bring it to me, please."

"Here is a nice yellow one in her size. Now what?" Amber said minutes later after retrieving a jump suit.

"Thanks, wait here," Cynthia said, stood and walked down the hall a few feet, stopped and pressed a hidden button on the wall beside the transparent wall, opening a small door. She inserted the jump suit and closed the door; immediately, the yellow jump suit dropped into the cell across from Heather.

"Yellow, not my color, but thanks anyway. It is already warmer in here and the jump suit does look more comfortable than this skintight outfit I have on. Any men out there? I would like to change?" She asked.

"Just us girls, but I will fix it so we can't see you undress too," Cynthia said and then tapped the keys to make the wall solid again. "Heather, we will be back shortly, don't go anywhere."

"Yeah, right," Heather said to the wall.

Upstairs in the control room, the sergeant on duty picked up a microphone and pressed two buttons which connected him to the intercom within the facility.

"Mr. Pierce, we have an incoming aircraft. They have identified themselves as Whiskey Charlie four eight three, she is one of ours."

"Control, allow them to land and send a greeting party to the runway to see who it is and advise," Davin Pierce said into the intercom microphone in the galley. "Did they say who was on board?"

"No, sir."

"Did you ask?" Davin asked.

"Yes, sir, but they wouldn't say. They didn't want to say over the air waves."

"Okay, double their greeting party, armed and you know the drill. I will be right up," Davin said and then hung up the intercom. "Looks like we have unexpected guests; Bryan, Mona, would you care to join me?"

"Sure, let's go," Mona replied not waiting for Bryan to say anything. "It's been pretty dull around here; a little excitement would be nice."

Sally sat quietly in her chair watching the three depart and munched on her desert of apple pie, thinking, *'This place is really awesome. I need my gun.'*

They had been watching her a bit more closely since Amber and Cynthia had returned from wherever they had Heather locked up. *'Do they know who I really am? Do they suspect anything? What did Heather tell them? Maybe it is time for me to make my move; I was tasked to get to the control room on level six, but that looks like it is nearly impossible. Decisions need to be made; and I need a gun. Maybe I can take pretty girl's gun; she has been eyeing me ever since I got here. Maybe a little seduction is in order. And she has two guns; that would make it easy. Yeah, pretty girl is an easy target. Graves needs to get in here and I need to make it happen, but how,'* Sally thought to herself.

"Hey, soldier, I need to use the bathroom, can you direct me?" Sally said in a very sexy voice, one she had not used in many years, not since she worked as a high-priced call girl on the Vegas Strip.

"Sure, come with me," the young female soldier tasked with guarding her replied and then turned toward the door.

"Are you going with me?" she teased.

"Yes, I am not supposed to let you out of my sight," she answered as they walked down the hall.

"You take this pretty seriously, don't you?" she teased seductively.

"Yes, I do, so don't do anything stupid, I would hate to have to shoot you. The restrooms are just over here," she said pointing toward the two doors on the right.

Fifteen minutes later, Sally emerged from the restroom alone. Her guard was tied up in the restroom, unharmed; but had also completed her mission of letting Sally get her weapon and escape. Sally had succeeded in getting the next phase of her plan, getting weapons and a bullet proof vest.

Up in the hanger, the welcoming committee was waiting for the Gulfstream to shut down its engines and allow its passengers to disembark. Minutes later, the engines spun down, and the door opened; seconds went by before Andi and Ivy stepped out.

"Okay, everyone, these are welcomed guests; you are dismissed," Bryan ordered the welcoming committee of armed soldiers.

"Welcome to North Dakota," Davin said as Andi stepped onto the ground in front of Davin. "Are you the only two on board?"

"No, we brought a close friend; he will be right out," Ivy said quickly and then gave a hug to Davin, Bryan and then finally to Mona. "Great to see all of you."

"We were very worried when you had your bad accident and didn't know for sure if Helen could put you back together again," Davin said smiling.

"Unlike Humpty Dumpty, when all his king's men could not repair him, Helen is a miracle worker and she actually made me better, and then added a few things to Andi to hopefully make him better too," Ivy said smiling.

"Is one of the things she gave you, a sense of humor?" Bryan asked.

"Yep, mine works better than Andi's but his is coming along slowly."

"Hey, I resemble that," Andi commented.

"That's resent that, Andi. Come we have a lot to talk about and very little time to act," Davin said. He turned and headed toward the door. "Sergeant, see that the bird is fueled, and the crew given a place to rest and some food."

"Yes, sir," the sergeant replied and rushed toward his ground crew to issue orders and to greet the crew.

Monica Teach, also known as Monica Henshaw, according to the name on her second birth certificate. It was the name given to her by the doctor and his wife when he stole her from her biological mother, Connie Young Cutler. Connie's married name was Connie Cutler; and when she divorced, she dropped the Cutler and returned to her birth name of Connie Young. When she met and married Davin Pierce, she was Connie Young and never told him about her first marriage and the birth of Monica. She finally broke down and told Davin the entire story when they found the documents and birth certificates on board the Soviet submarine that was recently discovered. Connie was in the process of telling Amber about her half-sister when things got heated and she never finished the story. Amber found out when she met with Monica in Hawaii. Every family has secrets. Some should never be disclosed; and others need to be. This secret needed to come out and sooner rather than later.

"Davin, I need to bring you up to speed on some other little secrets this facility holds. Will you come with me and Mona? I would rather show you than just tell you. What I am about to disclose is Top Secret Codeword and you know the drill on that, I will have you sign some non-disclosure docs first once we get inside to the outer office. Please come with me and leave your cell phone and other electronic devices on your desk, please," Bryan said when he entered the office that Davin was using while at the facility.

"Okay, boss. Anybody else joining us?" Davin responded wondering if he was the only lucky person to join in.

"Nope, just you for now. We may consider Amber and Connie, but for now just you," Mona responded as they followed Bryan out of the office and down the hall to the elevators. He pushed the button to call for the elevator, but Davin noticed he pushed both up and down buttons together. They were on the fourth level and the elevator arrived within seconds; the door opened, and they entered. Bryan opened the emergency phone box and removed the phone, pressed six numbers, and inserted a credit card, looked inside the box, got his eye scanned, and then the back of the elevator opened. Davin had no idea that the back could open; it looked solid to the naked eye.

"Follow me," Bryan ordered as the three of them looked down the extremely long hallway.

"How long is this hallway?" Davin questioned as he looked at the shiny tile floor and light green painted walls and what appeared to be no end to the hallway.

"Two point six miles, but don't worry we have transportation," Bryan said and touched a hidden panel on the left wall about ten feet from the elevator door. A sliding door opened to expose two electric golf carts. "Climb on old man."

"Watch it; I may be old, but I can still kick your butt," Davin commented jokingly, knowing he had only half a chance in whipping up on Bryan.

"Anytime, Davin. I will have Mona stand in for me to make it almost fair."

"No way, I couldn't beat her in a fair fight; and I know she doesn't fight fair," Davin continued to joke with his friend.

"Look, enough of that, we have some serious things to discuss once we get to the end of this hallway. Sit back and enjoy the ride."

"Can you tell me a little about where we are going, and how long this secret has been here?" Davin questioned as they rode along quietly.

"This section was built at the same time the rest was refurbished. We needed to be able to house certain items away from the main facility for logistical reasons and safety. You will understand a little more once you see everything. We are going up to level two; you don't notice it, because we are climbing up the ramp at a very slight angle. Once we arrive, we will be at the east end of the runway, but still in the mountain side. Even though we are at level two, we are still over one hundred feet below the surface, mainly because we are under the mountain that you saw as you landed or took off on our runway, the one just to the left of the end of the runway," Bryan said as he started to brief Davin.

"Okay, we are under the mountain beside the eastern end of the runway, which is a lake most of the time. So, what is under this mountain?"

"Don't be so impatient; you will see in a few minutes."

Arriving at the end of the hallway, they were met by a large blast door, measuring ten-foot-high by twelve foot wide, that looked to be very solid. Mona walked over to a panel, opened it, pressed her hand to a screen, leaned in for an eye scan, inserted a card, and typed in six numbers.

"Wow, a lot of security to get in; what if you had to get in quickly?" Davin asked as he watched the procedure.

"That is another secret which you will learn about in a few minutes," Bryan said as the bolts retracted, and the door started to swing open quietly. Davin saw that the door was at least two feet thick and was constructed like a bank vault with multiple bolts that extended at least three feet into the frame around it.

Bryan and Mona walked into the dark area beyond the door and signaled for Davin to follow. Mona reached over and turned on the lights. The lights came on in sections starting with the ones directly overhead and continued for what looked like a mile or more.

Davin could hardly believe what he was seeing sitting directly in front of him. "Wow, is that a Blackbird?"

"Yes, but not your ordinary SR-71 Blackbird. The original design was to be a high-altitude bomber with extreme speed, but most ended up being spy planes; this one is both, a spy plane with a working bomb bay and targeting system. She can carry four nuclear bombs and deliver them anywhere on earth quickly. We also have two F35 Super Stealth Fighter/bombers, two FA-18 Super Hornets, and one G-7 Corporate Gulf Stream business jet with long range tanks. All in flyable shape and ready to go at a moment's notice. There is also a storeroom full of munitions and bombs."

"Damn, who else knows about this?"

"Now you, of course me and Mona, along with the flight crews, ground crew and six-person security team. Oh, there is one other item you need to know about."

"Isn't this kind of overboard. You have four FA-18s and four F-16s in the other hanger, are you preparing for war or what?"

"I will answer that, Bryan. Yes, those are our main defense force; but if we need to go bigger and badder, then we open the mountain and launch these. And of course, there are the missiles," Mona commented.

"Missiles?" Davin looked confused.

"Yes, missiles. This facility was originally built back in the 60s as a ballistic missile launch silo and had one ballistic missile. Once fired, the site would be abandoned or something like that. The powers in office at the time thought that was a poor use of a missile silo; so, once they built the first one, they built twenty others around the country. Not a bad idea, but again, once they launched, what became of the silos? This one here became what you know of back down that long hallway. But in the late 80s, we modified this place; added seven more silos, all controlled from the room on level 8, the level very few people know about. Three of the silos are at the back of this hanger buried in the mountain and can be ready to launch in about a half hour."

"Damn," Davin commented looking around the hanger and at the four doors on the back wall. "I assume those four doors give you access to the silos?"

"Yes, and the fourth is the backup control room. Do you want to see it?" Mona replied and started to walk toward the back of the hanger.

"Sure."

After about an hour of touring around the huge hanger, they stopped at a small room with a sign on it that indicated it was the breakroom. Bryan paused before opening the door and looked closely at Davin and said, "Behind this door is the most guarded secret within this facility, I don't want it to get out so you can never leave once we enter. Are you okay with that?"

"What? After all this you…" Davin started to say when Bryan opened the door and Davin looked in to see a very comfortably decorated breakroom, with computers, terminals, large screen TV, over stuffed leather sofas and chairs along with a full kitchen.

"Got ya! Come on in, I need a cup of coffee. And you can meet some of the team," Bryan said as they entered the room and saw six of the team relaxing comfortably around the large room, some sipping coffee, others reading or on the computer. "Everyone this is Davin Pierce, Director of Covert Operations, CIA, and you know Mona. Is that coffee fresh?"

"Made it about an hour ago, so pretty fresh. How's it going boss?" one of the team spoke up from across the room.

"Fair to midland as it were. You have heard about the pandemic going on in the world and we are all stuck here for a bit longer," Bryan commented as he poured coffee for Davin, Mona and himself.

"Yeah, but we are doing fine down here. No worries," Sergeant Henry commented from his computer.

"Bryan, why show me all this now. Do you know something I need to know to prompt this exposure?"

"Yes, Mona, would you like to explain it to our boss."

"Wait a second, when did I become your boss?"

"About two hours ago," Mona replied. "You may want to sit down," she said as she pointed to the table in the corner.

Back in the main facility, Amber and her team were discussing their next move in the pursuit to capture Ted Graves and his team of miscreants.

"Wait, are you saying that we are to wait right here until he comes to us?" Heather stated as she read the recently arrived message from Josh Randal, director of the CIA.

"Yes, due to the pandemic which is now kicking everyone's ass out in the world, we are to stay here. All indications are that Graves is planning an attack on this facility in the next couple of days. We are to prepare to stop that attack, which means we stay here, safe from the virus, and hopefully able to stop Graves from taking this facility," Amber replied to her team.

"We heard a rumor that Monica Teach is your half-sister and is out to kill you and your family; is that true or just hear say?" Heather asked.

"Yes, she is my half-sister, but I am not sure about the killing part. There are too many variables in the equation that don't add up. She had her chance more than once and didn't do it; she also told me in Hawaii that she didn't want me dead. So, to answer your question, I don't have a good answer. She may not be who she says she is, could be an imposter using the holographic generator to fool us. I just don't know but will be watching my back just to be safe; and I expect all of you to have my six."

"That needs not be said, we have your six and always will," Dan answered for everyone, smiling.

"Thanks. Now let's get some rest while we can. Things may heat up real fast if we are not careful," Amber said as she stood to leave.

Her team followed suit, and all headed for their assigned rooms for rest and to prepare their equipment, weapons, and other items for a potential attack.

Down in the hidden hanger

"Davin, we received a message from Josh just before we came in here. He has been ordered by the President to assign you as Director of Operations of this facility. Bryan and I are to report to you. We have never had a director of operations before. Bryan has always been in charge and has been running things quite well; but they feel, that since you are stuck here with us, that you should be put in charge of the whole place," Mona started to say as Bryan walked over to Captain Chancy Davis who was sitting in front of the big screen TV watching a Harry Potter movie.

"But why? I think Bryan has been doing a great job here, and I don't want to take over. He is in charge and I will follow his lead," Davin protested.

"That may not work, Davin. Bryan is not going to be here; he has been ordered to report to Washington to take over as Director Homeland Security. He protested but lost; the President wants this to happen. It is supposed to be temporary, but you know how that is in Washington. It is kind of like that song *Hotel California*; once you check in you can never leave."

"Not sure I like this set up; why not you take over as lead?" Davin asked.

"I'm going too as assistant director," Mona replied.

"That means I can never leave here."

"No, all it means is that you are here until we return, or a replacement is named," Mona confirmed.

"Still don't like it, what does Josh say about this?"

"Not a happy camper."

"I would suppose he is not very happy. I just moved into the Director of Covert Operations there; guess I can run it from here." After he thought about this for a brief moment, he then asked, "When does all this take place?"

"Seven days from now," Mona replied and then got up, walked over to the refrigerator, and pulled out a couple of cold beers.

Seconds after she made her statement, red lights started to flash, and a siren began to blare out its warning.

"What the hell?" Bryan yelled. "Code Red, get your men ready, Captain... Let's go, NOW!"

Bryan, Mona, and Davin started to run toward the exit and the long corridor to the main facility as he picked up his internal walkie talkie and depressed the send button. "What is going on?" he yelled.

"Six Blackhawks just landed on our facility and are unloading troops, heavily armed," came the response.

"Lock us down!" Bryan ordered and immediately all the entrances to the facility bolted shut and locked. All the ventilation shafts also locked down preventing any access into the facility.

"Getting a call from HQ," the operator said in a rather calm voice, as if this was nothing but a drill and he knew about it.

"Who?" Bryan asked as they entered the long hall and boarded the golf cart to return to the main facility.

"Josh Randal."

"Put him through, did you verify it's really him?"

"Voice recognition confirms and so does the location and number he is calling from. The line is secure and encrypted," came the response from the operations control room.

"Hello, Josh. What the hell is happening outside that prompted your call?" Bryan asked calmly.

"Is Davin and Mona with you?" Josh asked.

"Yes."

"Put me on speaker and stop your golf cart. We need to talk," Josh ordered. He then paused until he figured they had stopped and were waiting for an explanation.

"Okay, we have stopped, what is going on?" Davin yelled across the cart to the walkie talkie.

"Calm down; you have probably noticed several Blackhawk helos landing upstairs; don't panic. Stand down your troops, they are NOT attacking. They are your perimeter defense and are there to protect you. I tried to call earlier and could not get through. Don't know why, but your system may be compromised. We are secure for the moment but check to be sure you haven't been compromised. The bottom line is those troops are a company of Special Forces troops from the 82nd Airborne Division. They will bivouac upstairs and provide added security. Things are happening around the country about which we are not happy. And we may lose control if we don't take steps to safeguard certain facilities, yours being one of those."

"Hold one, so I can alert control that this is not an attack. Be right back," Bryan said. He quickly switched channels and told control to stand down from red alert, and then switched back to Josh.

"Okay, we have stood down; now, next time let us know before they arrive, please."

"Again, sorry about that mix up, but I got tied up with your brother and he insisted on sending you the troops and did it before I had a chance to call you. And hopefully, there will not be a need for a next time. Now, stay safe out there; and one more thing, your appointment to temporary Homeland Security director has been changed. You stay where you are and keep Davin out of trouble. You know how he is, trying to save the world all the time," Josh said and waited to disconnect.

"Now wait a minute boss, I don't always, well mostly always, I guess, try to save the world; but you have been with me most of the time, so you are to blame too," Davin yelled back to his friend and boss.

"Oh, yeah, forgot about that part. Be safe my brothers," Josh said and then broke the connection.

"I guess we are in this together; let's go meet our guests," Davin said and then looked at Mona and smiled, thinking the troops were going to love seeing her. "Mona, maybe you should grab a jacket or floppy shirt before we visit our guests."

"Why, I think this outfit suits me well," Mona protested looking down at the tight low-cut t-shirt and skinny jeans she had on.

"Yes, baby, you look incredibly awesome, and to a group of soldiers in the field you are awesome eye candy; but we don't want them to get the wrong idea. You are taken; so, please before we meet the troops, put on at least a shirt," Bryan insisted.

"Okay, all right, I will stop by our room and get a conservative blouse," Mona said smiling, knowing full well that Bryan loved her and only wanted her to be safe even from the potential stares from the troops.

"I suggest that you tell Amber and her team that we have troops and to dress appropriately," Bryan instructed Davin as they rode back to the main facility.

"Roger that, as soon as we get back," Davin agreed.

"Dad, what is going on out there, it seems like we have a bunch of soldiers setting up camp around us. Are we going to be attacked or what?" Amber asked her dad when he, Bryan and Mona returned to the mess hall.

"Not really sure at the moment, but the President and Josh believe we may be; and with that virus starting to run through the country like a wildfire, we just have to settle in for the long haul. The soldiers are here to protect the facility and us, of course. We will set them up with the kitchen and facilities in the house above, so they will not be coming down here, except for the commander and his immediate staff. Always keep your people close and armed. We have weathered storms worse than this and survived. Your experience with the hurricane in New Orleans is a good example of your resolve. Now, get your people together and explain to them what is happening; and by all means, no one is to venture to the surface for any reason without clearing it with me, Bryan, or Mona. Everyone needs to partner up and travel anywhere within the facility or on the surface in at least pairs, no exception."

"Got it, dad. Can we have dinner together tonight? There are some things I need to discuss with you in private?" Amber asked.

"Sure, is six o'clock good for you? Is your mom invited?"

"Yes, please bring her," Amber said. She then turned and left the mess hall to find her team, who were supposed to be in the theater watching a movie.

"Be careful; I feel this is just the low before the storm," Davin said and then turned to Bryan and Mona and continued. "What next old man?"

"Hell, I don't know, maybe check the arms room; or better yet, let's get a drink and talk about what could happen, put a plan in place, and then watch it go up in smoke when the shooting starts," Mona said joking.

"Sounds like a plan, your place or mine?" Davin agreed.

"You got cold beer and scotch?" Bryan asked.

"Both, let's go."

Back in California

"Dad, did you hear about your general friend in Washington?" the holographic Allison, his daughter asked when she entered her holographic father's office, dressed in a white almost shear blouse and a short pair of orange shorts, barely covering her bottom, and black leather knee high boots.

"No, what happened to him?" Ted answered before he looked up and did a double take on his daughter. "What are you dressed for, a go-go dance party?"

"No dad, this is just a cover up, I'm going out to the pool and didn't want you to go into shock with the tiny bikini I have on under this," she commented. She then turned her holographic device off and was standing there as The Colonel before continuing, "Well, your general has submitted his resignation and disappeared. Just fell off the grid as it were."

"That is interesting; they must have known that he was working for us, convinced him to resign his commission, and go into hiding. We will just have to locate him and make sure he doesn't talk. Send, ah... Robert to come in and see me. I have a job for him."

"I don't think so; I will take care of it myself," The Colonel stated.

"Colonel, I know you are the boss, but do you want to take the chance of getting captured or killed before we finish this. If you get caught, they will put you in jail for a very long time; and we're not ready for that."

"Ah, dad, didn't know you felt that way," The Colonel turned back into Allison and said in her sexiest voice.

"Let Robert do it. If he is killed or captured, we will miss him, but will continue to move forward. Now go work on your tan or whatever you are planning on and have Michelle join you. She can keep the men away from the pool while you burn yourself."

"Okay, I like her," Allison said as she turned and started to leave the office. She stopped abruptly before exiting, and asked, "Ted, what do you think we should with Miss Monica?"

"Not sure just yet; she is still needed, at least for a while longer. Then maybe we take her for a little cruise," Ted Graves commented casually.

"I don't want to kill her; she hasn't done anything wrong. Just because the FBI, CIA, and all those other organizations think she is bad, she really isn't and shouldn't have to die," The Colonel as Allison said and then left the room.

'Maybe she doesn't but, well, maybe,' Ted Graves thought to himself.

Minutes later, Robert Sanchez knocked on the office door and let himself in without waiting for a reply from Graves.

"Robert, good, that was quick. Did Allison tell you what I needed?" Graves asked when he looked up and saw Robert.

"No, she didn't, just said you wanted to see me ASAP," Robert replied as he sat in the chair across from Graves.

"Remember our old friend Admiral John Fitzgerald Hancock?" Graves asked.

"Yeah, heard he went rogue on us; spilled his guts about everything you are trying to do. Want me to take him out?"

"First, you must find him. I'm not sure if we should kill him; he may still be of use. He doesn't know everything I have planned; only the stuff that required his assistance. So just locate him; and, well, then I will have something else for him to provide the CIA and FBI. Something that will turn the tides as it were," Graves ordered.

"Roger boss, I will let you know when I find him," Robert agreed and then stood to leave. He paused for a moment at the door and turned to look back at Ted Graves, a holograph of the Ex-president of the United States and criminal mastermind wannabe while thinking, *'He never suspected; damn I'm good.'*

Walking back toward the main part of the house, Robert paused at a closet and opened the door to look inside at himself; then he turned off the holographic device and became Allison again, wearing the tiny bikini she had on under the projection of Robert. Robert was actually tied up in the closet and unconscious, thanks to a little drug she had slipped to him in his morning coffee. She would dispose of his body later, after her father left the house. She would need help, but that was the easy part; half of the men that worked for Ted were really working for her. There was a very large ocean, just outside, and a properly weighted Robert would disappear forever, never to be found. The next problem to solve was to ensure her fake dad was captured by the FBI, or someone; she didn't want him dead, just gone from her life. Death, of course, was an option. Only she knew his true identity, and it would soon be exposed to the FBI. Her true identity would never be known though, because she was an android and could be anyone at any time.

Walter Reed Military Hospital

"How is our guy doing?" NSA Director Wilson asked the doctor on duty as he approached the Intensive Care Unit.

"Patient Winho is doing fine; we will be moving him out of isolation tomorrow. Temperature is done and vitals almost normal. He is one very lucky fellow; we have reports of other cases around the country and they are not doing as well. Don't know why he is recovering so fast but are very happy that he is. There have been twenty-seven reported deaths from the same virus and over four hundred cases reported. The CDC has declared it a pandemic and are taking steps to ensure the spread is contained," the doctor reported.

"Is there a vaccine for it?"

"None that we have, we are trying many different treatments with minimal success."

"You have other cases here?" Wilson asked.

"Yes, six are in the ICU and one down in the morgue. Lost him this morning. Older gentleman with multiple physical problems, he didn't have a chance. I need to leave now; have patients to check on. You can visit Shan if you like; just don't open the tent around him, and wear a mask when you go in," replied the doctor.

"Understand," Wilson agreed. Minutes later, Wilson entered the isolation room where his agent was, watching the television. "Winho, isn't it about time you got out of that bed and back to work; we have a country to protect," Wilson said joking around.

"Would love to boss, but the doctor said no. Besides that, the nurses here are awesome, beautiful, fun and, well I would like to stay a while longer and enjoy their company," Winho replied smiling.

"How are you feeling?"

"Fine, a little tired and some tight muscles but overall doing fine."

"You are one of the lucky ones; this virus has killed several already. So, you just take it easy and get your strength back. I need you up to full capacity. We have a situation, and you may be the only one to handle it," Wilson commented.

"Me, why me? I am just a junior agent; you have many more experienced agents on staff," Winho asked looking confused.

"You have been to China and know the country. Besides, I have asked the CIA if they could help, but their top four Chinese agents are not available presently, and that leaves only you. When you get out of here, I will explain further. The doctor said you are being moved out of here tomorrow for a regular room and should be released in a few days. So, to repeat myself, get well and back to full strength as quickly as possible; your country needs you.

With that being said, I will be back in two days to pick you up," Wilson said and then turned to leave.

"Wait, sir. Maybe they can release me today."

"Not a chance, not until the doc signs you off as healthy. Get some rest. That's an order," he said and then left the room.

Way up north

"Davin, what the hell is going on? Why are we in lock down?" Connie questioned.

"Well, the short answer is we have been getting reports of a possible pandemic with a very nasty virus up there; and also, intel has indicated that our old friend Ted Graves is about to do something very stupid, and we are the target of that stupidity," Davin told his wife.

"But you said earlier that we have a company of soldiers from Ft. Bragg up there providing protection and we are deep in the earth with limited access; what's there to worry about?"

"Everything, Graves knows the lay out of this place. He knows all the little secrets, how to get in, and much more. We must be careful. Going out there is dangerous right now. The soldiers up there will be brought in after the medics check each one for a possible virus infection; and even when down here, they will be kept in the main hanger for their safety and ours. There is a mini mess hall there; and we have provided cots and everything they will need to sustain life for months without trouble. They will be allowed to exit the hanger to the outside for patrols, fresh air and smoke breaks, but they understand this is a necessary precaution for every one's safety," Davin replied before he took a sip of his now cold coffee.

297

"At least they get to go out; what about us?"

"As long as we stay within the fence we can go out," Davin confirmed.

"Good, I would go crazy staying down here and not be able to see the sun or moon."

"You will see both of them once we make sure the perimeter is safe. And that is up to our new guests. They are here to protect all of us."

"Can I go up now?" Connie asked.

"No, not now. There is a storm up there and it is raining pretty heavy; maybe in an hour or two when the storm passes. Let's take a walk. We can go up to the house without going outside and watch the rain for a bit."

"Allison, I just received a message to get the company jet ready for departure but didn't get a destination," Ted Grave's corporate pilot told Allison as she walked out of the villa.

"North Dakota to start, then on to Washington, DC. I have to visit an old friend," she commented as she walked past the pilot and headed toward her private guest house located across the lush green garden.

"As you wish, we will be ready in an hour; come on out when ready," he replied to her back as she walked on. *'She is turning into a royal bitch,'* he said under his breath as he turned.

"I heard that," she yelled back, "And just remember who is in charge."

Twenty minutes later, she had finished her shower and stood naked in her room. She was picking out outfits to pack thinking about how long this mission would take and what would she need to complete it. She thought she would bring something sexy to tease the Admiral. She threw skinny jeans, several sexy blouses, high heal shoes and other sexy items she thought would help into her travel bag. Then she opened her gun safe and retrieved her favorite pistol, a Glock Model 30 compact forty-five caliber which held ten rounds. It was small and lethal thinking that was just what she needed for part of her mission. She also grabbed a box of ammo and a small holster to slide into her belt at the small of her back. Perfect, now a backup pistol, a Colt Mustang, 380 caliber, six shot, looks a lot like a Colt 1911 forty-five that has been around for centuries, only smaller, yet deadly. She slowly dressed to travel. She slid on a pair of jeans, mini boots, a white bra and an almost transparent loose-fitting blouse; slipped the Glock into her belt in the small of her back and an ankle holster just above her boot, hidden by her flared jeans.

After checking the time, she decided to have lunch and see her father before flying out.

"Dad is there anything you need before I leave?" Allison asked her father when she entered his office without knocking first.

"No, where are you going?" he asked without looking up from the document he was reading.

"Shopping, need to get a few things; I thought I would run down to Rodeo Drive and spend some of the money we have," she joked.

"Okay, don't spend too much. And bring me lunch from that Mexican place we like, couple of burritos, and well, you know what I like."

"Sure, got to go, be back soon," she lied, knowing full well that he would not be here when she returned. He had made an appointment which she knew he wasn't going to miss.

After checking the time on her watch, she saw she only had an hour to get to the airport. She walked out to her white convertible 2020 Corvette ZR1, which she loved and never would part with it. She climbed in, started the 750 horsepower 427 cubic inch engine, and listened to its roar. She loved the power it had and the freedom it gave her.

Allison left the driveway and headed to the airport instead of Rodeo Drive. She would leave her car in the hanger where it would be safe until she returned. Driving south from her father's complex. she passed the four SWAT team trucks heading north. She waved to them as they sped toward the home, she had lived in for the past four years.

Deep down, she hoped her father would not resist and just let himself be captured.

Unknown to either Allison or Ted, not too far from the estate, another Allison Graves had other plans for the wheelchair bound Ted Graves. Sitting in an older Chevy Malibu, three blocks away, she watched as the real Allison drove by. She was watching to make sure the real Ted Graves didn't leave the estate, when she saw the helicopter take off from behind the estate to fly Ted to the airport fifteen minutes after Allison departed, leaving the estate empty.

"Graves, plan B, now; Graves and Allison left the estate and the SWAT Team is almost there," the fake Allison, aka The Colonel, informed her fake father. Thinking to herself, *'This may work out much better than plan A.'*

Home of Ted Graves

The FBI SWAT team entered the property of Ted Graves without incident, and immediately surrounded the house to prevent anyone from escaping. The lead SWAT officer walked up to the front door and rang the doorbell. The door slowly opened by a young female dressed as a French maid.

"May I help you?" she asked the heavily armed officer.

"Yes, we are here to see Mr. Graves; is he home?" he asked.

"He is in his office. Please come in, I will let him know he has visitors," she responded politely.

Behind her, the officer saw four men each holding a weapon; but as he started to raise his M-4 rifle, they immediately lowered theirs and set them on the floor, presenting no resistance.

"Thank you," he said. As he started to enter, he signaled for four of his team to follow.

"This way; Mr. Graves office is in the back. No need for your weapons; he knew you were coming and is not going to resist," she said as she led the way to the office, knocking on his door when they arrived. "Mr. Graves your guests are here."

"Come on in; I have been expecting you. Please have a seat, we have much to talk about. Would you and your team like some coffee or refreshments?" Graves offered politely.

"No, sir. We are here to arrest you for crimes against the country. Would you please come with us?" the officer said quietly, looking very confused.

"Sure, but may we talk for a few minutes first. I have a few things to say before you cart me off to jail." He paused and then asked his maid, "Sophia, will you please bring in some coffee and see that his team gets some refreshments."

"Yes sir, right away," Sophia said and then left the room.

"Okay, Mr. Graves, what do you want to say? Make it quick. We have another job to do in an hour," the officer said as a joke.

"You may want to hold off on that one for a while after you hear what I have to say," Graves said and then added. "By the way, Officer Higgins how is your family?"

"Wait, I didn't tell you my name and what has my family got to do with you?" Higgins asked growing angry at the insinuation.

"Everything, just about everything. You see, right now while you are sitting here in my office overlooking the Pacific Ocean, my team is at your home waiting for my signal to kill your wife and children. And more of my people are at the homes of every member of your team waiting for my order to do the same. Now do I have your attention?"

"How do I know you are telling me the truth," Higgins asked becoming very agitated at the statement and thought of his family being killed.

Graves just smiled and then picked up the remote control from his desk and aimed it at the tv screens behind him and pressed the button turning them on. There were six monitors with six individual pictures on each showing armed men surrounding the homes of each member of Higgins team.

"Isn't technology just great, Officer Higgins," Graves stated.

"Okay, you win; we will leave and not bother you," Higgins said not believing his eyes, but knowing it to be true when he saw his home on the monitor and the five-armed men dressed in black outside his home. "What if I just shoot you right now?"

"That will not do any good; your family will be dead before you leave this room. And besides I am not here, what you are looking at is a holographic projection of me. The house is empty; everyone you have seen coming in here have been holographic projections. Now if you want to live and for your families to live, you will stand up and leave my house now. Goodbye Officer Higgins. Oh, before I forget, Ms. Monica Teach is not here; I will release her soon. Now leave my house," Graves said and then his projection disappeared along with the desk and chair he was sitting on.

"Let's get out of here, this place gives me the creeps," Higgins said as he rushed out of the office and out the front door. "Stand down and load up, we are leaving," he told his team.

Los Angeles International Airport General Aviation Terminal

"Is my plane ready?" Allison asked her pilot when she drove into their private hanger on the south end of the airport.

"Yes, fueled and ready. What is our destination? I need to file a flight plan," her pilot asked.

"Fargo, North Dakota," she replied.

"Did you know your father just left in the Citation?" he asked as he started to walk away.

"No, where was he going?" Allison asked looking very confused.

"Didn't tell me; he was just here and had Sophia fly him out. Didn't know she was a pilot until today."

"Our maid is a pilot," Allison replied becoming more confused. "When you file a flight plan, can you find out where he was heading?"

"Sure, be back in a few minutes; go ahead and get on board when ready," he replied and then walked into the terminal building to file their flight plan and find out where Graves was headed.

'I knew he had an appointment with Josh Randal but that is tomorrow; where is he going today?' Allison thought to herself. *'Where the hell he is going? Oh well, he didn't' say he was leaving today; maybe the appointment got moved up.'*

Fifty-five minutes later Allison was sitting in the back of her Gulfstream VI business jet enjoying a glass of red wine when the pilot announced that there was a storm on their route and he would be diverting to the west a bit to avoid it and the ride might get a little rough as they passed the storm.

"Just what I need now, a storm and not knowing what my father is up to. No flight plan filed and off with the maid," Allison said to herself almost loud enough for Melodie to hear her.

"Did you say something Ms. Allison?" Melodie asked from the galley.

"No, nothing important Melodie; could you bring me some more wine?"

The flight continued for another hour when the captain said, "Miss Allison, we have to head a little further west to avoid this storm and shit..." the captain yelled just as the left engine quit. "We just lost an engine, buckle up we are descending and looking for a place to set down."

"Now what more can go wrong with today?" Allison said to herself and Melodie.

Melodie strapped in across from Allison as the business jet lost altitude. As they passed through twenty thousand feet, the right engine quit, and they had no third engine to rely on. Flying dead stick in a business jet was no easy task and the pilot and co-pilot were fighting the turbulence and descent as best they could. They saw below them a vast forest and mountains; they looked on the charts and out the window for a safe place to land, and could not find anything, no roads, lakes, fields, nowhere to set down a large business jet safely. Finally, after seeing an old fire road cutting through the trees, the pilot made the decision to land on it. It didn't look wide enough for the jet, but at least it was fairly straight.

After many attempts to call Mayday without any response, the co-pilot gave up and concentrated on landing the plane.

As it crashed through the trees, the plane's wings were torn off. The plane finally settled onto the dirt ground with a loud crash. The pilot and co-pilot had slowed down as best they could without having engines to help. They used flaps and landing gear to slow them down, but still hit the ground at over a hundred miles per hour. All landings of any size aircraft are considered controlled crashes and this one was no different except it wasn't as controlled as they had planned.

Once the wings broke off, the fuselage started to slide down the road. It plowed up dirt and trees and stopped two hundred yards after it first hit the ground. Luck was on their side, the plane did not explode because the fuel tanks were ripped off with the wings and the fuselage tanks were empty, as were the wing tanks.

After quickly unstrapping, the pilot and co-pilot bolted out of the cockpit to the cabin to ensure their passengers were alive, and then popped the cabin door open. All four exited the plane, expecting it to explode. Besides multiple cuts and bruises, no one was seriously hurt.

"Wow, what a ride; that was fun, let's do it again," Allison commented as they stopped running about a hundred feet away from the wrecked plane.

"Not funny," Melodie said almost smiling at the joke. "You're bleeding."

"Yeah, not funny. I suspect that this accident was not an accident," the pilot said looking back at his broken plane.

"What do you mean?" Allison asked as she sat down on a tree stump.

"The fuel gauges said we had half a tank of fuel in both wing tanks and a full fuselage tank. That plane should have exploded if there was any fuel in the tanks, but it hasn't. I believe someone messed with the gauges, and we ran out of fuel which caused the engines to quit. I need to go back over there to find out and get our survival gear. You stay here; we will get what we need. And if the bird is safe, maybe we can stay inside until that storm over there passes over us, unless you want to stay out in the rain," he commented just as the rain started to come down.

"Bleeding is the least of my worries, by the way, so are you," Allison commented.

Minutes later, after standing in the pouring rain, the pilot yelled back to Allison and Melodie, "Come, it is safe here. Get in the cabin," as he and the co-pilot stepped back into the cabin.

"Good, my suitcase is still here; I will get us some dry clothes," Allison said as she and Melodie stepped back into the cabin. The pilot pulled the door closed behind them, to maintain the temperature inside. After retrieving her suitcase and pulling out some dry clothes, she and Melodie took turns in the restroom to change and dress their cuts.

"We have another problem," the pilot stated when he returned from the cockpit.

"What's that?" Melodie asked.

"The emergency locator beacon transmitter has been disabled, and it will be very difficult to locate us in this forest. I don't know if anyone received our Mayday calls; we received no response at all," the pilot commented.

"What else can go wrong with this day?" Allison asked nobody in particular.

"Well, if you must know, we have food and water for about three days; and we have lots of beer and wine," Melodie stated. She then turned to the pilot and asked. "How long will the batteries hold out?"

"Battery power should last at least a week without recharging; we could run the generator if we had fuel, but we don't have any. So, it could get cold in here at night. We have blankets; and if we keep the door closed, it should stay warm. But the air will get pretty stale; this is a pressurized cabin you know."

"Okay, when the rain stops, we can maybe build a fire and the smoke will alert someone and they will come to investigate," the co-pilot said.

"While we wait, I could use a cold beer, Melodie," the pilot requested.

"Make that four, we are alive, dry and lost, but we have beer. What else do we need," Allison said, sat down, and continued talking, "Someone sabotaged my plane to get rid of me. I don't think my father would do that, but who? Does anyone have a signal on their cellphone?"

"That is a question that can't be answered right not, but I will help you find out who and then we can deal with them," the pilot said getting an agreement from everyone as they sipped their cold beer. Everyone checked their cellphone and saw that there was no signal on any service. They must be too deep in the woods and mountains to get a signal.

"No signal, well, when the rain stops, maybe we can climb up one of these mountains and get a signal and maybe get out of here. They will be looking for us, but with this bad weather they will not have much luck; and the trees may be blocking a view from any plane that may fly over us. I would say we are screwed until the weather moves out," the pilot said and then took a long chug of his beer.

"Captain, maybe we should unlock the weapons cabinet, and have everyone get a weapon. There may be bears or mountain lions up here and I would prefer that nobody gets injured any more than what we have already been. We need to survive and get out of here," Allison recommended.

"I agree completely, but as long as we are in here with the door locked, I think we are pretty safe, for now," the pilot agreed. "Here are the keys," he added placing the key to the cabinet on the table.

CIA Facility North Dakota

"Mr. Pierce, we just received this message from Fargo Flight Center, they have lost contact with a business jet and believe it has crashed in the mountains. They are asking for assistance from anyone in the area that can assist in a search. They did receive a Mayday call but lost tracking because of the storm; no emergency locator beacon was activated," the communications sergeant stated as he walked up to the table that Davin, Connie, Bryan, and Mona were sitting at in the mess hall.

"What's the weather like upstairs?" Bryan asked.

"Pretty nasty, heavy rain, low clouds, zero visibility, not good to fly or even be in right now. Predictions are that it is stationary and will be like this for several days. Not much hope of launching any aircraft safely," the sergeant replied, "I got an update just before coming down here. Sir, it is not recommended to launch any type of rescue, according to the National Weather Center. Oh, I forgot to say, the winds are gusting from 60 to 85 miles per hour. Really nasty storm out there, sir."

"Doesn't sound good for any survivors of that downed jet, if they survived the crash that is," Connie commented.

"No, it doesn't, aren't our choppers all weather equipped?" Mona questioned.

"Yes and no, they can fly with the terrain mapping equipment and do a search, but you still have to look out the window for the crash site and with zero visibility that just won't work," Bryan replied, "Not much we can do until the storm lets up and we can launch a rescue mission. Even putting troops on the ground is not a good idea since we don't know where to even start to look, the area around us is all forest and mountains, very few roads, mostly old mining or fire roads which haven't been maintained in years and nothing much else, maybe a few old mining cabins if they haven't fallen down already."

"Sergeant, keep us posted on the weather and any reports from Flight Watch; if the weather breaks, we will go looking but not until," Davin ordered. Davin looked at Bryan and asked, "Is there any way with all the electronic gizmos you have downstairs that we could have tracked that plane before it crashed. Don't you record all the activity in the area for review later?"

"Yes, but not everyone here knows what we can do. Let's go down and look at the tapes, maybe we got them on radar," Bryan answered quietly.

"Can I come too?" Connie asked.

"Sure, bring Davin with you," Bryan said and then stood and started for the door.

An hour later, they had looked at the recordings from the radar and other tracking instruments they had available and discovered a flight from a business jet with the transponder code they were given by Flight Watch only to find the plane did go down in a very heavily forested and mountain area. Landing a plane there safely would be a miracle, and extremely difficult to reach by land or air while the storm continued. They would just have to wait; and the survivors would have to hang on until they were able to reach them. It would likely be days before a rescue party could reach the area in which they may have gone down. The plane was at 3,500 feet above the valley floor and flying in and out of the radar because of the mountains, when radar lost them completely. This would put the possible crash site in about a twenty-five-mile radius from where they dropped off the radar. The mountains in that area reached altitudes of over 9,000 feet. They were lucky to have been able to pick them up as they descended. If they survived the crash, they were on their own.

"It looks like they crossed into Canada and were heading more northwest when the radar lost them," Bryan commented looking at the charts and radar image.

"That could pose a problem. Some of those areas have not been mapped or traveled for years; they could be in a real world of hurt. But the Canadian government will let us do a rescue op, if we show them the track the jet flew and possibly provide assistance when needed," Davin commented. He looked at Connie, "Can you contact your friend up there? Tell them the situation and see if they will assist."

"Sure, I will need a secure line," Connie agreed and then looked for Mona or Bryan to respond.

"Mona, take Connie up to comms and get her set with a secure line," Bryan asked his partner.

"Let's go, this will take a while," Mona said and then she and Connie left the control room.

Oval Office, Washington DC

"Mr. President, this just came in on the virus," Secretary of Defense Harlen Jones said as he walked into the Oval Office. Harlen Jones was the recently appointed Secretary of Defense, six foot two inches tall, a black American, retired Colonel from the Air Force as a fighter pilot and resembled Morgan Freeman in many ways, attitude, looks, the way he spoke. If you put the two together, you might not be able to tell which one was Morgan Freeman.

"What now, Harlen?" the president asked his friend.

"A break in the possible pandemic, seems that a young oriental agent from the CIA had contracted the virus while in China, actually bringing it back with him. He is recovering at Walter Reed and is providing his blood to synthesize an anti-body. But the high point to his recovery is that black coffee is suspected as being the magic drug that helped cure him."

"Black coffee?"

"Yes, black coffee, seems as though the coffee beans have a chemical that literally kills the bad parts of the virus and the patient will get sick but not to the point of dying, just a mild case of the flu which is easily treatable with other drugs," Harlen replied smiling.

"So, no pandemic. Do they drink the coffee or have to take it in some other way?" the president asked.

"Drink it, black and strong. Then they will be monitored and given the necessary drugs to counteract the flu," Harlen stated confidently.

"That is the best news I have heard in a month. Did the troops get settled in up in North Dakota?"

"Yes, and Bryan says thanks; he wasn't sure what was going on until you called. Well, you know how your brother is."

"Yeah, kinda like me in many ways."

Deep in the mountains in Canada

"Captain, since we are stuck here for who knows how long, at least tell me your names, so I don't have to say, 'Hey you' all the time," Allison asked of her pilot.

"Sorry, Ms. Allison, I thought you knew, since your father hired me weeks ago. My mistake. My co-pilot is Jaime Longstreet and I'm Ralph Potter, no relation to Harry," he replied referring to Harry Potter of movie fame. "We have been flying you around for several weeks now, sorry for not introducing ourselves to you."

"Pleasure to finally meet the two of you, who have been under my employ for weeks. I guess I should have stepped into the cockpit to see who was up there. By the way, nice landing. You kept us alive and I appreciate that more than you know," Allison said and then turned to Melodie and thanked her for being alive and with her now.

Looking at her pilot and co-pilot she had to wonder and then asked, "Are you two a couple?" thinking that a beautiful young pilot flying corporate aircraft may have a male friend in the business also.

"Actually no, we are just flight partners, the position came open and I applied just like Ralph did. After hours of interviews and a flight test by Ralph, I was hired. We have only known each other for a few weeks," Jaime replied blushing a little. She stood five foot three, nearly perfect body, not overly endowed but just right, a bit smaller than Allison but well proportioned. Her red hair was pulled back into a ponytail and her bright green eyes indicated that she might have some Irish blood in her.

"Melodie, what about you; do you have a guy waiting for you at some airport?" Allison was full of questions, mostly to pass the time and a little because she just wanted to know about the people she was possibly going to die with.

"Yes, I have a husband and two wonderful children back in Arizona. I just hope I can see them again soon. This accident was not on my dance card, but happy we are still all alive," Melodie replied, and then asked, "We know who your father is, but nothing about you; can you, or will you, tell us about you?"

"Not much to tell, I was born and raised in a private boarding school. My father was president of the United States, as you know, and though he was pronounced dead over 20 years ago, he was not killed as the government thought. He brought me back into his life a couple of years ago and I have been helping him rebuild the businesses he owns. And yes, the rumors you have heard about him being corrupt are not true. He was falsely accused before he fled for his life. There were people in the government that wanted him out and would and did do everything in their power to ensure he was removed from the White House. Anything you have heard recently is not true; he did not kidnap anyone, blow up anything, or commit any crimes. The people behind all that are still in power and are doing all those things making it look like my father is the criminal. He is not the criminal and I am trying to prove that. This accident or sabotage is just another attempt to stop me and my father."

"If what you are saying is true, and I have no reason to not believe you; then we are in deep trouble here. Those that sabotaged this plane, may be on their way here to make sure we did not survive," Ralph commented, then picked up the keys to the weapons locker and walked back to unlock and distribute weapons and ammo. "Melodie, do you know how to use a gun?"

"Yes, grew up in the country and am a damn good shot," Melodie commented as she took a Barretta 92F semi-auto pistol and an M-4 from Ralph. "Do you have a choice of weapons, Allison?"

"I have my two pistols already; just give me an M-4 also. I like those, lots of bullets and easy to reload," Allison commented quickly. "I think we need to post a guard and not everyone sleep at one time. I will take first watch. Ralph, maybe you take second with Jaime and then Melodie. We have foul weather gear in the back to keep dry."

"I suggest positioning ourselves on top of the fuselage, for a better view of the area; won't be able to see far with all the trees, but I will take some items out and set up some noise traps to alert us if anyone is coming."

"Wow, what a group, three women and a man to defend ourselves. Do you think we stand a chance?" Melodie commented.

"Yes, better chance than most; we have weapons and know how to use them. We also may want to leave the plane when the rain stops and move to higher country. Better view and they may know where we crashed and are heading here right now," Jaime added to the mix.

"You're right Jaime, lets pack up some supplies and get out of here," Ralph agreed.

"But not leaving the crash site may also be our only salvation; if the good guys come looking, they will expect us to be here, not on top of some mountain," Melodie said not agreeing with Jaime.

"Hell of a situation. Let's hold out here; at least we have supplies, cover and hopefully the good guys will find us first," Allison said and then finished off her second beer.

"Davin, the rain is letting up and we have three of the choppers fueled and ready to go. Do you want to ride along?" Bryan asked as he entered Davin's temporary office.

"Sure, let me gather my gear and be right with you. Oh, did you hear about the pandemic scare," Davin replied.

"No, what's going on with that?"

"Not much, according to your brother; they have found a cure already and it is readily available around the world. Can you believe it, coffee, strong black coffee kills the nasty part of the virus and most patients only get a mild case of the flu, which is easily cured with a couple vaccines that have been around for years," Davin reported, and then added, "I'll be ready in a few minutes; meet you at the hanger."

"We will wait for you, but don't be too long; those people need help and we are the closest to them. I have already cleared crossing into Canadian air space, and we will be joined by a couple Canadian Search and Rescue teams. We may need them, that is a big uncharted area with lots of trees and mountains," Bryan commented as he turned to leave the office.

Twenty minutes later, all three Blackhawk helicopters were heading northwest toward the last known position of the downed business jet. As they approached the Canadian border, the pilot of the lead Blackhawk received a call on guard frequency that the two Search and Rescue helos were on station and already establishing a search pattern and for Davin's three to take the western three sectors.

"Seeker Two and Three this is One," the pilot of Seeker One called the other two Blackhawks.

"Two here."

"Three here, what's the plan?"

"We are entering the search area, Two and Three go to your areas and stay in contact. Report any possible sightings," Seeker One ordered and then switched to the inter-aircraft communications. "Gentlemen and ladies, we are in the search area; look out the window and let's pray we see something to lead us to the crash site. I'm going to run the grid now," the pilot stated. He then started his run between the mountains, turned on his ground radar and a piece of gear that is not normally on a military helicopter, known as a metal detector to most people, except this one could detect metal from an altitude of 500 feet. Flying his Blackhawk at three hundred feet above the terrain was risky, but it would give them the best chance of locating the crash site. Of course, it might also pick up anything that was metal which could slow down the search investigating each piece of metal they detected. But that was the chance they must take.

Four hours into the flight they had discovered six burned out cars, two trucks, and four downed aircraft. All of which had been there for a long time; and except for two of the aircraft there were no bodies. Unfortunately, two of the crashed aircraft had the remains of the pilot in one and four bodies in the other. Their positions were recorded, and they would report them to the Canadian Search and Rescue for recovery of the bodies. One of the cars also had a body, but it wasn't human; the remains of an Elk were stuck in the windshield. The driver must have survived and walked out of the forest after the crash, which was near the only road through the area; the car was resting fifteen feet from the road.

"This is going to take a while, with all the junk down there. Any reports from the other searchers?" Davin asked the pilot.

"No, sir. A few possible but nothing yet," the pilot replied. "Stand-by we have another helo in the area that is not part of our search, attempting to contact them now," the pilot said and then switched to a frequency that the other aircraft should have been listening to. "Unidentified aircraft this is Army Search and Rescue Seeker One, do you copy?"

No reply from the unidentified helicopter. The pilot called several more times without getting a response; switched to intercom again and told his passengers that he was breaking off the search to investigate the unknown aircraft.

Minutes later, Seeker One pulled up and over a mountain peak at 800 feet above the ground and saw the unidentified aircraft at about 300 feet above the ground and hovering.

"What the hell?" the pilot said to himself, "What do you think?" he asked his co-pilot.

"I think we found our crash site and they got here first. What do you want to do?"

"They haven't seen us yet; let's just slide up beside them and get their attention," the pilot said. He informed his passengers of what he was seeing and stopped moving forward when the other helicopter turned. The side door opened, and a large machine gun slid out and opened fire on the ground.

"What the hell?" the pilot yelled, "Open the side door and slide out the M-60. They are firing on something on the ground, possibly our crashed plane. Eight heavily armed commandos were fast roping to the ground. We have to stop them!" he yelled to his passengers and dove his Blackhawk toward the attacking old Huey, UH-1 helicopter.

"We don't have an M-60, this bird is unarmed," Davin yelled back.

"They don't know that."

"What do we have?" Bryan asked.

"Just our handguns and a flare gun," Davin replied as he looked around the cabin for anything to defend themselves with other than handguns.

"They are pulling away. Their troops are on the ground." After pausing, he continued, "I'm going to hover near there; you guys get out. Use the bucket and wench."

Seconds before he got low enough to let them out, bullets from the mystery Huey slammed into the Blackhawk. The pilot turned abruptly to the right to avoid the rapid fire from the old Huey helicopter. He knew he could outrun the Huey but could not outrun the bullets streaming up at them.

"Mayday! Mayday! We are taking fire and are evading as best we can. Mayday!" the co-pilot yelled into his microphone. Seeker Two had weapons and immediately turned toward the mayday call, receiving coordinates via the radar.

"We're going down, hang on!" the pilot screamed to his passengers. "Losing oil pressure in number one; number two just quit. HANG ON!"

The four in the back immediately tightened their harnesses and looked out the window at the thick forest below them. The crash would come quickly since they were only 800 feet above the terrain.

The Huey turned and were heading straight for them, they had no defense except to crash and to hopefully survive the impact through the trees.

On the ground, the passengers of the downed business jet took up defensive positions around their aircraft and opened fire on the attacking commandos. Knowing they were out gunned and outnumbered they fired relentlessly killing three of the attackers instantly. The commandos seeing their prey was armed and returning fire, took cover and radioed their ride to open fire on the crash site again, not knowing they had left to fight off an attacking Blackhawk.

Seeker One crashed through the trees, breaking off treetops and rotor blades, rolling over several times before the sudden stop on the forest floor. More bullets struck the Blackhawk as each team member unstrapped and rolled out of the broken fuselage. The pilot reached over to his co-pilot only to find him dead from multiple bullet wounds. Blood ran down his face and into his eyes and nearly blinded him; but he was able to unstrap and get out of the chopper along with his four passengers. As they ran away from the Blackhawk, they looked for cover from the machine gun firing on them. Luckily the forest was thick and provided them with cover. After reaching about fifty yards from the Blackhawk, they stopped and assessed their situation. Davin helped Connie, and Bryan almost carried Mona to safety. They were safely hidden from view from above where they stopped to rest and assess their wounds.

"The biz jet is about three hundred yards that way; there must be survivors based on the amount of gun fire coming from there," Davin commented. Davin looked at

Connie who was holding her arm tightly and asked, "Are you okay?"

"No, I think my arm is broken. You're bleeding," Connie replied.

"I'm okay just a scratch."

"No, it's not, let me look at it," Bryan said as he looked at Mona leaning against a tree. She did not look good, blood covered over half her body. Bryan started to check Davin but stopped to check on Mona. "Not good, you need medical attention; you have, well, Captain, do you have contact with Seekers Two and Three?"

"Stand by," the captain responded and pulled his emergency radio out of its pocket on this flight vest. "Seeker Two and Three, do you copy?"

"Seeker Two, kind of busy right now. Be right with you," Seeker Two responded as he was in pursuit of the Huey. "I have a rogue Huey shooting up the forest and about to teach him a lesson. Seeker Three is on his way and will pick you up."

"We are about fifty yards south of Seeker One. We have injured and one dead," the captain reported.

"They are on the way, Seeker Two is armed and chasing down the Huey."

"Davin, your wound is not serious yet, but you need medical soon too. Captain, we need to get over to the biz jet and help if we can. Let's go! Davin you stay with the ladies in case they circle around."

"Okay, I'm not going to be much good in a firefight anyway. Go!" Davin ordered. "Be careful."

Bryan and the captain took off toward the firefight that was raging several hundred yards away; the trees gave them protection from any stray bullets and cover as they got closer.

"How many mags do you have Bryan?" the captain asked.

"Two extras, one in the pistol, 15 rounds each," Bryan replied quietly.

"Good, between us we have almost 90 shots, make each one count, we may have only one shot before they come down on us."

"This isn't my first rodeo, cap," Bryan replied becoming a bit annoyed with the good captain. "Guess you don't know me very well, US Army Ranger, 82nd Airborne, retired Lt. Colonel."

"Sorry, didn't know. I don't read the files on everyone. Okay then you call the shots, I'm only a lowly captain," the pilot apologized.

"No problem my good captain, you had no idea as to my experience; you lead, I know how to follow orders."

"If you insist; why don't we circle around behind the bad guys and see if we can make a difference in this little shoot out?"

"I think that is a great idea, lock and load," Bryan replied as they slowly moved closer to the commandos. "Look they are hunkered down behind those downed trees and whoever is at the crash site is doing a great job of holding down the fort. Let's wake up the bad guys."

"You stay here. I'll move about 20 feet to the left, and we can get them in a crossfire. Head shots if you can, they look like they have body armor on and no helmets. Pretty dumb move if you ask me."

"Okay, move out, Cap," Bryan agreed.

Three minutes later, the captain took his first shot, taking down one of the commandos. Bryan also fired and another commando fell dead. That was the only shots they were able to get off; they did not know there were two commandos further back and they had opened fire on Bryan and the captain immediately. The captain was hit in the shoulder before he was able to dive for cover. Bryan also took a shot in the leg, but was able to return fire from his position, wounding another commando. Within minutes, the shooting stopped when the captain and Bryan were surrounded and captured by the remaining commandos. The survivors of the biz jet crash were running low on ammunition and had taken several serious hits. Allison's pilot was wounded but alive. Within minutes, they were also surrounded and had to surrender or die. They were hoping they were not going to be executed but had little choice, with ammunition almost gone and little chance of survival in an extended firefight.

"It's gotten pretty quiet over there; I hope the guys are doing okay," Connie commented.

"Doesn't sound good; you girls stay here. I'll go check," Davin said as he stood and then leaned on a tree.

"I'm in better shape than you Davin, I'll go," Connie said seeing her husband in great pain and bleeding again.

"You're not in too good of shape yourself, and Mona is unconscious. I'll go."

"None of you will go anywhere. Please sit-down Mr. Pierce," a voice ordered as a man appeared holding an M-4 pointed at them.

"Okay, you won't get an argument out of me," Davin said and sat, placing his Colt 45 pistol on the ground in front of him, as he watched another man step out from behind a tree. "What took you so long, we have injured.

"We had to find a safe place to land, our Blackhawk is not equipped with a rescue bucket," the first soldier said. "We are parked about a half mile away; some of the boys went to the biz jet. Don't know what is going on over there, but it should be cleared up shortly. As for the Huey, it got away. The guys they dropped off are either going to die or surrender shortly," the soldier reported. "Stand by, I need to check in with Seeker Three."

"Seeker Three this is Two, do you copy?" the soldier spoke into his handy talkie.

"Loud and clear, Two, what's your status?" the response came a second later.

"Several injured, need medivac, bad guys are all down. Repeat, area is clear of bad guys. Come on in and pick up the injured; we will recon the area for other survivors. Landing site two clicks to the north; you will see Seeker Three on the ground there, large enough for you to land. Over."

"Roger Two, be there as quickly as possible, out," Three responded.

"Mr. Pierce, as you just heard medivac is inbound. Two of my men will stay with you; the rest of us need to check and secure the area, be back shortly," the sergeant stated. He and three of his men followed heading toward the downed business jet. They checked the bodies of the bad guys as they passed them.

The firefight did not last long, and all but two of the commandos were killed. Those two were transported back to North Dakota along with the passengers and crew of the crashed biz jet.

"You're Allison Graves, aren't you?" Bryan asked the young lady sitting across from him in the Blackhawk as they flew back to North Dakota.

"Yes, but you knew that before you came looking for us. What are you going to do with us?" Allison replied as she sat there holding her damaged right arm.

"First, we are going to get you and your crew some needed medical help; then once you are cleaned up and in some fresh clothes, we will sit down for a long talk. I hope by then you will be in a talkative mood. Mr. Pierce and I have a lot of questions and want some truthful answers. Is that okay with you, Ms. Graves?" Bryan stated and then turned to Davin who was laying on a cot strapped in. He was not doing well, but nobody was in great shape.

Bryan was shot in the shoulder, Davin took two hits to his right side, Connie broke her leg during the crash, and Mona had multiple cuts and bruises along with a broken shoulder. As for the crew of Allison's jet, Allison had a broken arm along with multiple cuts and bruises, Melodie faired the best with only cuts and bruises, Jaime was shot in the leg, missed the artery, and her pilot Ralph had two gunshot wounds to his left arm and shoulder. The commandos did not fare as well when the team from Seeker Three caught up to them; all but two were killed. Their bodies would be recovered by the Canadian Search and Rescue team. The Canadian crash investigation team was on their way to the crash site to determine why Allison's jet crashed, but if Ralph was correct, the plane was sabotaged and a tracking device would be found when the investigation team arrived. That is the only way the commando's Huey could have found them so fast. The doctor on Seeker Two along with his medics patched up everyone as quickly as possible so they could be transported back to North Dakota.

The Canadian government was not very happy that there had been a firefight in their forest but were pleased it was contained quickly. The mystery Huey disappeared and was found abandoned in a small isolated airfield in Montana. The Huey had been reported stolen from an airport in Idaho.

Back in North Dakota

"Amber, you may want to go to the hanger, the Blackhawks are about fifteen minutes out and you mom and dad are injured," the communications sergeant told her when he approached in the mess hall.

"Hurt, how?"

"I don't have the details, but the doctor radioed to ask for the medical team to be in the hanger and some guards to stand by. That's all I know," he replied and stepped back as Amber stood and ran from the mess hall. Watching her run, stirred feelings in him and he knew that she was way out of his league, but it didn't hurt to dream.

Within minutes, Amber was running down the hall toward the elevator which she needed to take up to the second level which had the long hall connecting the main facility with the hangers. Not stopping for anything, she ran as fast as she could, slipped on the polished floor, and fell but recovered quickly. After she reached the elevator, she rode it up and then ran down the hall toward the hanger.

Amber arrived at the hanger just as the first Blackhawk was landing. A team of medical personnel and corpsman were standing by to get the injured out of the helicopters and into the medical bay as quickly as possible. Standing behind the medical team, Amber waited until the Blackhawk touched down and then she bolted toward the Blackhawk. The door slid open and what she saw was horrible. There was blood everywhere in the helo; her mom and dad were sitting stiffly in the back. When Davin saw Amber, he raised his hand to stop her approach. He wanted the severely injured removed first; he and Connie were hurt, but not life threatening. The medics grabbed the stretchers and immediately placed them on the gurney, rolling them quickly away from the spinning rotor blades so the doctors could perform a quick exam of each injured passenger.

Davin, Connie, and Bryan slowly climbed out of the helo; Mona was on one of the stretchers.

"Dad, Mom are you okay?" Amber questioned as she saw her parents wrapped in multiple bandages.

"We're fine. Just a few nicks and scrapes. Bryan go check on Mona, we can handle this," Connie said seeing that Bryan wanted to help his friends.

"Right," Bryan said and then hurried over to his partner. He was stopped by a medic and ordered to sit. The medic saw that Bryan's wounds were bleeding and he was leaving a trail of blood as he walked toward Mona.

"You need to stop right now, sir. Ms. Mona will be fine; she is in good hands. You are bleeding all over the runway and at the rate it is coming out, you will pass out in about four more steps," the medic stated.

Bryan was becoming very dizzy and looked at the medic with concern in his eyes; he then passed out, collapsing on the runway.

"I need a hand over here," the medic yelled to anyone within ear shout. Seconds later, two soldiers arrived and helped lift Bryan onto a gurney. "Thanks guys, will you help push him to the elevator; we need to get him to the med bay ASAP."

Davin tried to stand and help, but he was too weak to assist and was helped back down to the gurney he had sat on waiting for the doctor to come check on him and Connie.

"Captain, when the other helo lands there is a Ms. Allison Graves on board along with her pilots and cabin assistant. Please get them to medical; have guards with them the entire time; and when released from medical, bring all of them to the mess hall. I will be there, I hope. if not, just stay with them until I catch up. I need to talk to them; and remember, guard them the entire time. Do not let them out of your sight. Also, send someone to get Ms. Sally and our guest from the lock up; bring all of them to the mess hall and keep a guard on all of them. Oh, yeah, Sally may have a weapon, she relieved from one of her guards. Please take it back and secure it. I was told it wasn't loaded by the guard who lost it."

"Got it, sir," the captain replied and then hurried off to do as he was asked.

"Doc, I can get to med by myself; can we get a wheelchair for Connie. Her leg is bleeding, and she is having

329

trouble walking?" Davin asked the doctor that was examining him.

"Got two coming over right now. One for each of you," the doctor replied and then helped Davin and Connie into their new rides.

Two hours later, Davin, Connie, and Bryan were sitting in the corner of the mess hall chatting about the events of the day.

"Here are our guests, now," Bryan commented. "Bring them over here Captain."

"Ms. Graves, please have a seat. We need to talk about a great many things, but first, captain where are our other guests?" Davin asked the captain.

"On their way, wanted to ensure these four were comfortable first," the captain replied. "Should be here in a few minutes. Do you want them here with these four or should I keep them over on the other side for a bit?"

"Get them some food and drink and have them sit over on the other side of the hall until we call for them, Thanks Captain," Davin replied pointing to the empty tables on the other side of the mess hall.

"Let me introduce us. I'm Davin Pierce, this is my wife Connie, the manager of this facility is Bryan, along with his partner Mona, who is down in the med bay right now. Okay, now who are you four?"

"I'm Allison Graves; you know my father Ted. This is Ralph Potter, my pilot, Jaime Longstreet, co-pilot, and Melodie my flight stewardess. We were heading to Fargo and were detoured because of weather, and then, well Ralph can explain what happened. Please, Ralph," Allison said to introduce everyone and turn the conversation over to Ralph.

"Mr. Pierce, the weather as you know was unexpected and very severe. We had to fly due north to avoid it; and once we were vectored into Canada and were talking to the Canadian flight following, we lost an engine. Within seconds, the second one flamed out. We tried everything to restart. The instruments showed we had fuel, but I believe, and NTSB up in Canada will back me up when they finish their investigation, that the gauges were tampered with and we did not have any fuel. We were sabotaged and we were not supposed to survive. Lucky for us we did, and luckily, your team found us. Those men were there to make sure we were dead, and we thank you for your assistance."

"Allison, do you have any idea who might want you dead?" Bryan asked.

"Let me tell you a little more, something you may only have an idea about, but are wrong on many counts," Allison stated and then looked across the room at Sally and Heather being brought into the mess hall. "Be careful of those two; they don't work for me or my dad. They only think they do."

"I don't understand what you are getting at, please explain," Davin asked.

"Mom, I do have a question that you never answered," Amber said looking at her mother sitting quietly across from her.

"What is it, Amber? Oh, wait, I know what you are going to ask; come with me for a moment and I will tell you all you need to know." Connie said, stood up and started for the door.

"Okay, I still don't understand, but I'll follow," Amber said as she followed her mother out the door and down the hall. Once they reached the elevator, Connie pressed the button for down and waited in silence.

"What's the big mystery, mom?" Amber questioned.

"Hang on, you will see in a few minutes." Connie said as she entered the elevator and pressed four.

Upon reaching level four, they exited and walked to room 409. After they entered and Connie closed the door behind Amber, Connie indicated to Amber that she should sit down.

"You can come out now," Connie said quietly while facing the back of the room. They both watched as Josh Randal, her brother walked into the room.

"Hi, mom. You finally told her. Hi, sis," Josh commented and then hugged his sister.

"Only your father, Josh, me, and now you, know of this. As you can see, he wasn't killed. Some of the stuff in the safe were the documents that indicated he was not killed and that he was working under cover for the company. The Colonel probably knows now, because he broke into the safe and found the birth records for Monica and the documents about Josh. So, Josh can come out of hiding. For the past several months, he has been working under cover with Josh senior."

"But why the deception; I'm your daughter. Don't you trust me?"

"We trust you, but we had to make it look real. You are a good actor, but to be sure we had to keep you in the dark, sorry, honey. It had to be that way." Connie said and started to cry.

"But mom, how did you do it?"

"Trust me, it wasn't easy; but that is why you haven't seen me much over the past few months, I have been Josh's contact and had to stay out of everything to maintain my cover too."

"Why popcorn?"

"Because it is explosive, and I couldn't think of anything else to tell you at the time," Connie said with a little laugh.

"I don't know everything but will tell you what I have discovered. My father is not who you think he is. Four days ago, I went to talk to my father and noticed something was not quite right with him. He had been in a wheelchair for several years now and suddenly I caught him walking around his office. He tried to explain to me that the doctors told him he needed to walk some every day to keep the circulation in his legs moving. I didn't question him further on that, but there were some other minor things that did not set right with me. I believe the man in my fathers' office was an imposture, using that damn holographic machine to disguise himself. I used one to disguise myself as one of the top men that worked for us as security and being him, I was ordered to hunt down and kill an Admiral Hancock. The person I posed as is locked in a closet back at the estate, he is not injured just sleeping off a pile of sleeping pills. Is this making any sense?"

"Yes, continue," Bryan said for the group.

"Well, I got a call from one of my trusted security men and he told me that the FBI stormed the estate and confronted my father, but my father was on his plane heading to Washington to meet with Josh Randel. It is all confusing, but he can't be in two places at once, even using a holographic device, can he?"

"Technically, yes he can," Davin added.

"Okay, say he was on his plane flying to Washington when the FBI stormed the estate. Could he have been there as a holograph talking to the FBI?"

"Yes, it is possible, not likely but possible," Bryan confirmed.

"I am Allison Graves; daughter of past President Ted Graves and I have not committed any crimes. Someone looking like me and acting like me has been committing all the crimes you have me down for. And my father, since his recovery from being blown up, has turned his life around and not the criminal you say he is. Someone is using the holo device to impersonate him and me to commit those crimes. I can't prove it, but you must believe me, we are innocent. And those two over there, Sally and Heather have been duped also; they think they are working for my father and me, but they are really taking orders from the impostor."

"I'll be right back," Davin excused himself without explanation.

"Mr. Pierce you have to believe me, we are innocent," Allison pleaded.

Everyone sat quietly waiting for Davin to return which he did ten minutes later, smiling. "Your father is sitting in Josh Randal's office right now and he is not using any holographic device. He is in his wheelchair and Josh says he is there on his own free will. So, if you are here and he is there, and we also just got a report that your father was seen boarding a plane in New York about an hour ago, that confirms part of your story. Does Sally and Heather know they have been duped?"

"I really don't know. These people are very good and have been playing us and you for months," Allison replied.

"One other very important question," pausing for a second, Davin asked. "Where is Monica Teach? And is she anyway involved in this deception?"

"Monica is also very innocent and has been safely housed in a woman's prison in Arizona. We found out she was being transported to Arizona to be held there by the fake Allison or rather The Colonel posing as me, so we intercepted her people and replaced them with ours, took her from them and put her in a very safe place. She agreed to it because we could not keep her safe without a lot of guards, so the prison was the best choice. The warden is a family member and has been taking good care of her. Just so you understand she came to my father asking for protection. She said she didn't trust the FBI or government in general, too many people turn up dead. I will give you the location, but you probably already know where the woman's prison is. But you will need to know how to get her out; my aunt will protect her with her own life if necessary."

"Okay, then, we will have her picked up and brought here," Bryan stated. He then turned back to Davin and said. "Do you believe all this?"

"In a strange way, I do. It is starting to make sense," Davin replied prior to asking Allison to give him the information he needed to get Monica safely away from Arizona. Once she gave him that, he got up and left the mess hall again, to make a secure call to the Phoenix Office of the FBI to speak with a personal friend of his there.

"Good afternoon, Jake. How is the oven down there?" Davin asked his old friend about the 118-degree weather that Phoenix was having today.

"Just peachy, Davin, what prompted this call. You know I'm on coffee break," Jake joked.

"I have a little mission for you; have you got your GO bag packed?" Davin stated and then filled Jake in on the details and asked if he could get right on the pickup and delivery of one Monica Teach to North Dakota. Davin said he would send the company jet down to pick her up.

"All set, Jake Larsen will handle everything in Arizona," Davin reported when he returned to the mess hall. "Is it time to inform our other guests of what is going down. Or do you think we need to do some more research?" Davin asked Bryan.

"Research of course. I'll be right back," Bryan said, got up and walked over to the closest refrigerator and retrieved six beers. He then signaled one of the guards over with Sally and Heather to come get some for himself and the two women. "Bring them over to our table once you get them some drinks. Oh, get yourself one too, but don't leave the room, keep an eye on them. And only one beer each."

"Research," Davin repeated taking a beer from Bryan as he passed them around.

"Now, Ralph Potter, you are their corporate pilot; have you noticed anything strange about Mr. Graves or his daughter? Melodie and Jaime, you can add anything also if you would be so kind," Davin added.

Potter told of a few strange things that confirmed what Allison was saying about having an imposture. He said there were times he would be talking with Ted Graves and then twenty minutes later Graves would ask the exact same question of him. Almost like Graves was losing his mind and could not remember things happening around him or there were two different people. Potter didn't think much of it at first, but then now that he was in on Allison's story it was making sense that there was an imposture of Ted Graves.

"Wow, this is getting deeper by the minute. Okay, say we believe everything you have told us; your father, you and Monica are innocent of all crimes and even our two new guests here, Sally and Heather have been duped into believing they are working for you and your father. What do we do with them? Although they were following orders, they may have killed someone."

"I think Ms. Sally and Heather need to stay locked up, even though they were following orders from the impostures; they did commit crimes and need to be punished," Davin stated. He then looked at the head guard and said, "Take them down to the lock up, after they finish their drinks; and lock them up for now. We will figure out what to do with them later."

"Yes sir," the sergeant answered, finished his coke, looked at his partner and cocked his head toward the door indicating it was time to go. They left with their prisoner moments later. Heather tried to protest but didn't get much sympathy from anyone as they were escorted out of the mess hall.

"Now as for you four. We will give you a place to sleep; you have free roaming privileges on this floor only. Any attempt to leave this floor without an escort will cause you to be locked up in our secure jail down below. I will tell you that you are on the fourth floor of this facility and you need a pass key to exit through the stairs or elevators. So, as I said, stay on this floor, come to the mess hall, movie room or any room on this floor. We are not putting guards on you for now. Is that understood?" Bryan ordered. "Now come with me and I will assign quarters to you; each room has a closet with clothes. Some may fit; there is a variety of outfits. Feel free to change into anything that you feel comfortable in. Dinner is usually served at five, and I believe we are having steak tonight, or you have a choice of other entrees. Just ask our chef, she will fix most anything for you. Now come along."

After Allison and her pilots left, Melodie stayed to talk with Davin and Bryan.

"Okay Melodie, what have you got for us?" Davin asked his deep cover agent, "You have been deep for too long; are you still with us?"

"Davin, dear, you know damn well I am still a company girl and always will be," Melodie answered and then paused to take a sip of her coke. "Everything Allison told you is true; there is another Allison out there and the best I can guess is she is an android, but not like Andi and Ivy. She has been programed to kill. She has a male human posing as Ted Graves, and he has a holographic device to complete the show. From what I could find out she goes by the name of The Colonel and nobody knows what she really looks like on our side anyway. Maybe some of her people do, but every time anyone outside her organization saw her, she was Allison Graves, or some unknown person and we could not track her. She is very good at hiding her identity and that of her Ted Graves. So, to help with this mystery, I am at a loss and can't provide any more than the story Allison told you. It is true to the best of my knowledge."

"Damn, we are no further along than we were a year ago," Bryan commented.

"Did I hear correctly that we bombed Iran?" Melodie asked.

"Yes, somehow the fake Ted ordered our fleet in the Med to drop two nuclear weapons on Iran and pretty much ended hostilities with them. Mostly because there isn't any government left and their nuclear program is just a pile of radioactive sand," Davin replied.

"So, what is our government doing?"

"We, like we have done to so many countries, are sending aid and relief to Iran, there will be no war, just a rebirth of a nation. Hopefully one that is not hostile and will work to make themselves better without starting a war," Davin commented. He then looked at Bryan and added, "Do you have anything you want to add? This lady needs to get cleaned up and rested."

"Nothing at the moment, but is it possible that Rocky Soto or his techs built this new android and programed it to come after you and Randal?" Bryan asked.

"Very possible and we do have a list of possible bad guys that could be working with this android," Davin said looking very worried. "Here is the list of ones we know that are still out there," he said as he handed Bryan the list.

"Sonja, last name unknown, Max the mouse, also no last name, Greg Conway, Richard Clark, Ward Phillips and one that is not on this list, is Horatio Soto. He is supposed to be under Witness Protection, but my source says he has been missing for several months and they cannot locate him. He may be a suspect too, or just dead."

"Dad," Amber interrupted as she walked up.

"Yes, Amber."

"I can contact Val in Hawaii and see if she has any leads on the break in at the house there and maybe link those to what we know," Amber said referring to Lt. Valerie Lake of Hawaii Five O.

"Good idea, make it so, number one," Davin said and then added, "I have always wanted to say that."

"Dad, grow up," Amber said and then walked over to order some dinner.

"Is it dinner time already? Melodie, get some rest, we can talk again later," Davin commented and looked at his daughter walking over to the window to order dinner. "Guess it is time to eat, what do you think, Bryan?"

"Works for me, can't do much else right now. Pandemic, and storms, and bad guys all over, what else can we do?" Bryan agreed and then stood just as Chilly his German Shephard came in followed by Mona his partner.

"Just so you know guys, Monica Teach is on the company jet heading this way. She should be here in a couple of hours," Mona stated and then followed the guys to order dinner and drinks. "Ivy and Andi will be right up too; they are down in the gym beating each other up again."

"I guess we can solve those problems on another day. Today is done," Bryan stated.

"Yeah, we still have a couple of pretty nasty bad guys out there and no idea who or where they are. But we do have an inside man and will know soon. Until then, time for food." Davin commented and followed everyone over to order dinner. "Has anyone seen Connie and Amber?"

"Here they are, what's up Connie?" Mona said as she saw Connie, Amber and a young blonde man following. "By the way, Sally and Heather have confessed to their connection to The Colonel and will be picked up by real US Marshalls in a few days; we have to transport them to Fargo for the transfer. Exactly what they will be charged with is still undetermined, but they will face some jail time."

"Sounds like a plan." Bryan acknowledged.

Davin smiled when he saw the three of them together knowing now that his only daughter had been brought up to date on the entire operation. "Let's eat."

"Hey, it's a good day when we all make it through and are still alive. We survived another day." Bryan commented while smiling. He then ordered a Rib Eye steak medium rare.

This is not the end.
It's just the beginning of the story about Amber Pierce and her half-sister Monica Teach.
The following is an excerpt from Sisters, Book 11 in the continuing saga of the Pierce family.

Sisters

It had been three months since they left the safety of the North Dakota facility and now it was time get back to work. Things had quieted down somewhat after the attempt on Allison's life and the return of Monica to her place in the Pierce family.

Amber's brother Josh was now off on his undercover work and she would not see him again for a while, but she knew he was reasonably safe as he posed as a drug dealer in Thailand while he tried to uncover The Colonel's connection to the drug Sexiticy. Her duties were to help with Monica and Allison to discover who The Colonel was and to stop him or her at all costs.

The sun had not been shining for days, rain and foul weather was on the forecast for the next two weeks. It was typical Florida weather for November. Standing in the rain at the side of the grave of her long dead parents was Monica Teach. She was looking down at the parents she had only known up until she turned sixteen when they were both killed in an accident. Her father was not in that grave, it was the man that stole her from her mother at the hospital where she was born. She forgave them of the theft, because they gave her a good life and treated her very well, not to mention they left her extremely rich. When she found out that her real father was a direct descendant to Blackbeard the pirate, she, at first, was ashamed of her heritage, but then realized it was something she could not change but her name was. Getting it legally changed to Monica Teach was a bit of a hassle, but worth it. But that proved to be a problem. Someone, or something as it were, decided to kidnap her and use her name in a trip down the criminal mile. She was to be blamed for the death and destruction of many crimes and there was no way she could stop it without the help from her sister and her family, Amber Pierce.

Amber stood beside Monica and listened to her story and felt very sorry for everything that Monica had been put through. She was safe now, at least mostly safe. With the help of her father, Davin Pierce, and Josh Randal, both CIA, and a little push from her biological mother, Connie from the FBI, the charges were dropped and removed from Monica's record.

Allison Graves, the daughter of past President presumed dead Ted Graves, help in getting things cleared up with Monica and got records and charges dropped for her and her father, Ted.

All seemed to be going in the right direction; there was only one major problem left to solve. Who was behind all the deception and crimes that Monica, Allison and Ted were being charged with? Those people were still out there and as of today the CIA, FBI, and local police had no idea who they were. The use of the newly invented personal holographic generator had proven to be a nightmare.

"Monica, you are home now, and we will find out who is behind all this." Amber stated as they stood there.

"I know, Amber, but it is so unsettling to me. I grew up believing these two people were my parents and when I found out who our mother was and you were my sister I was relived, but also very scared that the person posing as me would really kill you and our mother. I didn't want that to happen. I want to find this person and with your help and Allison's, we will stop them, kill them if need be." Monica stated then turned and started to walk back to the car.

"Time to go, Allison." Amber said to the young woman standing next to her.

"Yeah, right, let's go. I need to call my dad; he may be able to help locate these imposters." Allison said and then followed Amber up to the waiting car.

An hour later, the three ladies were sitting in Amber's hotel room waiting for Davin and Connie to arrive. The thought that was going through each one's mind was how were they going to beat someone that has been two steps ahead of them for the past couple of years. Was there a mole in the company or FBI; were they just smarter than she was? There had to be a way to find them.

Stay with our three ladies to discover the truth and how they break into the deception.

Characters

Amber Pierce – daughter of Davin and Connie Pierce, CIA

Davin Pierce – Assistant Director CIA, Covert Operations

Connie Pierce – Assistant Director FBI Washington DC office

Josh Pierce – Twin brother of Amber Pierce

Josh Randel – Director CIA

Stephanie Randel – Agent CIA

Monica Teach – Great Grand daughter to Blackbeard the Pirate

Hannah Brickman - Terrorist

Seth Conners, Station Chief London

Julie Thompson, CIA agent

Reginald Knight, chief inspector from MI-6

Howard Smythe, Scotland Yard, Homicide Section

Horace Blackstone, Inspector Scotland Yard, Counterintelligence Section

James Wittman, MI-6 agent

Major Brent Miller – helicopter pilot in Vietnam

Henry White – CIA Agent

Diane Bear – CIA Agent

Doctor William Hun – Emergency room doctor Da Nang

Todd Black - CIA Agent Vietnam office

Ginger Burns - CIA Agent Vietnam office

Donald Vickers - US Marshall

Jake Miller - US Marshall

Michelle Brooks - passenger

Heather Newton - US Marshall

Sally Howard - Ex-call girl and model

Allison Graves - daughter to past President Ted Graves

Ted Graves - ex president

Admiral John Fitzgerald Hancock – Director at Department of Defense

Robert Sanchez - bad guy, assassin

Phillip Wilson – NSA Director

Shan Winho – NSA Agent from China

Melodie – Flight Stewardess Allison's airplane

Sophia – Pilot and maid at Graves Estate

Tony Sanford - President of the United States

Jaime Longstreet – co-pilot on Allison's plane

Ralph Potter – pilot on Allison's plane

The Colonel – Terrorist Leader

Betty Young – Connie's mother

Lt. Colonel Hal Moore – 1st Battalion 7th Air Cavalry

Marvin Grossman – CIA Agent

Cecil Hunt – CIA Agent

Bryan Forest – North Dakota CIA Facility Manager/Agent

Mona Vale – Assistant ND CIA Facility Manager/Agent

Miquel Sanchez – Drug Dealer, Gun Runner, Human Trafficker

Admiral "Bear" Henderson – retired

Mary Henderson – Josh Randel's secretary and daughter to Admiral Henderson

David Henderson – Lt Commander of Nuclear Submarine

James Wittman – MI-6 agent

Clyde Hines – CIA Agent

Barbara Hines – CIA Agent

Major Brent Miller – Huey pilot in Vietnam

Rhonda – Miller's co-pilot

Valerie Lake – Hawaii Five-O Police Lieutenant

Ivan – co-pilot on Graves Gulfstream business jet

Louise – Stewardess/CIA Agent on CIA business jet

Malcom Drumming – Senior FBI Agent

Pamela Grayson – FBI Agent

Natalie Graves – Warden at Federal Woman's Prison Arizona

Carlos – works for Ted Graves

Simon Rafferty – CIA Team Chief Virginia Office

Cynthia Flower – Section Chief CIA Denver Office

Phillip Gentry – CIA Agent Denver

Heidi Cruz – CIA Agent Denver

Monty Jorgenson – CIA Agent Denver

Dan Weston – Detective Denver Police

Megan – CIA Agent Denver

Kathy - CIA Agent Denver

Lenora Henderson – Secret Service Agent

Jules – Chef at North Dakota facility

Jerry – Airport Executive Lounge attendant, New Orleans

Harlen Jones – Secretary of Defense

Jake Larsen – FBI Agent, Phoenix Arizona office

Submarine pen

From Wikipedia, the free encyclopedia

Surrendered German U-boats moored outside the Dora 1 bunker in Trondheim, Norway, May 1945

A **submarine pen** (*U-Boot-Bunker* in German) is a type of submarine base that acts as a bunker to protect submarines from air attack. The term is generally applied to submarine bases constructed during World War II, particularly in Germany and its occupied countries, which were also known as **U-boat pens** (after the phrase "U-boat" to refer to German submarines).

Background

Among the first forms of protection for submarines were some open-sided shelters with partial wooden foundations that were constructed during World War I. These structures were built at the time when bombs were light enough to be dropped by hand from the cockpit. By the 1940s, the quality of aerial weapons and the means to deliver them had improved markedly.[1]

The mid-1930s saw the Naval Construction Office in Berlin give the problem serious thought. Various factions in the navy were convinced protection for the expanding U-boat arm was required.

A Royal Air Force (RAF) raid on the capital in 1940 plus the occupation of France and Great Britain's refusal to surrender was enough to trigger a massive building programme of submarine pens and air raid shelters.

By the autumn of 1940, construction of the "Elbe II" bunker in Hamburg and "Nordsee III" on the island of Heligoland was under way. Others swiftly followed.

General

It was soon realized that such a massive project was beyond the *Kriegsmarine*, and the Todt Organisation (OT) was brought in to oversee the administration of labor. The local supply of such items as sand, aggregate, cement, and timber was often a cause for concern. The steel required was mostly imported from Germany. The attitudes of the people in France and Norway were significantly different. In France there was generally no problem with the recruitment of men and the procurement of machinery and raw materials. It was a different story in Norway. There, the local population were far more reluctant to help the Germans. Indeed, most labor had to be brought in.[2] The ground selected for bunker construction was no help either: usually being at the head of a fjord, the foundations and footings had to be hewn out of granite. Several meters of silt also had to be overcome.[3] Many of the workers needed were forced labor, most especially the concentration camp inmates supplied by the *Schutzstaffel* from camps near the pens.

The incessant air raids caused serious disruption to the project, hampering the supply of material, destroying machinery, and harassing the workers. Machinery such as excavators, piledrivers, cranes, floodlighting, and concrete pumps (which were still a relatively new technology in the 1940s) was temperamental, and in the case of steam-driven equipment, very noisy.[4]

Bunkers had to be able to accommodate more than just U-boats; space had to be found for offices, medical facilities, communications, lavatories, generators, ventilators, anti-aircraft guns, accommodation for key personnel such as crewmen, workshops, water purification plants, electrical equipment, and radio testing facilities. Storage space for spares, explosives, ammunition, and oil was also required.

Types of bunker

Four types of bunker were constructed:

Covered lock

These were bunkers built over an existing lock to give a U-boat some protection while it was at its most vulnerable – i.e. when the lock was emptying or filling. They were usually constructed with new locks alongside an existing structure.

Construction bunker

Used for building new boats

Fitting-out bunkers

After launch, many U-boats were fitted-out under their protection

Shelter for operational boats and repair bunkers

This was the most numerous type. There were two types that were built either on dry land or over the water. The former meant that U-boats had to be moved on ramps; the latter enabled the boats to come and go at will. Pumping the water out enabled dry dock repairs to be carried out. Some bunkers were large enough to allow the removal of periscopes and aerials. There is no truth in the rumor of an underground bunker on Fuerteventura in the Canary Islands. This story was gleaned from a similar situation in Le Havre in France when captured U-boat men were interrogated by the British.[5]

IJmuiden

IJmuiden (Dutch pronunciation: [ˌɛiˈmœydə(n)]) is a port city in the Dutch province of North Holland and is the main town in the municipality of Velsen. It is located at the mouth of the North Sea Canal to Amsterdam, and lies approximately 17 kilometers (11 mi) north of Haarlem.

The internal capitalization in the city's spelling is because **IJ** is a digraph in Dutch, and is therefore sometimes considered to be a ligature, rendering it a single letter.

The port of IJmuiden is a deep water port suited to fully laden Panamax ships, and fourth port of the Netherlands.

Second World War

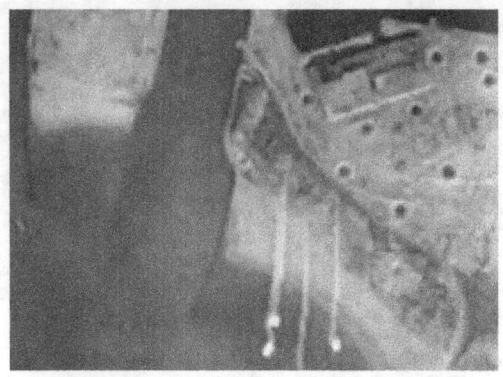

Still taken from a <u>United States Army</u> film, shot during the bombing of the German bunker *Schnellbootbunker BY (SBB2)*, February 1945.[6]

After the German <u>invasion of the Netherlands</u> on 10 May 1940, the Dutch Royal family left the country from IJmuiden in the late evening of 12 May, some on board the British <u>destroyer</u> <u>HMS *Codrington*</u>, <u>Queen Wilhelmina</u> left on board <u>HMS *Hereward*</u>. The quays at IJmuiden were crowded at that time with people desperate to be transported across the channel, sometimes at great expense. During the German occupation, the canal was out of operation and the Germans destroyed most of IJmuiden to create what they called *Festung IJmuiden* (Fortress IJmuiden), a heavily defended area in which the entire civilian population had been removed.

IJmuiden became the site of two separate fortified pens constructed by the German navy (*<u>Kriegsmarine</u>*) to house their *schnellboote* (fast torpedo boats, known to the <u>Allies</u> as <u>E-boats</u>)[7] and *Biber* <u>midget submarines</u>.[8] The older structure, codename *Schnellbootbunker AY (SBB1)*, was protected by a 10-foot (3.0 m) thick concrete roof.[7] The newer one, codename *Schnellbootbunker BY (SBB2)*, had 10–12 feet (3.0–3.7 m) of concrete, with a further 2–4-foot (0.6–1.2 m) layer separated by an air–gap.[Note 1][8]

The E-boats laid up in the shelters during the day, safe from air–attack, and put to sea under cover of night to attack Allied shipping.[7] The pens were priority targets after <u>D-day</u> as the torpedo boats they protected were a considerable threat to the supply lines serving Allied forces in western Europe and were subjected to repeated air attack. This included four attacks by No. 9 Squadron and No. 617 Squadron of the Royal Air Force, during which a total of 53 of the five–ton, Tallboy earthquake bombs were dropped.[9][10] There were also two attacks in 1945 by the American air force with rocket–powered Disney bombs, specialist weapons designed to penetrate fortified, concrete bunkers that could resist conventional bombs.

Captured German U-boats

Ia Drang, Viet Nam

From Wikipedia, the free encyclopedia

The **Battle of Ia Drang** was the first major battle between the United States Army and the People's Army of Vietnam (PAVN), also referred to as the North Vietnamese Army (NVA), and was part of the Pleiku Campaign conducted early in the Vietnam War. It comprised two main engagements, centered on two previously scouted helicopter landing zones (LZs), known as LZ X-Ray and LZ Albany. The first involved the 1st Battalion, 7th Cavalry Regiment and supporting units under the command of Lieutenant Colonel Hal Moore, and took place November 14–16,

1965 at LZ X-Ray, located at the eastern foot of the Chu Pong Massif in the central highlands of Vietnam. The second engagement involved the 2nd Battalion, 7th Cavalry Regiment plus supporting units under the command of Lieutenant Colonel Robert McDade, and took place on November 17 at LZ Albany, farther north in the Ia Drang Valley. It is notable for being the first large scale helicopter air assault and also the first use of Boeing B-52 Stratofortress strategic bombers in a tactical support role. Surrounded and under heavy fire from a numerically superior force, the American forces at LZ X-ray were able to hold off and drive back the North Vietnamese forces over three days of battle, largely through the support of both air power and heavy artillery bombardment, which the North Vietnamese lacked. LZ X-Ray was considered an American tactical victory, as the Americans claimed an almost 10:1 kill ratio. At LZ Albany, however, an American battalion was ambushed in close quarters. They were unable to use air and artillery support due to the close engagement of the North Vietnamese, and the Americans suffered an over-50% casualty rate before being extricated from the battle. Both sides, therefore, were able to claim victory in the battle.

The size of the clearing at LZ X-Ray meant that troops had to be shuttled in, the first lift landing at 10:48. The last troops of the battalion were landed at 15:20, by which time the troops on the ground were already heavily engaged, with one platoon cut off. Faced with heavy casualties and unexpected opposition, 1st Battalion was reinforced by B Company 2nd Battalion 7th Cavalry. Fighting continued the following day when the LZ was further reinforced by A Company 2/7 and also by 2nd Battalion 5th Cavalry, and the lost platoon was rescued. The last Vietnamese assaults on the position were repulsed on the morning of the 16th. As the Vietnamese forces melted away, the remainder of 2/7 and A Company of 1st Battalion 5th Cavalry arrived. By mid-afternoon 1/7 and B Company 2/7 had been airlifted to LZ Falcon, and on the 17th of November 2/5 marched out towards LZ

Columbus while the remaining 2/7 and 1/5 companies marched towards LZ Albany. The latter force became strung out and, in the early afternoon, were badly mauled in an ambush before they could be reinforced and extricated.

The battle at LZ X-Ray was documented in the CBS special report *Battle of Ia Drang Valley* by Morley Safer and the critically acclaimed book *We Were Soldiers Once... And Young* by Harold G. Moore and Joseph L. Galloway. In 1994, Moore, Galloway and men who fought on both the American and North Vietnamese sides, traveled back to the remote jungle clearings where the battle took place. At the time the U.S. did not have diplomatic relations with Vietnam. The risky trip which took a year to arrange was part of an award-winning ABC News documentary, *They Were Young and Brave* produced by Terence Wrong. Randall Wallace depicted the battle at LZ X-Ray in the 2002 movie *We Were Soldiers* starring Mel Gibson and Barry Pepper as Moore and Galloway, respectively. Galloway later described Ia Drang as "the battle that convinced Ho Chi Minh he could win".

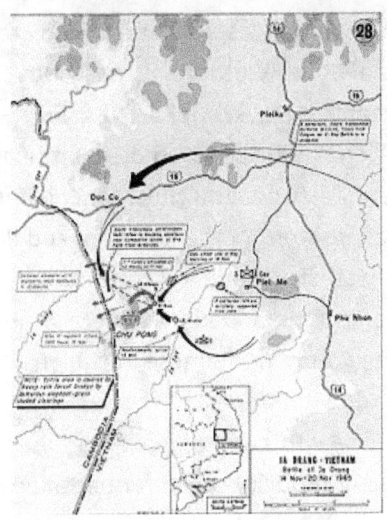

Background

By early 1965, the majority of rural South Vietnam was under limited Viet Cong (VC) control, increasingly supported by Vietnam People's Army (PAVN) regulars from North Vietnam. Military Assistance Command, Vietnam (MACV) General William C. Westmoreland had secured the commitment of upward of 300,000 U.S. regulars from President Lyndon B. Johnson and a build-up of forces took place in the summer of 1965.

Viet Cong forces were in nominal control of most of the South Vietnamese countryside by 1965 and had established military infrastructure in the Central Highlands, to the northeast of the Saigon region. Vietnamese communist forces had operated in this area during the previous decade in the First Indochina War against the French, winning a notable victory at the Battle of Mang Yang Pass in 1954.[12] There were few reliable roads into the area, making it an ideal place for the communist forces to form bases, relatively immune from attack by the generally road-bound ARVN forces. During 1965, large groups of North Vietnamese Army regulars moved into the area to conduct offensive operations. Attacks to the southwest from these bases threatened to cut South Vietnam in two.[13]

357

By 1964 North Vietnam had established the B3 Front in the central highlands of South Vietnam. By early November 1965 three PAVN regiments – the 32nd, 33rd and 66th – and the H15 Local Force Battalion had been assembled in the area. The B3 Front commander, Maj. Gen. Chu Huy Man, planned to target South Vietnamese positions in the Kon Tum and Pleiku provinces. The city of Pleiku was the location of the South Vietnamese II Corps headquarters, commanded by General Vinh Loc, who had at his disposal nine South Vietnamese battalions: four ranger, three airborne, and two marine.[14]

The U.S. command saw this as an ideal area to test new air mobility tactics.[15] Air mobility called for battalion-sized forces to be delivered, supplied and extracted from an area of action using helicopters. Since the heavy weapons of a normal combined-arms force could not follow, the infantry would be supported by coordinated close air support, artillery and aerial rocket fire, arranged from a distance and directed by local observers. The new tactics had been developed in the U.S. by the 11th Air Assault Division (Test), which was renamed as the 1st Cavalry Division (Airmobile).[15] The division's troopers dubbed themselves the "Air Cav" (Air Cavalry) and in July 1965 began deploying to Camp Radcliff, An Khê, Vietnam.[16] By November, most of the division's three brigades were ready for operations.[17]

The U.S. deployment caused the B3 Field Front Command to bring forward an attack on the U.S. Army Special Forces Plei Me camp, some 45 km southwest of Pleiku, which was originally planned for December. The assault was instead launched October 19 with only two Regiments, the 32nd and 33rd, instead of the planned three, before the Air Cavalry troops were combat ready. The plan was to attack the camp with the 33rd Regiment while the 32nd Regiment would lie in wait to ambush the South Vietnamese relief force that would inevitably be sent from Pleiku. Once the relief force was destroyed, the two regiments were to join and take the camp.[18] The initial attack was repulsed with the help of strong air support, and a small relief force reinforced the camp on

358

the morning of the 22nd. The main relief force, advancing south from Pleiku on route 6C, was duly ambushed at 18:00 the next day. After a two-hour battle the ambushing forces were beaten off, but the South Vietnamese, discouraged from moving any further, set up a defensive position, and did not reach the camp at Plei Me until dusk on the 25th. The North Vietnamese forces withdrew west towards the Chu Pong Massif.[19][20]

At the end of October, after the siege of Plei Me was lifted, General Westmoreland ordered General Kinnard to take his division on to the offensive and seize the initiative in Pleiku province.[21] Initial operations were conducted by 1st Brigade, and on November 1 they captured a North Vietnamese aid station south west of Plei Me. Further engagements over the next few days revealed the arrival of the North Vietnamese 66th Regiment. Having taken increasing casualties, 1st Brigade was relieved by 3rd Brigade, the handover being completed over the period November 7–12.[22]

On November 11, intelligence source revealed the disposition of the three NVA regiments: the 66th at vicinity YA9104, the 33rd at YA 940010 and the 32nd at YA 820070.[23][24] On November 12, the 3rd Brigade was given orders by General Larsen, IFFV Commander and General Knowles, 1st Air Cavalry Division Forward Headquarters Commander to prepare for "an air assault near the foot of the Chu Pongs",[25] at 13°34'11"N 107°40'54"E, 14 miles (22 km) west of Plei Me.

On November 13, 3rd Brigade Commander Colonel Thomas W. Brown, acting following the order issued by Gen. Larsen, IFFV Commander and Gen. Knowles, 1st Air Cavalry Division Forward Command Post Commander, met with Lieutenant Colonel Hal Moore the commander of the 1st Battalion, 7th Cavalry Regiment, and told him "to conduct an airmobile assault the following morning"[26] and to conduct search and destroy operations through 15 November. Meanwhile, an ARVN intelligence source by intercept of radio communication indicated that some NVA B3 Field Front recon elements and transportation units had already moved out of their assembly areas to attack the Pleime camp.[27]

Biographical Information on David McIntosh

David spent over 25 years with Army Military Intelligence, working in Electronic Warfare and communications, retiring in 1996 as a Master Sergeant (E-8). His career dealt with ground and airborne electronic warfare equipment and operation. I was head trainer on several Airborne Electronic Warfare aircraft and ground operation equipment. Some of my more interesting assignments were in locations such as Japan, Hawaii, Panama, and Saudi Arabia (Desert Storm), to name a few. He has been working in the telecommunications and military intelligence collection field for over 30 years. His career spans many areas of information protection, information acquisition, systems security, government security planning and implementation. As a civilian he taught graduate school classes in Network and Systems Security for Webster University.

David holds an MBA, BS in Business and AS in Aerospace Technology. David is a pilot, scuba instructor, writer, semi-professional photographer and father of 4, which have produced 11 grandchildren.

David's hobbies include writing, flying, travel, photography, sports cars, sailing, woodworking, and camping. Presently he is travelling around the country in his motorhome with my wife and German Shepherd, enjoying our great country and writing novels.

www.ingramcontent.com/pod-product-compliance
Lightning Source LLC
Chambersburg PA
CBHW070406260626
47161CB00001B/295